"Go back to sleep, Raine."

Macauley's voice was flat.

"Why are you leaving?"

He squeezed his eyes shut tightly, seeing her face in his mind, glad as hell that she couldn't see his. Why did she have to push this, make it harder? Then, on the heels of that question, came another. Why the hell should she make this easy for him, for herself? If he'd learned one thing about this woman, it was that she didn't shirk unpleasantries. She insisted on the truth, all of it, not sparing herself or anyone else.

The truth. Didn't he at least owe her that much? After every oath he'd violated, after what he'd taken from her, here, last night, he at least owed her the truth, no matter how brutal.

D0360669

Dear Reader,

Happy Valentine's Day! And as a special gift to you, we're publishing the latest in *New York Times* bestseller Linda Howard's series featuring the Mackenzie family. Hero Zane Mackenzie, of *Mackenzie's Pleasure*, is every inch a man—and Barrie Lovejoy is just the woman to teach this rough, tough Navy SEAL what it means to love. There's nothing left to say but "Enjoy!"

Merline Lovelace concludes her "Code Name: Danger" miniseries with *Perfect Double*, the long-awaited romance between Maggie Sinclair and her boss at the OMEGA Agency, Adam Ridgeway. Then join Kylie Brant for *Guarding Raine*. This author established herself as a reader favorite with her very first book—and her latest continues the top-notch tradition. *Forever, Dad* is the newest from Maggie Shayne, and it's an exciting, suspenseful, *emotional* tour de force. For those of you with a hankering to get "Spellbound," there's Vella Munn's *The Man From Forever*, a story of love and passion that transcend time. Finally, Rebecca Daniels wraps up her "It Takes Two" duo with *Father Figure*, featuring the ever-popular secret baby plot line.

Pick up all six of these wonderful books—and come back next month for more, because here at Silhouette Intimate Moments we're dedicated to bringing you the best of today's romantic fiction. Enjoy!

Yours,

Leslie Wainger
Senior Editor and Editorial Coordinator

Please address questions and book requests to:
Silhouette Reader Service
U.S.: 3010 Walden Ave., P.O. Box 1325, Buffalo, NY 14269
Canadian: P.O. Box 609, Fort Erie, Ont. L2A 5X3

KYLIE BRANT

GUARDING RAINE

Silhouette®

INTIMATE™MOMENTS®

Published by Silhouette Books

America's Publisher of Contemporary Romance

If you purchased this book without a cover you should be aware that this book is stolen property. It was reported as "unsold and destroyed" to the publisher, and neither the author nor the publisher has received any payment for this "stripped book."

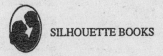

SILHOUETTE BOOKS

ISBN 0-373-07693-2

GUARDING RAINE

Copyright © 1996 by Kimberly Bahnsen

All rights reserved. Except for use in any review, the reproduction or utilization of this work in whole or in part in any form by any electronic, mechanical or other means, now known or hereafter invented, including xerography, photocopying and recording, or in any information storage or retrieval system, is forbidden without the written permission of the editorial office, Silhouette Books, 300 East 42nd Street, New York, NY 10017 U.S.A.

All characters in this book have no existence outside the imagination of the author and have no relation whatsoever to anyone bearing the same name or names. They are not even distantly inspired by any individual known or unknown to the author, and all incidents are pure invention.

This edition published by arrangement with Harlequin Books S.A.

® and ™ are trademarks of Harlequin Books S.A., used under license. Trademarks indicated with ® are registered in the United States Patent and Trademark Office, the Canadian Trade Marks Office and in other countries.

Printed in U.S.A.

Books by Kylie Brant

Silhouette Intimate Moments

McLain's Law #528
Rancher's Choice #552
An Irresistible Man #622
Guarding Raine #693

KYLIE BRANT

married her high school sweetheart sixteen years ago, and they are now raising their five children in Iowa. She has enjoyed writing since grade school, when she used to pen stories to amuse her younger sister.

Always an avid reader, Kylie became interested in writing again a few years ago. After her twins turned four, she finally managed to steal enough time alone to get started.

When she isn't busy with her job teaching learning-disabled students, she's reading, at the computer, or attending her sons' sporting events.

For Dad,
who has always believed in me

Prologue

She ran through the night with a speed born of terror. She could hear his heavy footsteps behind her. He was close, very close. She could feel his breath on her neck, imagined his arms reaching toward her. Sobbing, she tried to put on a burst of speed, but her legs seemed wooden, unresponsive. They couldn't move her fast enough, far enough to avoid him.

He caught hold of her long hair and yanked her to a painful stop, and then his weight hit her, knocking her to the ground. He loomed over her like a shadow born of the total darkness around them. She fought wildly, with a strength belied by her youth, fed by her panic. There was a single hopeful instant, when she thought she could get away from him. And then her eyes fixed on something in his hand coming toward her face, before her head exploded in pain....

She came awake with a start, bolting upright in bed, hauling in huge breaths of air to fill lungs as starved as a runner's. She pulled the sheet and coverlet up to her chin, and wrapped it around herself to still the shaking in her limbs. Even as she made the motion, she knew it was in vain. The chill skating over her skin wasn't due to the temperature, but to the deep, pervasive cold spreading within her.

The darkness in the room was broken only by the faint glow of the moon shining through the window. The night seemed even more oppressive than usual, more sinister. Eleven years had passed since she'd regarded the darkness with anything less than fear. In that time she'd learned ways to deal with her lingering phobia.

But none of the tricks she'd devised, not the deep breathing or the mental gymnastics would help her tonight, she knew. It wasn't only the old nightmare that had her shaking in her bed like a child, it was the one being revisited on her daily. Dawn wouldn't bring an end to her fear anymore, because the specter from her sleep had been transferred to daylight.

Her eyes went to the window, as if she could search out her tormentor in the night outside. She couldn't make herself think of the darkness rationally when she knew someone was out there. Someone was watching, weighing her terror, planning yet another move against her.

She huddled in her bed, unable to stop trembling. She could no longer deny what was happening in her life, couldn't shake the feeling of forboding.

The very real nightmare from her past had begun all over again.

Chapter 1

Simon Michaels surveyed the man seated across from him from beneath lowered gray brows. No wasn't an answer he ever accepted gracefully, and certainly never from a man who looked as disreputable as this one. "Surely you could postpone your vacation." His tone changed his words from a suggestion to something approaching a command.

"I could," Mac O'Neill agreed, "if I wanted to." He crossed his arms lazily, leaned back in his chair and added, "But I don't." He paused to note the mottled red color his answer brought to Simon Michaels's face before going on. "I told you on the phone, my partner is perfectly capable of handling your security problem, whatever it may be. If that's not acceptable, you'll have to find another company."

Only the fact that Simon had been a good friend of Mac's father had convinced Mac to at least show him the courtesy of this visit. But no amount of pleading was going to change Mac's vacation plans. He hadn't taken any time off since starting his company, and after four years he was burnt out to the core. This trip wasn't for pleasure only, although he was going to do his damnedest to fill it with such. A man too long on any job made mistakes. In his line of work, miscalculations could cost lives.

It was his attitude as much as his words that triggered Simon's temper. "Dammit, Mac," he thundered, slamming his hand against the top of the polished teak desk. "What difference does it make if you spend this month lying on a tropical beach, or the next? What are you planning that could possibly be so damn important?"

"What I'm planning," Mac replied bluntly, "is to get tanned, drunk and lucky. And not necessarily in that order. I just hope a month is long enough."

Simon snapped his mouth shut, not for the first time reconsidering his selection of Mac for this particular problem. He needed to be absolutely sure that the person he hired was a gentleman, as well as damn good at his job. Unfortunately, in this case, the two qualities seemed to be mutually exclusive. Macauley O'Neill, or Mac to all but the unwise, had the experience necessary for the job, but Simon remained unconvinced that the man wasn't as morally corrupt as he sounded. Nothing about his appearance was reassuring. The look in those blue eyes was sharp enough to cut glass. His dark brown hair was worn much too long, and it didn't appear as though he'd shaved that day. He looked like a good man to have at your back in a fight, and a bad one to cross.

Simon squelched his misgivings. He needed Mac O'Neill, needed that uncompromising toughness and experience. There was too much at stake to change his mind now, at any rate. He'd have to hope that the memory of his friendship with Mac's late father would temper any less admirable qualities the man had.

He relaxed in his leather chair again, reassessing his strategy. It was obvious that Grady O'Neill had bequeathed to his son his damnable Irish stubbornness. But Simon had had plenty of experience getting around Grady over the years, and he didn't doubt his ability to persuade his son. "It occurs to me that I've been unfair to you." He spread his hands expansively. "Here I'm asking you for a commitment before I've even outlined the job." He paused invitingly, but when Mac didn't respond, he continued. "You know how close your father and I were when we were growing up."

"That's the only reason I'm here, and not already on a plane headed south."

The man nodded, as if in appreciation for that consideration, but Mac wasn't fooled by his affable pose. When Simon Michaels wanted something, he got it. That's what Grady had always said, torn between admiration and disapproval. And it was clear that Simon wanted Mac. It just wasn't clear for what.

"I don't think you've ever met my daughter, Raine," Simon said. He gestured to the wall behind him. "That's her in the picture with her mother. She was about fourteen when that was taken."

Mac gazed at the picture impassively. There was actually very little to see of the girl. The portrait showed Lorena Michaels, Simon's wife, smiling a warm, sweet smile, with a girl's silhouette in the background. He examined her delicate profile and heavy fall of hair for another moment before shifting his gaze back to Simon.

The other man was still studying the picture, and his face had visibly softened. He collected himself after a moment and faced Mac again. "Most men would move heaven and earth for their children, and I'm no different. I know that's how I feel about Raine. And the boys, too, of course, but..." He shrugged. "They're men now, capable of solving their own problems. But Raine has always been special, and now she's in trouble." His gaze was level as he added, "That's why I called you, Mac. I need your help to keep Raine safe."

Mac crossed one leg to rest his ankle on the opposite knee. "From what?"

"My daughter's being harassed. God knows how long it's been going on—she doesn't like to confide in me. But I recently found out that she's been receiving threatening letters, phone calls, that sort of thing. I think she might be the target of a stalker, and I don't mind telling you, I'm scared for her. She's too damn trusting for her own good. If this person, whoever it is, decides to step up the intensity of this unpleasantness, Raine would make an easy target."

"You could call the police."

Simon snorted. "She did that, of course, but they've been no help. Came by her house a couple of times, asked some questions and left. They haven't even been able to find out who's behind the harassment, much less get it stopped. I called the detective in charge of her case, and all I got was a runaround. The bottom line is, my daughter remains in real danger."

"So you decided to take matters into your own hands," Mac concluded. That fit with what he knew of Simon Michaels. He wasn't a man to sit idly by when he or his were threatened. According to Grady, he was overprotective to a fault. Mac recalled his father saying once that Simon went through all the newspapers before his wife read them, removing any news that might upset her.

"I decided to put the matter into *your* hands," Simon corrected. "I've been following your successes. I know your company is growing rapidly, and you have quite a reputation in the field. Your experience in military intelligence gives you a unique background, you must admit. Walt Hightower is still singing your praises for the way you discovered that bomb in his office complex. You saved him several million dollars."

Mac ignored the flattery and leveled the man a look. "It does sound like you could use a security expert. But it won't be me. If you refuse to let my partner do the job, you'll have to find someone else."

"I'm willing to make it worth your while." Simon named a sum that would put a sizable dent in the mortgage on Mac's company, with enough left over to buy some of that fancy equipment his partner, Trey Garrison, was always talking about. But Mac remained unmoved. He'd never been a man who could be bought, although he wasn't surprised Simon had tried. He'd met the man only twice previously, despite the friendship that had existed between him and Grady. Yet everything he'd heard about Simon indicated that he was a man who got what he wanted.

But not this time.

Mac uncrossed his legs and rose lithely to his feet. Simon looked surprised, then, as understanding dawned, grim.

"Sorry I can't help you, Simon," Mac said, not bothering to sound in the least regretful. "But I can recommend another company that's very reputable."

"How's your mother doing, Mac?" The smooth words, delivered in that innocent tone, could be mistaken as polite if one didn't have a suspicious nature.

"She's doing well. Real well," he responded shortly.

Simon shook his head in remembered sorrow. "She took Grady's death hard. I don't remember ever seeing a person grieve like that before. Of course, you didn't make it back until after the funeral, but your mother had a very difficult time coping with all the arrangements. When she called me I was glad to help out."

Mac gave a tight, humorless smile. The wily old bastard was really turning the knife now. "My father was right about you," he said in a deceptively mild voice. "You *can* be a real son-of-a-bitch."

Simon chuckled. "Grady never pulled any punches. A person always knew where he stood with your father." He sobered. "He'd want you to do this, you know that, don't you, Mac? We were like brothers growing up, your dad and I. We always stayed in touch. I know how upset he was about your decision to join the military. But he was proud, too. He knew you were damn good at your job."

It was what Simon didn't say that kept Mac rooted to the floor when common sense advised him to head for the door. Unspoken was the fact that Mac and Grady had never agreed on the intelligence work that had kept Mac out of touch for months at a time. That same work had prevented him from hearing of his father's death until after Grady had been in the ground a week.

There were many people across the globe who would swear Mac O'Neill didn't have a compassionate, human bone in his body. Simon Michaels was sitting before him banking on the hunch that Mac had at least one. And with the unerring accuracy of a master, he'd honed in on the biggest regret in Mac's life. Even acknowledging the finesse with which he was being manipulated didn't detract from the guilt that flooded through him. The last time he'd seen his father, his parents' small house had reverberated with raised voices and slamming doors. Mac had crashed out of the house that day in a fury, never guessing that it would be the last time he'd see his father. Grady had died two months later, victim of a heart attack.

The hell of it was, Mac knew Simon was right. Grady had been fiercely loyal to his family and friends. He'd have moved heaven and earth to get his son to help Simon. And it was this realization that caused Mac to pause. It was a poignant truth that it was impossible to make amends to a dead man.

It was a psychological reality that Mac couldn't help but try.

He sank slowly, reluctantly, into his seat. "Exactly what do you have in mind, Simon?"

To the older man's credit, he didn't show his satisfaction by so much as a flicker of an eyelash. "I'm sure you'll want to tighten up the security at her home. And then—" his voice hardened "—she'll need around-the-clock protection. I don't want the bastard who's behind these threats to get anywhere near her." Frowning, he added, "I wanted her to come home until this thing was resolved, but she wouldn't hear of it. Raine used to be a very amenable girl, but over the past few years she's developed a real independent streak."

"How old is she?"

"Twenty-six."

Mac raised one eyebrow. "Old enough to deserve independence, I'd think."

"Maybe," Simon agreed reluctantly. "God knows, she's accused me often enough of being overly protective. But she can't deny that she needs help now, as much as she'd like to."

"You could always cut off her allowance," Mac said cynically. "That would bring her back in a hurry."

For the first time, Simon looked a bit uncomfortable. "I don't give her an allowance. She wouldn't take it, and she hasn't any need for it. She's an artist, and her paintings are enjoying some modest success. She's able to be financially independent. A couple of years ago she bought a house that sits on five acres in the San Fernando Valley."

Mac didn't doubt that the fact stuck in Simon's craw, since her success put her outside of his control. He also suspected that Simon was downplaying his daughter's accomplishments. Although the house Raine Michaels had bought might not match this Burbank home for glitz, any property in the Valley wouldn't have come cheaply.

The thought of spending the next few weeks at that home in the Valley made his back teeth clench. Nothing would have given him greater pleasure than to tell the man before him to go to hell. "All right," he said, his tone little more than a snarl. "I'll go out there and recommend the necessary security measures."

"And you'll see to those measures yourself?" the older man prodded.

His jaw tight, Mac gave a short nod.

Simon gave a slight smile. "I'll call Raine and tell her to expect you. I trust your judgment, Mac. If you assess the situation and can honestly tell me that she's in no danger from this weirdo, well, then I'll go along with you. But if there is even the remotest possibility that her safety is in jeopardy, I'm trusting that you'll be there to watch over her as long as is necessary."

Mac mentally said goodbye to his plans for spending the next month with solicitous, well-endowed blondes and bottles of Scotch for companions. Maybe if he was lucky this case wouldn't take up too much of his time. If he could get it tied up in a couple of weeks, then his much-needed vacation wouldn't have to be canceled, just postponed.

With any luck, his role as glorified baby-sitter for Raine Michaels would be of blessedly brief duration.

* * *

The next day Mac was swinging down from the sleek black pickup that had his company's logo painted on its side. He stopped for a moment after he got out, eyes narrowed against the bright afternoon sun as he studied Raine Michaels's home. Compared to most he'd passed on his way through the Valley, this one was completely unpretentious. Unlike most of its neighbors, it was two-storied and had a large wooden porch running across the front. A double garage was attached. The paint was blindingly white, the contrasting trim painted black. Pots of bright red geraniums lined the porch steps.

Mac didn't go immediately to the door. Instead, he walked all around the house, noting the spacing of the windows, the doors, the overgrown brush close to the house. When he'd reached the front again, he turned slowly around, squinting in the direction from which he'd come. There was a semicircular drive, each end leading to the road. He frowned when he counted half a dozen cars parked haphazardly along the drive. He'd obviously arrived in the midst of some kind of party.

He climbed the steps and knocked at the screen door. When no one came to answer, he repeated the action. The seconds ticking by stretched into minutes. Mentally cursing, he pushed the door open and walked inside. He let the screen bang behind him, further announcing his presence, although there didn't seem to be anyone around who would care. He sauntered through the spacious hall, stopping to look through each doorway.

The first room on the right appeared to be a den. The walls were lined with bookcases. Two men sat hunched over a table there, arguing vehemently. Neither looked up at his arrival. Mac went on to the next room, which he guessed to be a family room. A large curved sectional couch sat in front of a TV and entertainment center. One wall sported a large stone fireplace with a huge mirror hanging over it. An ornate grandfather clock stood in a corner. The room was empty.

In the large kitchen he found a pretty blond woman sitting on the counter, swinging her feet while she talked on the telephone. She raised her eyebrows at him and smiled, her look full of appreciation as it trailed over his dark green shirt and jeans-clad thighs. But when he asked, "Raine Michaels?" she merely shook her head at him and continued her conversation on the phone.

The dining room was empty, but he found seven more people in what had probably at one time been a living room. It had obvi-

ously been converted to a studio, with bare floors and a wall of
windows. Several easels were set up, with four men and three
women sitting before them, all immersed in their work. "Where
can I find Raine Michaels?" he asked. Only one person in the room
looked up at his words, and she merely shrugged. In growing irritation, Mac exited the room and started up the open stairway. He
wandered freely through each of the four bedrooms and two baths
upstairs, finding all of them empty. He passed a young couple in
the hallway, but as had happened downstairs, neither person
questioned his presence.

The remaining door was closed, so he banged on it with one
knuckle before pushing it open. The room appeared to be yet another studio, with an easel set up in front of a window. The young
man standing before it had his back to the door and didn't look up,
although the squeak of the old hinges made no secret of Mac's entrance. Tiring of the search, Mac determined to end it. "Hey, kid,"
he drawled. "Where can I find Raine Michaels?"

Stiffening at the sound of his voice, the person didn't immediately answer.

Mac's patience snapped. "Look, sonny, I'm not asking for the
secret of life here. Just one quick answer. You *do* know the woman
whose house you're in, don't you?"

"Intimately," came the wry response, as the person turned
around.

When they were face to face, Mac was immediately aware of his
mistake. This was no boy, although with the slight build beneath
the oversize man's shirt she wore, he could be forgiven his as-
sumption. And she was no kid. At first glance Mac would have
pegged her age at eighteen or twenty, but after a closer look he re-
vised his estimation.

Although her face was smooth of wrinkles, her eyes belied her
apparent youth. Large and thickly fringed with long, thick lashes,
they were the color of antique gold coins. But more surprising than
their color was the incongruous look of age in them. He'd seen that
look before, in the eyes of the people left alive mourning their
bombed village and dead families. Then the woman blinked, and
Mac was left wondering if what he'd thought he'd seen in them was
a trick of the light.

His intense perusal was interrupted by her next words. "I'm
Raine Michaels. How can I help you?" Her tone was polite,
slightly interested, and ignited what was left of his temper.

"Are you always this polite to people you don't know?" He kicked the door shut behind him with the heel of one boot, and leaned against it, arms folded.

Her eyes flickered, but when she answered her voice was even. "I try to be. Why? Is there some reason I should be rude to *you?*"

He noted that the calm in her voice was at odds with the slight trembling in the hand still holding her paintbrush. "I'd think there's plenty of reason to at least be careful, yeah. From what I've noticed of this place so far, you're lucky all you've had to contend with are some notes and phone calls. Because there's absolutely nothing stopping some nut from walking right into your house."

"Apparently not," she murmured, turning slightly from him to lay her brush down. She picked up a rag and wiped off her hands. "Why don't we quit talking in riddles and get to the point? Who are you and why are you here?"

"The name is Mac O'Neill."

Mac O'Neill. The security expert her father had sent over. Raine let out a breath she hadn't been aware of holding. Tremors of adrenaline still vibrated through her veins, warring with relief at his introduction. The suddenness with which a stranger had appeared behind her had left her undeniably shaky. She turned around, studying him warily. She should be relieved that he was here, but somehow she was less than reassured. His pose against the door should have seemed indolent, but instead she was given the impression of barely leashed power. He didn't offer his hand, and she was fervently grateful. She was oddly reluctant to touch this man, even in greeting.

"I didn't bother to call first because your father told me you'd be expecting me," Mac said. "He's pretty concerned about your safety, you know, and well he should be. Your home is about as secure as a goldfish bowl in a room full of cats."

She put the rag down. "Yes, I have been expecting you. But when Dad called he didn't mention when you'd be coming." And he'd also neglected to mention that the security expert he'd hired for her would look right at home on the front line of the L.A. Raiders. Her eyes wandered over him furtively. He had to be all of six feet, and he looked as solid as steel. His shoulders seemed to fill his shirt, to stretch it. His chest was broad, tapering to a masculinely narrow waist and hips.

Realizing her eyes were lingering on those hips, she jerked her gaze to his face. His hair was a thick, glossy brown and shone with occasional highlights from the sunlight that was still streaming into

the room. It appeared as if he had forgotten to keep his last few
appointments with his barber. He wore it unfashionably long in
back, but the style seemed to suit him. This wasn't a man who
could wear a preppy haircut. He hadn't had a close encounter with
a razor in the recent past, and the masculine stubble on his face did
nothing to detract from his tough appearance. His nose had been
broken at least once, and judging from the set of that stubborn
chin, he'd had it coming.

The thought put a tilt to her lips, one that quickly faded when
she looked into his eyes. Unconsciously she drew in a breath and
took an involuntary step forward, angling her head for a better
look. Narrowed at her now in annoyance, they were a startling
shade of blue. Ice blue, the artist in her decided. The exact hue of
the ice below the surface of the thick Alaskan glaciers.

Mac stared at the woman before him. From behind, clad only in
that oversize shirt, tight-fitting jeans and barefoot, she'd looked
every inch the urchin. But he never would have made the mistake
of thinking her a boy if she'd been facing him when he first saw
her. The portrait in her father's office hadn't shown her in detail,
but Mac recognized the delicate features, the straight, dainty nose
and pouty mouth from the picture. The long hair was gone,
though, and worn much shorter than his. A very light brown, it was
cut short on the sides and back, and left longer on top. If it wasn't
for those huge, haunted eyes, she'd never draw a man's second
glance.

"So, Mr. O'Neill," she interrupted the silence. "I'm sure you'll
want to take a look around and write up some suggestions. I'll give
you time to do that, and we can talk when you're finished."

He would have told her that he'd already started that process if
he hadn't observed the way her gaze flicked to her painting. Irritation filled him anew. He was accustomed to his clients at least
hearing him out, but it looked as though he would need to vie for
her attention, and damned if he was going to do that.

"How much time will you need?" she asked, and though she was
again looking at him, he could tell her mind was on her work.

"A couple of hours should do it," he replied.

"Great." There was no mistaking the satisfaction in her voice.
"While you're looking around, I'll take advantage of this light.
Oh, and if anyone should stop you, tell them to speak to me."

He could have told her that the odds of anyone in this house
paying any attention to him were singularly improbable, but she'd
already half-turned away from him, picked up her brush and

dabbed it onto her pallette. He stared hard at those narrow shoulders, not certain whether to be amused or furious at his obvious dismissal. After another moment he shook his head wryly and left the room. He'd take the time she'd mentioned, and he'd make those notes. And then he and Miss Raine Michaels were definitely going to have that talk.

Oh, yeah, they'd talk. And he had a feeling that she wasn't going to like what he had to say to her. Not one damn bit.

Mac's solitary investigation of Raine's property didn't do much to improve his mood. Although there was evidence that some security efforts had been taken, none of the work seemed recent. There were plenty of outdoor lights installed on the garage. But any third-rate burglar could open her door locks with little effort. As it was, it took Mac less than twenty seconds to pick the dead bolt on her front door, but he credited himself with better than average skills in that area. The back door wouldn't be a problem, either, although one probably wouldn't bother to pick the lock. A well-placed kick would splinter it. He studied the antiquated alarm system. He guessed it had been put in at the time the house was built. It had been one of the best systems available when it was installed, but technology changed, and so did the skills of thieves. It would need to be replaced with one much more sensitive.

Of course, he thought dourly, the best system in the world wasn't going to do much good if she continued to leave her doors wide open.

He kept busy jotting down notes for the next couple hours, wandering about the property at will. It wasn't until late afternoon that someone actually questioned his presence. And the question wasn't suspicious in nature, but rather interested.

He'd come into the house after a thorough look at the grounds. In the hallway he came face to face with the blond woman he'd noticed on the phone earlier.

"Well, hi, you're back." Her words were accompanied by the same slightly flirtatious smile she'd thrown him in the kitchen earlier. "Did you ever find Raine?"

He gave a short nod. "I found her. Who are you?"

The woman didn't seem put off by his curt manner. "Sarah Jennings," she answered. "I'm a friend of Raine's. And you are?"

Mac looked past her through the doorway into the study. The same two men he'd seen there earlier were still in conversation, this time at normal volume. "Mac O'Neill. I'm doing some work for Miss Michaels." He turned to her and noted the avid curiosity in her blue eyes. She was pretty, he noted detachedly, tall and slender and much closer to the image he'd had of what Simon's daughter would look like. "Tell me. Are all these people here today friends of Miss Michaels?"

She shrugged. "Friends, acquaintances, employees. Raine usually has a full house."

"So I've noticed," he murmured. He gestured to the men in the next room. "Who are they?"

Sarah stepped around him and peeked into the room. "Oh, that's André Klassen and Greg Winters, Raine's agent and accountant. Both of them are here a lot, and they absolutely detest each other. They come to talk to Raine and stay to disrupt the tranquillity the rest of us seek here." She turned to him and rolled her eyes. "They rarely agree on anything."

"And all the others I've seen wandering about?"

"They're probably art students from the university. Raine volunteers there occasionally, and she's sometimes a guest speaker for art classes. She's kind of befriended a few of the students and lets them come here to take advantage of the peace and the view to work. Sometimes the sessions turn into impromptu lessons."

Mac studied her for a moment. "And where do you fit in, Sarah Jennings?"

She dimpled at him. "Anywhere I want, usually. Raine and I met in college, and we've been friends ever since. We're both artists, so we have a lot in common. And now that I've answered *your* questions, answer one of mine. What kind of work are you going to be doing for Raine?"

A voice interrupted them before Mac's silence could be interpreted as rude.

"Mr. O'Neill is the man Dad called about, Sarah," Raine replied as she came down the stairway. She'd gotten rid of the oversize man's shirt, and her red cotton T-shirt was tucked neatly into the same jeans she'd been wearing earlier. Her feet were still bare. "He has a security company and will be giving me some suggestions." She cocked her head at Mac, newly aware that she had to look up a long way to meet his gaze. "Sorry I took so long, I kind of lost track of time. I'll make dinner and we can talk while we eat, if that's okay with you."

Sarah's eyes widened comically. "You're going to cook?"

Raine noted the flicker of unease her friend's disbelieving tone brought to Mac's face and shot Sarah a reproving look. "I can cook. You'll stay, too, won't you?"

Sarah shook her head. "I've got a date, so I should be heading home to get ready. I might be back tomorrow, though."

Her departure seemed to herald some sort of mass exodus for the rest of the visitors in the house, or so it seemed to Mac. He was seated at the kitchen table, his notebook in front of him, and Raine was moving about the room with lithe, sure motions, setting out ingredients for supper. Each time Mac started to speak he was interrupted by yet another person stopping in to bid Raine goodbye. To each she issued a dinner invitation. The ones who seemed about to accept quickly reconsidered after a pointed look from Mac. In the end, it was just him and Raine in the kitchen.

Intercepting some of the looks Mac shot at her friends did nothing to settle Raine's nerves. She wasn't used to dining with strange men, and she'd counted on Sarah's presence at dinner to help her cope with that anxiety. She didn't relish the thought of being alone in the house with Mac, no matter what his occupation was. But after ignoring him all afternoon, she owed him the civility of listening to his security suggestions. She couldn't honestly even say she'd been immersed in her work. Once he'd left her studio upstairs, she'd been unable to concentrate on the painting that had seemed so important only minutes before his arrival. She'd found herself mixing paints for the next few hours, attempting, without much success, to duplicate the pale turquoise hue of his eyes.

That distraction from her work was uncommon enough. Her response to this stranger, as a man, was even more rare. He made her nervous. That in itself wasn't unusual. It had been more than a decade since she'd been able to face being alone with a stranger without anxiety. But, as with her fear of the darkness, she'd long ago found ways to deal with that phobia. This man was different, though. He caused more than nerves, he forced . . . an awareness of him. She didn't recognize it, couldn't identify it, but it was there, nonetheless. And the unfamiliarity of that feeling heightened her confusion.

You are certainly in a state today, she scolded herself. Without a second thought, she took two large steaks from the freezer and set them in the microwave to thaw. It was easy to see that her customary light dinner of a salad or soup wouldn't go far in filling Mac up. She snuck a glance at him. He'd helped himself to one of the beers languishing in the back of her refrigerator, and he was watching her over the top of the bottle. Those cool, pale eyes seemed to look right through her, as if he could read her apprehension and divine his part in its origin.

That steady gaze of his was positively unnerving. "So, what's your real name?" she blurted, trying to distract him. Waiting for his answer, she took out the steaks, seasoned them and set them under the broiler before readying some potatoes to bake.

He cocked an eyebrow at her. "You think I'm using an alias?"

With a quick smile, she shook her head. "No, I mean, what's Mac short for?"

"What makes you think it's short for anything?" he countered.

She put the potatoes in the microwave, set the timer and began to fix a salad. "Because I can't imagine any mother in her right mind holding a newborn baby in her arms, looking down at him lovingly and calling him Mac."

At his silence she glanced at him. "Is it a secret?"

Her light tone belied her interest. He surprised her and himself by answering reluctantly. "My full name is Macauley. I go by Mac."

"Macauley," she repeated softly, pausing in her preparations for a moment. "Macauley O'Neill. Sounds like a poet."

His lips twisted with something that could not pass for a smile. "Hardly."

She had the food on the table a short time later, and Mac tasted the steak cautiously. She was watching him with amusement in her odd-colored eyes, and he knew she recognized his wariness. Finding the steak edible, he dug in. Actually, despite Sarah's remark, the meal wasn't bad, he thought judiciously. Of course, it was hard to ruin a steak or potato, and his appetite hardly ran to the finicky. He'd had to exist too long on field rations to be difficult to please, even after four years out of the military.

Mac made no attempt at conversation during the meal, and after a few stilted efforts, Raine, too, fell silent. She watched as he ate with swift, economical movements. Something told her that he wasn't used to sharing a meal with another person. That much, at least, they had in common.

When Mac had finished eating and had declined the rest of her steak, she carried her plate off the table. He surprised her by doing the same, setting his plate down on the counter. She shot him a surprised smile. "Thanks. You're handy to have around."

"I intend to be," he informed her. "And I may as well get started. I'd like to get my things unloaded before dark."

She blinked. "You mean to leave some equipment here?" Shrugging, she said, "Sure, I guess so. You can put everything in the garage. It can be locked."

"It can also be unlocked pretty easily," he said. "Along with just about every other door and window on your property. As a matter of fact, Miss Michaels, I'd say you're in desperate need of my services. This house isn't the least bit secure."

Setting the dishes in the dishwasher and wiping off the counter, she agreed evenly, "Obviously I've reached a similar conclusion myself, or you wouldn't be here. So tell me, Mr. O'Neill, just what are you going to recommend, how much is it going to cost me, and how long will it take to get done?"

He watched her move gracefully around the kitchen. Her words were very bottom-line, and completely at odds with the attack of nerves he'd observed earlier. "Oh, I think most of it will be pretty painless stuff. We'll have to replace the doors completely, as well as all the locks, and set up a new alarm system. That will include new glass in all the windows," he added, "because they'll need to have alarm wires running through them, too."

She didn't react until he spoke of the windows, and then she looked up, instantly wary. "I bought this place for the view, and I won't have that spoiled. If you're going to recommend bars over the windows, you can forget it." Security bars were common in the larger cities of California, but Raine wouldn't consider them. Their sight always left her uncertain whether they worked to keep others or made prisoners of those inside.

It wasn't until she'd mentioned the bars that Mac realized he hadn't planned to suggest them. He barely knew this woman, yet he'd instinctively known she'd refuse the idea. "You won't notice much difference in the windows," he assured her. "The glass will be thicker, but the wires will be almost invisible."

She frowned slightly as she thought of her haven being turned into a welter of activity, with workers wielding hammers and power drills. Not for the first time, she cursed the weirdo who had targeted her for a special brand of harassment. It had taken her years to reach the point when she felt comfortable living alone. And until the calls and letters had started, her home had been her refuge. She was no longer able to feel completely safe here, and she resented that fiercely. Peace of mind was something most people took for granted, but reaching that state had been a milestone in her life.

She only hoped that the measures Mac O'Neill implemented would be enough to restore it.

"All right," she said. She turned to face him resolutely. "I'd like you to go ahead with your suggestions, and as quickly as possible. How long do you think I'll have to put up with your crew?"

Mac frowned slightly. He was getting a real bad feeling about this job. Or, considering what it had cost him so far, an even *worse* feeling. Something told him that Simon had left a great deal out in his last call to his daughter, and Mac mentally cursed the man. "You'll be rid of my crew in a few days," he said deliberately. "But I'll be around a bit longer."

Raine lost her breath at his next words.

"I'm going to be living with you."

Chapter 2

Raine felt as though she'd had the wind knocked out of her. "Living with me?" she echoed faintly. *"Here?"*

For the first time since he'd left Simon Michaels's office, Mac felt a glimmer of satisfaction. At least he wasn't the only one unhappy with this situation. "You're very astute," he drawled. "Since you're the one in need of protection, and you live here, this is where I'll be. Until I've assured myself and your father of your safety, that is."

"No!" Raine set the broiler in the sink with more force than necessary. Grasping the edge of the sink tightly with both hands, she closed her eyes and took a calming breath. What he was suggesting was impossible. In a quieter tone, she said, "I do not need to be protected. Not this way. And certainly not by..." *A man... this man.* "By one of my father's hired flunkies," she finished.

"I'm nobody's flunky," he replied sotto voce. She looked up and was surprised to find him close, very close. It was his unexpected nearness that had her taking an involuntary step back, not the underlying steel in his voice. But his eyes tracked her movement, and she knew he'd drawn his own conclusion about it.

Caught in the beam of those ice blue eyes, Raine was momentarily transfixed. They were really the most amazing color. The artist in her couldn't help but be fascinated. And the woman in her... well, it had been so long since she'd listened to the woman inside that she wasn't certain she'd recognize the voice. But something in her responded to him. She was too honest with herself to admit otherwise. The realization only complicated the situation.

He reached toward her, and her head jerked wildly, another unconscious action she damned immediately, another one seen and noted by that all-observant gaze. His arm continued its journey toward the sink, turned on the faucet and allowed the hot water to run over the dirty broiler she'd slammed down there.

Raine turned away, shaken by her reaction to the man. Belatedly she attempted to pick up their conversation. "I apologize if I offended you with my choice of words. But I live alone. Your staying here is out of the question."

He misread her trepidation. "Concerned about appearances?" he mocked. "Somehow, in light of your troubles, I think that's a little foolish, don't you?" He watched her with a slight furrow still etched in his brow, wondering not for the first time, just exactly what Simon *had* told her. Not much, apparently. Not enough to encounter the total resistance Mac was getting from her now. The old bastard was shrewdly presenting her with a fait accompli, leaving the dirty details to Mac. Even though he'd spent his career dealing with the fine art of dirty details, he wished Simon was within punching range. He was getting the feeling that the depth of his daughter's opposition was just one in a long list of items Simon had glossed over when filling Mac in on this job.

Heaving a disgusted sigh, he turned to face her, leaning against the counter. "Look," he said flatly. "We'd better get this all out in the open, even though you're probably not going to want to hear it. Hell," he added under his breath, "I *know* you're not going to want to hear it. But I won't be leaving until I've thoroughly investigated these phone calls and letters you've been receiving. I was hired by your father to secure your house and to make sure that the wacko who's been threatening you doesn't get close enough to hurt you. Once I'm certain you're in no danger, I'll be out of your hair. You'll be free to do whatever it is you like to be alone to do out here, and I'll be on a beach in the South Pacific, working on an allover tan with someone much happier about having me around."

He stopped then, his explanation complete, but Raine was looking at him in disbelief. The fact that he appeared no more pleased than she about this state of affairs didn't make her feel any better. "I still can't believe this. He hired you to be my body-guard, didn't he?"

He lifted one shoulder. "If you want to call it that."

She shook her head incredulously. "What are you, a cop or something?"

"Or something," he agreed. "My partner and I own a firm called Security Associates. Our jobs entail different things for different people, but our priority is to keep our clients safe. It's obvious your father didn't give you the whole story on the phone, but you did agree to have me come here, remember?"

Oh, she remembered, all right. And she could now see how easily her father had manipulated this arrangement She'd already reached the conclusion that she needed to hire someone to assess her security needs. With all she'd had to do lately getting ready for her upcoming show, she had, in a rare moment of dependence, allowed her father to choose a reputable security company for her He'd done that, and more. He'd used her acquiescence to set his own plans in motion.

But this... She found it difficult to comprehend how her father could be this callous about her feelings. To hire a stranger—a man—to stay here with her, to live with her, if only for a short time... whatever could he have been thinking?

The answer, of course, was that her father hadn't been thinking, at least not about what had happened eleven years ago. He *never* thought about that, had never dealt with it. He reacted to the here and now. He'd determined what was needed, and he'd arranged it, leaving her, as usual, to deal with it as she would.

She waited for panic to set in, to crowd aside her anger at her father's machinations. Under no circumstances could she allow a stranger to move into her home, no matter what his motives were. The man was here, but that didn't mean he had to stay.

"Mr. O'Neill," she began resolutely.

"Mac," he corrected. "Just Mac."

"All right—Mac," she agreed. "You probably don't know my father well, but this sort of... shall we say *misunderstanding* is common for him. I neither need nor want a bodyguard, and I will not pay for those services. I am in need of your security advice, however. I'm sure we can work something out in that area." She watched him warily, hoping he'd agree. She couldn't afford to take time away from her painting right now to investigate another security company.

Mac turned his back on her then, already bored with the scene. He wasn't a man who avoided confrontation, but arguing held no appeal for him. Her show of stubbornness would change nothing. He shut off the water in the sink, reached for a scraper beside the faucet and began scrubbing the broiler.

"I've already been paid for this job, Miss Michaels, by your father. That means we do this his way. It'll be a hell of a lot easier on all of us if you'd just give in gracefully this time."

He'd struck a nerve, although, with his back to her, he was unaware of it. Raine had stopped giving in a long time ago, and despite what he thought, it had been a difficult habit to break. It had been necessary in her long quest for independence, and she wasn't going to backtrack now. She had tread many miles on the path of least resistance before discovering that it didn't lead anywhere she was particularly interested in going.

"Whatever he's paying you, I'll double it," she announced baldly. "Go ahead with the other security measures we discussed. Then you can get on that plane, and I'll deal with my father."

"No." He rinsed the pan and dried it with a towel hanging above the counter. "Where do you want this?"

"What do you mean, no?" she demanded. "Darn it, turn around and look at me. What's my father given you to make you this unreasonable?"

He did face her then, and impatience was written on his hard features. "It's not what he's given me, it's what I gave him. My word. I won't leave until I'm sure you're safe, and that's final. Drop it, Raine."

She stared at him in frustration. He stared back implacably. She was the first to look away. "A bodyguard is an extreme measure, I can assure you. The police haven't seemed all that concerned about a few notes and phone calls, since no actual physical threats have been made. If you'd just talk to them, you'd understand."

"They probably won't talk to me," he responded, startling her. "I'll call the detective in charge, of course, but I'm pretty sure it will be useless. Information on cases like these is shared on a need-to-know basis." Experience had taught him that the police would pump him for any information he could give them on the case, but would be damn reluctant to share any of their own. "You'll have to fill me in on what's been going on since the threats began, and I'll be talking to the people who spend a lot of time out here. I'll draw my own conclusions." He set the pan on the stove and turned to face her again. "If I decide that you're in no real danger, that's what I'll tell your father."

Raine considered his promise. A part of her, one she hadn't wanted to listen to, had wondered just how secure a few more bells and alarms were going to make her feel. But this man's word would be something else entirely. If he was able to stay long enough to see the work through, he'd have enough information at his disposal to judge her situation accurately. And if, at that time, he was able to assure her she was safe, she knew she'd believe him.

The mere thought of having him in such close proximity had all her nerves quivering. And she wasn't totally sure that it was only her wariness of strangers, and of men in general, that caused such a response. There was something disturbing about Mac—no, *Macauley*—O'Neill.

She chewed her bottom lip. His sheer size and uncompromising stance were intimidating. There was no reason to trust him, and with her history, trust didn't come easily. Could she really risk the resurgence of all her old fears by letting this man stay?

Could she risk sending him away?

"All right," she said slowly, struck by the finality of her words. "You can stay."

His face was impassive. He obviously hadn't expected the outcome to be any different. "When we start working, I'll need access to the entire house and everything in it."

"My studio," she informed him firmly, "is off-limits."

"There may be wiring that needs to be done," he warned. "And when we get to the windows . . ."

She winced a little, already dreading the day that the one haven left to her would be disturbed by workers and pounding hammers. "I'll understand when work needs to be done there."

He watched her intently for a moment more, but she seemed to be sincere. He gave an abrupt nod. "All right, then." Obviously finished, he turned and headed for the door.

"You can move your things into the first bedroom on the right," she called after him, a little surprised at the rustiness of her voice. He didn't acknowledge her words, and a moment later the front door closed behind him.

Leaning weakly against the counter, she wiped her damp palms on her thighs. She felt as though she'd just been run over by a steamroller. Already she was having second thoughts about her decision. She didn't imagine that they'd be her last during his time here. But it would only be for a while, she assured herself. Surely it would only be a couple of weeks before things would get back to normal and Macauley O'Neill would be out of her life. Whoever was harassing her was certain to be caught soon, and then she could finish her paintings for her show in peace.

The thought of a stranger, this man, living in her house seemed to affect her with temporary paralysis. His presence filled her with so many tumultuous emotions, it was impossible to sift through them all. But even in the midst of that turmoil, her thoughts were curiously distracted. Her mind insisted upon painting pictures of Macauley on the beach he'd mentioned.

Working on that all-over tan.

Two days later Raine was in the den with her accountant, and her patience was wearing thin. "I don't know, Greg, do whatever you think is right. I trust your judgment. Whatever you recommend is fine with me."

Mac stepped into the room in time to hear her words, and his mouth twisted. Apparently Raine's accountant was given a much freer hand than her security expert, and he'd bet that Greg hadn't had to drag those concessions from her the way Mac had.

"You're not even listening to what I'm telling you, Raine. Just take some time and study this portfolio I'm putting together for you."

"Why in heaven's name do we have to do this now?"

Mac leaned against the doorjamb, eavesdropping unabashedly.

Raine tossed a file folder on the desk frustratedly. "I hired an accountant, Greg, so I wouldn't have to be bothered constantly with these matters. You know how busy I am getting ready for this next show. Can't we discuss this when you have it completed?" She got to her feet in barely restrained impatience and paced a few steps away.

Mac couldn't help noticing that though her hips were narrow, her bottom had an unmistakably womanly curve. He pushed aside the unwelcome observation and spoke deliberately. "Raine."

Both Raine and Greg turned at the sound of his voice. Mac noted Greg's annoyance at the interruption. He'd spoken to the man yesterday, questioning him at length about his knowledge of the threats. From the amount of time Winters spent here, Mac was beginning to wonder if Raine was his only client. She was obviously his favorite one. The man was only a few inches taller than she was, with thinning, sandy-colored hair and earnest brown eyes that were fixed on her. Mac thought he read more than a professional interest in the man's gaze. "I need to talk to you."

"We're right in the middle of—"

"That's okay." Raine interrupted Greg's irritated statement with undisguised eagerness. She laid a hand on the man's arm placatingly. "I really do have to talk to Mr. O'Neill, Greg. Just go ahead and finalize those plans. I'll look at the file when you have things ready to be signed."

Greg threw Mac a glance rife with frustration, but picked up the file folder and placed it in his briefcase. "I might as well get back to my office, if you're going to be busy," he said stiffly. "I'll talk to you about this later. And I'm going to insist that you hear me out before you make any final decisions."

Raine waved goodbye and, when he'd left, looked at Mac. Her uneasiness at having him in the house had ebbed a little. She rarely saw him. Though she was an early riser, he was earlier. When she got up in the morning he was already in the family room, which he seemed to have taken over for his own uses. Without a word to her he'd moved in a large desk, chair and a computer, all of which must have come off one of the trucks loaded with materials that were arriving hourly.

Although some of the natural edginess she'd felt at having him here as a prolonged guest was wearing off, that didn't mean *he* didn't bother her. Even from a distance he'd still proven to be something of a distraction. Though she'd gotten back to her current painting, more than once she'd found herself wandering to a window overlooking the driveway, watching him supervise the unloading of supplies.

Nor could she keep her eyes from lingering on him now. He seemed to have a perpetual shadow of whiskers on that rock-hard jaw, and she wondered at it. Her knowledge of men's beards was nonexistent, but it seemed to her that at some time he would have to appear either clean-shaven or with the start of a beard. The dark clothes he was wearing, combined with his perpetually slightly disheveled appearance, gave him a look that was lethally dangerous. She didn't recognize the skitter of electricity that vibrated down her spine every time she got this close to him. It wasn't fear, but it was an uncomfortable sensation, nonetheless. His presence was too overpowering. Her first instinct each time they were together was to put an additional three feet between them. She held her ground. She'd given up running years ago.

Giving him a wry smile of gratitude, she said, "My hero. You just saved my sanity. Greg is a dear, sweet man, but listening to him talk money makes me want to run screaming into the sunset."

Closing the door behind him, Mac sauntered across the room and sank down into an easy chair. "He's right, you know," he said. "You can't sign things without reading them—that's the height of stupidity."

Her eyebrows climbed at his insinuation. "I always read the papers," she replied tartly. "But only once. I don't share Greg's enthusiasm for debating endlessly about money-market accounts and tax-deferred bonds."

"Sounds like he has quite a bit of power." He gave her a level look. "It's a little naive to put all your trust in one individual. How do you know he won't take off with your money?"

"I thought the point of hiring experts was to let them do what they're expert at," she responded sweetly. "Or so you've told me." She walked past him and sat on the couch.

"You're too trusting," he said flatly. "That's probably what's gotten you into this mess to begin with." She wrinkled her nose at him and curled her legs gracefully beneath her. The supple movement drew his unwilling gaze for a moment. She was once again dressed in jeans, which hugged her tiny curves faithfully. Her feet were bare. He tried to remember if he'd ever seen her wear shoes, and couldn't recall that he had.

"No use trying to be diplomatic," she said dryly. "It's obviously a strain for you. Did you really have something you needed to discuss, or did you just want to insult me?"

"I wanted to warn you," he replied. "I've gotten just about everything I need to get started installing the security system we talked about. There will be workers arriving within the hour to start on the job."

He certainly didn't believe in wasting time, she mused. Somehow, that didn't surprise her. "You wanted to give me enough time to barricade myself in my studio?" she asked, only half-joking.

No hint of amusement showed in his ice blue gaze. "I want you to stick around until they arrive. If that's no bother."

He needn't have added that last phrase, as if he was concerned with politeness. She wasn't fooled. It had been a order, not a request. Not for the first time she wondered where he'd acquired that tone of authority, the presence that said he was used to issuing orders and having them carried out. She didn't quite believe that it all stemmed from his current job, although that would certainly add to it.

"What do you need me for?"

His gaze narrowed. He'd just witnessed her giving Greg Winters carte blanche with her money, for Pete's sake, while he was expected to debate each step he took to keep her safe. He'd had more difficult clients before, and some much more irritating, so he couldn't quite put his finger on the reason she could so easily spark his usually banked temper. He put it down to the fact that his mood had been approaching dangerous since her father had first coerced him into this job.

The explanation he gave was terse. "I want you to meet each of the workers who'll be around for the next few days. Get a good look at them so you'll remember their faces."

An unexpected chill ran down her spine. "You mean so I'll recognize them," she interpreted slowly.

He nodded. "After today, if you see any new faces around here, you find me, pronto. That shouldn't be too difficult, since I won't be far from your side for the duration of this case."

She blinked at him, the lights in her golden eyes dimming. And then she looked away. Her voice, when it came, was quiet. "You think someone might actually come into my house and threaten me?"

He heard the nerves beneath the even tone, but he didn't bother to sugarcoat his answer. "We won't be taking that risk." Not waiting for an answer, he went on. "I've spoken to the police." As he'd assumed, the detective had been unforthcoming about the investigation, saying that he'd discuss it only with Miss Michaels. Mac had gotten most of his information from Winters and Klassen the day before, when he'd interviewed the people who came and went so freely here. Both men had been visibly reluctant to speak to him. "Winters said he saved a total of four letters, which were eventually handed over to the detective. How many others have there been?"

"At least that many."

"When did they start?"

Raine pulled her knees up in front of her and clasped them with her arms. She felt the sudden need for something solid to hold on to. "The phone calls began about a month ago, but only lasted a few days. Then the letters started. At first I tried to ignore them. After all, the calls stopped by themselves, and I thought the letters would, too." She could feel disapproval emanating from him, although he remained silent. "André pointed out that the letters started a week after articles about me had appeared in the newspapers and in a magazine," she informed him. Grimacing, she added, "When you're in the public eye, you draw a lot of attention. Not all of it's positive."

She was reciting word for the word the same line Klassen had given him yesterday. Mac hadn't liked it any better then. He wondered if Klassen was the reason she didn't take action on the threats sooner. He'd taken an instant dislike to the self-important agent, with his impeccable suits and carefully groomed hair. The feeling had been mutual. "I would think that would be all the more reason to take safety precautions," he drawled.

She looked away. She was uncomfortably aware that the first response she'd had to the letters was denial. Facing the danger had been too much like facing a reflection of her past. She despised herself when she took the easy way out, but that was exactly what she'd done by embracing André's assurances that the letters were the products of a crank. She'd tried to be strong, as André had urged, until the nightmares returned, reminding her insidiously that inner strength was no match against a person intent on doing evil. "When they continued, I got more and more spooked. So did everyone else. I suppose that's what drove Greg to save the ones I eventually turned over to the detective last week."

Mac flipped open the notebook he'd been holding and glanced at the scrawled phrases he'd jotted when questioning Winters. " 'You're nothing.' 'Why should you have it all?' 'You're headed for a fall.' 'Your days are numbered.' " He looked up and saw that her cheeks had grown a shade paler as he'd read the messages out loud. But she met his gaze squarely. "Were all of them in this vein?"

"More or less."

"How about the phone calls? Did you recognize the voice?"

She shook her head. "It was always a whisper, but the message was pretty much the same. My harasser apparently isn't very creative."

He ignored her feeble joke. "When did the last letter come?"

"A week ago."

"Do you have any idea at all who might be sending them?"

"Detective Ramirez already asked me that, and the answer is no." The way he was firing the questions at her made her feel she was being interrogated. Certainly he was being as thorough as the detective she had talked to. "The calls always came late at night, and the letters have all been in my mail."

That brought up another interesting point. "When the detective talked about the letters you'd turned over to him, he didn't mention anything about envelopes." And no amount of questioning had garnered much else from the man, either. Mac had left the police headquarters frustrated, although he'd known what to expect. He doubted even Trey Garrison's accomplished finesse would have been enough to pry more information from the close-mouthed Detective Ramirez.

"I was upset by the first few letters," she explained carefully. Nothing in her tone hinted at the panic she'd experienced upon receiving them. "André was concerned that I was getting too agitated, and right before my upcoming show." She added wryly, "Very inconvenient timing, you see. Anyway, he offered to take care of them, and I let him. I wasn't aware Greg had saved some of them until later. There was nothing remarkable about the envelopes, believe me. They were white and standard size, addressed to me." She smiled faintly. "All the printing looked computer generated. Nothing so dramatic as messages made up of cutout letters from newspapers, if that's what you're getting at."

"Think about those envelopes," he urged, his turquoise gaze intent. "Where did they come from?"

Misunderstanding his meaning, Raine frowned in annoyance. "I already told you, I don't know who—"

He shook his head and interrupted her. "No, I don't mean *who* sent them. What city did they come from? What did the postmarks read?"

Comprehension came swiftly. And then, as she tried to remember, foreboding followed. "I think," she said slowly, "I'm almost certain that some of them had L.A. postmarks."

"Some of them?" he questioned sharply.

She shrugged helplessly. "I don't recall whether I noticed the postmark on every single letter."

Inexorably, he questioned, "Don't recall what the postmark was stamped, or don't recall whether every one had a postmark?"

"Well, of course they had postmarks," she asserted. Under that unrelenting gaze, she moistened her lips. Darn it all, the man had a way of making her feel like she was a sandwich shy of a picnic. "I mean, I assume they all had one."

At this disclosure, his eyes closed briefly, as if in pain. "Do me a favor, will you?" he asked through gritted teeth. "Quit assuming things. You are in danger here, and some of it is because you *assume* too damn much."

Her jeweled eyes were wide, watching him guardedly. He didn't give a damn. This piece of information put a whole new light on the case, and he didn't like the possibilities. He didn't like them at all.

Mac struggled to rein in his temper. "Let me get this straight. All the letters were found in your mailbox." At her short nod, he went on. "You know this, of course, because you bring your own mail in daily." His voice sounded slightly hopeful.

Raine opened her mouth to answer, then, at his knowing gaze, snapped it shut again.

He gave a humorless smile. "Somehow I thought not. So all the letters were found *among* your mail, which is brought in the house by..." His voice tapered off, an invitation for her to continue.

She felt like giving him a swift kick instead. She was finding she liked his sarcasm even less than that expressionless mask he adopted most of the time. His thoughts right now were all too apparent. "I usually bring in my own mail," she informed him tartly. "But on occasion it's brought in by André, Greg or Sarah."

"Or one of the endless stream of art students who wander in and out of here at will?"

"No."

"No?"

Raine glared at him. She knew what he was insinuating, and the fact that hindsight had proven there was some truth to his concerns didn't make her feel any more kindly toward him. She defended herself. "Look, I don't spend a great deal of time downstairs during the day. I'm usually in my studio. I have two more works to get done for my upcoming show. I'm involved in endless meetings with André and Greg and you can't believe how many other people."

"You've been careless," he stated evenly. "And whether you like to admit it or not, the possible lack of postmarks on some of the letters changes everything." His eyes were icier than usual. He had a mental vision of his vacation sprouting wings and flying away. "It means that this jerk may have already been closer to you than you want to admit. Close enough to have placed a letter in your mailbox, anyway."

She swallowed hard. "We don't know that."

"But it's a possibility, and we'll have to act on it. I'd strongly advise you to invest in a fence across the front of your property, one with motorized gates."

She rubbed her hands over arms that were suddenly chilled. "A fence?" she repeated dumbly.

He nodded, watching her reaction closely. "I'll bring in some catalogs, and you can pick out a style you like. The doors and windows will take only a week or so to install. The fence will be a bigger project. I may have to order some of the materials, but that shouldn't be a problem."

She wasn't concentrating on his words. It took all her strength to keep from screaming her opposition. Memories flooded her, reminding her of the time she'd moved with her family to Burbank as a teenager. The house had come equipped with all the latest electronic features, to keep them safe, her father had assured her. As if it had happened yesterday she remembered the first day she'd stood inside the drive. The gates had closed behind her with a gentle, irrevocable *snick*. It hadn't been a feeling of safety they'd generated in her that day. Instead she'd felt like a prisoner. If her father had had his way she'd still be living behind those protective barriers, protected from harm and from life in general.

"No," she whispered, as much to the memory as to Mac.

He leaned forward, his arms on his hard thighs, his face implacable. "Yes. That's exactly what you're going to do, Raine, and you know why? Because you put me in charge here, and until this thing is over, I'm calling the shots." He lifted a hand to stem her response. "You said you'd listen to my ideas once I'd assessed the situation. Well, here they are. Lady, you're in real trouble. You can't brush these threats off as the work of some crank. Cranks lose interest quickly—they don't keep harassing their targets indefinitely. And you can't rely on the police to help you, because they don't have a thing to go on, especially without the envelopes. I doubt this case is a real high priority with them at this point, anyway. No one has actually been hurt." His pause was full of meaning. "Yet."

She sprang up from the couch. "You're deliberately trying to scare me." And he was succeeding admirably. All the panic she'd managed to suppress from the time the threats began was all too close to the surface now. Which of course meant that she hadn't been suppressing it at all, hadn't been dealing with it, as André had insisted. She'd been getting through the last few weeks by denying its existence.

Until the nightmares had made even that feat impossible.

"You should be scared," he agreed bluntly. "That's what I've been trying to tell you. Because all the alarms and fences in the world can't make it impossible for someone to get to you, if that's what he really wants."

His words affected her like a dash of ice water. She paced away from him, giving herself time to recover. "Careful there, Macauley, or you'll talk yourself out of a job."

"Not quite," he returned tersely. "Because the rest of my job is to make sure no one *does* get to you." She whirled around then to face him, and her look of utter dismay was enough to tell him that she'd interpreted his meaning accurately. "As I said, you could spend a fortune securing your home and property and still not be completely safe. You're taking the kind of precautions that would make wise choices for anyone living out here. The rest of the job will be up to me."

She interpreted his words correctly. "How long . . . do you plan to stay?"

"As long as it takes," he said flatly. "Until this nut is stopped, you're in danger." After a pause, he added, "I've already informed your father."

"Great," she muttered. She dug the tips of her fingers into the back pockets of her jeans, feeling as tautly drawn as a wire. There was definitely nothing calming about this man. But in fairness to him, she had to admit that he didn't soft-pedal bad news, either. She grudgingly respected that. She preferred to face reality head-on than to be coddled from it. The knowledge that she hadn't been doing a particularly good job of that recently wasn't too comforting. "I should probably warn you to expect calls from my brothers, William and John. No doubt Dad has already filled them in, and they take their roles of big brothers extremely seriously."

Mac didn't bother to inform her that he'd already spoken to William. And she was right, her brother had been outraged that Raine hadn't taken action immediately. Mac even agreed with William's description of his sister, up to a point. There *was* something almost otherworldly about Raine at times, as if she was detached from the details of life. But he'd noticed that was usually when she was preoccupied with her painting. He was beginning to believe that her family tended to underestimate her. There were other times when she could be unbelievably tenacious. Especially when she was arguing with him.

He shrugged mentally. Actually, this scene had gone better than he'd had a right to expect. She'd hadn't been thrilled with his news, but she hadn't refused to cooperate, either. "This won't last forever, Raine. And it shouldn't interfere with your painting. I'll answer the phone and bring in the mail." That drew an arch look from her, which he chose to ignore. "You'll need to keep your outside engagements to an absolute minimum, but if you do have to go anywhere, I'll go with you."

She was silent, surveying the floor in melancholy resignation. His next words shattered that mood, however.

"Of course it will be necessary to restrict your visitors. The house will be declared off-limits to guests."

At his words she could feel the walls from her childhood spring up and begin to close in around her. "That is out of the question!"

Mac watched her from beneath hooded lids. Her eyes were spitting golden sparks at him. "You think so?"

"I draw the line right there." She approached him and said fiercely, "Dammit, Macauley, I'm not going to let you turn me into a hermit!"

He frowned impatiently. "Call me Mac. And it's necessary, Raine."

She continued as if he hadn't spoken. "My friends are always welcome in my home. If André and Greg can't come here, that means I'll have to spend more of my time going to their offices for meetings. That will take me away from my painting and make your job more difficult." She could tell by the way he considered her words that she'd made a valid point. She pressed on. "And I can't just tell the students they can no longer come here to paint. The peacefulness here is inspiring. I'm not going to rescind my invitation."

"If you won't, I will." His voice was impatient. He should have known she wouldn't give in easily. "It's not going to be all that peaceful around here, with all the work my men will be doing, so they won't be missing much."

"I refuse to alter my life any more than I've already agreed to. Don't you understand?" She tried to reason with him. "If I let this weirdo completely change the way I live, I've also let him win. I won't do that, Macauley—I can't. It's taken me too long to take control of my life. I won't give it up now."

He didn't know which annoyed him more, her continued use of his given name or her obstinance. "You're overreacting. We're not talking forever here, just a few weeks at the most. You're not giving up your life to someone, but a little healthy dose of fear has done wonders to keep some people alive."

"And too much stifles them to the point that they might as well be dead," she retorted. "If a person isn't experiencing life, she isn't living it, either."

His temper snapped at her stubbornness. He rose swiftly to his feet and crossed to her in two long strides. "What you're experiencing here, lady, is something most people go out of their way to avoid." His voice was close to a shout, but she didn't back down, and her gaze was just as furious as his. Jerking her chin up with one hand, he bent down so that his face was inches from hers. "You talked about being scared earlier, Raine, and you sure as hell should be. There's a sicko out there who's trying to get your attention. Trying to frighten you, and baby, whoever it is might already have been close enough to be on your property. Remember that the next time you think about bucking me. Maybe it's someone you know, maybe not. Maybe he walks right into your house, and he's welcomed here, or maybe he hides in the shadows. He could be out there at night, watching this place, watching you—"

"Stop it!" she cried. His taunting words painted a scene straight out of her nightmares. The stress she'd been under for the past few weeks seemed to gel, and for a second it was all directed at this man. Her fingers clenched into fists and she pushed hard against his chest, punctuating her words. "Just—stop it!"

Chapter 3

Raine became aware of her actions at the same moment Mac gathered both her fists into one large hand. She stared at him in shock, her body frozen by her loss of control. Their gazes melded.

Her eyes were pure amber now, and he was struck with the realization that the look he'd thought he'd recognized in them upon their first meeting hadn't been a fluke. For an instant they were full of anguish. Why the hell did she try to pretend to be unaffected by all of this? Because she was far from unaffected, that was clear. She was close enough that he could feel her heart racing, her body quivering.

She tugged at her hands, but he didn't release them. She looked down, wishing to escape from that speculative regard. She was afraid of what he'd see. He was so observant she felt like a butterfly impaled on a pin beneath that searching stare. Certainly she had all too good an idea what he might find if he looked hard enough, if he was perceptive enough.

He released her wrists, and she immediately turned away from him. It really wasn't a question of whether or not the man was perceptive. She had a sinking feeling that very little got by Macauley O'Neill. She moved toward the fireplace and pretended an intense interest in its decorative oak mantel.

"I'm sorry," she said in a low voice. He said nothing, and she still wasn't controlled enough to turn around and face him again. She forced a shaky laugh. "I can assure you that I only attack someone once a week, so you're safe for the next several days."

He remained silent, and she angled her head around to peek at him. He was expressionless, watching her silently, and her throat went dry. She'd never met anyone so difficult to read, and she suddenly wondered why it seemed so important to know what he was thinking.

When he did speak, he didn't mention her loss of control or her apology. "If you'd think about this rationally, you'd admit that it makes sense to limit the number of people who have access to you." He was silent for a moment, thinking swiftly. Then he said grudgingly, "Maybe we won't have to bar guests completely. If André and Greg are still allowed in here, will you agree to tell the art students to stay away?"

It shocked her a little to hear him suggest something that sounded very close to a compromise. She had the feeling the concept was foreign to him. She considered the offer. "I'd want to be able to see Sarah, also."

His tone was unmistakably sarcastic. "You have meetings with her, too?"

"No," she informed him evenly, "but she's a very dear friend of mine. And she's been having a rough time lately dealing with her younger brother. It's affected her work, and she needs me for support."

"Fine," he snarled, at the end of his patience. "André, Greg and Sarah will be allowed in. No one else, except my men and your family."

It was clear he was already regretting the concession he'd made. She wondered at a sudden compulsion she had to soothe him. "William and John don't get away from the city more than once a month, and I just saw them last week. And I usually visit with my parents at their home. My mother suffers from a chronic heart ailment, and she hasn't been well lately. As for the students..." She hesitated, uncertain what she would tell them to keep them away. She was loath to let them in on the threats. Perhaps it would be enough to let them know how hectic things would be, with Mac's work crew around. "I'll take care of contacting them," she said finally.

Mac crossed to the desk in the corner of the room and rummaged through the drawers until he found a notepad and pen. Then he came back and sat down. "All right, that's settled. Now I need for you to give me a complete list of the people who have been in and out of here lately." It wouldn't have to be a regular guest wreaking havoc on Raine's life. Anyone who could come and go at will had the opportunity to place those notes in her mail. It could be, as he'd pointed out, someone who was welcomed to the house. It could also be someone completely unknown to her, but first he was going to have to work through process of elimination.

She would have liked to ask why he needed the names, but after a look at his face decided not to push her luck. She knew intuitively that his temper was still simmering. She began with Sarah, Greg and André. They were by far her most frequent visitors. She named several other friends who stopped in occasionally, and included the art students. He asked for the name of the courses and the instructors for whose classes she'd been invited to speak. Finally, after racking her brain for a while longer, she shrugged. "That's it, I guess."

"You're sure?" he pressed. "Are all the people I saw here in the last couple days on this list?"

She looked blank for a moment. "I suppose so. I have to confess, I don't always know myself who's here. If my work's going well I sometimes don't come out of my studio until dusk." She wasn't about to relay that he'd provided an unusual distraction several times already.

He folded up the list he'd written. "Things will start changing around here immediately."

That sounded ominous. Raine looked at him distrustfully. "Exactly what does that mean?"

"It means that I'm going to hold you to this agreement we've hammered out," he said bluntly. "And it means that you're going to have to trust me to do my job, and stop starting a war every time I suggest something that's for your own good." He cocked an eyebrow. "Is that clear?" he asked.

For her own good. She couldn't count the number of times she'd heard that phrase in her childhood. "What is clear," she announced, gritting her teeth, "is that you've got ego where your brain should be. If you think I'm never going to question a suggestion you make, you'd better think again. I'm not a trained seal."

"Not well-trained, no," he put in.

She glared at him. He stared implacably back. That remark was the first hint of humor she'd noted in the man, and at any other time she would have been pleasantly surprised by it. She'd always thought that a sense of humor was the only thing that made life bearable at times. She hadn't expected to find one in Macauley O'Neill. He seemed too tough, too jaded. But since his humor was veiled and sarcastic and directed at her, she was less than amused by it.

"You're hilarious," she informed him. "But I still expect to be consulted before you make any major changes around here."

He ignored her verbal rebellion. Already he regretted backing off on the issue of her visitors. Her argument about allowing Greg and André here made sense. But he knew she regarded the concession as a compromise, and would expect future ones. She'd be disappointed—that wasn't the way he worked. He was here to do a job, and he wasn't about to run each of his ideas by her over afternoon tea and get her approval. Compromises didn't necessarily keep people alive.

Not for the first time, he wished that his partner, Trey Garrison, was handling this job. He had infinitely more patience, and could even trot out some charm when it was called for. No doubt he could have long talks with Raine Michaels and convince her that every idea he had was her own. Mac lacked the ability and the inclination to do so.

He frowned at the woman before him, looking back so defiantly, and wondered why on earth she annoyed him so much. It shouldn't matter to him that she questioned his every move, even though he knew damn well that her accountant and probably her agent had freer rein. And he was protecting *her,* for Pete's sake, not just her money or career. Most likely it was just that Raine Michaels was turning out to be a big pain in the butt, at a time in his life when he had even less patience than normal for dealing with big pains.

"Well?" she prompted, interrupting his musings.

"Consider yourself consulted," he said shortly, and turned to leave the room. Over his shoulder, he added sardonically, "But I'll sure let you know the next time something comes up that's open for discussion."

Raine stared at his departing back, openmouthed. That man, she fumed, was totally insufferable. She shouldn't be surprised, since her father had recommended him so highly. No doubt it was considered an admirable trait by Simon Michaels. But it was a bit wearing on her. She walked over to a nearby chair, kicking its leg childishly. She winced as the resulting pain reminded her that she was, as usual, barefoot. She sank into the chair, rubbing her toes, a wry smile pulling at her lips. Every action had a consequence. If she had learned anything in her life, it was that. The thought quickly had the smile fading from her face.

The phone rang then, and she startled. It was silenced abruptly after one ring, indicating that it had been picked up somewhere else in the house. She caught a look at her reflection in the mirror over the fireplace, one hand held to her heart, eyes as wide as a deer's caught in the headlights.

Get a hold of yourself, Raine, she scolded herself mentally. First she'd fallen apart in front of Macauley O'Neill, and now a ringing telephone was spooking her. She took some deep breaths and sat down in the chair, folding her legs under her. Her eyes went to the window. The expanse of green lawn gently rolling to the road, and the walnut grove in the distance, painted a scene that never failed to calm her. Today, however, its usual peace was jarred by the sight of yet another truck rumbling up the driveway toward her house.

She turned her gaze away, troubled. The unceasing activity surrounding her home was impossible to ignore, as were the reasons for it. She'd tried to relegate the need for Macauley O'Neill, or someone like him, to the furthest corner of her mind, telling herself she had energy only to focus on her work right now. But brutal self-honesty was a trait she tried to cultivate, and it forced her to admit that she'd been playing ostrich for the last few weeks. In not allowing her fear from the past to take over, she'd failed to respond appropriately to the threats at all.

Raine swallowed, self-doubt welling inside her. She'd worked very hard to overcome most of the demons that had haunted her for years. But somehow, today, her modest triumphs over the shadows in her past seemed trivial, like so much window dressing to disguise a vacant storefront. Shivering, she wrapped her arms closer.

Staring sightlessly at the wall, Raine wondered bleakly whether she had the courage to face being the target of someone's malice yet again.

"Raine." Mac's voice held a note of impatience. He'd looked all over the whole house, fully expecting to find her in her studio, doing that work she was always claiming she was behind on. He hadn't expected she'd still be in the room in which he'd left her, staring into space.

She turned her head slowly to look at him, but didn't get up.

"The crew has arrived. I'd like you to meet the men who'll be doing some work here for the next few days."

She took a deep breath, then rose. "All right."

He glanced at her sharply as she passed by him on her way to the front door. Her tone was subdued, as was her manner. He'd grown weary of her constant debating with him, but he thought that he'd prefer it to the way she seemed now, as if a light inside had been snuffed out as easily as a candle flame by careless fingers.

He wondered if he'd been too rough on her earlier. He didn't have a lot of polish, and he made little effort to hide the fact. When her bravado had been stripped away, she'd revealed real fear. Mac shook his head and followed her to the door. He couldn't expend any remorse for that. Getting her to admit a threat existed had been necessary to enlist her cooperation. It was damn near impossible to protect a person who refused to recognize the seriousness of the situation.

He followed her out on the porch. "Over here, everyone," he said tersely.

Raine slanted a look at him as the men moved immediately. No wonder he ordered her around as if he was a drill sergeant. If he was used to commanding this kind of reaction from the people around him, she was probably lucky he hadn't assigned her to hard labor for being insubordinate. Despite her dismal mood, her mouth quirked at the thought.

Mac ran through the introductions quickly. What would have seemed a courtesy by any other man was clearly not, in this case. He turned to her and said curtly, "Take a good look at their faces."

She obeyed, smiling at each of the men in turn. "Hi," she said to the crew assembled. "I understand you're the guys who are going to make my life unbearable for the next few days."

Most of the men smiled, some responded.

"Only for a little while, ma'am."

"We'll try not to be in your way long."

"Yeah, then it will be up to Mac to make your life unbearable."

Raine turned to look at the man at her side consideringly. "A role I'm sure he'll fill nicely," she responded in a wry voice, and they laughed.

Yet another man walked up then, in time to hear the exchange. "You won't be the first to have that opinion of ol' Mac, here," the man said. "He doesn't waste a lot of energy on charm."

"That's your area, not mine," Mac agreed. He made a motion with his hand, and the other men dispersed, going back to their task of unloading equipment. The man to whom he'd spoken leaned forward with his hand extended toward Raine.

"Trey Garrison, Mac's partner. As you can probably figure, I'm the brains of the outfit."

Raine laughed and shook his hand. "If that's so," she said, casting a look at Mac, "then I'm scared to death. Macauley's mind clips along at a rate faster than the speed of light, and I'm not always thrilled with the things it comes up with."

Trey's eyebrows lifted at her use of Mac's full name. "Sounds like you've been busy, then," Trey addressed his friend, climbing the steps toward them. It wasn't until the two men stood side by side that Raine was struck by an incredible similarity between the two, a similarity that owed nothing to the physical. Oh, they were both tall and broad through the shoulders, but Trey's hair was black, his thickly lashed eyes a glittering emerald green, and his chin bore a deep cleft.

She observed both men carefully, her artist's eye charmed even as her mind puzzled over their resemblance. She'd give anything to paint them like this, standing side by side, or, better yet, profile to profile. Both were frankly wonderful specimens of manhood, and she was grateful that such examples were wasted on her. But it was much more than their physical attributes that she'd wish to convey in a picture. There were edges to Macauley that he made no effort to hide, and she thought she could discern such edges in Trey also, although he made attempts to disguise them. Though he was still smiling, amusement didn't touch his eyes. They remained watchful and alert, and somehow Raine knew that although he was looking at her, his attention was equally attuned to their surroundings.

That intense observation was what reminded her most strongly of Macauley, she decided. Both men gave her the uncomfortable feeling that she'd been sized up in the space of an instant, and neither gave away their reactions to that sum. There were auras of strength and power surrounding them, as if in any crisis these men could be counted on to take control. They hadn't gained that presence by years in the security business, Raine knew that instinctively. Something much more dangerous, much more lethal had shaped these men, had left indelible marks on their psyches. She wondered why it suddenly seemed so important to her to find out just what those experiences had been.

"Did you come to work or to satisfy your need for amusement?" Mac asked his friend.

"Well, since you're so rarely good for laughs, I must have come to make myself useful," Trey answered. "Thought I could use this time to discuss the rest of our cases with you, if you can spare a few minutes?" This he directed to Raine, and she snapped out of her reverie to answer.

"Go ahead, I'm on the way to my studio, anyway. It was nice meeting you, Mr. Garrison." She turned to walk away but hadn't gone more than a few steps when she was stopped by Macauley's low voice.

"Raine."

Ignoring the way the two syllables of her name took on a life of their own when uttered by him, she turned to look back inquiringly.

"If the phone rings, I'll be answering it."

Her lips pressed together at the reminder, one that had been completely unnecessary. He'd already made it crystal clear in the study earlier just how thoroughly he would be taking over her life. Her amber gaze clashed with his icy blue one for a moment. Then she broke the contact, looking beyond him to address Trey with a brittle smile. "See? Not only do I get around-the-clock protection, I get a free secretary thrown in, too. Your company offers one heck of a deal."

Both men watched as she turned on her heel and strode into the house, and then Mac let out a sigh. "Let's go into the house. I've got sort of an office set up on the first floor."

Upon entering the family room, Mac sank down into the desk chair and indicated for Trey to pull up a seat.

"I think I noted a bit of hellcat in that last exchange," Trey remarked. "What's going on?"

"It's a long story," Mac answered, his voice sour. "Suffice it to say that Simon Michaels did a number on me when he hired me, and his daughter is continuing in the fine tradition of her old man."

"You think this job was overreaction on Simon's part?" Trey asked. "Or was he right to be alarmed?"

Mac rubbed the back of his neck reflexively. "He definitely had reason for concern. From what I can gather, the police haven't gotten too far. There hasn't actually been a physical threat made, but the tone of the letters was nasty enough. There's every possibility that she's in real danger."

"So what's with her attitude?" Trey jerked his head toward the door. "Either you haven't convinced her of the risk or you've failed to bowl her over with your smooth manner."

It was a long-standing joke between them that Mac's personality could cause the kind of friction needed to light a match. *Real*, Mac called it. *Abrasive* was a term Trey threw around a lot. The humor of it was that the two of them were more alike than different. Trey just knew how to use the pretty words to cover up what he was really after. Mac believed in calling a black one-eyed jack a spade.

"You'd definitely have been better in this job than me," he admitted without rancor. "I knew that from the start."

"Not necessarily," Trey argued lazily. "That terse, dictating manner of yours might actually be considered by some women as godlike. It just apparently hasn't convinced Raine Michaels that you have her best interests at heart."

Mac's fingers drummed restlessly on the desktop as he leaned back in his chair. "I don't think that's it, at least not all of it," he said. "I actually got through to her a while ago. Despite her attitude, I think this whole mess really has scared her. But she's determined for some reason to hide that fact from me, and maybe from herself, as well. That's the angle I can't figure out."

Lifting a shoulder, Trey asked, "Does it matter? You can handle things here, can't you? Raine doesn't look big enough to give you too much trouble."

Mac snorted at that, but remained silent. His partner had no idea just how much trouble Raine Michaels could be, and he'd be hard-pressed to explain it to him. She hadn't actually *done* anything, after all. It wasn't her fault that everything about her seemed to bother him in some inexplicable way. No, that was due more to his need for a vacation than anything else.

"How busy are you right now?" he asked his partner. "Have you taken on any more cases in the last few days?"

Trey gave him a rundown of current clients, the approximate length of each case and the manpower and equipment needed for each.

Mac nodded. They were pretty busy, busier than he would have liked at the moment. They had been expanding fairly rapidly in the past year, and hiring more men as needed. It sounded as if every one of them was going to be kept active for a while.

"I spoke to a Detective Ramirez, who's in charge of Raine's case."

"Did you get anywhere?"

Shaking his head, Mac replied, "Got the usual confidentiality runaround. Not that I expected any different. He wouldn't say what leads, if any, he's been following. I have no idea whether or not he's run checks on some of the people closest to Raine."

"Do you suspect the threats have been made by someone she knows?" Trey asked.

Lifting a shoulder in response, Mac answered, "It's a place to start. I don't like not knowing anything about the people who have access to her. I'd like to get some information on a few of them. It won't be easy. The comings and goings around here resemble a subway station." He handed the list to Trey.

Trey perused the names, a frown marring his brow. "How many of these people are in and out of here in a day?"

"Lots," Mac answered dryly. "She isn't even sure who comes some days. When she's painting she's kind of in a world of her own."

"Okay," Trey said, pocketing the list. "I'll see if I can pull some strings, get these names run through the police computer for records."

"I won't even ask how you'll get that accomplished." Mac knew from experience that Trey would know someone on the force, most likely a woman, who would be only too happy to do such a favor for him.

"Anything else?"

When Mac shook his head, both men rose. "I'll get on this right away, then," Trey promised. Walking across the room, he asked, "What kind of artist is Raine Michaels, anyway? Have you seen any of her work?"

Mac shrugged indifferently. "She paints."

Trey looked at him with mock patience. "Very astute, Mac. I'd gathered as much when you spoke of her pictures. Are these hers on the wall here?"

They moved to examine the paintings Trey indicated. "Looks like these are all hers," he noted, looked at the signature in the corner. Each was signed simply *Raine*. Each bore the unmistakable stamp of the same artist.

Both men examined the paintings, four in total, in silence. "She's talented," Trey said, his voice tinged with surprise. "I haven't heard of her before. Is she shown anywhere?"

Mac shrugged. He didn't have the interest that Trey did in the creative world. "She's got a show coming up soon," he said. "She's been getting ready for that. She has an agent, if that means anything. André Klassen." He nodded in the direction of Trey's pocket. "He's on the list."

Trey's eyebrows rose. "He's no slouch, either. He wouldn't take her on if she didn't show promise. And if these pictures are a sample of what she can do, she'll go far."

Mac studied each of the pictures in turn. All were done in a similar manner. The scenes were slightly out of focus, as if they were being viewed beneath water. Each painting depicted people, in crowds or as couples. He looked closer at one that showed a man and woman standing side by side in what, at first glance, would seem to be intimacy. It was only upon closer examination that he noticed each had a hand reaching for the other, and the hands weren't quite touching. That one point seemed to accent the slight distance between the two, adding to the overall effect of incredible yearning. "You can barely make out the features of these people. Why'd she smudge them up like that?"

Trey chuckled. "You're a philistine, you know that? It looks as if Raine Michaels favors a form of Impressionism. An artist who does it really well doesn't need everything in the picture to be clear in order to convey emotions and a message."

Taking one last look at them, Mac wondered if the almost surreal view of reality in the pictures was indicative of Raine's grasp of the world. If so, it depicted almost perfectly the person described by her family, a woman who saw things differently, who reacted to events with a maddening naiveté. He couldn't deny the effectiveness of the technique in her paintings. He was no art patron, but even he could feel the emotions she'd captured there. Such a viewpoint in her personal life, however, could be downright dangerous.

He turned away from the pictures. He couldn't afford to think of Raine as more than a client. This glimpse into her perception of the world around her made her seem too human, more than a case. Emotionless objectivity was the quality he brought with him to each job, the quality he was paid handsomely for. Somehow that element receded in the presence of her talent. He made sure his eyes avoided the paintings as he walked Trey out of the room and through the front door.

* * *

Raine woke up, her heart pounding, chills chasing up and down her spine. Panting, she pulled the sheet closer around her, scooting up to lean against the white wicker headboard.

The nightmare was back.

Her body was trembling with the aftershocks, her mind still frantically reassuring itself that it had only been a dream, it wasn't real, it wasn't happening all over again.

Wrapping her arms around herself, her eyes went wildly to the window, latching with desperation on the full moon, the bright stars. It was always easier when she could concentrate on the night's natural light, when the sky was bright despite its blanket of darkness.

She concentrated fixedly on the brilliance of the moon. It lit the sky with almost dusklike shadows. It wasn't really dark at all. Not really. She needed to believe that, *had* to believe it to quiet the pounding of her heart. It hadn't been a night like this one that she'd been dreaming of. No, then the sky had been utterly black, and she'd had to depend on the streetlights' artificial glow to guide her way.

That night had given her a lasting fear of the dark, but she'd since learned plenty of ways to compensate for that fear. She was using one now. If this didn't work, the switch to the lamp at her bedside was within easy reach. The night-light she'd long relied upon was still in the drawer of the table next to her bed.

She didn't reach for either. Already the deep breathing she used was calming her, the chills chasing over her skin were lessening. Before the letters started, it had been years since she'd had the nightmare. Now it was coming with increasing frequency. It wasn't difficult to figure out what had triggered its return. Reality had an ugly taint to it these days.

She waited silently in the bed, her head propped wearily against the headboard. Though the effects of the nightmare eventually faded, she knew from experience that she wouldn't be able to sleep. Not yet. After a time, she clicked on the lamp and slipped from her bed. Padding to the door in bare feet, she flipped a switch that turned on the light in the hallway. Some fears could be faced, she knew, and conquered. But such feats took time, and she hadn't been willing to wait until her fear of the dark disappeared before she'd bought her own home. She'd simply hired an electrician to wire her house so that she'd never have to walk into a dark room.

Reaching the end of the hallway, she turned the light on inside her studio from a switch mounted outside the door. She pushed open the door and strode quickly to the painting she was working on. It was the second to the last one she needed for the show, and overall she was pleased with its progress. She went to a table in the corner of the room and selected some paintbrushes. A flash of movement at the window caught her eye, and she was drawn slowly to it, peering into the darkness. At first she saw nothing but shadows, and then she could discern a figure moving. Her throat went dry and her breath seemed trapped in her chest. Who was out there? Was it the same person targeting her for a mind game of cat and mouse? Would she wake in the morning to a new sick message in her mailbox or elsewhere in her home?

Even as those questions echoed in her head, she began to breathe freely again. Because she recognized who was down there, knew the identity of the person even though she could make out little more than movement and shadows.

It was Macauley, and he was pacing the small patio at the back of her house. She could tell by the impatient stride, the set of the shoulders. She couldn't see his face, but she knew she was right. He was also awake tonight, and the knowledge gave her an odd sense of kinship. She watched as he walked across the patio and back, over and over. He moved as a man tormented, as if he, too, had nightmares that kept him from sleep, kept him from peace.

She backed away from the window, feeling as though she was guilty of spying. Raine had no way of knowing what sent him outside at this time of night. He could have been working off some restless energy built up from the day. For all she knew, this was his way of dealing with a particularly pesky problem, striding back and forth in the moonlight until a solution appeared.

But somehow she felt it went deeper than that. Maybe her own experience had her assigning like motivations to the man, but she thought he moved as a man driven. Driven into the night to exorcise demons that preyed on the unconscious mind. She was familiar with those demons, and felt an immediate empathy for him.

She didn't know what kind of ghosts were haunting Macauley O'Neill. She didn't know what past experience had molded them. But she knew without a doubt that they existed.

Chapter 4

The hammering of the workers reverberated through the house for the next few days. And despite her promise to remain understanding about the noise, Raine frequently felt on the verge of screaming. On the day the work had begun she'd been surprised to see Macauley come into the kitchen at breakfast. When he'd handed her a package of earplugs she'd laughed and thanked him. But after three days she was no longer laughing. For the fourth time that morning men had tromped across her studio and were currently working at removing the glass from her windows.

She finally admitted defeat. The earplugs had helped mask the noise coming from the rest of the house, but they couldn't cover up the sounds in this room. Nor could she work with the constant visual distraction. She'd be getting no work done that day, so she cleaned her brushes and left. Wandering through the house, she noted similar noises coming from all directions.

The job was actually going much more quickly than she'd imagined. Already half the house sported the new glass Macauley had spoken of. The tiny wires running through it were scarcely noticeable. The front door had been replaced and adorned with a shiny new deadbolt. Men were at work in the kitchen taking that door down, also. Raine sighed silently. She couldn't deny that the

precautions made her feel more secure. Yet they were also a blatant reminder of why she'd felt unsafe to begin with.

Wandering outside, she noted a car coming up the drive. She
shaded her eyes against the bright morning sunlight, trying to detect the identity of the driver. A quick grin crossed her lips when
she recognized Sarah's bright red sports model. Eagerly, Raine
started down the steps to greet her friend. If she couldn't work, the
next best thing would be to spend some time talking to Sarah. Her
quirky sense of humor was just what Raine needed today.

"Hi," Sarah called as she climbed out of the car. She paused
after slamming the door and looked toward the house. "I just
knew that a trip out here was in order this morning. And look at
the sight of all those half-naked men." Several of the workers had
shed their shirts in the warm sun. She sighed appreciatively. "I
must have a sixth sense about these things."

Raine laughed and came around the car to give her friend a quick
hug. "I arranged it just for your benefit, too. That's the nicest
thing about you—it takes so little to make you happy."

Sarah's return smile was forced. "I wish that trait ran in our
family."

Immediately, Raine sensed her friend's mood. "What's the
matter? Is Joe in trouble again?" Joe was Sarah's brother, younger
by six years. Their parents had died when Sarah was nineteen, and
she'd raised Joe herself. He'd been in and out of scrapes for the
past few years, and Sarah was constantly worried that someday he
was going to land himself in something she couldn't get him out of.

Lifting a shoulder in response, Sarah simply said, "Joe is Joe."
She smiled slightly. "Someday he'll grow up and become a responsible citizen, right?"

Raine wasn't so sure about that. She'd had occasion to observe
Joe quite a bit over the years, and she thought he'd been spoiled
beyond belief, first by his parents and then by his sister. Several
times she'd suspected Joe was to blame for some odd bruises on
Sarah's face. But when she'd mentioned her suspicion once, her
friend had become angrier than she'd ever seen her. It was the only
time they had quarreled, and Raine had learned to leave the subject alone. Although she wanted desperately to help her friend, she
respected the boundaries she'd set.

She said only, "How can he miss with a sister like you to look up
to?"

Sarah agreed with mock solemnity. "That's exactly what I keep
telling myself." She nodded toward the house. "It really looks like

things are starting to happen here. Mac doesn't mess around does he?''

Turning to face the house, Raine agreed dryly, "He makes things happen, all right, although I'm sure under different circumstances he does more than his share of messing around." Her tone gave the words an unmistakable connotation, and Sarah widened her eyes in mock disbelief.

"Raine, I'm shocked! You're starting to sound as bad as me!" She laughed. "I'm having more of an effect on you than I'd imagined possible."

Quick color flared to Raine's cheeks at her friend's teasing. The words, as well as the thought itself, had been totally unlike her, and she wondered uncomfortably where they'd come from. It wasn't like her to idly speculate about a person's sexual habits, and she certainly hadn't given any conscious thought to Macauley's. At least she hadn't believed so until she heard her own words a moment ago. She curled her fingers into her palms in sudden tension. Stress was definitely taking its toll on her.

"I don't see Mac with the others." Sarah was looking at the men. "I don't suppose you arranged to have him appear half-nude for me, too?"

"Sorry."

"Shucks. Something tells me that would definitely be a sight worth seeing." She turned to Raine. "What are you doing out here, anyway? I expected to find you holed up in your studio all day."

"I would have been." Raine sighed. "But there have been men traipsing through it all morning, so I finally gave up."

"No wonder you're so glad to see me," Sarah remarked idly. "Since Mac spread the word that your place was off-limits to the students, it must seem deserted in there, even with the crew you have working."

But Raine didn't hear the last part of the sentence. "Mac told the students what?" she asked in a carefully measured tone.

Sarah shot her a look. "Didn't you know? I ran into Cindy Zeller on campus, and she told me. Apparently Mac called the professors of all the art classes you help with occasionally and told them to spread the word to their students. Everyone was real bummed out, and of course they didn't understand, since Mac gave the teachers no details. I assumed it was because he didn't want to have to deal with a bunch of people tromping in and out of here while so much work was going on. To tell you the truth, I wasn't all that certain what kind of reception I'd get here myself."

For the first time in her life, Raine could physically feel her blood pressure rising. The sensation was quite incredible. She, who had spent most of her childhood doing as she was told, rarely lost her temper. She hadn't needed to. And later, when she'd started asserting some independence from her family, she'd known intuitively that a show of anger wasn't going to accomplish anything. But if she wasn't mistaken, it was anger she was feeling now. More than that, really. What she felt was closer to white-hot, boiling rage.

How dare he! Even after she'd told him repeatedly that he was to consult with her about any decisions he made, he did this! Upon the heels of that thought came the memory of the conversation they'd had about just this thing. He hadn't given her any promises about doing as she had requested. As a matter of fact, he'd been quite rude about it. But this settled it. She and Macauley O'Neill were going to come to terms. Right now.

"Will you excuse me?" she said distractedly to Sarah, already striding away. "I've got to talk to Mac about something."

"Sure." Sarah waved her away and began to wander in the direction of a shirtless workman. "I can amuse myself."

Raine ran up the steps and into the house. She found Mac at the desk he'd had delivered, sitting in front of his laptop computer, speaking on the phone. She stalked across the room and slammed her hands on the desktop, leaning toward him. "You and I need to talk," she said through gritted teeth. "Hang up—now."

He hadn't turned at her entrance, and he spared her only a glance before continuing his conversation.

Raine's jaw clenched at his nonchalance. Here he was rearranging her whole life, and he acted as though nothing out of the ordinary had happened. He was probably busily making some other arrangements to make her life even more unbearable. "Now, Macauley," she repeated firmly.

He glanced at her again, and his mouth flattened in annoyance. "I'll call you back, Trey. I have to attend to something." He listened for a moment and then said, "Well, then you call me when you can. That'd be easier, anyway. I'm not going anywhere."

Those words fueled Raine's anger. No, he wasn't going anywhere, was he? He was staying right here, running her life and being obnoxious about the way he did it. He took his time turning off the phone and setting it down in front of him. Then he turned fully to face her. "What's your problem?"

"My problem?" she exclaimed incredulously. "The question is, what's *your* problem? Do you have a control fetish, is that it? Are you utterly incapable of following directions? Or don't you understand English?"

He didn't respond, just leaned back in his chair and studied her from beneath hooded lids. His composure shredded her own even further.

"I specifically said that you were to discuss your plans with me before you did anything," she said, seething. "And I told you that I wanted to be the one to contact the students about staying away for a while. So will you please tell me why you felt it necessary to do it yourself?" She smacked both hands against the desktop and turned away to pace a few steps. Then she whirled back. "What is it with you, anyway?"

Mac lazily watched her work herself into a full-blown lather. She'd had a pretty good start on it when she came storming in here. He'd expected this confrontation, though he hadn't especially looked forward to it. But he did find it interesting watching her. Her eyes were glittering with fury and shooting gold-edged daggers at him.

He swallowed a sigh. God save him from natural disasters and temperamental women. There wasn't a lot a person could do about the first, but he did his best to avoid the second. That's why, in his leisure time, he always sought out simple, uncomplicated females. They might get upset over a broken nail, but they were damn easy to distract from their disappointment. Raine Michaels was as far removed from those women as it was possible to be. Not only did she lack the voluptuous curves he looked for in a companion, she was not, by any stretch of the imagination, uncomplicated.

"Is that what has you all hot and bothered?" he asked shortly.

She took a deep breath. Screaming at him was not the answer, and it wouldn't satisfy her, anyway. She'd like to take a punch at that hard jaw. She had a feeling she was far from the first person who'd had the urge. "Why did you leave the message at the college for the students to stay away from here? I ordered you not to."

His eyes narrowed at her choice of words. "I don't take *orders* very well," he said in a deadly tone.

She didn't flinch before the threat in his voice. Nor did she retreat. "Apparently not," she ground out. They glared into each other's eyes for several long moments. Neither blinked until the phone in front of Mac rang. He snatched it up with movements made jerky with irritation. "O'Neill," he snapped into the receiver. After a moment he said, "You'll have to call back." He pushed the button to end the call and fairly slammed the phone on the desk.

Her mouth firmed at the autocratic way he'd answered the call. He hadn't identified her residence. It was as if he'd taken over the telephone wires to her house, too, and that only added to her anger. "Who was that?" she demanded.

"Klassen."

"Did you plan to restrict my calls, too?" she asked sarcastically.

"Until we get this ironed out, yeah," he answered, his jaw clenching.

"The only thing we have to iron out, is your attitude," she informed him. "You deliberately went against my wishes. And it better never happen again."

"You said you'd contact the students, but you haven't, have you?"

Her silence was all the answer he needed. "I wanted to talk to the professors you mentioned, so it was easy enough for me to pass the message on at the same time. Apparently you didn't take me seriously when I told you why we needed to restrict your visitors. If you can't see how stupid it is to allow any bozo on the street easy access to you while you're being threatened, you need your head examined."

"I'm not stupid!" She hissed the words at him. "I just think you're overreacting! I would have told the art students the next time they came out here, although it does seem pointless—I know I'm not being threatened by one of them! For heaven's sake, what possible motive would they have?"

"Take your pick," he replied tersely. "Anger, envy or just plain craziness. Or it could be good, old-fashioned lust." At her incredulous expression, he cocked an eyebrow sardonically. "Spurn any suitors lately, Raine?" He watched her sputter in response to his words.

"I haven't— I don't— There aren't— You're nuts!" she finally finished in frustration. "You are so far off base, Macauley!"

"Mac." He bit out the word. "Call me Mac."

She ignored him and went on. "Someone saw an exhibit, saw my name on the news or picked me at random for this sick little game, but it isn't someone I know! And it definitely isn't one of those poor students, who probably think I'm angry at them for some unknown reason, because I doubt you bothered supplying them with a reasonable explanation!''

"It's done," he said dismissively. "And it won't be undone. I was hired to protect you the best way I can, and I don't answer to you, Raine, I answer to your father. You're welcome to call and complain about me, but something tells me my actions would have his wholehearted approval."

"If you think that commends them," she said scathingly, "think again."

"It doesn't matter. While I'm in charge here, I'll do things my way, and if you don't like the way I protect your delicate little tush, that's too damn bad. Maybe when this whole thing has been solved you'll be able to see the bigger picture."

"The big picture I see is of an arrogant jerk who thinks the term 'security expert' is synonymous with God!" she shouted.

"Um, excuse me." A voice spoke from the doorway.

"What?" Mac and Raine snapped the question simultaneously.

Sarah smiled, took one look at both their faces and said, "On second thought, I think I'll just leave you two alone a while longer. Since you're getting along so well and all."

She retreated, and Raine took a deep breath. No doubt their raised voices had reverberated through the house, even with the sound of the work being done there.

"Look," Mac said, forcing his voice to a more even tone. "I'm not saying you have to turn into a hermit. I'm just trying to limit your visitors to a small enough number that I can do an adequate job of ensuring your safety."

"I suppose I should be grateful that you've at least eliminated my closest friends from your list of suspects," Raine replied caustically.

Mac said nothing, just looked at her.

Her eyes narrowed. "Don't tell me, let me guess. You don't trust them, either."

"I don't trust anyone," he said flatly. "And neither should you. At least not until this is over."

Her anger began to ebb as she digested his words. They were easy enough to believe. He didn't trust anyone, and she'd been able to tell that the moment she met him. It was in his guarded manner, his expressionless eyes. What was more difficult to understand was why that realization would make her heart ache. She'd wondered on occasion if he was capable of human emotion at all. And then she would remember the sight of him pacing her small patio in the middle of the night. Something rode this man, and that fact assured her at least that he felt *something*. A man totally without conscience didn't have trouble sleeping at night.

He was regarding her with those startling blue eyes that revealed nothing of his thoughts. He must think she was the most difficult client he'd ever had, and she couldn't totally blame him. She knew how contradictory it seemed, her making him fight for every inch he gained in his efforts to protect her. She just didn't know how to explain the renewed fear she felt in the process. It was as if each gain he made came at a cost to her hard-won battles against the terror of her past. Each concession she allowed made the fear stronger, her defenses weaker.

"I understand what you're trying to do," she said, looking away. Her voice was almost a whisper. "But, Macauley, I made a choice a long time ago not to let a lousy experience dictate how I live. I tried it your way once, tried to go through life keeping people at a distance, to shield myself from possible hurt." She hesitated for a moment, then met his gaze squarely. "It nearly suffocated me. I can't live that way. It's not who I am. And it wouldn't guarantee that I'd be totally safe, either. There's always a possibility that some crazy who's going to tear my life in two is right around the corner. And if that happens, what would I have gained by not allowing anyone to get close to me all those years?"

Something in her eyes caught his gaze, held it. She was an enigma, this woman, and he'd never much cared for enigmas. They always nagged at him until he'd figured them out. This wasn't the first time he'd wondered about her, about what made her tick. He already knew she wasn't a daddy's girl, content to live off her father's money until a suitable match came along to support her. And at times like these he was unable to assume that she was little more than a slightly ditsy artist. She sounded wise beyond her years, even if he didn't necessarily agree with what she was saying. That ancient look was back in her eyes, the look that was a match for the darkness in his soul. And because it reminded him of things he'd much rather forget, he deliberately turned away.

The phone jangled then, and he answered it. "Who is this?" he asked bluntly. After a moment, he held the receiver out to her. "Harold Bonzer," he said, a slightly questioning note in his voice.

She snatched the phone out of his hand. "Hello, Harold," she said, her voice warm. She walked away from Mac, talking softly.

He sat down in front of his desk, listening to the one-sided conversation. He was able to discern that the man had something to do with the art world. They were discussing Raine's paintings and the upcoming show. He didn't remember hearing the man's name before, however. It was impossible to tell from Raine's manner just what the man was to her. Her voice was cordial, but she seemed to treat everyone with the same warm manner. As a matter of fact, she usually behaved as though she was the hostess at some damn tea party—except, on a few notable occasions with him.

His lips twisted in a sardonic little smile. He'd bet Raine Michaels had experienced a broader range of emotions since he'd come into her life than she had in years, but somehow he thought she wouldn't appreciate that fact.

Her conversation with Harold over, Raine set the phone down on the desk in front of him.

"Who's Harold Bonzer?" he asked.

"He's been my benefactor," she replied. "I owe the success I'm enjoying largely to him. I met Harold through Sarah, when he was sponsoring a show for her, and he offered to take a look at my work."

"He can't be the only reason you're successful." Mac surprised her, and himself, by saying it. He nodded toward her paintings on the wall. "You're good. At least Trey seems to think so, and he knows a little about that sort of thing."

"Thanks for the vote of confidence, but there are lots of starving artists out there who are good," she observed wryly. "I'm lucky Harold took a liking to my work. I don't think André would have been interested in me otherwise."

"Just what does a benefactor do?" he asked, leaning back in his desk chair.

"Harold got me hooked up with André. Together they arranged a show for me at a local gallery." She shrugged. "Some of my things started to sell. It helped that people knew Harold Bonzer was buying my paintings himself. He's a well-known name in the art world, and when he takes an interest in an artist, it usually helps launch a career."

"What about Sarah Jennings? Did he help launch her career, too?"

Raine nodded. "He's helped get her shown, and she's doing very well. She's had it kind of tough. She's been raising her brother since her parents died."

"How did Sarah feel when her benefactor started taking an interest in you?" he quizzed.

Her gaze flew to his, startled anew at his perception. "I think," she responded slowly, "that it hurt her feelings at first. But she's okay with it now. And she had a show last year that he was instrumental in arranging. Of course, she's a very talented sculptor. That's one of her pieces on the mantel."

Mac's gaze flicked in the direction she indicated, then to her. "Where's Bonzer live?"

"In L.A."

"Mac." They both turned when they heard the voice. One of the workers stood in the doorway, Raine's mail in his gloved hands. "I thought you'd want to take a look at this."

"Bring it over here and put it down, Mike." The man obeyed, while Mac pulled open a desk drawer and withdrew a pair of plastic gloves. He drew them on, then flipped through the mail deliberately. He handed all of it to Raine except for one long envelope.

She peered over his shoulder. "It has a postmark," she said, half to herself.

"But no return address." Mac looked at the man. "Thanks, Mike." The man nodded and left the room. Mac opened the letter cautiously and withdrew the single sheet of paper.

The room seemed to grow eerily quiet. Even the hammering outside had momentarily stilled. From the corner of the room, the ticking of the grandfather clock seemed intrusively loud. Raine's heartbeat sped up until she was convinced that the sound of its pounding was discernible in the near silence. Her palms grew clammy, and she had to force herself to watch over Mac's shoulder as he unfolded the letter. Time crawled interminably as he unfolded it once, and then again.

Her breath came out in a rush, the first she'd been aware that she'd been holding it. "An invitation to visit my aunt's cottage in Maine," she said, aware of the note of relief in her voice. Now that the moment was over, her foreboding seemed silly. "Pretty dangerous."

Mac folded the letter up, then handed it and the envelope to her. "Not this time," he reminded her soberly.

She stared at him silently, reading his meaning. No, not this time. And maybe not the next. But one of these days, another threat would arrive, couched in terms just a bit more sinister than the last. That certainty remained unspoken between them.

The phone rang again, and Raine turned as he answered it. She wandered away from the desk to stare sightlessly out the front window. The bright California sunshine, the lush green grass, the walnut trees on the edge of her property—they all seemed so ordinary. Cars drove by occasionally on the ribbon of road in the distance, and with even less frequency on the road in front of her place. Even the men working outside could seem harmless, as if they were involved in a normal construction job, if she didn't know the events that had triggered their presence here.

Her eyes went toward the line of trees. They signaled the end of her property line. She had five acres, most of it covered with a soft blanket of green grass, and it was an open invitation to bare feet. As a child she'd loved to slip her shoes and socks off and just run, flat out, as fast as she could on just such a stretch of grass. She'd run as far and as hard as possible, until she would drop, panting and laughing, into the grass. Then she'd roll to her back and watch the clouds float by until she got enough breath to do it again.

She'd tried that when she was older, when she felt weighted by problems with no solutions except those that would come from within. But the feeling wouldn't die that she'd been running away from something, something she carried with her always. The day she'd finally faced that fact was the last time she'd indulged in that particular fancy.

Aware that Mac had hung up, she turned to him quizzically.

"That was Trey," he said soberly. "He had some information for me, and I'm sure you're not going to like it. You may as well come over and sit down."

She didn't immediately obey. Anything Macauley thought she wasn't going to like, she was pretty sure she was really going to *hate*, and she was suddenly loath to hear it. She ran a hand over her short hair in an unconsciously nervous gesture. Then, biting her lip, she drew herself up straighter and headed over to him.

Mac observed her closely. She'd had to visibly gather her defenses, and he wondered for a moment if he was doing the right thing in sharing this information with her. He still didn't know just how strong Raine Michaels was, how much she could withstand before she broke down. He'd already witnessed her upset once, when he'd deliberately pushed her.

But he had the feeling that that time had been unusual for her, just as her temper of today had been. And he guessed that she wouldn't welcome him hiding something from her, at any rate.

She returned his gaze with one of her own. "Well, you may as well get this over with," she said, striving for lightness. "Unless, of course, you're trying to rack up extra popularity points for drawing out the misery."

He didn't crack a smile. Holding out a piece of paper on which he'd jotted down notes, he said, "These are two of the names from the list of art students you gave me."

Raine looked down, then at him. "I remember. Why?"

"Trey has been doing some checking on all the people on the list."

Raine frowned. "Do you mean to tell me," she said, her voice ominous, "that you've been prying into these students' lives?"

He didn't blink. "That's exactly what I mean. And it's fortunate he was able to get to it so soon, and damn lucky he has the contacts he does in the police department. Both of the people on that list have been in trouble with the law."

She stared at him, momentarily at a loss. She was caught between renewed anger at the lengths he'd gone to and a sudden sense of unease. "What..." Her voice sounded rusty. She cleared her throat and tried again. "What did you find out?"

"Andy Radcliff was accused of date rape three years ago, when he was a freshman in college. The case never went to trial because the girl abruptly refused to testify."

"You mean she recanted?" Raine asked slowly.

"No, I mean that she suddenly changed her mind about going through the trial process." He watched her carefully. "That's not the same thing."

Her face was completely composed, but he noted that one of her hands clenched and opened, over and over. "What else?"

"Sally Jessup is on probation for vandalism. Seems she got angry at one of her professors and did about a thousand dollars' worth of damage to his car."

Raine took a deep breath as she absorbed the news. She didn't know Andy and Sally any better than she knew the other students. That was to say, she was on speaking terms with them, but they were acquaintances. This news was a surprise to her, but it shouldn't have been. She'd been warned often enough of the dangers of taking people at face value.

But it had been a conscious decision to ignore that advice. She hadn't intended to take foolish risks, but she'd wanted to live her life free of the kind of suspicion of people that could choke spontaneity from her. And she had felt alive again, making her choices based on what was right for her and not necessarily on what was safest, what was smartest.

That fact was apparent.

She didn't feel scared right now. Regardless of the news he'd given her, she somehow couldn't imagine Andy or Sally were to blame for her harassment. She just felt sad. She knew that she wouldn't be able to forget this, wouldn't be able to look at the two in the same light as before. Right or wrong, her perception of them would be colored by what she'd learned today. And the next time she would be just a little less trusting.

"I'm not saying that either of them has been linked to your case," Mac surprised her by saying. He'd seen the color slowly recede from her cheeks, and her hand abruptly stilled on her thigh, as if she'd just become aware of its action.

"What you're saying," she said woodenly, "is that I've been taking an unnecessary risk by allowing people I don't know well to come into my home. Especially in light of the threats."

Mac hesitated. There was something about her demeanor that made him a little cautious about pushing her much further. She was composed, but she was a little *too* composed for his liking. She looked as if she could shatter at one more word from him. At the same time, for once she was listening, and maybe this moment was what it was going to take to wake her up. With that thought in mind, he answered deliberately. "Yes."

"That's what you've been saying all along, isn't it? I guess I owe you an apology."

He felt as though he'd been poleaxed. "An apology? What the hell for?"

"For questioning your actions. I can see now that they make sense. I should have seen it before." She hesitated. When she finally finished, her voice was flat. "I didn't want to see it."

"Are you saying you'll quit fighting me now?" His tone was cautious. Whatever had brought about this abrupt about-face, he was going to take advantage of it. His job would be a hell of a lot easier if he didn't have to constantly convince her to listen to him.

"That should make your day, shouldn't it?" she said with a fixed smile. "And now, if you'll excuse me, I'm going to see if the men are finished in my studio." She turned and walked swiftly out the door.

He watched her go with a frown furrowing his forehead. He'd won a valuable concession just now, he knew. In her current frame of mind she was going to be much more amenable to work with. But somehow he couldn't summon up any satisfaction about that.

He shook his head, but it didn't help dislodge the memory of that wounded expression on her face. Not for the first time in their brief acquaintance he was responsible for dimming the bright light from her eyes. Before she left they'd looked haunted again, vulnerable. He couldn't quite put his finger on what he'd seen in them.

And he couldn't help feeling like a bastard for being responsible for it.

Chapter 5

"So how's the piece coming along, Raine?" André walked into the kitchen, where she was sitting at the table with Greg. Despite the early hour he was impeccably dressed in a three-piece suit with a silk tie. "No problems, I hope."

Raine caught the look of dislike Greg sent the other man, and inwardly sighed. After the scene with Macauley last night, she wasn't in the mood for company, nor did she feel like playing referee between her agent and her accountant. But Greg had shown up early this morning, before Raine had had breakfast, and it would have seemed churlish not to offer him coffee. He'd accepted with alacrity and had seemed quite contented chewing a blueberry muffin and drinking cup after cup, saying little.

Actually, when he wasn't lecturing her on money-saving skills, Greg never did have much to say. Raine had noticed before that he had a tendency to stumble over his words a bit, then become tongue-tied into an awkward silence. It was an oddly endearing quality, one that made him...

Safe. The word hissed mockingly in her mind, but she dismissed it. She usually filled in the silences with light chatter and questions to draw him out a bit. But she wasn't doing too well in that department today. Sleep would have been a welcome visitor last night, but had remained elusive for hours. Today she was having trouble forming coherent sentences, much less sparkling breakfast conversation.

"The painting is coming along fine," she said, lying a little. It had been progressing well until yesterday, when she couldn't get into her studio. There was no reason to tell André that. He already worried too much over the endless arrangements for the showing. If he thought anything was going to slow her progress on the paintings, he'd have a heart attack right on her kitchen tiles, and that was definitely something she wasn't up for today.

André frowned, peering at her more closely. "You look a bit peaked, Raine. Are you sure you're feeling all right?"

"For Pete's sake, Klassen," Greg said irritably, "what a great thing to say to a woman. Are you afraid your precious schedule will be thrown off if she was to get sick for a day?"

André smiled a tight, humorless smile. "And you have so much expertise, my friend, in how to talk to women, don't you? What are you doing here again, anyway? Sometimes I wonder who runs the office while you spend your days here."

"André, Greg, please." Raine's voice was tired. "Just quit. André's right, I didn't sleep well last night, and I'm really not in the mood for this." She smiled to soften her words. "I know the two of you enjoy sharpening your fangs on each other, but my stomach isn't up to bloodshed this morning, okay?"

Mac came to the doorway then, in time to hear her last remark and to disagree with it. She made it sound as if the two men engaged in a casual conversational duel to pass the time, when in fact there was a competition afoot here. He was surprised she couldn't see it. He'd sensed it the moment he'd met the two, watching them vie for Raine's attention. At least Klassen's interest seemed to be professional, as overbearing as it was. But Winters was definitely interested in more than Raine's tax withholdings.

He shook off the irritation that accompanied the thought and spoke. "The men are finished in the studio, Raine. They shouldn't be bothering you again."

All heads swiveled toward him. "All right," she answered with a slight smile. "But I'll use the earplugs, just in case."

He gave her a short nod and disappeared toward the front door.

"What did he mean by that?" André demanded. "You haven't been able to use your studio, Raine? Are you still going to be able to complete your work on time? Damn, I knew that man was trouble. He and his crew have been a constant distraction, haven't they? Why in heaven's name don't you send them away until after the showing?''

"Oh, and I suppose Raine's security can wait until then, Klassen?" Greg put in caustically. "Easy to see where your priorities are."

"It's equally easy to see where *yours* lie," the man answered sharply.

"That's enough, both of you!" Raine snapped. They looked at her, mildly surprised at her unusual display of impatience. "I'll be able to finish the painting in the next few days, André. Mr. O'Neill has been careful to disturb me as little as possible." She didn't mention that the man had a way of *disturbing* her that had nothing to do with the work that was being done on her house. She didn't even like to admit that to herself.

"When will O'Neill be done around here?" Greg asked. "Seems like he's taking a long time to put in an alarm system."

André nodded in agreement.

Raine hesitated. She was loath to discuss Macauley's role as her bodyguard. André had already decided the letters were meaningless, and a disclosure would only upset him. He considered anything that took her mind off her work at this point as a major aggravation. Greg was just the opposite. He'd worried over the threats incessantly. Knowing how seriously she was taking them would only cause him more anxiety.

"There's a bit more to putting in a security system than any of us realize," she finally said. "And Mac's been replacing doors and windows, as well. But things around here should be straightened out soon."

"I hope you're right," André said. "Well, I'll leave you to work." He gave Greg a pointed look, and the younger man rose reluctantly from the table even as he glowered at the other man.

"I suppose I should go, too," Greg muttered. "Thanks for the breakfast, Raine. I, uh, just came out to see how you were doing." He shrugged self-consciously. "Haven't talked to you in a few days."

Strangely touched, Raine smiled gently at him. "I'm fine, Greg, really. And thank you for coming this morning. You know you're always welcome, both of you." Her look encompassed the two men.

Greg nodded wordlessly and sent a look at André. The older man remained rooted to the floor. It was obvious that he wasn't leaving until Greg did. "You haven't gotten any more of those letters, have you?"

"No."

"Or phone calls?"

"No, nothing, Greg. Everything's been fine."

"Because if you want, I can come out here each day and get the mail in for you. I don't like the thought of you opening those by yourself."

"Mac already does that for me, Greg, but thanks anyway."

Greg didn't look happy at that piece of news, but he finally nodded and walked out of the kitchen.

Showing the two men out the door, Raine breathed a sigh of relief. She didn't remember ever being in a bigger hurry to get rid of them. Her nerves were definitely a bit frayed this morning, and dealing with their animosity was beyond her today. She'd never quite figured out just where that animosity sprang from. The two really shouldn't have many matters they needed to collaborate on. But each insisted on butting into the other's side of her business, and after months of playing peacemaker, Raine had finally given up. They appeared to *like* to bicker, and as long as she didn't have to listen to it she just shrugged it off. Today, however, it had been particularly exasperating.

She headed for the stairs. Already the hammering was beginning outside, but she would retrieve her earplugs and go to her studio. If Macauley was right and she wasn't disturbed, she'd be able to get quite a bit finished on her painting. Today she was in need of the kind of solitude and peace she was able to attain only when lost in a world of her own.

"Mr. O'Neill, may have I have a word with you?"

Mac turned quizzically to face André Klassen. "In a minute," he responded. Turning to the workman he'd been talking to, Mac continued the instructions he'd been giving the man. The worker listened intently, nodding a few times in understanding. When he was finished, Mac faced André.

"What's on your mind?"

Klassen stepped out of the way quickly, narrowly avoiding two workmen walking by carrying some long planks. "Maybe we'd better go inside," he suggested. "I don't want to have to shout over this racket."

Mac looked at him, noting how incongruous the man looked in his Saville Row suit and five-hundred-dollar shoes amidst the organized chaos of the workers. Turning on his heel without a word, he led the way to the house. He didn't really have time for this, but it would be better to get Klassen out of the path of his men before that Ivy League haircut was creased by a two-by-four. Leading him into the study, he stopped in the middle of the room and turned to him.

"I wanted to talk to you about Raine," André began. He waited, but when Mac made no response, he continued. "This whole mess you're creating here really couldn't have come at a worse time, actually. You do know she's getting ready for a show, don't you?"

"I'd heard something about that," Mac answered sardonically.

"You probably aren't aware, then, of the amount of work and concentration that goes into something like this." The man made a dismissive gesture with his hand. "No one is, really. But I handle practically everything, so there's little Raine has to do except paint her exquisite pictures."

When Mac still said nothing, André felt compelled to explain further. "She cannot accomplish that, Mr. O'Neill, with you and your men constantly underfoot. This incessant noise must be a serious drain on her concentration, and I'm going to have to ask you to cease it at once."

Mac crossed his arms and rocked on his heels. He'd seen plenty of men like André Klassen, self-important and certain of their own power. He'd never lost his amusement for them, however. He shook his head wryly. Locations in the world were different, but its inhabitants never were. He was a master at sizing up people, analyzing their goals and predicting the lengths they would go to achieve them. This man wasn't even a challenge. "'Fraid I can't do that, Klassen," he said laconically.

The man frowned. "I'm going to have to insist. You may start again as soon as the show is over. Heavens, you may start as soon as Raine is finished with the last piece she's doing. But you must see that she's unlikely to finish as long as she's surrounded by all this commotion."

"The work will proceed on schedule," Mac answered. "You don't have the authority to give me orders. You're Raine's agent, right? Stick to selling her paintings. That's your job. Her security is mine."

André's mouth tightened. "I'm more than her agent, O'Neill. I make a lot of the decisions around here. I decide what is appropriate for Raine, and I know a lot more about her well-being than you do."

"Is that so?" Mac asked softly. "Then maybe you'd like to explain one of those decisions to me. Winters told the police detective that the first few letters and phone calls weren't reported because you told Raine not to bother. Care to explain to me why that qualifies as the appropriate decision for her?"

The man replied coolly, "I was merely trying to protect her. She didn't need to be worrying about some crank letters when she was busy with her work. She agreed with me."

"I know why she agreed with you, and I have a real good idea why you suggested it in the first place. It doesn't have anything to do with the fact that you didn't take them seriously. You didn't want *her* to take them seriously, because you were afraid they'd affect her work, and that, in the end, would affect you." Mac bared his teeth in what could not pass for a smile. "How am I doing so far?"

"If you think for one minute that I was primarily considering myself, you're insane, O'Neill," André returned angrily. "I was acting in Raine's best interests then, and I am now. I'm telling you to get rid of these men and clear out of here!"

Mac's eyes were slits. He walked closer until he was inches away from André. "You don't make decisions around here, Klassen. Don't kid yourself. You never did have that right. I may not know Raine well, but one thing I've learned damned quickly is that she likes to call her own shots. My men stay, I stay, and the work continues. You have nothing to say about it. Are we clear on this?"

"We'll see about that," the man said between clenched teeth. "You're overstepping your bounds here, O'Neill. You're way out of line."

"I've never been in line, Klassen. I leave that for guys like you." He walked past the man and went out the door. Jogging down the steps, he approached the crew. The man was no threat to the work getting done here, Mac knew that. Klassen's only recourse would be to go to Raine or, barring that, to her father. Neither avenue would do him any good. Mac's lips curled in a grim smile. He'd like to witness the scene if Klassen attempted to push Raine about the changes being made to her home. Would she go head to head with him, the way she did with Mac, or be more placating? So far, he'd been the only recipient of her temper as far as he could see, but somehow he'd bet that being told what to do wasn't something

Raine Michaels accepted easily from anyone. For that fact alone, he almost wished that Klassen would go to her.

But apparently the man had thought better of that idea, as well, because a moment later he got in his foreign sports car and roared down the drive, narrowly missing the black pickup heading toward the house.

The truck pulled up in front of the house and stopped. Mac walked over to greet his partner. "Hell, I see you more now than I did before I started this job," he gibed.

"Lucky son of a gun," agreed Trey. "Actually, I'm on my way to a site and just swung by to see if you needed anything. I didn't know I was in danger of getting sideswiped by some crazy." He stopped to peer at Mac. "That driver didn't happen to be someone who had just finished a conversation with you, did he?"

"You're so funny."

"And right," Trey said surely. "So who did you bowl over with your usual smooth manner this time?"

"That was Klassen. He was telling me to call off the work because it might distract Raine from her painting. Which might take some money out of his pocket," he added caustically. "The man's all heart. First he talked Raine out of reporting the harassment to the police, and now he's trying to cut short her security measures."

Trey raised his eyebrows. "Makes you sort of wonder if he has any other reason for wanting to keep this whole thing hush-hush."

Mac looked at his friend with sardonic amusement. "Don't ever kid yourself, Garrison. Your mind is just as suspicious as mine."

"I know that. I'm just better than you are at covering it up. Besides, I've been asking around and I'm hearing rumors that Klassen is having money problems."

"What kind of money problems?"

"I've heard from several sources that he's overextended himself, and his cash flow isn't, shall we say, flowing. That would explain why he's so anxious for Raine to have a successful show. As her agent, he stands to make a nice profit from anything she sells, and she has been selling well lately."

Mac silently examined what Trey had said. It made sense, in light of Klassen's almost fanatical demand to leave Raine alone. But the man would have to be one selfish bastard to convince Raine and Winters not to go to the police, if his sole interest was that Raine finish her paintings on time. Of course, Mac continued to muse, nothing he'd noted about Klassen today would be at odds with that supposition.

"All right," he said slowly. "Keep asking around. Have you heard anything about Winters?"

"Haven't talked to many people who have heard of him," Trey answered. "He was an accountant in a big corporation, but he left three years ago to start his own business. I don't know what kind of reputation he has. But I'll keep asking around. Someone in the business has to know him."

Mac made a mental note to ask Raine how she'd first met up with her accountant. Okay, thanks. I owe you one."

Trey grinned. "That's how I like it, pal." They spoke of business a few more minutes before he took his leave. As Trey drove away, Mac's eyes went up to the windows of Raine's studio. Was she working? Had she been able to wipe out everything that had passed between them the day before and concentrate on her painting? Or was Klassen right in assuming that she needed absolute peace to paint? Somehow Mac didn't believe that. He'd witnessed her strength of will on several occasions since he'd met her. Her father, too, had spoken of it. Mac didn't know how Klassen had formed his opinion of Raine's delicate nature, but he was betting the man's perception was incorrect.

More and more, he was getting the feeling that Raine Michaels was a lot stronger than people gave her credit for.

Sitting on the floor of her studio, Raine stretched one leg out in front of her and touched her nose to her knee several times. Then she switched legs. After a full day of painting, her back was full of knots, the muscles tight. The exercises helped loosen them at the end of the day, but didn't always complete the job. Today, no matter which way she bent and stretched, those knots weren't going away. Spreading both legs out, she bent forward, touching her forehead to the floor.

After a brief knock, the door to the studio opened, and she raised her head to meet Mac's impassive gaze.

"Drop something?" he inquired.

Rising to her feet gracefully, she shrugged her shoulders first one way, then another. "Working the day's kinks out," she explained.

He didn't respond. Seeing her bent in those impossible contortions had made his throat go dry. Out of nowhere came images of her in other, more intimate positions. Those narrow jeans of hers should have been constricting her movements, but she moved as easily as though she was wearing a leotard. On the heels of that thought came a sudden desire to see exactly what Raine would look like in such an outfit. He'd seen her in nothing more revealing than jeans and T-shirts.

He gave himself an impatient mental shake. It had been a while since he'd had a woman, but not *that* long. His taste in women ran to those with far more obvious physical assets than Raine possessed. And when he was on a job, there was no room for idle imaginings.

"My muscles get stiff standing here for hours," she explained. "I'm tempted to put in a hot tub to do the job for me. That would be easier than the exercising."

Without conscious thought Mac walked toward her. She looked surprised and not a little wary at his approach.

"Turn around," he ordered.

She stared at him, not obeying.

He turned her gently, then grasped the top of her shoulders. Using his fingers to massage her neck, his thumbs rubbed deeply and rhythmically around her shoulder blades.

Every muscle, every nerve in her body froze. Her heart stopped for an instant, then doubled its beat, the blood pushing rapidly through her veins to pound in her pulse. Her brain screamed at her feet, ordering them to run. They remained rooted in place. Raine stood fatalistically, incapable of movement. She waited for the silent scream to grow inside her until it beat at her temples, demanding to be released. Already her breath was coming in short, quick bursts, as if she'd broken from her frozen state and run as far and as swiftly as her mind commanded. She couldn't swallow around the knot in her throat. She waited for the nightmare to spring to life, in Technicolor reality.

Because this was so like her dreams. There was a man, a big man, standing behind her, out of her sight. He was touching her, and she couldn't move, couldn't pick up leaden feet and flee. She had run before, on that dark, haunting night, as though her heels were on fire, but she hadn't gotten far, no, not far enough. She took a deep, shuddering breath, and her wide-eyed gaze went to the window.

She blinked confusedly at the still bright sunlight streaming in. It wasn't dark outside. It should have been dark. The sky had been black that night, and so it was repeated in faithful detail in her nightmares. She shook her head dazedly. But this wasn't a nightmare. The hands on her body weren't hurting, they were soothing. She concentrated fiercely on the rhythmic movement at the top of her spine. Her breath was released in an odd little sigh. Her heart continued to beat wildly, but the silent scream welling inside slowly dissipated. She was still tense, but movement had returned to her limbs. She shifted her feet slightly. The past was vacuumed away, back to the niche where her mind kept it. Instead Raine concentrated on the most amazing thing that had happened to her in years. Someone was in back of her—no, not just someone, a man. He was touching her, and she hadn't screamed, she hadn't involuntarily reacted in a way sure to embarrass her the next moment. The confusion she felt now was from a very different source.

It was a moment before she realized the hands on her shoulders had dropped away. Turning slowly, Raine gazed at Macauley with a sense of wonder. How was it that this man could accomplish what no other could? What was there about him that could tame her reactions when she couldn't control them herself?

"You *are* tense," he commented. "I wasn't much help." He didn't know what had had him reaching for the woman, anyway. It was totally out of character for him. But somehow, coming in here and seeing her like he had had forced him to react before he'd made the conscious decision to do so.

Her voice was soft when she answered him. "Yes. You were." She stared at him for another long moment, wondering how he had managed to short-circuit her customary reactions. Shaking her head slightly, she said, "And I intend to pay you back. With dinner."

He was already shaking his head. "I don't expect you to feed me."

Raine cocked her head at him. "How do you eat at your other jobs? As a matter of fact, how have you been eating since you got here? I haven't fed you since the first night."

He shrugged. "The men always bring me something. And I just stopped in here to ask you to come down with me so I can explain the alarm system." He hadn't answered the first part of her question, and from the looks of him he didn't intend to. But it didn't matter.

"Well, your men won't be around forever, although—" she rolled her eyes "—it feels as though they already have been. You might as well start eating when I do. I'm a passable cook, as long as you don't expect anything fancy."

He didn't. But he also didn't want to...what? Be in her company any more than he had to be? That was ridiculous. He'd been busy supervising the work, making sure it got done as quickly as possible, and he really had been eating on the go. But she was right. There was quickly coming a time when the men would be done and he'd need to eat. It wasn't unusual for him to eat with a client, though it had been a while since he'd done protection work like he was doing for Raine.

He'd never liked that aspect of the job, to tell the truth. Trey handled most instances like this, when one of them was required to stay close to a client. Mac lacked the will or the interest needed to soothe fears, to get on an informal footing with people he would likely never see again. He looked at Raine. Her eyebrows were raised, and she was no doubt drawing her own conclusions. He gave in gracelessly. "All right, just tell me what time you want to eat at night. Don't expect me for breakfast or lunch, though. I don't have time to sit down to a meal more than once a day."

"Good," she said, amusement lacing her voice. "Because I don't have time to fix one more often."

"Can I show you the system now?"

She followed him downstairs to the front door. He indicated a panel that had been ensconced on the wall. "Every door and window is wired into this system. The lock has been changed on this door, and a dead bolt added. The side and back doors also have dead bolts. The same keys open all three doors. Once you open the door with your key, you have two minutes to get to this panel and type in a code you'll select. If the code is typed in correctly, the alarm will stay off. If not, it will sound, and loudly."

Raine studied the panel, fascinated in spite of herself. Across the inside cover of the panel door was a tape emblazoned with the name of a well-known alarm and security-system company.

"Once the alarm sounds, it will simultaneously ring this company." Mac tapped the name she'd been reading. "You'll have a contract with them that guarantees they'll have someone at your door in less than twenty minutes."

"Why both kinds of alarms?" she questioned.

"Protection," he said bluntly. "Noise has been known to scare off would-be intruders. And if it doesn't, the contract ensures that you'll have someone out here to check on things. The same thing with the windows. If one is broken, the wires running through it will also trigger the alarms. I can program the panel right now, if you're ready."

"Ready?" she asked, at a loss. "What do I have to do?"

"Give me six numbers that mean something to you, so you'll be sure and remember them. Lots of people pick a date, but if you do, try to stay away from the obvious ones like your birthday. We don't want someone to look up basic information on you and come out here and be able to get into your house."

After a moment, she recited six numbers to him. Mac programmed them into the panel, and the red light went on, indicating that the alarm was activated.

"What happens if I don't get to the panel within two minutes?" she asked interestedly.

"The alarm will go off, and the company will dispatch someone over here. Try not to let that happen too frequently," he advised dryly. "They'll add a charge to your bill for unnecessary trips."

"It would make more sense for them to call first," she said logically. "Or for the owner to be able to call and tell them there's been a mistake."

"This company doesn't operate that way anymore," he said shortly. That was why he used them. That phone call could be made under duress, and there was no way for the security guard to know for sure if services were really needed. "It makes them more expensive, but I think they're worth it." He opened the door and motioned for her to precede him. On the porch was a stack of bright yellow signs, with the name of the security company written across them in bold black letters.

"No," she said flatly, understanding his intent before he spoke a word. "I will not have those strewn across my lawn like forgotten campaign posters."

He gave her a hard look. "They can be effective. Most burglars have been at their trade for quite a while. They're familiar with the names of the systems. This one's reputation is the best. It could convince a would-be intruder to try his luck elsewhere."

Her lips firmed and she didn't say anything. She didn't care what Macauley's reasonings were. As soon as he was gone from here, those garish signs would be in the trash. She had to live with the intrusion of security panels and alarms, new doors and windows. She wasn't going to let the rolling splendor of her lawn be spoiled.

Mac led the way around the corner of the house. She gasped, for the first time noticing that the wild honeysuckle bushes had been cut back from the house, the vines had been pruned to practically nothing, and all the bushes had been shorn. "We had to clear the brush away from the house," he explained tersely, seeing her reaction. "You can't afford to have anything around the house or windows that would be large enough to conceal a person. You don't want any unpleasant surprises."

"No, but I'm sure getting plenty today," she muttered under her breath. If he heard her words, he ignored them.

"The flowers were left alone, for the time being. As long as they don't get too tall, they shouldn't be a problem." He read her mutinous expression accurately, and lectured, "You're going to have to think like this, Raine. Start making some decisions based on what would be safest for you."

Safest. She regarded the word with irony. She wasn't sure how safe she was ever going to feel in her home again, after this ordeal was over. She felt as though it had been violated, first by whoever was sending the letters and now by the security measures. It would probably never again seem as sacrosanct a haven, and she felt a melancholy regret.

"I plan to add several more security lights," he went on. Glancing at her, he said, "We really didn't have to do much rewiring. Some had been done fairly recently."

"I had it done right after I bought the house," she confirmed. Though she'd been anxious to move in right away, there hadn't been near enough lighting for her to feel comfortable here. She'd had all new wiring done, with several more electrical plates installed.

She wondered if Macauley had thought it odd when he'd seen all the light plates in her house. The electrician she'd hired hadn't made any attempt to hide the fact that it was one of the strangest requests he'd ever had. But it had been worth it to be certain that she would never have to walk into a dark room.

There would come a time, she hoped, when such measures would no longer be necessary, when she wouldn't fear specters hidden by the dark. But until then, she'd taken the necessary precautions to make certain that she would never be trapped in the darkness again.

Chapter 6

Raine looked up from the grilled chicken breast she was cutting. Macauley was eating steadily, giving her no idea of his opinion of the meal. Her lips tilted upward. She guessed he was enjoying it. He wasn't saying a word, but he was devouring the chicken, rice and potatoes she'd prepared. The garden fresh peas, she noted, were left at the side of his plate. She made a mental note not to prepare them again while he was here.

His eyes caught hers then, and he put his fork down. "Sorry. Didn't mean to eat like a ravenous animal."

She shook her head, still smiling. "It's nice to see you enjoy the meal." He ate like he did everything else, she observed, silently and efficiently. "There's another chicken breast here." She offered the plate to him, and he speared the meat, dropping it on his dish.

"I don't get much chance to enjoy someone else's cooking," he admitted. "I usually order takeout or have to make do with my own concoctions."

"What do you cook?" she asked curiously. As she'd done the grilling she'd decided that it would be a shame to waste the lovely evening, so they were eating on the patio.

He finished chewing and swallowed. "Well, my menu's kind of limited. Mostly I stick to meal choices one, two, three or four."

She laughed. "What in heaven's name are they?"

"Meal one is chicken noodle soup with rice and mushrooms added." Raine made a face, and he shook his fork at her. "Don't knock it, it's pretty good. Then meal two is hamburgers and French fries. Meal three is a steak and potato and meal four consists of kitchen-sink stir fry."

"Don't tell me," she said, "you throw everything in except—"

"The kitchen sink." He nodded. "Right."

"Everything but peas," she noted, nodding at his plate.

"You caught me," he said without apology. "Even now that I have choices, I'm not finicky. There's not much I won't eat, and haven't. But I draw the line at peas."

Finicky would hardly describe his appetite, she mused. He'd eaten everything else she'd put in front of him. "What do you mean, now that you have choices? Has that been a recent change?"

He mentally cursed his verbal blunder. That was exactly why he hated these assignments. He didn't know how to make the kind of casual dinner conversation that would keep his clients happy, and he damn well didn't want to talk about himself. Four years out of the field had dulled his senses. He would never have made a slip like that before, or he wouldn't have lived to get *out* of the field. But it wasn't as if it mattered anymore. The only thing that bothered him was how quickly old habits were slipping away from him. He needed that vacation even worse than he'd thought. Wiping his mouth deliberately with his napkin, he said finally, "I was in the military."

She cocked her head, startled. She couldn't picture his hair in the short-cropped style still favored by most branches of the service, but his answer made sense when she considered his discipline and bearing. He must have been a commissioned officer, and that would explain the tone of voice he used, the one that commanded instant respect. Still, she was having difficulty reconciling the idea of this man taking orders from anyone. No matter how far he had risen in the ranks, he'd still had to answer to superiors. She shook her head unconsciously. It didn't make sense.

His eyes caught the movement. "What? You don't believe I was in the Army?"

"I don't think it was just the Army, no," she admitted, her gaze steady. "There had to have been something more to draw you to a life like that. I have a hard time imagining you joining up for the chance to jump when someone else demanded it. You're disciplined, but not a follower." She didn't notice the stillness that crossed his features at her words. "There had to have been something . . ." She stopped then, her eyes widening. "Military intelligence?" she said in a whisper, but it wasn't really a question. She was right, she knew she was, though there was no flicker of agreement on his face. Undercover work would have drawn Macauley O'Neill. The danger would have lured him; living on the edge would have sustained him. It would also explain how he acquired that still watchfulness of his, that solitary manner. The lone life would have forced him to rely only on himself. No wonder he bit out commands in that terse voice of his. He was used to ordering lives to suit himself, as means to an end.

"They must have recruited you right out of high school," she said in a quiet voice. "Or was it on a college campus?"

He stacked their plates economically, walking away from her into the kitchen. She followed him to the doorway, and then leaned against the doorjamb. He set the dishes in the sink with a clatter and went to the refrigerator, opening it and extracting a long-necked bottle of beer. He offered her one and she shook her head. He must have had one of his crew stock her refrigerator, she realized for the first time. She rarely thought to buy beer, never having acquired a taste for it. Usually there were some strays in there, leftovers from a guest. He'd taken his bottle from a six-pack.

He still hadn't answered, and she realized suddenly that he had no intention of doing so. He walked deliberately toward her, but she didn't move. Stopping inches from her, he stared into her face. His mouth was set in a firm straight line, and his eyes were hooded. The masculine stubble on his chin was at eye level, and for an instant she experienced an overwhelming urge to reach up and touch it, to scrape it with her fingernail. How would that roughness feel against her skin? she wondered a little dizzily. Dragged across her cheeks, or her lips? Or lower?

She caught her breath at the uncharacteristic thought. She'd never been attracted to tough-as-nails, emotionless men, not that she could ever remember meeting one before. To be truthful, she'd really never been overly attracted to any man. Safety had always been the number-one quality she looked for in a date. She'd faced that fact squarely years ago. She'd tested her wings—there was no other phrase for it—on two men in her life. They'd been little more than boys, really. But this was no boy in front of her, nor was he safe. She didn't know why, then, standing this close to a man who emanated danger and hands-off, would make her throat clutch.

"May I?" His words were rusty.

Her gaze traveled fascinatedly, watching his mouth form those words, to his eyes, back to his mouth. Had he read her mind, captured her errant thought and determined to make it his own? Then he moved and his meaning became clear. She shifted out of his way on legs that suddenly seemed wooden. Mac brushed by her and walked to the patio. Pulling a chair around, he set it down facing the west, apparently with the intent of taking in the sunset.

She took a deep breath and followed him out the door. She sat in a chair near his. Silence prevailed for a time as they watched the sun sink in brilliant splendor. "Simple pleasures," he murmured after a time. Turning his head lazily to her he added, "I can see why you bought this place. The view is great."

She nodded, tucking her feet under her on the chair. "The smog isn't as bad out here. And it's peaceful without being too isolated. I loved it the moment I saw it. I barely gave the electrician time to complete the work I hired him to do before I moved in." She looked at him consideringly. "Where do you live?"

"I have an apartment." He shrugged. "I'm not there much." Certainly it wasn't a home, not the way her house was. It was pretty sterile, now that he thought about it. But he didn't have the faintest idea how to go about making it any other way, and damned if he was going to hire one of those high-priced decorators with double-breasted suits and ponytails to come in and do it for him. He wasn't really interested in matching color schemes and draperies, but it would be nice to come home to something more than a refrigerator and a bed. Maybe some pictures on the wall would help. He would want something he liked, something he wasn't going to get tired of looking at. Hell, maybe he'd even buy some of Raine's paintings. Though he hadn't any idea of their worth, he had money saved. And he already knew that he liked the ones he'd seen.

But maybe that wouldn't be such a wise choice. He was anxious to walk away from this job, and when the time came, he didn't want any reminders of it, or of her. The knowledge that such reminders would disturb him was irritating but undeniable.

"How long have you been out of the Army?" she asked.

After a brief hesitation he answered her. "Four years."

"I was right, wasn't I?" He turned to pin her with a look. "About your being in the intelligence branch?"

"Drop it, Raine."

"Is the reason you don't want to talk about it the same reason you decided to quit?" she persisted.

"I said drop it." His voice was clipped.

"Something plagues you at night," she said softly. "I've seen you pacing out here. I couldn't sleep, either, and I watched you. Was it the intelligence work you did, is that it?"

If the woman had one ounce of self-preservation she would be retreating. Right now every sense she had should be screaming a warning to her. Men a hell of a lot bigger had been known to quail before his temper. She was either unaware or unafraid of it. He didn't know which was more galling.

"What the hell do you know about it?" he snarled.

She met his gaze steadily. He was angry. No, more than that, he was furious. At her. Because she wouldn't back off and let him remain in that emotional cave he isolated himself in. It should have frightened her, the thought of this man angry. He was dangerous-looking at the best of times. Right now he was lethal. Yet his temper had a curiously calming effect on her. It was a rare sign of emotion from him, and for some reason she wanted to stoke it. Wanted to force him to respond as a man, not as a machine.

"I know how every regret a person has can compound at night until it threatens to choke you. I know that fear uses the daylight to hide and the darkness to prowl in." Her voice dropped. "And I know that people who can sleep do, and those of us who can't usually have a reason."

He rose from his chair so suddenly it clattered behind him. "You don't know what you're talking about," he growled. "You think your ivory-tower existence has prepared you to talk about regrets? Lady, you don't know what regret is. Up to now, the biggest fear in your life has been whether you'll sell well enough for Klassen to keep you as a client. Hell, you don't have the sense to be scared when there's a real threat out there. You let Klassen talk you out of reporting those letters at first because you wanted to believe him. You couldn't even make a decision about it until Winters forced you to!"

She looked away then, but he didn't relent. He had her on the ropes, and the thought gave him a savage delight. She'd poked and prodded at him like a child tormenting a puppy, and then had the guts to compare the two of them. The little girl from California, the successful artist, had nothing in common with Mac O'Neill.

"I'm saying that a person doesn't have to be in military intelligence to—"

"It's called covert operations, baby, and most of the time it has damn little to do with intelligence." His face was savage. "Do you know what that job entails, hmm? It doesn't involve nine-to-five office hours pushing papers across a desk. It's carried out in the searing heat of deserts halfway around the world, and in jungles with air so thick you can barely breathe. People don't matter there, obtaining goals does.''

"And did you attain your goals?" she asked almost soundlessly.

"I did my job."

The tone was flat, the words bleak. And she knew in that moment she had been right about him. She'd sensed that something rode this man, sensed it as only someone who'd been in that kind of pain herself could have done. And she felt for him, felt all the unspoken despair behind his outburst.

He clenched and unclenched his fists, angry that he'd allowed her to goad him into this admission, feeling as though she'd stripped away protective layers to reveal the ugly black center of his soul. And because he felt exposed, because he was uncomfortable with his own disclosure, he attacked. "What is it with you? You can't find enough problems in your own sheltered little existence to keep you occupied? Do you need more to get inspiration for your work, is that it? Concentrate on the creep who's harassing you, that should be trouble enough for anybody. Anybody with the sense to feel caution, that is.''

"There's a difference between not noticing danger and not allowing it to ruin your life. I'm sure you realized a long time ago that it's not the threats from without that keep people running, that scare them the most. It's the ones we carry inside us."

He stared at her wordlessly, his eyes arrowing into her. Where did she come up with these ideas? From what he knew of her, from her father, she'd had the sheltered upbringing of a society princess. He remembered something Grady had said once, that Simon Michaels protected his wife against anything in her life that might be unpleasant, and he figured the man had done the same for Raine. Certainly his voice when he spoke of her had been full of feeling. He had been concerned enough about her safety to hire Mac.

So what had happened to Raine Michaels along the way that would give her these kinds of insights?

"What is it about you?" he murmured, gazing intently at her.

"We're alike, you and I," she answered, and the truth of those words struck her violently. For some reason she'd felt it at the beginning—there was something she recognized in Macauley O'Neill. Something that had struck a chord in her. It wasn't a solely physical attraction, though she was only beginning to recognize that, too, existed. It was some element she hadn't been able to put her finger on until she'd seen him pacing alone in the moonlight. Now that common thread seemed to wrap around her, coaxing her to draw closer to the man, in spite of every self-protective tendency she'd ever had.

How else could she explain what had happened this afternoon? Over the years, it had been a carefully unspoken rule in her home that no one walked up behind Raine without announcing himself first. No one reached out a hand toward her unless he was standing in her view. And nobody *ever* put hands on her without her permission.

So what had happened earlier? Had she given Macauley tacit permission to touch her? Where had that acquired reaction gone to? And why had it disappeared under the touch of this man?

The thoughts echoed in her head, disturbing her. Each step she'd taken to regain a normal life had been met before with quiet self-satisfaction. She could go out now and not come home until after dark. She didn't like to, the discomfort was still there, but she could do it. She could stand in a line with someone behind her, and as long as that person didn't touch her, no one would be embarrassed. It might still make her sweat, the hairs on the back of her neck might prickle, but she could do that, too. She should be thrilled that she'd finally conquered yet another one of her fears this afternoon, but instead it filled her with confusion. Why should this man be the one to release her from that plague?

She took a step away from him, and then another. For the first time she felt afraid of him. Not physically, no, but emotional fear, that was something else. Why she should feel this close to a relative stranger was a question too complex to answer.

"Whatever similarity you think you see between us is in your imagination," he said harshly. "You're being threatened, I'm here to protect you. It's as simple, as basic as that. Don't start romanticizing anything about this. Romantic is the last word that should be used to describe someone like me." He turned on his heel and stalked into the house.

Raine picked up the chair he'd knocked over and leaned against it. She would never have guessed that being threatened by a maniac would help her combat yet another inner fear. Somehow she knew that Macauley would object to being thanked for her self-improvement, but the credit was indeed his. And that meant that he had some strange connection with her. One she was still at a loss to explain.

* * *

The next evening Raine and Mac ate in silence. The only time he spoke at all was to answer some question she put to him, and finally she gave up the effort. He seemed determined to maintain a distance from her, and she suspected that meant she'd been closer last night with her probing than he felt comfortable with. Whatever the cause, she respected his withdrawal for what it was. She hadn't meant to pry, but that was exactly what she'd done.

"Looks like I owe you another apology," she said tentatively.

He hesitated in his chewing for a fraction of a minute. "What for?"

"I pushed last night, and I didn't respect your privacy." She made an expression of self-deprecation. "All the things I hate having done to me. My brothers accuse me of using my sense of honesty as a weapon and beating people over the head with it. I hope I didn't do any lasting damage."

He swallowed. And then, unwillingly, his mouth quirked in an almost smile. "I'm still in one piece."

"Well, good," she said lightly. "I'd hate to think that you were one more victim to my mad, impetuous quest for pushing people over the edge. I was beginning to think you weren't going to talk to me anymore."

Actually, he'd given that idea some thought, and it had its merits. But he should have known that it would be a useless tactic with Raine. Last night she'd gotten him furious enough to strangle her, and tonight she was charming him with her self-effacing humor. He wasn't a man easy to charm, but she did it so easily, so effortlessly. The wry humor, usually directed at herself, and the huge eyes, full of whatever emotion she was feeling at the moment, were incredibly beguiling. They would have enchanted a less cautious man, drawn him irresistibly closer. He wondered why it was that he hadn't been tripping over her admirers. She was attractive enough, although she didn't seem to give her looks any great thought. She didn't move with the conscious invitation of a woman aware of her power over men, but she was graceful. Some men would be attracted to that slim, delicate body and offbeat sense of humor. Where were those men? Were they all blind, or stupid?

He stared at her silently for a moment. Right now her eyes reflected her sincerity. They were perfect mirrors for whatever emotion she was feeling at the moment, as easy to read as a child's. He'd observed fear in them, determination and anger. He's seen them teasing, warm and friendly. But whatever she was feeling didn't control her; just the opposite, in fact. He was coming to realize that she was a master at tamping down her most bothersome emotions until she'd conquered them. She had a kind of courage that was difficult to resist, and recognition of that made him edgy. Women like her weren't for men like him, and the fact that he even had to remind himself of that was proof that the job here was getting to him. *She* was getting to him.

She raised her eyebrows then and he realized belatedly that he'd been staring. He shook his head. "Don't worry about it." Changing the subject smoothly, he asked, "I've been meaning to ask you where you met Greg Winters. How did he come to be your accountant?"

She smiled in remembrance. "He was taking an art class at night at the university. I had been a guest speaker, and he'd asked my opinion of a painting he was doing. A bunch of us ended up going out for coffee, and he and I started talking. He told me what he did and convinced me that I could use an accountant." She shrugged. "I agreed to let him take a look at my finances. They were really a mess. I mean, I don't really have the time or the inclination to look into money markets and that kind of thing. It bores me."

Mac frowned. "You didn't hire him just like that, did you?"

She felt a flash of irritation, which she pushed away. After all, he didn't sound half as judgmental as her father had when he'd found out. He'd wanted her to fire Greg right away and turn her financial matters over to Simon's private accountant. It had been one more thing they'd disagreed about. Meeting his gaze squarely, she responded, "Greg gave me references, and I checked with all of them. He really knows his stuff."

"So he's a better accountant than he is an artist?" he inquired lazily.

She opened her mouth to answer, then shut it. "Much better," she agreed impishly. "He has as much artistic skill as I have financial brilliance. So actually, we suit pretty well."

But not as well as Winters would like, Mac thought silently. He made a mental note to check with Trey on anything else he might have found out about the man. There was nothing in Raine's voice when she spoke of him to suggest more than friendship on her part. Yet Winters's feelings for Raine were as transparent as glass. From the conversation he'd overheard in the kitchen several days earlier, it was apparent that even Klassen had picked up on them.

The doorbell rang then, and they rose simultaneously. He reached out and captured her wrist. She sent him a silent, questioning look, ignoring the tingling in her skin beneath his fingers.

Giving no explanation, he moved in front of her, then proceeded into the house. She heaved a sigh of resignation. For a few minutes she'd almost forgotten the real reason for his presence here.

"Mac, good to see you again. Where's my daughter?" Simon Michaels stepped through the door Mac had opened, clasping the younger man's hand in a hearty shake. Spying Raine coming down the hall he said, "There you are, Raine. I hadn't heard from you recently, so I thought I'd stop by and see how things are going. Your mother had planned to come, too, but she didn't have a good day today."

Concern flared immediately at the mention of her mother. "Has she taken a turn for the worse?"

Simon waved a placating hand. "Now, don't worry, honey, she's fine. She just tried to do too much today, and got overtired. You know how I'm always telling her to take it easy. She'll be more rested tomorrow."

Raine wasn't convinced. For as long as she could remember, her father had been protecting his wife, watching over her health with an almost solicitous care. He was capable of overreacting to a normal day's tiredness, and he was just as capable of glossing over the real state of his wife's health to avoid alarming Raine. She chewed her lip for a moment, surveying him. "I think I'll call her," she said. "Unless you think she's asleep already."

"Excellent idea," he said heartily. "Hearing from you will perk her right up." As she walked toward the phone on Mac's desk, her father cleared his throat. "Why don't you go to the kitchen, Raine? Then you can talk as long as you wish and we won't bother you. Go ahead," he urged as she studied him suspiciously.

She flicked her gaze at Macauley. He inclined his head slightly.

Aware that she was being manipulated, she decided that her concern for her mother was most important at the moment. She turned and left for the kitchen.

As soon as she'd exited, Simon turned to Mac. He'd noted the look the man had shared with Raine but didn't comment on it. "Well, why don't you give me a progress report, Mac? Have there been any more threatening letters?"

Mac shook his head. "Not so far." He gave the man a rundown on the security precautions that had been completed to date.

"That sounds well and good, but what about this maniac who's been threatening her? I called that damned detective again, and he's no closer than before to solving this thing. I get the feeling it isn't exactly high on his list of priorities, either," Simon added disgustedly.

"I've talked to him, too," Mac said.

"Well? What do you think?" Simon demanded. "God knows, the beefed-up security can't hurt, but she remains in danger until the person sending these letters is caught. Surely you realize that."

"What I realize," Mac returned, in a deceptively mild voice, "is that you set me up when you got me to come out and look things over." He propped himself against the edge of his desk, crossing his arms.

Simon gave him an impatient look. "What do you mean? I told you that Raine needed your services."

Mac nodded judiciously. "You did. You said you wanted me to come out, make her home safe, and judge just how much danger she's in."

"And that's just what you've done. I don't know what else you're talking about."

"You counted on the fact," Mac continued softly, "that once I was here I'd talk Raine into my staying. That's one little fact you forgot to mention, Simon. That you'd forgotten to mention the extent of my job when you spoke to her."

The man didn't bat an eyelash. "What I counted on," he corrected, "was you. That you'd come here and take care of things. And you're doing fine, so far. Hell, son, if I hadn't known you were the man for the job, I wouldn't have hounded you into taking this case."

Mac ignored the flattery. "You tried to manipulate me," he said flatly. "And Raine." He paused for a moment, letting the words sink in. "Don't try it again."

Simon's jaw clenched. The look he'd intercepted between the man and Raine took on a whole new intimacy, and he didn't like it at all. "You don't speak for my daughter, O'Neill."

"I think I do," Mac contradicted. "At least in this instance. And you know it. That's why you took so long to come by. You were waiting for her to cool down a little before you talked to her again."

"I've been busy, and I knew I could trust you to get things done."

"There isn't anything else that you've forgotten to tell me, is there, Simon?" Mac asked caustically. "I've never been much for surprises."

There was a moment's silence as their eyes clashed. Simon looked away first. "You know everything you need to about this case, more than I know, most likely. I have a hell of a lot more faith in you than I do in that overworked detective downtown. You'll take care of Raine for me, and she'll get back to the life she was meant to have."

Mac faced him impassively. "And that is?"

Simon waved a hand carelessly. "Raine needs a husband. She's a sweet girl, and sooner or later she's going to meet a nice, respectable young man and settle down. I've introduced her to several promising young executives myself. It's only a matter of time before she chooses one and marries."

The words were harmless enough, but Mac knew there was a message in them for him. A nice young man good enough for Raine would win Simon's vote for son-in-law. The description could never be applied to the likes of Mac O'Neill. He shook his head in bemusement. Simon really had the most incredible gall. Mac was good enough to keep his daughter safe, but if it hadn't been for the threat hanging over Raine's head, he knew without a doubt that Simon would have preferred Raine didn't get within ten miles of him. And the hell of it was, he couldn't fault the man for feeling that way. What he didn't understand was why Simon thought it necessary to issue the subtle warning in the first place.

Raine's entry into the room interrupted Mac's thoughts. "Mother's nurse said she was asleep. I'll get in touch with her tomorrow."

"You do that, honey. And now I'd better go. I have to stop by the office for some files I need to work on tonight."

"I'll walk you to your car," she offered firmly.

"No, that's not necessary—"

"Oh, but I insist," she said, hooking her arm through his and leading him out. "You and I haven't really had a chance to talk. And there's so much I have to say to you."

Mac's face lit with amusement. Simon was going to get an earful, that was certain. And somehow he thought Raine might just come out on top in this particular skirmish. Having been on the receiving end of her temper a time or two himself, he couldn't help relishing the thought of Simon taking his turn.

* * *

Raine sat in the porch swing long after her father had gone. As dusk began to turn to night, she got up and flipped the switch that should have turned on the porch light. Newly installed floodlights shone across the lawn. She tried another switch, and a spotlight that must have been mounted on the top of the house began sweeping the area with a moving beam. Muttering to herself, she gave up and went back to the swing. Macauley had forgotten to explain the extent of the changes he'd made. Feeling like a stranger in her own home, she stared pensively at the shadows.

A couple hours later she was still there. Mac stood in the doorway watching her for a moment.

"Hi," she said softly, looking up at his arrival. He'd obviously started getting ready for bed. He was shirtless, and she was entranced by the sight of his bare torso gleaming in the partial darkness.

He leaned against the doorjamb. "You going to turn in soon?"

She lifted her shoulder in a shrug. "Not yet. Why don't you join me? Porch sitting is very relaxing, you know."

"Is that a fact?"

She nodded solemnly. "It's almost a lost art. Come here, I'll show you." She got up and crossed over to him, taking him by the elbow and leading him to the swing. He stood by it, eyeing it suspiciously.

"The first rule of porch sitting is to situate yourself in the most advantageous place possible," she lectured him with mock solemnity. "This swing will do just fine." She gave him a slight push and he reluctantly sat down on its slatted seat. "Then, you just sit yourself down . . ." She sat next to him. "Just so." She pushed off the floor with her foot and sent the swing moving slowly through the air.

After a moment he turned to look at her. "And then what?"

"And then—" her voice was filled with laughter "—you wonder what your neighbors are up to."

He gave a sound that might have been a chuckle. She turned her head swiftly, captivated by the sound. She caught the remnants of a smile on his firm lips. Her eyes fell to his jaw. For the first time since she'd met him, he was clean-shaven. "You shaved," she gasped.

He rubbed his chin. "I'm not a complete savage. I shave every night," he said, half defensively.

Every night. The words conjured up an intriguing mental image. She could picture him, torso bare, leaning toward the mirror, moving the blade up his throat in smooth, sure strokes. She imagined him wiping the foam from his face, slapping on the after-shave she could detect. The vision dripped with sensuality. Shaving at night spoke of habit. A habit acquired so a man didn't abrade a woman's softer skin with a day's worth of whiskers. She took in a shuddering breath, and changed the subject.

"What did you and my father talk about tonight?"

"What's been done around here," he answered vaguely.

She arched her eyebrows, waiting for him to go on. When he didn't she prompted, "And did he approve?"

What a question. Simon's approval of the measures he was taking to keep Raine safe had been easily apparent. His warning had been equally so. "He seemed to." After a pause he said, "Is there something wrong with your mother? You and your father seemed rather concerned."

She gave a gentle sigh. "My mother has a genetic heart condition that worsens with age. She almost died having me." Her voice softened, and she added, "My father has always protected her, and my brothers and I tried to do the same. We never upset her if we can help it. Stress aggravates her condition."

"No wonder he seemed so worried about her."

When he didn't go on, Raine said wryly, "You can't fool me. My father didn't come over here to discuss Mother. He grilled you about this whole mess, and about me. I know him well, remember. That's why he got me out of the room."

"Were your ears burning?"

"Still warm," she said, turning one to him. "See?"

Without conscious volition, one long finger reached out and traced the shell-like contours of her ear. It was dainty, just like the rest of her.

Raine turned her head toward him, so his finger touched her cheek, her lips. He left it there for a moment, rubbing softly across that pouty mouth. He felt her mouth open slightly beneath his finger, and he experienced a sudden urge to bend down and press his lips against hers, to see if the easy warmth that was so much a part of her would extend to her kiss. He bet it would. Kissing Raine might be one way to chase the chill away from his own dark soul. Her warmth would spread, stamping out the coldness inside of him. He pulled his hand back at the thought.

Nothing and no one was that warm. He'd been cold for so long he was numb from it. And it was more likely that the ice in him would spread to *her*. That would be all he needed, one more thing to feel guilty for.

And he *would* feel guilty, he thought with a glance at those wide eyes gazing at him. He was hired to do a job here, and no woman would interfere with that. He hadn't needed Simon's veiled warning earlier to remind him. He couldn't maintain his objectivity in this case if he got involved with her. But he could no longer deny that the temptation was there.

That ancient resignation he sometimes observed in her eyes still puzzled him. At times he felt compelled to unlock the secret of the ghosts he saw there. But he hadn't attempted it yet, and he wouldn't. He didn't need to learn anything that would draw him closer to her, tempt him further. It wouldn't be fair, after all, since he fought his own inner battles alone.

But despite those shadows he suspected existed, she managed to radiate an uncommon, pure innocence. Perhaps that was what beckoned to his jaded soul the most, the recognition that something rare was waiting inside her, just within his grasp.

He knew he should get up then, go into the house. But the swing's rhythmic movements were lulling, and the company was sweet. He felt a wistful yearning that coaxed him to stay even when he knew he should go. Moments like these had been forgotten long ago, but now memories were stirring, and so were other emotions, some better left undisturbed.

He sat in silence next to her, drinking in the night sounds. After a while Raine pulled her feet up beside her and leaned her head against the slatted back. Mac stretched out his arm, and she relaxed against it trustingly.

Staring out into the night, he felt an unusual contentment. It was peaceful to just sit and look at the stars with a woman by his side. A woman who didn't demand anything from him, not even conversation.

There was something seductive about such a woman, something that beckoned to him. He almost believed that she could banish the darkness inside him. Thinking like that was dangerous. *This woman* was dangerous.

But she was also enchanting, intriguing.

She sighed and moved a little against his arm. He allowed his arm to tighten around her shoulders as he breathed in her scent.

Captivating.

Chapter 7

Three days later Raine was staring at a blank canvas. She needed to complete one more painting. But inspiration had, for the moment at least, deserted her. Usually she was able to look out her window for a few minutes, then close her eyes, and an idea would start to take shape. These days, all she could focus on outside her window were those ugly yellow signs dotting her lawn, the trucks and the piles of materials out front.

Today's scene was different from last week's. There were only two trucks out front, and the noise had shifted. Currently it was coming from the roof. Directly above her, in fact. In frustration she left the room. No one seemed to be in the house, a far cry from the way it had been before Macauley O'Neill had come into her life. The phone rang as she was on her way out the front door.

She walked swiftly to the library before remembering his order that she wasn't to pick up the phone herself. But he certainly didn't seem to be around to answer it. His shirt was lying across a chair. The walkie-talkie he carried to keep in contact with the men was on his desk. After the briefest hesitation, she crossed the room and picked up the receiver.

"Raine Michaels?"

A feeling of trepidation began to form at the pit of her stomach when she heard the unfamiliar voice.

"Yes, this is Raine Michaels."

"This is Dr. Dietz, calling from the emergency room at St. Joseph's Medical Center."

Her fingers clenched the phone more tightly, guessing what the next words would be, wishing helplessly that she could stop them.

"I'm afraid your mother has been brought in by ambulance, Miss Michaels. The ER crew is working to stabilize her now, but..."

Tears formed in Raine's eyes, and she closed them tightly, as if she could shut out the words. This wasn't the first such phone call she'd received. But her mother's health had been precarious before, and she'd always managed to pull through. Always. The word repeated itself in her brain in a litany, even as she forced her question out between numb lips. "What's wrong?"

"Cardiac distress, Miss Michaels. Your father is with her now, and he asked that I contact you and your brothers. I'd recommend you get here as soon as you can."

A sob broke through then, and Raine closed her lips tightly for an instant, to stem the rest. "Yes," she agreed finally, once she was sure her voice would work again. "Tell him I'm on my way."

"Check with admissions when you get here, Miss Michaels. They can direct you from there."

She didn't wait for anything more. She dropped the receiver in the cradle and ran to the door. Once there she realized she didn't have her keys, and ran halfway back inside the room, looking wildly about for her purse. The tears streaming down her face weren't helping her search any, and she wiped at them frustratedly. Her fingers curled into her palms, and she forced herself to take a deep, calming breath. It wouldn't help her parents to have to deal with their daughter's hysterics once she arrived at the hospital.

Calmer, she went to the hallway closet and took her purse from the shelf on which she always kept it. Extracting the keys, she hurried to the garage and backed her white Lexus into the drive. She'd reached the road at the end of the drive when she remembered Macauley's instructions about going nowhere without him.

She deliberated for only a frantic moment before turning onto the road in front of her house. No doubt he was up on the roof in the middle of the melee, and she definitely wasn't going to take the time to join him up there and explain. She could call him from the hospital. Biting her lip, she prayed to God that she wouldn't be too late.

She turned off onto a secondary road and began driving toward the Golden State Freeway. The freeway would help her avoid the traffic snarls that seemed to occur like clockwork. Worry gnawed at her as she drove. Her mother hadn't suffered an attack in over two years. The intervening time had lulled Raine into a more complacent frame of mind. It had been easy to let herself believe that the worst was behind them and that Lorena Michaels would actually get better. Wiping her eyes, Raine glanced in her rearview mirror. A large blue car was following her closely, and she eased up on the gas a little, intending to let the driver by. The car sagged back.

She bit her lip, her attention returning to the road ahead of her, cursing the amount of time it would take her to reach the hospital and her mother. Her foot pressed down more firmly on the gas.

A bump against her rear fender jolted her from her worry then, and her gaze flew up, shocked. The car in back of her was on her tail again, and even as her hands tightened reflexively on the wheel, the car banged into her again. Despite her grasp on the wheel, her car pulled to the right.

"What's the matter with you, are you crazy?" she shouted at the reflection in the rearview mirror. She righted the car and looked wildly about but there were no other vehicles in the vicinity. She sped up, hoping to outrun the lunatic in back of her. But the other car kept pace, then pulled alongside her. She sent wide eyes over to the car, and her view of the driver made the situation seem even more unreal. Her attention was jolted to her own car as the blue vehicle started edging toward her own. Instinctively, Raine lifted her foot from the gas and started to brake, but she wasn't able to avoid the collision.

The car hit the side of hers with a screeching sound as metal ground against metal. The Lexus was far smaller than the other vehicle and lurched violently to the right. She pulled the wheel to the side frantically, barely able to stay on the road. She threw one more panic-stricken gaze at the other car before it hit her again. This time she slammed on the brakes as she felt her right wheels hit the sandy shoulder of the road. This pulled the car even harder to that side. Before she had a chance to react the blue car slammed into hers again. Raine pulled on the wheel, but the force of the impact sent the Lexus around in a dizzying circle before it flew into the ditch at the right of the road and crashed into a palm tree.

Seconds or minutes ticked by before Raine was aware of anything again. She raised her head groggily, suddenly realizing that it had been resting upon the air bag, which the accident had activated. Glass from the broken windshield littered the dash and the front seat. Shards dropped from her body as she sat up straighter, and she raised a shaky hand to her temple. Her shoulder harness hadn't prevented her from hitting her head hard on the side window. Releasing the button for the seat belt with trembling fingers, she opened her car door and stumbled out, almost sprawling to the ground. She stood up on unsteady legs, swinging her gaze up and down the road frantically. The blue car had vanished.

She blinked, disoriented. The sunshine was still pouring down brightly, birds were still flying overhead. Everything seemed bizarrely normal in the world. But things weren't normal at all. Just moments before she could have been . . .

She could have been killed.

Her teeth started to chatter despite the warm air, shock setting in, adding to the chill skating up her flesh. She was never sure how long it was before she made her way to the side of the road and waved her arms weakly at an approaching car. It slowed to a stop beside her. The driver listened to her disjointed explanation and promised to call a state trooper to help her.

She went to her car to wait. Leaning against the fender, she wrapped her arms tightly herself. Whoever had been in that old blue car had deliberately tried to push her off the road.

She wondered numbly if that was all the driver had set out to do.

The hospital doors swung open wildly as Mac pushed his way in. Stopping at the front desk, he asked a few terse questions of the nurse standing there, before she pointed to a waiting room behind him. He turned and his ice blue gaze swept the area swiftly before catching sight of Raine sitting in the corner with another nurse and a state trooper. As he strode over to them, a muscle jumped in his jaw. A livid bruise marred one side of her delicate profile and a good-size bump was above it. He pushed past the nurse and squatted in front of her. One finger tipped her chin up gently, then turned her face from side to side. His mouth was a hard, tight line. He dropped his hand and covered both of hers, which were clasped tightly in her lap.

"You look like hell, kiddo," he told her.

She smiled tremulously. "I feel a lot better than I look. I think."
Actually, she hadn't seen a mirror, but as she'd tried to convince the trooper, and the nurse in front of her, she felt fine. The terror

of her ordeal was not the most pressing matter on her mind. "Please, Macauley, I have to find out about my mother. She's here somewhere, they called me, and no one will help me. ..." Her voice cracked. "I have to know how she is."

Her confused explanation made little sense, but he responded to the lambent plea in her golden eyes. "It's all right, everything's fine," he said soothingly. "Calm down and tell me what happened."

"She insisted that I bring her here to St. Joseph's right away," the trooper interjected. "I figured from the looks of what was left of her car, that was a pretty good idea. But now that she's here, she won't let a doctor check her out." He shook his head and lowered his voice, clearly believing that Raine was delusional. "She keeps insisting that her mother is here, and real sick. Then she gave us your number, so I called you. Maybe you can help her see reason."

"She is here," Raine said firmly, her voice pulling Mac's gaze to her own. "I got a phone call from Dr. Dietz, calling at my father's request, asking me to meet him here for Mom. I didn't have time to find you. ..." Her voice faltered a little at the grim look on his face. "I planned to call once I got here."

Mac fired a look at the nurse, who was standing silently by. "Did you check this out?"

"Yes, sir, I did," she explained patiently. "No one by the name of Lorena Michaels has been admitted or treated in the emergency room." Her voice was firm when she added, "And there is no Dr. Dietz on our staff."

The nurse's words lent an even more chilling interpretation of the recent events. Mac closed his eyes briefly, mentally cursing himself for ever leaving Raine alone, even in her own home. It was not, he thought savagely, opening his eyes and taking in her battered demeanor, a mistake he would ever make again.

"But there has to be a Dr. Dietz," Raine explained wearily. She looked at Mac. "He called me."

Mac gazed steadily at her, watching comprehension slowly dawn on her face, and with it, fear. His hands tightened around hers as she swayed a little in her seat.

"He called me," she repeated in a whisper.

"Yeah, sweetheart," he agreed in a savage tone. "He sure did." The bastard had called her, had set her up. And then she'd had an accident that could have killed her. He'd never much cared for coincidences. Her hands trembled a little in his, and he loosened his grip, for the first time aware of how tightly he was holding them. She looked as if she had taken another blow as awareness began to settle in. But then she raised her chin slightly and made a deliberate effort to compose her features.

A corner of his mouth went up. The lady had guts. That had never been more apparent than right now.

"You need to be seen by a physician, ma'am," the nurse standing on the other side of Raine said kindly. "And then if everything is all right, your husband can take you home and pamper you shamelessly. How will that be?"

"He's not my husband," Raine corrected her. "He's—"

"Not taking you home until a doctor sees you," Mac put in firmly.

"But—"

"While the doctor is tending to you, I'll call your father," he promised. "I'll ask him how your mom has been. And I'll need to let him know what's happened."

She was already shaking her head. "You'll just upset him."

"Raine." His voice was firm. "He has to know."

"And while he's putting your mind at ease," the nurse said, taking her by the elbow, "there's an examining room with your name on it."

Raine rose to her feet, but pulled her elbow from the nurse's grasp. "No." Her voice was strained. "I don't want to go in there."

"Now, ma'am." The nurse used a soothing tone, as if speaking to a recalcitrant child. "The sooner you come in with me, the sooner your—this gentleman can take you home."

Mac watched the scene silently, something about it bothering him. Raine's face was tight and drawn, not surprising under the circumstances. But the earlier composure he'd seen her fight for had faded, and her features were chalk white, her mouth flat. He couldn't shake off the feeling that something else was afoot here.

"Raine." His voice was soft. "Do you want me to come in with you?"

Her gaze swung to his and clung for a second. Then she looked at the nurse and the trooper. Impatience was starting to show on the nurse's plump face, and the trooper looked quizzical. She looked down then, trying to summon a little dignity.

"No." She spoke with visible effort, but her voice was even. "I can do this."

Mac looked at her closely, thinking her choice of words odd. But her jaw was firming again in determination. And without another word she allowed the nurse to escort her out of sight. Watching her leave, he had to fight the urge to follow. The trooper spoke then, snaring his attention.

"Well, I think she'll be all right. Seems a bit shaken up, but that's to be expected." His voice was matter-of-fact. He'd obviously noticed nothing out of the ordinary. "From the sounds of it, it was a hit-and-run of some kind."

Mac's gaze sharpened. "Were there any witnesses to the accident?"

The man shook his head. "None that stuck around. Miss Michaels claims another driver bumped into her from behind, then ran her off the road." He scratched his head. "Frankly, I wasn't too sure if she was dazed from the accident, or what. The whole story sounded a little funny."

Funny was the last adjective Mac would have used to describe any of the happenings of the day. One of his men had yelled for him on the roof when Raine's car had taken off, but she'd been out of sight before he could follow her. There had been nothing to do but pace in the office, cursing the day he'd ever taken this job. When the call had come from the trooper, his anger had taken a back seat to his concern for Raine. Despite assurances from the officer that Raine seemed all right to him, Mac hadn't been sure until he could see her for himself. And now that he'd seen her, he still wasn't certain.

Oh, she was on her feet, that was a good sign. And other than that nasty bump on the side of her head, she didn't seem to have sustained any permanent damage, as long as there were no internal injuries. But something wasn't right here. He'd seen what it cost her to pull herself together and go with that nurse. Even as his mind was trying to puzzle it out, the trooper interrupted his thoughts.

"Miss Michaels said she only got one quick look at the person in the other car."

That snared Mac's attention, and fast. "She can identify him?" What a break that would be in this whole mess. The thought came and went that his involvement with Raine Michaels would then come to an end. And not a moment too soon.

But the man shook his head. "Not really. Seems like the driver was wearing one of those Halloween fright masks and a pair of gloves. Guess that's not going to help us out at all in solving this."

Mac stared hard at him. A mask and gloves spoke of a person who had planned this whole scene. Someone who had called Raine to deliberately lure her out of the house. It would have had to be someone who knew of Lorena Michaels's poor health. Then the man had laid in wait to ambush her, to run her off the road.

A fiery knot of rage burned low in Mac's belly. This was quite a leap from a few phone calls and letters. This scheme spoke of cunning and cold-blooded intent. Raine could have been seriously injured, even killed if she hadn't been wearing her safety belt. Had that been the ambusher's intention?

In short, succinct words he described for the trooper the harassment Raine had been suffering, then gave him the name of the detective investigating the case. The trooper promised to call the man with a full report. Then he excused himself and left.

The man's exit left Mac with nothing to do but wait. And think. And his thoughts weren't pretty. His palms itched. He wanted to get his hands around the throat of the person responsible.

He smiled a cold, deadly smile. He was going to find the bastard who was threatening Raine. And then he would make damn sure he paid.

Mac sent a concerned glance across the front seat of the truck, taking his attention off the road for an instant. "I take it you don't like hospitals."

"Not since . . ." She caught herself, and after a brief hesitation answered, "Not much, no. But I got through it."

Again, her words struck him as odd. She sounded as if it had been entering the hospital, and not the accident itself, which had been the bigger strain that day. He returned his attention to the road and fell into a contemplative silence.

After a bit, Raine heaved a sigh and looked at him. So far he'd shown remarkable restraint, but she was expecting him to lambast her for her foolhardiness today, and the anticipation of the explosion was almost worse than the words themselves would be. "Go ahead and say it," she muttered.

One eyebrow rose.

"You know you're dying to. I shouldn't have left the house alone. I walked right into a trap."

Still he didn't answer.

"Well?" she demanded.

"I'd say that about covers it," he agreed.

"I was afraid for Mother, and I wasn't thinking as clearly as I could have," she defended herself. "You were nowhere to be found, nor were any of your men nearby. I didn't think I had time to track you down. There haven't been any letters since before you came, and I thought—oh, heck," she finished, sitting back and crossing her arms.

"You didn't think," he said flatly. "And not thinking almost got you killed. Chew on that for a while."

She wrapped her arms around herself, goose bumps prickling the skin under her fingers. "I can't think of anything else. I'm scared, Macauley. And I hate that," she added fiercely. "I hate feeling this way." Fear wasn't the only emotion she was feeling. Anger was beginning to simmer inside her, and she welcomed it. "What will happen to my car?" she asked abruptly.

He made a left turn onto the road that led to her house. "I imagine it's been towed by now," he said. "You'll probably hear something soon. Some estimates will have to be given, to see if it's worth fixing or if it will have to be totaled out. I didn't see the car, so I don't know what it looked like."

"It resembled a folded-up accordion," she said shakily.

He gave her a look then that reminded her, without words, just how lucky she was to have walked away from it.

Pulling up in front of her house, he came around to her side and helped her down from the truck.

"I'm really all right," she protested, as his hands settled on her waist.

"You may feel all right now, but I can guarantee that every muscle in your body will ache by tomorrow," he predicted. "You go clean up. I'll take care of supper tonight."

She stopped in her tracks and stared at him. "Meal one, two, three or four?" she asked suspiciously.

"I'll surprise you."

No doubt he would. He'd been a constant source of surprises since he'd come, uninvited, into her life. She'd interpreted the burst of awareness she'd felt as soon as he laid his hands on her waist without shock. Something happened to her whenever Macauley O'Neill touched her. And that, perhaps, was the biggest surprise of all.

Supper turned out to be meal number two, and Raine had to admit that the juicy hamburgers tasted delicious. They were again eating on the patio, and there was a glass of wine in front of her. She had refused it at first, but Mac had insisted.

"You need it," he'd asserted flatly. "You had a hell of a shock today, and this will calm your nerves."

It was easier to drink it than to argue with him. And after the first few times, she'd stopped protesting when he refilled her glass whenever she took a sip. Already a little of the tension from the day was seeping out of her limbs. She would have liked to go along with his plan, finish the meal and drink enough wine to complete the job of relaxation, but she wouldn't allow herself to shirk reality.

"So what happens next?" she asked quietly.

He didn't pretend to misunderstand her. "Next you give me your word that you're going to do as you're told, without question." He held up a hand to forestall her response. "The stakes have been raised, Raine. Big-time. We're not talking about a crank with a bad attitude toward artists. Someone is out to get you. And you're going to have to face the fact that it could very well be someone you know."

Her eyes got wide. "What makes you—"

"Think about what happened today," he cut in sharply. "Somebody knew you well enough to masquerade as a doctor on the phone. He knew just what button to push—the illness of your mother—to get you to abandon caution and go tearing out of your home. That doesn't speak of an anonymous crank, Raine. It tells me that you know this person, at least slightly. Who knows that I've been staying at the house?"

She shook her head. "No one. I didn't mention it because I was hoping..." Her voice trailed off. She'd been hoping that this whole mess would clear up before she had to explain to anyone. She'd thought that perhaps, once the security measures were completed, the letters would have stopped or the harasser would have been caught or... She shook her head. She was no longer sure what she'd thought.

But she was sure what she didn't believe. "I can't imagine how anyone other than my friends would know about my mother's health, and none of them would do anything like this. It's too ludicrous to contemplate."

He surveyed her over his beer bottle. She wasn't ready to believe that anyone close to her could be capable of this kind of evil. He couldn't blame her. It would be damn hard for most people to consider. He wasn't going to push her any further on the subject tonight. She'd already been through enough today, and had held up damn well, too. She was shaken, it had taken conscious effort on her part, but she wasn't down for the count. Raine Michaels had more moxie, more sheer guts than most men he knew. He couldn't help but admire that.

Setting the bottle down carefully, he said, "If you haven't told anyone that I'm staying at the house, whoever planned this thought he could get you out by yourself. So we're going to continue to let him think that. I've been putting my truck in your garage—I'll keep doing that. Once the workmen have left, we're going to let him think I've gone with them."

Her gaze moved to the horizon. The sun had long since gone down in a brilliant, glorious display. "You think that will draw him out?"

"It could."

"And then what?"

Mac chose his words deliberately. "Well, if we're real lucky the police will step up their efforts and find the person behind this."

She looked at him silently, waiting for the rest of his thought.

"If not," he said bluntly, "I'm going to have to get the bastard myself."

His tone was chilling and full of purpose. Their eyes met, and she had no doubt that he would do as he said. He would accomplish what the police had so far been unable to. He'd find whoever was responsible for harassing her, the person who had almost killed her today, and he would stop him.

Unquestioning certainty filled her at the realization. For the first time since she was fifteen years old, she had complete and total faith in another person. No, she corrected herself. Not another person. In one person.

Macauley O'Neill.

Raine came awake with a start, her heart pumping in a familiar terrible rhythm, her breath coming in pants. She should have known better than to try to sleep tonight. But she thought the long, hot bath Macauley had recommended, coupled with the glasses of wine, would work their magic on sore muscles and an exhausted mind. And so they had, for a while. Until a dream-induced replay had awakened her.

The red digits on the clock at the bedside glowed twelve o'clock. She'd been asleep less than an hour. Chances for a return to slumber were slight, at least for a while. She stared out at the night fixedly. The full moon of a few weeks ago had splintered to less than a quarter now, adding to the darkness of the sky. She took deep breaths, from long practice familiar with the tricks it took to calm a body in flight mode.

But the old tricks weren't working well tonight. Deep breathing didn't calm her nerves, didn't chase the chill from her skin. She wasn't sure what would.

Mac heard the ragged breathing coming from her room as he passed it on his way to his own. He poked his head in the door, unsurprised when he saw the small figure sitting up in bed, arms wrapped around her knees. "Raine." His voice was low. She didn't answer, and he took a reluctant step over the threshold. "Are you all right?"

She nodded, then, aware he wouldn't be able to detect the movement in the dark, tried to speak. "Yes."

The ache in her voice negated the meaning of the word. He came farther into the room, reaching for the light, but she forestalled his movement toward it.

"No," she commanded, her voice quiet but even. "Leave it off."

His hand hovered at the switch for a moment before dropping. He'd never questioned the extra light plates, but had been aware shortly after he'd first come here that extraordinary efforts had been taken so that Raine would never have to be in the dark if she didn't want to be.

He hesitated. Every well-honed instinct he had screamed at him to back out of this room. This woman needed nothing he could give her, because he was empty himself. His feet moved with a life of their own, rounding the corner of the bed.

Raine's eyes stayed trained on him as he moved through the room. He'd removed his shirt. Even in the dim moonlight that filtered into the room, it was easy to discern the power in his muscled torso.

"Can I get you anything?" The words hung in the air. He'd obviously been on his way to his room from the bathroom down the hall. She knew that he would be clean-shaven. Her nostrils flared in appreciation at the slight scent of soap and after shave.

She shook her head, and this time he was close enough to her to see the action. He crossed in front of the window, and she caught her breath. For an instant he stood there, silhouetted against the sky, a portrait of shadows, dark against dark. And then he continued his approach until he was standing next to her.

"I can't..." She took a huge breath. "I dreamed about today." She tried a laugh that sounded more like a gasp. "Why is it always scarier in the nightmare?"

Mac sat on the edge of bed gingerly. "Recycled adrenaline?" he asked.

"I guess."

"When something like this happens, a person is in shock, operating to a large extent on instinct. Survival takes over and emotions are left behind. I guess when we sleep the emotions take over."

"They say most people don't dream in color, did you know that?" she whispered. "But I know I do. The dreams are vivid Technicolor horror shows, every time."

The dreams. She wasn't talking only about tonight—couldn't be. But he knew what she was saying. The unconscious had a way of opening even the most tightly locked mental doors in the sleep process. And sometimes that produced unpleasant nocturnal phantoms.

He wondered about her nightmares. What would cause a woman like Raine to suffer from them? He knew from experience that guilt would do the trick, but she had nothing to feel guilty for, he'd bet on that. She was too sweet, too decent. No, something else had to have happened to her. An experience of such trauma that stress would induce a reenactment of it at night. He wanted to ask her about it, but knew he didn't have the right.

Her hand reached for his and squeezed it tightly. He stared at her, able to make out her features in the shadows. He understood what it was like to wake up shaking and alone in a sweat-soaked bed. He'd accepted it stoically as a part of his life. He hated to think of it as a part of hers.

Without conscious thought his mouth lowered. He wasn't a master at comfort, hadn't had enough gentleness in his life in the last fifteen years to remember how to convey it. But he knew she needed something from him. He ignored the voice inside him that said she needed more than he could afford to give.

His lips pressed against hers and his tongue outlined the silky moist seam of her lips. Again and again he traced delicately before bestowing a parting kiss at the corner of her mouth. When he would have drawn away, he became aware of the small, delicate hand that had risen to lie against his bare chest. It traveled upward with exquisite slowness, over his corded shoulder, around his neck to tangle in the longer hair at his nape. Then it exerted its own inexorable pressure to bring his mouth back to hers.

Mac hesitated for an instant, but she leaned forward, and he couldn't swear that he didn't meet her halfway in a kiss that was more than the first had been, much more. This time her lips parted slightly for him in an invitation he didn't want to resist. His tongue swept in boldly, staking a claim that he would have denied with conscious thought. Her mouth twisted under his, meeting his demand with one of her own. Her other hand joined the first, and she pressed his head closer.

Mac obliged, giving her the kind of pressure that he was craving himself. He leaned over her, obeying the pressure of her hands to lie full length next to her. She shifted to face him, and he became aware of the silkiness of her nightgown and of the small breasts pressed against his chest.

He broke the kiss then, his breath coming roughly. It was time to get out of here, time to run like hell. He couldn't do this to her, and he sure didn't need any further complications in his own life. He reached in back of him and grasped one of her hands, peeling it away from his neck and pressing it to the mattress. On the way his wrist touched her breast, and the contact sent an immediate electrical impulse to his groin.

He groaned, and she shifted again, either by accident or design. But the next movement his hand made wasn't to push against the mattress to leave. Instead he captured one silk-covered breast, fingers exploring urgently. It was fuller than he'd expected, filling his palm precisely, as if fitted for his touch. He rubbed his thumb over her nipple and she gasped, moving helplessly. He didn't try to think anymore. Thinking would have stopped this madness and he was no longer sure he wanted it to end. He made it a point to avoid women like her, forever women, pure of heart. A man like him didn't deserve such purity in a woman, didn't look for it. But tonight he was incapable of turning away from it.

He hooked a finger in the narrow strap of her nightgown and dragged it down her arm. Then, with great anticipation, he pulled it away from her to bare her breast. His breath hissed out as he viewed the small mound, the nipple tightly drawn, taunting him. He lowered his head again and took her into his mouth.

A broken cry came from Raine as she felt the hot, warm suction. Her nipple was unbearably sensitive as he sucked at it and lashed it with his tongue. When he pulled his head back, the cooler night air stung. Leaving his hand to comfort it, he turned his attention to its twin.

She murmured brokenly, clasping his head to her. So this was what it was like, she thought wonderingly, dizzily. This spiraling pleasure that bordered on pain, a delicious anticipation of . . . something. Something out of reach. One of his jeans-clad knees moved between her legs and pressed against her softness.

That pressure was stirring an answering heat, and Raine was no longer content to be the passive recipient of Mac's touch. She wanted to explore him. She couldn't get over the thrill of being wanted by this man. She wasn't completely inexperienced, but she'd never known these shivers of pleasure that skated across her skin in the wake of his fingers.

Her hands wandered across his wide shoulders, fingers flexing, testing the tensile muscles there. She lowered her hand to his chest, feeling the crispness of the dark hair covering it. She kneaded her fingers against him, like a cat, and he lifted his head from her breast to gaze at her. He pushed into her exploring fingers, and she obeyed the unspoken demand. Both hands stroked him, learning the exact boundary of the triangle of chest hair, fingers threading through it to massage its muscled planes. When one of her fingers glanced over the male button of his nipple, a harsh sound came from deep in his throat. Summoning up all her courage, Raine moved to flick her tongue at the nipple, then closed her teeth around it with delicate precision.

He withstood the exquisite torture for long moments before pressing her back to the mattress. One hand reached for the hem of her short gown and brought it up, over her head, tossing it aside. Now his hands could explore freely, and explore they did. Her skin was soft, as silky as the nightgown had been, and he couldn't get enough of her. Her legs were smooth and firm, and the thought of her wrapping them around his waist made his gut clench. He wasn't thinking anymore about how wrong this would be, how wrong he was for her. In the back of his mind he assured himself that he wouldn't allow this to get out of hand, but his hands sliding over her naked skin called him a liar.

She needed him tonight in a way he couldn't quite comprehend, yet recognized. He couldn't ever remember being needed this way before, and it was a seductive snare.

His hands were gliding everywhere, leaving a trail of heat in their path, but suddenly that wasn't enough for Raine. She clutched his back, rubbing her hands along his vertebrae with long, smooth strokes. She met the waistband of his jeans, then, and the tips of her fingers delved beneath the loosened band.

Mac rolled away, every last instinct he had screaming a warning. This had progressed too far, too fast. He'd feel like a bastard for calling an end to it now, but not as much as if he was to go through with this.

Raine's hands moved to his front and she pressed against him as her fingers played with the open button on his jeans. One hand tugged at his zipper and he groaned, catching the errant hand, but not before it finished its task. Bringing her palm to his lips, he pressed a kiss into its palm. "No, honey, we can't." Whatever else he'd been about to say was lost as her mouth opened over his, sealing the words with liquid fire. He pressed her against the pillows, the pressure of his mouth a tale of frustration. She accepted his kiss, reveled in it as his lips moved on hers without gentleness. Her other hand crept to the open fly of his jeans and touched the hard length of him. He groaned into her mouth, breaking the kiss and leaning his forehead against hers. She freed him from his briefs, her other hand joining the first to stroke him wonderingly.

He gritted his teeth against the urge to thrust into that sweet touch, but when he heard her soft sound of discovery, he knew he was lost. Her gentle fingers skated over his turgid length, as if laying claim to uncharted territory. One small hand slid down his shaft and cupped the heaviness at its base. Mac gave up the inner fight. He'd never be able to give her more than his protection, but he could give her this. He could give her tonight. Maybe it would be enough.

With swift, economical movements he shucked out of his jeans and briefs. But he wasn't too far gone to forget to pull his wallet out of his back pocket and remove a foil-wrapped package from it. He managed to roll the condom on and then took both her hands in his. Using his greater weight, he pressed her into the bed, caging her face with their hands, and lowered his mouth to hers.

Raine accepted his kiss, returning its wildness. Her body was bombarded with sensations, so many she couldn't identify them all. He was stretched out full length on top of her, and she welcomed the weight. If she'd been more aware she would have been surprised at how right his touch seemed to her, but her awareness right now took a different focus.

She wiggled beneath his hard, hair-roughened body, delighting in the slight abrasion. Mac raised himself on one elbow above her, and she dazedly opened her eyes at the cessation of his kiss. She gazed in silent wonder at the shadowy form above her, shoulders wide enough to block out the very slight light coming in the window. His features were shadowed, but she knew them. Her dark warrior. The camera in her mind clicked, freezing this picture into her memory. And then he moved, and all besides sensation was forgotten.

He stared at her, noticing again how small she seemed beneath him. He was a big man, and he didn't want to hurt her. She looked so fragile lying under him, but she didn't act fragile. Her hands were skating all over him, lingering on his buttocks, squeezing the tight muscles there testingly.

His head lowered to nuzzle her breasts, and his fingers moved between her legs. She started slightly at the contact, but he found the downy thatch of hair there and the nub of her desire. His palm pressed rhythmically against it. When her body moved helplessly, he sent a careful finger inside her moist channel.

She uttered a broken cry as he explored her. Her body reflexively clenched around him, and suddenly it wasn't enough. She whimpered when he withdrew, but he immediately moved to replace his finger with his sex. The anticipation was too much, and she bucked a little in impatience for his entrance. A hard, satisfied smile crossed his mouth at her eagerness, and he knew she was as ready as he was. He positioned himself between her thighs and, tightening his buttocks, began to enter her. Her gasp mingled with his groan. He reached down to capture one of her knees in his arm and gently pressed it back against her thigh. Taking advantage of the way the position opened her to him, he inched inexorably farther until she had accepted all of him.

Her breath was coming in little gasps against his lips. She was so silky tight, he could feel the delicate inner pulsations as she adjusted to him. He waited for a moment, savagely savoring the pleasure. Then he began to move.

Each movement sent him deeper inside her, and Raine responded instinctively, reaching for something that only he could bring her. Her hands skated along his shoulders and back, and her head tossed restlessly against the pillow, evading his mouth. He reached between their bodies, rubbing against the pleasure point he'd found earlier. His ministrations, coupled with the powerful thrusts of his body, combined to send the world skittering away. All she was aware of was Macauley, his muscled torso above her, his smooth jaw pressing against her own, his breath sounding in her ear. She moved more frantically beneath him, and he quickened the pace of his thrusts. No longer was he controlling the depth and frequency of his movements. He was out of control now, as much as she was, straining together in a frenzy that abruptly shattered as Raine crested.

Capturing her cries in his mouth, Mac surged heavily against her, once, twice and again, before the pleasure slammed into him. Waves of ecstasy crashed over him, washing away the icy shadows in his soul.

Raine came half awake as a sudden chill chased over her skin. She opened her eyes enough to see Macauley pull the sheet over her shoulder. She watched, silent, as he pulled on his jeans. The sky outside was a dull gray, signaling dawn's approach. His back was to her, and his movements were uncustomarily jerky. Slowly she slid up to a sitting position, a foreboding presentiment filling her.

"Macauley?" she whispered, and reached out to touch the smooth expanse of back exposed to her. He moved away from her touch, and she dropped her hand. More eloquent than any words, that flinch had heralded what was going to happen next.

"Go back to sleep, Raine." His voice was flat.

"Why are you leaving?"

He squeezed his eyes shut tightly, seeing her face in his mind, glad that she couldn't see his. Why did she have to push this, make it harder? Then on the heels of that question came another. Why the hell should she make this easy for him, for herself? If he'd learned one thing about this woman it was that she didn't shirk unpleasantries. She insisted on the truth, all of it, not sparing herself or anyone else.

The truth. Didn't he at least owe her that much? After every oath he'd violated, after what he'd taken from her, here, last night, he at least owed her the truth, no matter how brutal.

"Last night was a mistake." His words hung bleakly in the air. He turned to face her. She was sitting up in bed, her arms wrapped around her knees, reminding him with sudden clarity of how he'd found her last night.

She tried to inject her voice with a hint of humor. "I don't have a great deal of experience with these things, Macauley, but I'm fairly certain that I'm supposed to be offended at being called a mistake."

He winced at her words. "Not you, Raine." Never her. "I made the mistake. I was a fool to stay last night and a bastard to make love to you."

"You'll excuse me if I disagree." The words were soft.

He stared at her, wishing that he had the words to say to her, wishing he'd never touched her last night and at the same time

wanting to touch her again. "You should be mad as hell, Raine."
His voice was harsh. "My job here is to protect you, not to seduce
you. I lost my objectivity last night, and that's the worst kind of
error someone in my position could make. I swore I'd never let that
happen...." *Again,* he'd almost said, and barely bit back the word.
No one knew better than he did what happened when a man let his
guard down. That was what caused a man to make mistakes. He
didn't see what was right in front of him until it was too late. Much
too late.

"Don't turn this into a tragedy, Macauley." Her words were
sharp, but so was her disappointment, and she was helpless to keep
it from showing in her voice. "It doesn't have to be. It could be..."
More. So much more. She had just enough pride to keep herself
from crying out the words.

"You'll never know how much I regret this, Raine," he said, his
tone raw, before he turned and walked from the room. He headed
for the bathroom and turned on the shower. Stripping, he stepped
under the spray and adjusted the temperature until it was icy cold.
He was ironically aware that if he'd taken a cold shower about five
hours ago, he wouldn't be feeling like hell now. Standing under the
stinging spray, he cursed Simon Michaels for coming to him in the
first place.

But he knew where the blame really lay. He was the one who'd
made the choice last night to stay, when he'd known damn well it
was the last thing he should do. And he was going to be the one to
deal with the guilt for the same action. He almost welcomed the
guilt. At least he'd lived with that emotion long enough for it to be
a familiar companion. Sometimes he thought he'd felt it for so long
that he'd miss it if it was gone. Sometimes.

But he wasn't sure he wanted to know of the new boundaries
guilt could take when he thought of the look in Raine's eyes when
he'd left her. Taking advantage of her youth and innocence was
somehow too sordid for even him to deal with. She would have
been so much better off if he'd left her alone, so he could walk
away when this was over without having altered her life. Now he
knew there was no way that could happen. She was too young, too
inexperienced and too damn vulnerable.

Raine sat in her bed, motionless for long minutes after he'd left
her. She felt splintered, as though Macauley had taken something
of her with him when he walked out that door. She replayed his
words in her head, over and over. After a time, anger started to
override her hurt. Scooting out of bed, she marched to her closet

and took out a robe. Tying the sash around her narrow waist with furious motions, she headed for the door.

Mac had knotted the towel above his hips and opened the bathroom door to head back to his room. He was faced with a very angry Raine. He stepped aside, but she followed.

"I want to talk to you," she said belligerently.

"Later."

"No, now," she asserted, pointing a finger at his chest. "We have something to get clear between us, and it can't wait."

His mouth firmed at her insistence but he didn't move. She was mad. Well, she was sure as hell entitled. And he couldn't blame her for wanting to get even with him. How could he when he couldn't stand to look at himself in the mirror this morning? "All right, shoot," he said resignedly.

"Don't tempt me," she answered, her eyes spitting gold sparks at him. "I don't much like people making decisions for me, Macauley, and that includes you. You may be the chief of your company, you might have called the shots when you were doing whatever you were doing for the Army, but you are only responsible for your own choices. Yours. Period. You aren't responsible for mine. I am a reasonably intelligent adult, and I will accept the consequences of my behavior."

"What in hell are you getting at?" He crossed his arms impatiently.

She wished for the first time that she was taller, so she could yell at him face-to-face instead of at his chin. But she was angry enough not to let the difference in their sizes give her pause.

"What I'm getting at is this—you are here to protect me and to keep me safe from this creep, whoever he is. I accept that. But that's where your responsibility to me ends. I made my own choice last night to sleep with you, and if anyone was seduced, it was *you.*"

His mouth quirked in an almost smile. The sight of it made her even madder.

"Don't you dare laugh at me, Macauley O'Neill! And don't you dare take credit for my choices. I learned a long time ago that every action has a price, and I've been paying a price for most of my life. You aren't going to change that. I won't *let* you change it."

"Are you about done?" he inquired interestedly.

She pursed her lips. "Not quite. You have something you're carrying around on your shoulders, Macauley. I don't care how much you deny it, it's there."

The accuracy of her statement stung him. "And you're going to say that you can take care of that for me? Ease my immortal soul?"

She shook her head, biting her lip. Her voice lowered. "I can't help you with that. No one can. You're the only one who can fight your way out of the darkness, because you're the only one holding the key. But I won't let you add *me* to that load of guilt you're carrying around."

She met his frozen expression squarely.

"I refuse to become anyone's regret."

Chapter 8

The next week went by with an almost monotonous regularity to the days. Mac and his men finished their work on the house. The beams of all the floodlights they'd installed reached clear to the road. They were left on at night, filling it with a synthetic brightness.

Raine worked unceasingly on her final project. She'd never experienced such drive to complete a picture before, nor been such a perfectionist in her attempts. She began as soon as she got up each morning and worked late into the evening. It gave her very little time to be around Macauley, and that was a bonus.

She wasn't sorry for anything she'd said to him, but her words had added to the chasm between them. Or maybe she was giving herself too much credit. It was more likely caused by his unwillingness to let anyone too close. And she had a feeling that she'd been closer than he'd allowed anybody for a very long time.

Sarah stopped in twice, each time asking Raine to come out with her for lunch. Both times she'd hesitated, then refused. She used her work as an excuse, but the second time she'd turned down an invitation she was very much afraid that she'd offended her friend. Sarah hadn't stayed long after that, and Raine blamed Macauley for her friend's hurt feelings. Although she'd originally kept the

extent of his involvement from her friends, it was he who was insisting now that she keep his role as bodyguard from them.

Macauley. Just the thought of him made her throat clutch. She
didn't regret the night they'd shared, and she wasn't sorry she'd
told him so. What had been a mistake to him was still a source of
wonder to her. Her limited experiences with the opposite sex hadn't
taught her very much about men, and nothing at all about men like
him. Whether he wanted to believe it or not, he'd given her something very precious that night. In his arms the demons had been
driven back into the night.

Anger had failed to sustain her for long. She knew that he expected such an emotion from her, and that he put his own interpretation on it. But it wasn't hurt pride that wounded her each time
she looked at him. If anyone was hurting over this it was him, and
she was helpless to reach him. She knew that despite her words he
was still blaming himself for touching her, and although the
knowledge made her impatient, she hurt for him, too.

A knock on her studio door interrupted her work and her
thoughts. "Come in," she said faintly. Macauley rarely interrupted her work. She released a breath when she saw Trey
standing in the open doorway, and pushed away a feeling of disappointment.

"Hi." She forced herself to smile at him. He made an imposing
figure in the doorway, but his wasn't the figure she would have
liked to see there.

"Well, you don't look much the worse for wear," he said,
strolling into the room. "All recovered from the accident?"

"I was shaken up a little, but I wasn't hurt," she explained.

"I shouldn't be interrupting genius at work, I know, but I
couldn't find Mac. Do you know where he's run off—" He
stopped in midsentence, his eyes on her half-finished painting. He
walked toward it without another word and stood in front of the
canvas, staring at it through slitted eyes. Then he turned a speculative gaze on her. "This is a real change from your usual works."

"Yes," she answered shortly. She wished she'd thought to turn
the canvas before she'd issued an invitation for him to come in. She
detested people seeing her work in progress.

"But I like it," he hastened to assure her. Shaking his head in
admiration, he continued, "You're good, lady. Will this be for
sale?"

"No way," she answered quickly, without even having to think.

He gave a half-satisfied smile. "Somehow I didn't think so." Giving the canvas one last look, he said, "Anyway, I didn't see Mac around the house. Do you have any idea where he might be?"

She started to shake her head, then thought again. "Try the back bedroom. The light they installed on top of the house isn't working the way he thinks it should. They ran the wiring through the closet in that room. It's the last door on the right."

"Okay, I'll look for him there." Trey left the room and walked down the hallway. He met Mac just closing the back bedroom door behind him. Trey gave a long, low whistle. "You don't look so good. Baby-sitting detail getting you down?"

Mac gave him a sour look. "What are you doing here?"

"Now is that any way to greet your best friend? About your only friend, I hasten to add."

They walked downstairs together. "Don't kid yourself, I've got lots of friends."

"Name one," Trey invited. "Aside from the obvious, I mean."

"Go to hell."

Trey laughed. "Been there, Mac. Actually, that's where I met you."

"That's a fact," Mac agreed. Trey had also been involved in covert operations, and his and Mac's paths had crossed several times before that fiasco in Central America. It had been Trey who had hauled Mac out of the remains of the bombed building, Trey who'd made sure he got to a hospital. When Mac got the chance to retire his commission, he'd talked Trey into getting out with him. His friend had been leery of leaving the only adult life he knew. Mac always suspected he'd been addicted to the excitement, the adrenaline of the job. When they'd decided to put their own company together, Trey had committed only for a year. But four years later he was hooked. In their business there were enough risks to keep even Trey happy.

"I've been busy while you've been living a life of ease," Trey told him as they walked into Mac's office.

"Do tell."

"I finally found out where Winters used to work, and I talked to some people there. They all seemed to have the same opinion of him. Shy, quiet guy, good at his job."

"Why did he leave?"

Trey shrugged. "To start his own company. He wasn't fired— they were sorry to see him go. So I looked him up in the Yellow Pages and paid him a visit."

Mac gave him an interested look. "What did you find out?"

"Well, he's got some ideas on tax-deferred bonds that wouldn't do us any harm to look into. You know, when we get the mortgage on the company paid off, we're going to need some ideas like that, and I'm not so sure our accountant is up on all the latest—"

"Trey?"

The man stopped in midsentence and looked at him.

"Did you find anything out from Winters that would help the case?" Mac asked patiently.

"I was getting to that. Anyway, I gave him a phony name and said I was looking for a good accountant. He's eager and seems to know his stuff. He gave me some references to check out, and that's what I did."

"Bingo," Mac said softly.

"Yeah," Trey agreed. "Raine's name was one of them, of course. But I did talk to four others on the list, and one of them told me something interesting. I told each of the people that I'd heard Raine Michaels used Winters Accounting, and got no responses from three of them. But there was one guy I talked to who seemed to think that Raine was Winters's girlfriend."

Mac went still. "Where'd he get that idea?"

"From Winters. Apparently they'd met up in a bar and had a couple drinks together, and Winters started spinning some tale about Raine and him being real close." Trey shrugged. "The guy was given the impression that they were dating, and heavily." He looked at Mac quizzically. "Is it true?"

"No."

Trey lifted his eyebrows at his friend's emphatic tone. "You seem pretty sure."

Mac looked away, aware that more than his opinion had colored his answer. He wasn't going to give voice to the fact that the thought of Raine involved with anyone filled him with primitive urges. "I've observed them together," he said. "Winters hangs around her like a puppy dog, but she doesn't treat him any differently than she does her other friends."

"Maybe that's a problem for him," Trey suggested.

Mac considered the suggestion. "All we know is that the guy has a crush on her."

"Crushes have been known to take ugly turns."

"Yeah, they have," Mac agreed darkly. "But even before this news, I was already considering Winters, Klassen and Sarah Jennings as possible suspects."

"The woman, too?"

Mac looked grim. "All three of them are close to Raine. They've had access to her mail and her home. So did the art students, of course, but the other three would certainly be aware of the state of Mrs. Michaels's health. They'd know just what to say on the phone to send Raine into a panic."

Trey nodded. When Mac had called him to fill him in on the details of the accident, he'd sounded like hell. That was when Trey had started to get the feeling that his friend was a little more involved than he wanted to admit. He'd shaken off the feeling. Having a client almost get killed under your watch was enough to upset anyone. But the way Mac looked today spoke of a man under a strain of some kind, and Trey couldn't help wondering just what, or who, was causing that strain.

"Anyone could get that information on Lorena Michaels's health. If a person was really digging, they could find out all about Raine's family. Whoever is after her wouldn't necessarily have to be someone she knows."

Mac turned a grim face to his friend. "That's what makes this so damn frustrating."

"Have the police turned up anything on the car that ran her off the road?"

Mac shook is head. "Not a thing. No one has come forward about it. Anyway, I've decided to step up security out here. I'll have two men covering the property at all times."

"Do you think you'll need more?"

Mac thought for a moment and shook his head. "Not yet. I'm sticking pretty close to Raine in the house. I think two can cover the grounds all right. This case is getting more complicated than we'd first figured."

Considering his friend for a moment, Trey asked, "Are you sure that's all this is? A case?"

Shooting him a sharp look, Mac snapped, "What's that supposed to mean?"

Trey shrugged. "It just seems . . . personal. I wondered if there was any more to this."

"It's a *job*, Trey," Mac answered caustically. "And the sooner we get it wrapped up, the sooner I can get out of here."

His friend winked lasciviously. "The sooner you can get to that vacation and loose women you've been putting off, hmm? I can understand your hurry."

Trey's comments left Mac cold. He should be feeling anxious to get this resolved, for his own sake as well as Raine's. She deserved to live a life free of the kind of hell she was being put through right now. She deserved to be free of a man who would make love to her and leave her in the morning, confused and dejected. She deserved . . . a lot of things. And he wasn't a man who could deliver any of them. Except for one. He could find out who was threatening her and he could stop him. He'd take personal satisfaction in catching the guy himself and making him pay for turning Raine's life into a waking nightmare.

Mac walked Trey to his truck, waved him off, then jogged down to the mailbox. Grabbing the stack of mail, he walked slowly to the house.

He knew the letter as soon as he saw it. Waiting until he got into the house, he let it slide off the stack of mail onto his desk. He opened a drawer, pulled out some plastic gloves, put them on and picked it up, studying it closely.

Addressed to Raine Michaels with no return address, it did, indeed, sport a postmark.

"Gotcha," he muttered, and opened it carefully. His throat knotted when he read the message typed in big block letters.

You escaped this time bitch but next time you won't be so lucky.

He swore, a crooning litany of obscenities. The intent of the message was implicit, and he crumpled the paper in his gloved hand, fury flowing through him. Someone was out there, still plotting to get at Raine, planning the next move against her. Each letter she'd received had been more menacing than the last, and this one promised another attempt on her life.

Glancing down, he noticed the way he had the paper balled up in his fist. He laid it down and smoothed it out, a feral smile pulling his lips. Whoever was behind these threats had just made a huge mistake. Raine couldn't vouch for the other envelopes, but this one had a postmark, and that was going to help nail this bastard to the wall. He picked up the phone and dialed the police. He asked for the detective in charge of Raine's case and tersely told him of the latest threat. The man agreed to come by the next day and pick up the letter.

Mac hung up, grim satisfaction on his face. At last they had something to go on. And he was going to make damn sure the clue would be the first step toward freeing Raine from this siege of terror.

* * *

When Raine came downstairs to fix supper, she walked in on Mac in the midst of chopping vegetables. She stopped short in the doorway, her eyes traveling over the pile of dishes and empty wrappers. He was not a neat cook. Pieces of stray vegetables were on the floor, and her walls would definitely need to be wiped off.

He looked up and caught her eye. "Uh, sorry about this." He gestured to the mess. "I'll clean it up while supper is cooking."

"That's okay," she replied, amused. "I planned to hose down the kitchen tonight, anyway." She strolled into the room and snatched a carrot from a bowl. "To what do I owe this display of culinary expertise?"

He'd gone back to chopping. "I just thought it was my turn to cook. You seemed busy so I decided to get supper going."

"Uh-huh." She wasn't convinced. Seating herself on the edge of the counter, she filched another carrot. Munching, she considered him shrewdly. The only other time he'd felt compelled to cook something was on the night he'd brought her home from the hospital. She had a bad feeling about this. Something had happened today to elicit this thoughtfulness, and no doubt it was something that affected her. He'd barely looked at her since the night they'd made love, and conversation had been practically nonexistent.

Chewing reflectively, she decided that whatever the news was, it could wait. She was going to bask in the pleasure of watching him perform the mundane task of cooking in her kitchen. For a few precious minutes she was going to allow herself to pretend that Macauley was a different sort of man than he was, one free of regrets and dark places in his soul.

But then he wouldn't be the man who'd made such a huge difference in her life, and he wouldn't be the one she so desperately wanted a chance with. She watched, fascinated, as he wielded the knife with swift, economical movements.

"Are you going to sit there and eat the fruits of my labors, or do you want to actually do something constructive?" he asked after several minutes.

"I could help," she said judiciously, "but I rather enjoy watching you do it."

A small smile pulled at the corner of his mouth. "Here's a knife." He slid a smaller paring knife toward her. "You can chop up those mushrooms."

Lazily, she slid from the counter and did as he asked. They worked together in a companionable silence that made her wistful at its ordinariness. There was another side to Macauley O'Neill, one he refused to even recognize. It was the side that would put a meal together, in an awkward attempt to soft-pedal some bad news. A side that took a kind of wonder from the simple pleasure of sitting in the porch swing and watching the stars.

It was a side that would make love to a woman to comfort her, giving her gentleness in the only way he knew how.

She ached with the need to argue with him again, to press the point she'd tried to make the other morning after he'd left her. But she knew it would be useless. He was the only one who could find a way out of the shadows in his soul. She knew from experience that while others could try to show the way, he would have to be the guide on that particular journey. But she hated thinking of him living his life cold and alone, never letting anybody get too close to him. She'd tried to live that way herself and knew the damage it inflicted.

She let him get through the preparation and the entire meal before she asked evenly, "So, when are you going to tell me what happened today?"

He froze in the act of reaching for his glass, but only for an instant. The next moment he picked it up in a smooth movement and finished his lemonade. Setting the glass on the table with a deliberate motion, he met her eyes. "What makes you think something happened?"

She leaned forward. "Because I'm beginning to know you, Macauley O'Neill. Better than you suspect."

"If you knew me half as well as you claim to," he said with irritation in his voice, "you'd know that *nobody* calls me Macauley. Ever."

"Nobody?"

He shook his head.

"Not your mother?"

"Only when she's mad at me."

She wouldn't even try to guess at the frequency that occurred. "I'll bet you had a grandma who did. I'll bet she insisted on calling you by your given name. I'm guessing she refused to call you Mac."

He frowned at her, annoyed, wanting to deny it. How the hell had she known that? His grandmother O'Neill had insisted that Mac was no name for a boy, and she'd never called him that. She'd died when he was twelve, but he could still remember spending weeks in the summer at her home, eating freshly baked cookies and exploring her neighborhood. Odd, how Raine's slightly teasing words had brought the visions back so vividly. He didn't remember that carefree boy often. He'd been buried under years of living on the edge, where black and white blurred into an ugly shade of gray. Where right and wrong didn't seem like opposites, but like a flip of a two-headed coin.

"You're right," he said finally.

"About your grandma?"

He wasn't ready to admit to the accuracy of her guess. "Another letter came today."

Her face went still, the amusement wiped from it. He noticed the change grimly. It seemed as if he was always responsible for bringing that look to her face. Intentionally or not, he was the one who'd put it there. He'd had no choice in the matter, however. She wouldn't thank him for shielding her from the truth, and he wouldn't insult her by trying to do so.

She stood up abruptly. "I want to see it."

"There's nothing new in it," he said quietly, rising, too. "The detective will be here to pick it up tomorrow."

"I want to see it," she repeated.

He looked into her face for a long moment, then nodded. He led her silently into the office and over to his desk. "Don't touch it," he cautioned. "There's always a chance they could find prints."

Raine read it silently. Long after she'd finished reading the message, it reverberated in her head. She swallowed and looked at him. "Doesn't sound like it's going to quit anytime soon."

He watched her carefully, judging her reaction. "No."

She turned away from him, crossing her arms and rubbing them, suddenly cold. "So how long does this go on? Indefinitely? How much longer do I have to be careful of who I see and where I go?"

"I don't know."

"I mean, it's not that I'm trying to get rid of you," she said, trying and failing at a light tone, "but I'm sure you have a life you want to get back to. And then there's that vacation you were planning. You don't have time to stick around here indefinitely, either."

"I'll have two men patrolling the grounds, day and night," he said quietly. "The crew has already started work on the fence in front. And," he added without thinking, "I'll be here as long as you need me."

She gave a little laugh. "Macauley O'Neill, duty first, that's your motto, right?" She forced herself to stop then, doubting her ability to keep her next words from being shaded with the bitterness she suddenly felt. He'd stay for the job, out of duty, a sense of honor perhaps, but he wouldn't be staying for *her*. The difference was glaring.

"I won't leave until this thing is over." It was a promise, to himself as much as to her, and he meant it. It was all he could offer her, but he knew it wasn't enough. Not nearly enough. "We've got a postmark on the envelope, and that will give the police something to look for."

"What will they be able to learn from that?"

"The detective will probably turn the letter over to the Postal Inspection Service. Sending threats through the mail is a federal offense, and the U.S. Postal Service has their own investigators. It will give them one more avenue to follow, at any rate."

"When you talked to the detective, did he say if they'd found anything on the guy who ran me off the road?"

He shook his head slowly. "No one saw anything. They're checking up on stolen and abandoned car reports and checking out rental agencies. Something may turn up."

Raine turned and walked across the room to the window. Suddenly the pace at which the investigation was proceeding was overwhelmingly frustrating. She didn't want to spend one more hour, one more minute with these threats hanging over her head. The only reason she'd remained sane so far was the amount of time and energy her painting was requiring. And the presence of Macauley, of course.

He made her feel protected, she realized suddenly, in a way no one before him had ever been able to accomplish. She'd carefully chosen men in her life who were no threat to her physically or emotionally. Until Macauley O'Neill had rocketed into her life and shattered so many of her personal reservations.

He watched her stand, pensive and alone at the window, and damned the helplessness that filled him. "I shouldn't have told you about the letter," he muttered, full of self-castigation.

That got her attention. She whirled, eyes flashing. "Yes, you should have. You're here to protect me, but not to hide things from me. I can face what's happening in my life, thank you very much. You're not responsible for my mood. I choose to know every aspect of what's going on in my life, and I'm free to react to it! Don't treat me as if I might shatter if you speak too loudly or say the wrong thing. The only thing I can't tolerate is being treated like an invalid."

Admiring the way temper lit her jeweled golden eyes, he inclined his head. "An invalid is the last word I'd use to describe
you," he said soberly. The bruise from her accident had already
turned its rainbow shades of color and now was a faded yellow.
She'd never complained about it, or the goose egg she'd sported for
a few days. She might be small, but she had the inner strength of
any ten men he knew. A little temper was far less than he'd expect
to have to put up with in this situation. She was edgy, and he
couldn't blame her. Who wouldn't be edgy with some lunatic after them? Responsibility was a word she used a lot, but neither of
them could deny that he bore partial responsibility for her anxiety
level. If he'd never touched her, she'd damn well be better off now.
And so would he.

If he'd never touched her he wouldn't be filled with regrets for
the way he'd compromised them both, taking advantage of her
vulnerability and jeopardizing his objectivity. He wouldn't be kept
awake at night kicking himself for giving in that one time, for
snatching a chance to be held in the arms of this warm, caring
woman. And he wouldn't be calling himself every kind of fool for
not taking the time to go slowly with her while he'd had the chance.
It seemed a shame that he hadn't spent more time exploring her
small, silky body, finding all the places that begged for a man's
kiss. If he was going to make such a mistake anyway, why hadn't
he turned on a light, so his memory could have gorged itself on her
gentle curves?

Now he knew what her delicate breasts tasted like, how they fit
his palm, but he didn't have a complete picture in his mind. Were
the nipples pink? He'd had the points in his mouth but didn't know
if the firm mounds were a creamy white or tanned to a golden glow.
Did she have tan lines that he could have traced with his tongue, or
was the rest of her skin the same hue as her arms, the color of antique lace? He'd never have the opportunity for those answers now,
and he damned himself for still wondering.

But most of all, he damned himself for ever having touched her
to begin with.

"I'm going outside," she muttered, and moved toward the door.

"Wait. I was meaning to ask you about those paintings in the
back bedroom."

She froze in place.

"The men had to move them from that closet in there when we
were working. I can put them back now, but I thought I'd ask you
for sure. I didn't know if you planned to include any of them in

your show or not." Still she hadn't turned or spoken, and he frowned at the back of her head. "If they're pieces for the show, maybe you'd like them brought downstairs."

"No." Her answer was flat and sharp, and seemed to propel her into action. She headed for the door. "I'll put them back myself."

"You don't have to... Dammit, Raine, wait!" he commanded. Swiftly he followed her into the hall and up the stairs. "I'll put them back, I just wanted to make sure where you wanted them."

She acted as if she hadn't heard him as she walked swiftly through the upstairs hallway, flipped on the switch and disappeared into the bedroom.

He lengthened his stride, but even so, by the time he reached her, she already had her arms around one large canvas and was attempting to lug it across the room.

"Dammit, put that down," he ordered. "You don't have to do that."

"I can handle it, and I don't want you in my things," she snapped. He watched her stiff back frustratedly as she carried her awkward load toward the closet. Swearing under his breath, he walked to the stack of canvases and began to pick up the top one, intent on at least helping her if she refused to let him do the work for her.

But his hand froze as he reached for it, and for an instant his mind froze, too. Then he picked up the canvas and carried it, not to the closet, where Raine was still struggling to place the painting she held, but over to where he could stand directly under the light. This painting wasn't like any of the others he'd seen of Raine's. It wasn't only the technique that was different, it was the emotion expressed on canvas.

Rage. It was depicted in the picture, pure and unadulterated. He didn't know how an abstract work could show so clearly the emotion of the artist. But it was there, in every brush stroke, in each slash of color used. He carried it to the stack and started to flip through the rest of the canvases.

Grunting with exertion, Raine finally managed to shove the huge canvas into the closet without harming it or a back muscle. Straightening, she turned and saw Mac. He was on his knees with one of the smaller pictures in both hands, holding it up and studying it. She strode over and snatched it from him. Not wanting to meet that silent gaze, she swiftly put it in the closet with the first one. Once that task was accomplished, she found she had a very difficult time turning to face him again.

When she finally looked at him, Mac was studying each of the paintings in turn. She couldn't tell from his impassive features what, if anything, he was thinking.

But she was afraid she could guess. As good as he was at a poker face, she knew he saw things that others would much rather keep hidden. And as soon as those ice blue eyes met hers, she was certain she was correct. Awareness was in them, and understanding. But still his words, when he spoke, jarred her.

"When did you do these?"

She took a deep breath. "A lifetime ago." Finally sure that her legs would work, she crossed to him, reaching for the top canvas.

He grasped her wrist, stopping her. "What happened to you, Raine?" His voice was hoarse from suppressed emotion. "What in God's name happened to evoke this much anguish on canvas?" Because something earthshaking had, that was apparent. Even his untutored eye could detect the pain and trauma reflected in each painting, which she'd kept hidden away, out of sight.

She pulled her wrist from his hold. "Life happened," she snapped. "It happens to all of us, doesn't it? These paintings were my reactions to it at the time, that's all."

He rose slowly to face her. "Tell me." It was less a command than an invitation. She started to shake her head, then bit her lip. Didn't he have some right to know, after all? He'd been the one to chase away the nightmare the last time she'd been awakened by it. He'd been the one to comfort her. But truth was painful, and reality sometimes more so. Even the most well-meaning person would be repulsed at her sordid little tale.

She looked at him uncertainly. He was watching her, silently, not pushing. Just there. And she knew with sudden certainty that what she'd had to overcome in her past was a mere whisper to what he'd seen. What he'd done. Nothing she could say would shock him, and he'd already pushed her away physically. She had nothing to lose by telling him.

"As you can imagine, having met my father, I led a pretty sheltered childhood." Her voice was thin when she spoke. "He taught my brothers to look after their little sister. I was to be pampered, and protected from all unpleasantness. I was spoiled beyond measure, and totally confined. My comings and goings were regimented, and I never went anywhere unescorted." The smile she tried for failed. "That was pretty restrictive for a teenager who thought she was an adult.

"But I was inventive. The library was one place I could go without restriction, so many times I'd arrange to have one of my brothers take me there, pretend to go inside, then duck downtown with one of my friends. It got to be kind of a game, and if my brothers ever suspected, they never told. They didn't like having to watch me all the time, anyway. I think I cramped their style." She looked at Macauley uncertainly. He was watching her closely, his face absorbed.

Her gaze dropped. "There was this guy at school I had a crush on, and one night we arranged to meet. We walked around the mall a while and then he took me back to the library." Funny how she could remember the boy so clearly. Bill Sanders had been a major heartthrob among her friends, and when he'd begun to pay attention to her, she'd thought that every teenage god in the heavens was smiling down on her. "We were gone longer than I'd expected. It was almost dark when we got back. The boy offered me a ride home, but I told him I had to wait for my brother. I knew I'd never be able to explain arriving at my house in a boy's car. I wasn't even going to be allowed to date for another year." Her voice trailed off for a moment.

"I waited. It grew dark, and then darker. It was almost ten o'clock and I became convinced that I'd missed John somehow when he'd come to pick me up. I decided I'd walk home and make up a good story along the way for being late. It was one of those utterly black nights, you know? Clouds covered the moon, and if there were any stars out, they were hidden, too. It wasn't so bad near the library, but the way to my place went past a park, and there weren't many streetlights. There were lots of trees and hedges, creating all kinds of creepy shadows. I heard something behind me once, but when I turned and looked there was no one there. So I just kept walking, faster and faster, wishing with all my heart that I'd stayed at the library and called home."

She rubbed her forehead, where a headache had suddenly appeared. Even after all these years it was difficult to tell the story. Difficult to think about. "The man came out of nowhere." Her voice tapered to almost a whisper. "He jumped out and grabbed me from behind, and tried to drag me into the bushes. I fought him as hard as I could, and I got away once, but he caught me again. He grabbed me by the hair and pulled me back, and that time—" she took a deep breath "—I couldn't get away."

"Did he rape you?" His harsh tone was almost a snarl.

Her eyes met his wearily, and he saw in them the same tired, ancient look he'd been surprised to see in them several times before. Only now he knew the cause, knew it without her answer. And that knowledge sent currents of rage firing along his veins.

"Yes."

Chapter 9

Although he'd been half-prepared for Raine's answer, Mac was still jolted by it. His big hands clenched and unclenched on his knees. A red mist swam before his eyes, and he knew if it had been within his power he'd have made sure the man died for hurting her. A long, slow, merciless death.

She swallowed around the knot in her throat and forced herself to continue. "He grabbed a rock and hit me. I don't remember anything after that. I found out later that John and William had been looking all over for me. They heard me screaming, but by the time they got there, I was unconscious and he was on top of me..." Words clogged in her throat. She hadn't talked about this for a very long time, and she faltered at the mask of menace that had descended over his features.

Then her trepidation was wiped away when he reached out and pulled her into his arms, sinking back onto his haunches. Burying his face in her hair, he squeezed her tightly.

She'd been raped.

The stark, ugly truth pounded inside his skull. His fury was so great that he shook from it. He rocked her back and forth in his arms, soothing her, trying to calm himself, not sure if he was capable of either. One hand threaded through her hair, pressing her head against his chest.

Her voice was husky when she spoke again. "I woke up the next day after surgery, and the man was already in jail. William and John had caught him, and they provided the ID. He pleaded no contest. I didn't even have to go to court."

"How old were you?"

"Fifteen," she whispered.

He closed his eyes in pain. He could envision her at that age, all long, swinging hair and wide eyes. At an age when she should have been acquiring boyfriends and the art of flirting, her life had been shattered in a way that he could barely comprehend. The lessons she'd learned then hadn't been on new hairstyles and the mysteries of teenage boys, they'd been in the random cruelty of life, and how to pick up the pieces and go on.

He rose suddenly and reached for her hand, pulling her to her feet. She didn't question his sudden movement as he led her out of the room and down the stairs. He opened the front door and crossed to the porch swing, her wrist still in his hand. Then he sank down in one corner, and the tug on her wrist urged her next to him. They swung silently for a time, she exhausted from the retelling.

"Your father never said a word about this to me," he said tersely. "Not when he hired me, not later. Not one word."

"I'm not surprised," she said quietly. "He's never spoken of it to me, either." She watched the sun sink behind the horizon pensively. "My father loves me very much. But he spent his whole life trying to shield my mother and me from life. I think . . . he just couldn't deal with the fact that he hadn't been able to do that. Thinking about what happened to me was just too painful for him, and he couldn't talk about it. Not to anyone."

Mac frowned fiercely. "Surely your mother knew."

Raine shook her head. "There was no telling what the truth would have done to her heart. She was told I'd had an accident, but that I'd be all right. There was no other way my father could explain my absence from the house to her while I was in the hospital."

"He wouldn't let you talk to your mother about it?" Mac was amazed at her father's selfishness. Raine had been a young girl, confused and frightened, her body and spirit violated. Surely her mother would have wanted to know when her youngest child was in need. What kind of bastard would make that decision for someone else?

"I wouldn't do that," she whispered. "I couldn't handle it if she had another heart attack because of me. I couldn't take that chance. I talked to counselors while I was in the hospital."

"And after?"

"Afterward my father sold our house and moved us to Burbank. He thought getting me away from the place where it had happened would help in the healing process."

He'd thought it would be easier to forget that way, Mac thought bitterly. He remembered Grady's surprise when he'd heard his old friend had left from the area. Simon probably hadn't even told him the reason. As if, by keeping silent and moving away, he could erase what had happened.

"That's what I've seen sometimes, in your eyes." His voice was low. "I wondered what could have made you so strong. All through this case you've taken everything that's been thrown at you, and bounced back." He tipped her chin up with one finger. "You're a fighter, Raine. And you're also one of the strongest people I've ever met."

His words embarrassed her, especially since she knew how wrong they were. "I'm not brave, and I'm not strong," she contradicted, jerking her chin away. "You don't know how long it took me to get my life back to something resembling normal. You don't know how many times I failed." Her voice tapered off into little more than a whisper. "There's still so much I'm afraid of."

"Like hospitals?"

Her gaze flew to meet his, and he knew that he was right. "I saw you, remember? You didn't want to see a doctor, but you forced yourself to do it. You're facing your fears. That's what strong people do, Raine. They admit to them and go on from there. There aren't many people who could go through what you did and still accomplish what you have."

"You don't know," she whispered rawly. "You don't know how many times I was weak. How many times I took the easy way out."

"You kept trying, that's all that counts. And you succeeded."

She gave a short laugh. "You want to know how strong I was, Macauley?" Self-mockery laced her voice. "You want to know what a fighter I was? I tried to pretend everything was back to normal, to do what was expected of me. But no matter how hard I worked, I couldn't put my life back together. My family thought I was doing so well. But I'd become real good at pretending. And three days after my sixteenth birthday I swallowed a bottle of my mother's pain pills.'' Her voice was shaky. ''That's what real heroes do, right? Take the coward's way out. Escape the pain.''

She took a shuddering breath and looked at him. His face hadn't changed, and he hadn't pulled back. She noticed for the first time that both of her hands were held in his. She hadn't shocked him or disgusted him. Nor was his look pitying. He *hurt* for her, and he seemed to understand her pain and the long journey back from it in a way she didn't question.

''My father finally realized that he wasn't going to be able to make things all right by ignoring them. I started to see a therapist, and she showed me how to use my artistic talent as a therapeutic release.''

''The pictures in the bedroom?''

She nodded. ''I keep them to remind me of how far I've come. And of how much further I have to go.''

''Just how far do you think you have to go?'' he asked, his voice rough. ''Give yourself a break. You've experienced more than some people have to in an entire lifetime, and you're one of the most well-adjusted people I know.'' The corner of his mouth pulled up wryly. ''You can even put up with a war-weary bodyguard with no sense of humor. Not everybody could.''

''I had to start confronting my fears. I couldn't go through life letting them cripple me anymore. And things are okay. I'm not sure I'm ever going to be able to walk down a street at night whistling joyfully, but I'm coping with my fear of the dark.'' The next words were harder, but she knew they had to be said. ''I haven't always been fair to the people who have helped me along the way, Macauley. I had a couple of boyfriends since . . . the rape.'' She hesitated, unable to explain how carefully she'd entered into the relationships, how long it had taken her to learn to trust each man enough to be alone with him, not to mention being intimate. They'd been little more experienced than she, and she could see now that that had been part of the reason she'd chosen them.

''I met them in college,'' she continued, gazing into the dusk reflectively. ''I dated the last one two years before I finally broke it off.'' Her voice was mocking. ''It had finally occurred to me, you see, that it might be a tad bit unfair to him to be little more than a signpost on Raine's road to emotional recovery. He was very hurt, and I was never able to fully explain it to him. I had a hard enough time understanding it myself.''

He understood what she was telling him, but everything inside him rejected having that interpretation placed on their own relationship. He cupped her jaw in one hard hand, turning her face to his. One thumb raised her chin, and his face was very close to her own when he muttered fiercely, "That's not how it was with me."

She read the savage certainty in his expression and couldn't deny his words. "No," she whispered, trapped in the intensity of his gaze.

"I know that," he muttered. "You responded to me too freely, holding nothing back. There were no ghosts between us, Raine, and I sure as hell wasn't an *experiment* with you."

She shook her head blindly and returned the fierce kiss he pressed against her lips. He was right, of course; he was too experienced not to recognize it. And knowing what he did about her, surely he would guess just how deeply her feelings for him ran.

Breaking off the kiss, he whispered against her lips. "And your other fears?" he asked rawly. "The nightmares?"

"They don't come as frequently as they used to," she said simply. "Usually a stressor of some kind brings them on. But I've learned how to get through them, too."

He put his arm around her narrow shoulders and pulled her close, his chest tight. He'd seen that kind of bravery before in the service. Trey had shown it when he'd pulled him out of the ruins of the hotel in Central America, others when they'd fought for their families, their countries. But this woman could teach the most decorated hero a lesson. She'd been through hell, but she'd fought herself free. She could have remained sheltered and protected for the rest of her life. Her father would have seen to it, and nobody could have blamed her for seeking that for herself. But instead she'd chosen to confront life head-on, facing down fears the way soldiers faced the enemy. Except that she'd been emotionally unarmed, and vulnerable. And, for the most part, she'd done it alone.

No wonder she seemed to have the wisdom of an ancient scribe at times. And it was no wonder she was able to see so clearly into his own battle-scarred soul. Such courage filled him with awe. And something else. An emotion he couldn't, wouldn't, name.

They sat and watched the dusk turn into night. When Mac spoke again, his voice was quiet. "Have you ever tried self-defense courses? The lessons might give you a feeling of safety."

"I went to a few a couple of years ago," she answered. "I couldn't...the instructor was showing us how to get away from an attacker. He put his arm around each student's neck from behind. We were supposed to use what he'd taught us to strike out and twist away. But when it was my turn...I panicked." More than panicked, she remembered uncomfortably. She'd embarrassed herself and the instructor with her reaction. She'd never gone back. Another failure that pointed out just how far she'd yet to go.

But then she remembered the day not long ago when a man had been behind her, when he'd touched her and the usual reaction had been suppressed. She looked at him. "You might be able to teach me," she said consideringly.

"Me?"

"That day, in the studio." Her voice dropped to almost a whisper. "You massaged my back."

"I remember." His voice was hoarse. Touching her had been totally out of line and completely out of character for him. But his hands had acted without permission from his mind. "You didn't panic then, did you?"

"No," she replied softly. "I started to, all the old reactions were there, but it didn't happen." Her hand went to his face and she cupped his scratchy jaw. "That's when I knew," she whispered achingly. "I didn't understand why you had such an effect on me, Macauley. But I'm beginning to realize its something neither of us can control. I react to you in a whole new way. And I think if you were truthful with yourself, you'd admit that I have the same effect on you."

Mac's eyes were gritty from lack of sleep. They'd stayed on the porch late last night, late enough for Raine to fall asleep. He'd sat there for an even longer time, one arm wrapped around her, keeping her head pillowed against his chest. He'd carried her upstairs sometime during the night and put her to bed. After he'd pulled her shoes and socks off he'd stood there indecisively. Figuring she wouldn't want to sleep in her clothes, he'd stripped off her jeans and T-shirt. The sight of her clad in only her silky underthings had sent him fleeing from the room. And kept him awake most of the night.

He needed to take a shower, but instead he went to the kitchen and poured himself a cup of coffee. He'd put the machine on a couple hours ago when he'd started working in the office, and it looked like he'd have to make a second batch, since he'd drunk most of this one. He rinsed out the pot and started another. It would be ready by the time Raine woke. He didn't think she'd appreciate his original strong black brew anyway.

A knock sounded at the front door, and he strode to answer it. "Detective Ramirez." He stepped aside, allowing the man to enter. "Come on in."

"Mr. O'Neill." The man nodded in greeting. "Sorry to hear there's been more trouble." The detective was short and wiry, with jet black hair worn slicked back and a small, neat mustache. "How's Miss Michaels holding up?"

"Better than she has a right to. The letter is in here." He led the man into the office, to his desk. "It hasn't been handled since it reached the house," he said. "Maybe you'll find a fingerprint."

"We'd have to get real lucky," the detective said cynically. "We didn't get one clear print from any of the others." He studied the letter and the envelope for a second, then, looking up, he asked, "Is Miss Michaels around? I'd like to ask her a couple of questions."

"I'll get her," Mac answered. He looked in the kitchen, and not finding Raine, went upstairs and tried her studio. But that room was empty, as well. Moving quietly, he went down the hallway to her bedroom, easing the door open. If she was still sleeping, he wasn't going to wake her, no matter what the detective wanted. Her bed was empty.

Growing a little alarmed, he strode out of the room to the bathroom. "Raine?" He rapped at the door. "Raine!" The doorknob turned under his hand and he pushed the door open, confronting a very startled and very naked Raine.

She'd obviously just stepped out of the shower, and water trickled down her body in tiny rivulets. Her hand was frozen in midair, as if she'd been reaching for a towel when he'd walked in on her.

He stepped into the room without conscious volition and swung the door shut behind him. His throat closed at the sight she made. He hadn't had a chance to really look at her the night they'd spent together, but the sunlight was streaming through the window, and every lovely inch of her was exposed. His eyes took immediate, greedy advantage. Her breasts were high, as his hands had remembered, the mounds exquisitely formed. They had the delicate shadings of the inside of a seashell, all creamy white and coral. Her nipples were small and pink. They tautened under his perusal, and his loins tightened in recognition of her response.

His eyes dipped lower, tracing each delicate rib, the sweet indentation of her waist and the curve of her hips. Her pelvis was narrow, and he wondered how she had accommodated him. She looked too fragile to lay under a man and accept him fully, but he remembered in sensual detail how she had. The dark triangle between her legs held a hint of mystery. Her legs were shapely and slim, ending in delicate ankles that he knew he could bracelet with two fingers. His eyes moved slowly upward again, as if involved in the tactile exploration he was longing for.

"Macauley?" Her voice was trembling, aching.

He stepped behind her then, picking up the towel. Slowly he wrapped it around her back, both hands keeping hold of the ends. His eyes met hers in the mirror before them as he slowly dried her.

Her breath came in little gusts, and she leaned against his chest. Her eyes never left his in the mirror, and he could read her response in the way she trembled under his hands. He went down on his knees, dragging the towel down her body to catch the tiny rivers on her skin before they reached the floor. Rising again, he wrapped the towel around her, tucking the ends together over her breast. His hands didn't leave then, and he moved closer, giving in to the temptation to bury his face at her neck.

Her throat arched to him, and she gave a little gasp at the sharp, stinging kiss he placed there. "Macauley," she moaned.

Abruptly, painfully, he remembered what had brought him upstairs to begin with. He drew a shuddering breath and brought his hands to her shoulders. "Detective Ramirez wants to speak to you." His voice was raspy.

She blinked dazedly. "Now?"

"He's downstairs." His hands skated down her arms and up again before he dropped them reluctantly and stepped back. "Get dressed and come down. I'll give him some coffee or something while we wait."

She nodded mutely, and he turned abruptly, leaving the room.

Rejoining the detective, he told him, "She'll be down in a few minutes. Can I get you something? Coffee?"

The man shook his head. "Had to give up caffeine. Doctor said it was causing an irregular heartbeat. And I can't get used to that decaff stuff. I mean, if you can't enjoy that jolt of caffeine, why bother, right?"

Mac grunted. He'd experienced a jolt this morning, but caffeine had had little to do with it. Suddenly he felt in need of something to drink, something a lot stronger than coffee. He wondered if the detective would find the taste of a shot of scotch more to his liking.

"Want to help me with this?" the detective asked.

Mac reached for the plastic evidence bag and held it open. Ramirez pulled a glove from his jacket pocket, put it on, picked up the letter and envelope and dropped them both into the bag. Doffing the glove, he shoved it in his pocket.

"Thanks," he said, reaching for the bag. He sealed it deftly. "This one will probably go right to the postal boys. They have their own investigators for these kinds of things. They might come up with something interesting."

Raine came into the room then. "Good morning, Detective."

Ramirez turned. "Miss Michaels, you're looking good. Glad to see you weren't too badly hurt in that accident."

"I'm fine," she murmured, giving a quick look toward Mac.

Her hair was already drying, Mac noted. Soft curls were forming on top. She'd dressed quickly, in a pair of white shorts and a silk tank top. His eyes went to her throat, which was marred with the slightest hint of color left by his mouth.

"I've been wanting to talk to you, Miss Michaels, about the car that ran you off the road."

"Yes," she said, her voice husky. She cleared her throat and forced her gaze away from Mac, focusing on the detective.

"Do you think you'd be able to identify it?" the man asked. "Reason I'm asking is, we think we may have found the car. It was a rental and was abandoned about ten miles from where the accident happened. Guy drove it off the road into some bushes and left it there."

"A guy?" Mac asked, sharply.

"According to the records, a Mr. Ray Paulus rented it from the agency the day before the accident." He shook his head, forestalling Mac's next question. "The information on the application was all phony. And no one at the agency remembers the man well enough to describe him. He rented at an airport, so it was plenty busy there."

"I described it to the trooper who helped me," Raine said. "It was a blue four door. I'm afraid I don't know enough about cars to guess at the make, but it was older. There was a lot of chrome on it, and it was big. At least twice the size of mine."

"Do you remember anything else?" the man pressed.

"It had a hood ornament of some kind," she said slowly. "And the chrome on the front passenger door was missing."

"That matches with the one we've got," the detective said, satisfied. "I'll tell the boys to start going through it. We may be fortunate. It's hard for a person to be in a car and not leave something behind.''

"Assuming, of course, that the car was thoroughly cleaned before it was rented out last time," Mac murmured.

The other man grimaced. "Yeah, assuming that. But it's the best lead we've had yet. I'd like to get this wrapped up for you, Miss Michaels. Keep your fingers crossed."

While Raine walked the man to the door, Mac made a quick phone call. When she came back to the room, he asked her, "How would you like to go see your mom today?"

Her eyes lit with pleasure. "Really?"

"You'd have to go with me," he cautioned wryly. "But yeah. I need to talk to your dad, anyway. I just called him, and he'll stay home until we get there."

"Okay." But still she didn't move, just stood in the doorway and looked at him. The silence grew thick with awareness.

"Raine," he said softly. "Unless you're trying to tempt me to finish what I never should have started upstairs this morning, you'd better give me a little while."

Her voice was just as soft. "And what if I wanted to tempt you?"

He closed his eyes tightly. She had no idea just how much of a temptation she was. "Then I'd be an even bigger jerk than I already am."

She looked away, her mouth trembling.

"Go on now. Get ready to go. We'll be leaving shortly."

She nodded shakily, turned and left the room.

He took a deep breath. A man could be all kinds of a fool, but he wasn't sure he could have been any more foolish than to indulge himself the way he had upstairs. It wasn't going to make this case any easier. It wasn't going to make it simpler to do as he'd vowed and stay away from her, reminding himself just how bad he was for a woman like her.

And it wasn't going to make it any easier to lay in his bed, just down the hall from her at night. Sleep was only going to get more elusive.

After greeting her father briefly, Raine left the two men alone and went in search of her mother. Mac closed the door to Simon's office behind her and then turned to look at the older man.

Simon sat behind his desk and leaned back. "Sit down, Mac. I hope you've got good news for me. Do the police have any information yet about the lunatic who ran Raine off the road?"

Mac remained standing, surveying the man, and didn't answer. He couldn't. Not when his hands itched to punch the man in the jaw for the way he'd manipulated this situation from the beginning. And maybe even for more than that. Hell, yeah, maybe, he thought savagely, he'd like to get his hands around Simon's throat for the way he'd failed his daughter all those years ago, when she'd needed him most.

Impatient at Mac's silence, Simon quizzed, "Well? Has there been a new development, or not?"

Mac strode to Simon's desk and placed his palms on the top. "Yeah," he snarled, leaning across the surface toward the man. "There's been a development. But I'm the only one it's news to, and you know why, Simon? Because you deliberately kept it from me when you conned me into taking this job."

Simon never blinked. "What's on your mind, son? I told you everything I knew, which was damn little, I might add."

Mac's laugh was ugly. "Except that you forgot the most important detail." He paused meaningfully for a moment. "You forgot to tell me that Raine had been attacked eleven years ago."

The man actually paled. "How did you... What makes you think—"

Mac's palms slapped the top of the desk frustratedly. "Raine told me, Michaels! But she shouldn't have had to. I should have known, because I should have already had that information. *You* should have given it to me. And to the police! My God, man, didn't it ever occur to you that the pervert who hurt her before could be a major suspect in this current sick little game?"

"Yes," Simon replied sharply. He'd obviously recovered from his earlier surprise. "Of course it occurred to me! That's why I've had someone watching him twenty-four hours a day since I found out about those damn letters!"

Mac stared hard at him. "Tell me."

Simon heaved a sigh. "His name was—is," he corrected himself grimly, "Brian Burnett. He was twenty when he... attacked Raine. He spent four years in prison and then returned to Sacramento, where we used to live. Five years ago he moved to L.A. He works in a factory."

"Why the hell did you keep this from me?" Mac bit the words out frustratedly.

"Don't you think Burnett was the first person I thought of when I heard Raine was being threatened?" Simon snapped. "I didn't go through you and I didn't go through the police, I took care of it myself! I hired a man to find him and to see what he's been up to lately. He's been under constant surveillance. If one thing had pointed to his being involved in this mess, don't you think I would have done something about it?"

"What, Michaels? What would you have done? You're not the law, so there's damn little you could do about it. What the hell were you thinking?"

"I was trying to protect my daughter's privacy!" Simon shouted. He struggled visibly to calm himself. Then he went on in a quieter tone, "There was no reason to hand this information over to strangers. For pity's sake, man, I have many more resources at my disposal than that detective who's handling the case."

"You mean money," Mac put in cynically.

"Yes, I mean money. And the things money can buy. In this instance it bought me a background check on Burnett and weekly reports on his movements. What would the police have done? Questioned the man, *maybe*, and left it at that? If Burnett isn't responsible for these threats, I didn't want to take the chance of mentioning Raine's name to him again. I don't want him even thinking about my daughter and I sure don't want him coming near her."

Mac was silent. Simon hadn't changed a bit over the years. He was the same man who'd thought the best way to help Raine get over the rape was to keep silent about it.

He shook his head. Hell, maybe he wasn't giving the man enough credit. Simon was trying, in his own way, to protect Raine. And while Mac didn't agree with his methods, he at least could agree with the intent. But the fact remained that Michaels might have inadvertently put his daughter even more in jeopardy by not giving this information to Mac and to the police.

"Do you have the reports from your investigator?"

Simon unlocked a desk drawer and withdrew a thick file, dropping it on the desk. "Right here."

Mac reached across the desk for it. Flipping it open, he scanned the first few pages. Detailed logs had been kept of Burnett's every movement, including the people he met. Mac's eyes rose to meet Simon's. "I'm taking this with me," he said. "I'll make a copy of it, then I'm handing this over to the police."

"The hell you are!" the man thundered. He rose to his feet and leaned threateningly across the desk. "You'll follow orders, O'Neill, or you're off this case. I'll fire you!"

"You can try," Mac invited. "But just because you stop signing the checks doesn't mean I'll be out of the picture. I gave my word that I'd stay with Raine until this thing is over, and you can't stop me."

Simon glared at him. "You're as stubborn as your old man was."

"No," Mac contradicted. "I'm much worse. The stakes have been raised, Simon. There's no doubt that Raine was set up last week. Whoever called knew just what to say to take her off guard, to lure her away from the house. What's left of her car testifies to the dangerous twist this case is taking." He watched Simon visibly pale and drop into his seat. "Yesterday another letter came. The detective took it, and the envelope, back to headquarters. He'll be turning it over to the Postal Inspection Service. Their investigators may be able to use the postmark to pinpoint the locale the letter was mailed from. They need to be aware that Burnett is a suspect in the case. All the information we have has to be available to them. Otherwise you'll be tying their hands. That's not fair to Raine."

Simon rubbed his hands over his face. Suddenly he looked like a frightened old man. "I wanted to spare her this," he muttered. "If it hasn't occurred to her that Burnett could be involved, I don't want to get her thinking about it again."

"You can't protect her from her thoughts, Simon," Mac said quietly. The man still didn't seem to understand that his keeping silent about the attack hadn't helped Raine forget about it. Just the opposite, in fact.

Simon sighed and clasped his hands on the desk in front of him. He contemplated them for a long time before looking at Mac. "All right. I'll put this into your hands, all of it. If you think the police need to be told about Burnett—" he gestured to the file Mac was holding "—go ahead."

"I don't see any other way."

Simon nodded. "I'm going to continue with that investigator who's watching Burnett, of course."

Mac agreed soberly. "I'd like to see the weekly reports you get on him." He'd feel better himself knowing someone was keeping tabs on the bastard who'd hurt Raine.

He began walking to the door, but Simon's voice stopped him.

"Mac."

He turned inquiringly.

"I'm trusting you to keep my daughter safe."

Mac exchanged a long, meaningful glance with the man. Simon was putting full trust in Mac because he had no other choice. But Mac could understand his desperation. The promise he made then was a vow as much to himself as to the other man.

"I won't allow her to be hurt again."

Chapter 10

Mac went quickly through the file when he arrived at Raine's house. It was complete and detailed, and there was absolutely nothing in it to indicate Burnett's involvement in Raine's case. The day she'd been run off the road, he'd been followed going to work.

Mac picked up the phone, called Ramirez and told him about Burnett. The detective was noticeably unhappy about the information that had been withheld from him. Mac could understand the feeling. Promising the detective that a copy of the file would be in his hands in a couple of hours, Mac hung up.

The walkie-talkie on his desk crackled. "A car's coming up the drive, Mac. It's Sarah Jennings."

"Got it," Mac answered. He spoke to the employee a minute longer, giving him the job of copying and delivering the file. Then he rose and went to the front door. Sarah was just getting out of her bright red convertible sports car.

"Well, hi," she greeted him as she slammed the door. She raised a graceful hand to push her long blond hair from her face. "I'm surprised to see you still here."

Mac went out and leaned against a post of the porch. "You're not working today?"

She made a face as she bounced up the porch steps. "Oh, work. Today was too gorgeous to be stuck inside. I decided to come by and see if I could tempt Raine into playing hooky with me. Maybe we could drive along the coast, go to the beach.'' She gave an artful shrug. ''I'm open to suggestions. As long as it's outside.''

Mac frowned. ''Raine's up in her studio. She's pretty busy getting her last painting done for the show. I'm not sure she should be disturbed.''

Sarah opened her eyes wide. ''Well, listen to you! You sound like André's clone. He didn't send you out here to keep Raine's nose to the grindstone, did he?''

Mac snorted. ''Not hardly.''

''Well, what André doesn't know won't hurt him. And I'm going to take Raine with me, if I can manage to steal her away. She needs a break even worse than I do, with all that's happened around here lately.'' She cocked her head to look at him coquettishly. ''You're welcome to come along, if you like. I have absolutely nothing against sharing sunny California days with dangerously attractive men.''

Mac surveyed her through narrowed eyes. A month ago this woman's blatant interest would have been returned, tenfold. Hell, a month ago he'd have asked someone just like her to accompany him on that tropical vacation he'd been planning. But a lot seemed to have changed in the past few weeks, not the least of which was his preference for voluptuous blondes with bust sizes that rivaled their IQ. That was before he'd seen a pair of wide vulnerable eyes of the rarest gold. It was before he'd witnessed the gut-clenching sight of a woman who put herself back together time after time, no matter what life threw at her.

It was before he'd met Raine.

Not responding to her invitation, he pushed himself away from the post. ''Suit yourself. You can talk to her. She won't be going anywhere, though. I guarantee it.'' He walked into the house and entered the office.

Sarah raised her eyebrows at his terse response and ran lightly up the stairs and down the hall. Breezing into the studio, she said, ''Surprise! I hope you're going to be a little more welcoming than Mac was. He seems to think he's taken over André's job as your watchdog during working hours.''

Raine looked around at her entrance, smiled and put down her brush. ''Sarah!'' She picked up a rag to wipe her hands before going over to give her friend a hug. ''It's good to see you.''

''Yeah, well, maybe you better tell that to Mac. He was positively taciturn downstairs. Of course, I don't have anything against silent men. Not talking does leave their mouths free to do, shall we say, more *interesting* things, so they have their good qualities. And Mr. O'Neill has a few good qualities of his own.'' She paused to take a breath. ''What's he still doing here, anyway? How much more work is there to be done?''

Raine bit her lip at the question. It was as straightforward as Sarah herself and demanded an equally straightforward answer. She searched frantically for words that wouldn't be an out-and-out lie but would satisfy Sarah. Before she could think of any, Sarah's eyes lit on the half-finished canvas beyond Raine.

''Raine, this is a different painting for you. Does André know? He'll throw a tantrum if he doesn't.'' She fell suddenly silent as she recognized the person in the painting. She sent a surprised glance to her friend. ''So, that's what Mac O'Neill is doing around here. He's your live model, hmm?''

''Not exactly.'' Raine led her friend out of the studio and down the stairs, hoping she'd drop the subject. But no such luck.

''Well, there's certainly something more going on here than in-stalling a few alarms. Oh, don't worry.'' She waved her hand. ''I won't pry. But he's exactly the opposite of the men you've dated in the past. I hope you're not getting in over your head.''

''You're jumping to conclusions,'' Raine said flatly. Despite her need to give Sarah a reasonable explanation for Mac's continued presence, she didn't want to give her friend the idea that there was something romantic going on between her and Mac, either. Al-though she'd welcome the possibility, he'd made his feelings clear. And having Sarah blurt out something embarrassing in front of him would be even more humiliating.

''Now it all makes sense,'' Sarah said wisely. ''No wonder he was so darn protective of you when we were talking downstairs. He was afraid I was going to whisk you away from him today. When I mentioned kidnapping you and running up to the coast, he posi-tively glowered at me.''

''Sarah,'' Raine said in exasperation. ''The real reason Mac is here is—''

''Sarah's already guessed the reason, honey. No need to pre-tend.'' Mac was lounging in the doorway of the office. It was clear he'd heard at least part of the conversation. ''You're going to make me think you're ashamed of me.''

''I don't— I'm not—'' stammered Raine.

''Good.'' His voice was satisfied male animal, and so was the smile on his lips. He sauntered toward them and bent to press an intimate kiss against Raine's astonished mouth. Raising his head, he dropped an arm around her shoulders and addressed Sarah. "You're right, Sarah. If Raine is done working for the day, I'm going to claim the rest of her time for myself. Hope you don't mind."

Sarah was eyeing the two of them speculatively. "Not at all. If you can distract Raine from the craziness in her life lately, more power to you."

Raine smiled weakly and slipped out from beneath his arm. "I'm going to walk Sarah out to her car. I'll be right back."

Outside, Sarah sent her an amused glance. "No need to ask what you've been up to lately! He seems pretty possessive already."

"We've . . . we're really just getting to know each other," Raine answered lamely, mentally cursing Mac for the earlier scene.

"You don't have to explain things to me." Sarah laughed as she got into the car. "I'm just glad things are looking up for you, for a change." Her face grew sober. "They are looking up, aren't they, Raine? You haven't gotten any more of those letters, have you?"

"As a matter of fact—" Raine took a deep breath "—I got another yesterday."

"Oh, no!" Sarah exclaimed in concern. "Are you okay? It didn't upset you, I hope."

"I'm fine."

"Well, if you want me to come out and stay with you, just give me a call, Raine. Anytime. I don't like the thought of you here all by yourself, new security system or not." Sarah frowned. "Or maybe you should come to my place for a while. You know I've got plenty of room."

"I'm going to stay put. But thanks for the offer."

"Raine . . ." Sarah hesitated, visibly uncomfortable. Then she sighed and said, "Are you sure you're going to be able to get ready for your show on time? What I mean is, maybe you should think about postponing it. Heavens, no one would blame you with all that's happened to you lately."

"No." Raine's voice was determined. "I'll be ready in time for the show, and I'm not going to let these letters disrupt my life."

Sarah still looked unconvinced. "At least promise me you'll call if you need anything, all right?"

Agreeing with a smile, Raine gave her friend another hug before Sarah slipped into the car and roared away.

Raine's shoulders slumped. She wasn't cut out for this kind of subterfuge, and the pretense had taken more out of her than she'd realized. Of course, Mac's little act hadn't helped. When he'd dropped that kiss on her mouth, her knees had very nearly given out. Straightening, she turned to the house. There was a curious pain in knowing how easily he could slip into the role of lover. Especially in light of how stringently he'd been resisting just such a role since the night they'd made love.

At least, *she'd* made love. She knew it had been something much less for him, but she had to face, at least, what she was feeling. She'd wondered why this man had had such an effect on her, why he could circumvent her customary reactions on all fronts. Now she had to face the reason.

She was in love with Macauley O'Neill.

The acknowledgment brought more pain than joy. Because she already knew that the gift of her love couldn't be offered to him. It wouldn't be something that would elicit a like emotion. Instead, it would cause him guilt and regret. She didn't want to lay that burden on him, didn't want to add to the load of conscience he was already struggling under.

She climbed the porch steps. Mac was standing in the doorway, but he stood aside to let her by. She hurt with a curious kind of pain thinking of his touch a few minutes ago. Knowing he was pretending hadn't diminished the pleasure, and that made her feel naive and foolish. She said nothing, and headed up the hallway stairs.

"Wait," he commanded.

She stopped and turned inquiringly.

"I didn't hear the whole conversation, but she seemed to be grilling you pretty good. What did you tell her?"

"Don't worry," she said, her voice stinging. "She'd already jumped to the wrong conclusion and your little act was very convincing. Your talents are wasted in security. You ought to be on stage."

"Raine."

"What? Don't think I didn't appreciate your efforts on my behalf, because it *was* an effort, wasn't it? I hope you won't be called on again for a repeat performance. I don't know what the big deal is, anyway. Why can't I tell my friends that you were also hired as a bodyguard? What do you hope to gain by keeping that secret?"

"The element of surprise."

She rolled her eyes. "That sounds like something important in tactical warfare, but of little real value in this instance. I've told you, my friends are not involved in these threats. You don't really expect me to believe that one of them tried to kill me, do you?"

Her voice held a dare, and a note of vulnerability. He chose his words carefully. "The fewer people who know I'm here, the better. If the harasser thinks you're alone, and vulnerable, he might make a mistake. And if he does, I'll be here to nail him." Her only response was a long, cool look. He strode forward and snared her wrist when she would have turned and continued up the stairs. Something about the set of those narrow shoulders provoked a reaction from him.

"Don't turn your back on me, dammit. You want to know about effort? You want to see pretense?" His words were edged in steel. "It's an effort every damn minute, being in this house and not touching you again. Knowing just how big a jerk I was to ever lay a hand on you that night doesn't keep me from wanting more. Taking more. So don't talk to me about pretending. Lady, I'm acting for all I'm worth, and the act is wearing damn thin."

His jaw was tight with emotion, and more than anything she wanted to cradle it in her hand. "You don't have to," she said achingly. "I'm right here. You don't have to be noble. Just reach out and take what you want."

He dropped her hand. "I can't do that." His voice was bleak. "I don't have the right."

His words made her angry. "Forget rights, Macauley! You don't have to earn happiness, it just is! But you do have to reach out and take it when you have the chance, because it doesn't happen by every other minute. Don't throw it away." *Don't throw me away,* she cried silently.

"I've done a lot of things in my life," he replied. "My father could see what was happening to me long before I realized it myself. He tried to tell me often enough. 'Son,' he'd say, 'that job is eating you alive, from the inside out.' And he was right. I lost the capacity to tell which decisions were right because they were my job, and which were right because they *were*. But I know that walking away from you when this is over is right, because I don't deserve someone like you. You've had too much unhappiness in your life already, and I'll be damned if I'll add a broken-down soldier with an iced-over soul to your list. You can't fix what's broken inside me. You're good, honey, but even you aren't that good."

"No, I can't fix what's wrong," she agreed. "You have to do that. But what's the matter with my being by your side while you heal? No one knows better than I do how good it would feel to reach out during that time for someone standing with you."

"I can't ask that of you," he said, his voice flat. "And I won't. I have a little self-respect left." *Damn little,* he could have added as he turned and strode away from her, away from temptation. Just enough to remind himself that the second-best thing he could do for Raine Michaels was to stay as far away from her as possible.

The first was to keep her alive.

"I need some background checks done," Mac informed Trey. The two were sitting in front of Mac's desk, sipping beers. "Do we have anyone free?"

"Only me."

"You'll do."

"Gee, thanks," Trey said mockingly. "Your confidence is inspiring."

A quick grin flitted across Mac's face. "What can I say? I taught you all you know."

"My eternal gratitude for that two-minute lesson," Trey gibed. "Lucky I had so much of my own experience and natural ability that I didn't need much help from you."

"Well, I'm going to be needing help from you," Mac said, turning serious. "I'd like you to do some more nosing around into Winters's, Klassen's and Jennings's backgrounds. And see what you can find out about a Brian Burnett, currently of L.A., formerly of Sacramento. He's been out of prison—" he swiftly calculated "—about seven years. I want to know who he celled with in prison, and if he keeps in touch with anyone he met there."

"Where's Burnett come into this?" asked Trey, writing the name down in a notebook.

"He was convicted of rape eleven years ago," answered Mac grimly. "The victim was Raine Michaels."

Trey lifted his head to stare at Mac. "Eleven years? She had to be..."

"A kid. Yeah. And this bastard got out after four lousy years." He knew Trey would guess there was nothing objective about Mac's interest. His friend had been right when he guessed this case had become personal.

Briefly Mac told him of what he'd learned from Simon Michaels. "I've talked to the guy following Burnett. He's done a pretty thorough job investigating him. He knows what jobs he's had and where he's lived, and gave me a list of names of the people Burnett sees after hours. I'd like to do a little checking into those names, to see just what kind of cruds he hangs out with.''

"What was Burnett doing the day Raine was run off the road?"

Mac frowned. "He was followed to work. It couldn't have been him."

"That's why you want to investigate his cronies," Trey guessed. "You think he might have enlisted some help that day."

"He could have been establishing an alibi for himself while Raine was almost killed. Yeah, I think it's possible. From the report I got from Michaels's investigator, Burnett didn't exactly get rehabilitated in prison. He's been in and out of scrapes since he got out—nothing bad enough to get him sent back, but he's walking a fine line."

"Why would he all of the sudden decide to reenter her life this way?" Trey asked, frowning. "After all these years, what does he have to gain by terrorizing her?"

"Maybe he's been plotting revenge all along, to get even for the time he spent in jail. Hell, I don't know. He could have seen an article in the paper, or something about her on TV, and that set him off. Who could figure how a sicko's mind works?"

"He definitely needs to be watched," Trey agreed. "Good thing Michaels has someone on him full-time."

"Does the detective know about Burnett?"

Mac nodded. "I'm sure Detective Ramirez will be paying him a visit soon. But outside of the remote possibility that Burnett will break down and confess, I can't see what good it's going to do."

They lapsed into silence for a moment. Then Trey leaned back in his chair. "I paid another visit to Greg Winters."

Mac's gaze sharpened. "When was this?"

"Last night. Remember I told you I'd approached him at his office and pretended an interest in his services?"

"Yeah."

"Well, I thought it would be interesting to follow that up with a visit to his home. There were some legitimate questions I had about some ideas he gave me. He was surprised to see me, but he invited me in. And guess what I saw there?"

Mac raised his eyebrows quizzically.

"Pictures, man. Lots and lots of pictures, and all of them are of Raine Michaels."

Something clenched in Mac's gut. "What kind of pictures?"

"Nothing personal—they'd all been cut out from newspapers and one magazine spread. He's even got them framed. A whole gallery of them is displayed on the wall over his desk in the living room.''

Mac mulled this over. ''Did he mention them?''

Trey shook his head. ''Not until I did. But remembering what he told the one client, that he and Raine were real close, I wanted to see what he would say. So I pointed to them and said something like, is that your girlfriend? And, I'm not exaggerating, he actually blushed. Stammered around a little bit and then muttered something about being really good friends with her.''

''I don't like it,'' Mac said narrowly. ''It sounds as if he's developed a fixation on her.''

''But where's his motivation to harm her?'' Trey asked. ''It's not as though she rejected him, right? Or did she?''

''I don't know, but I'll find out,'' Mac promised grimly. ''Even if she did, though, why would Winters be the one who hung on to the letters that got turned over to the detective?''

Trey shrugged. ''I never said I had the answers. But I sure have lots of questions.''

''You and me both,'' Mac muttered.

''Okay,'' Trey said, looking in his notebook. ''You told me earlier that you wanted criminal checks on Klassen, Winters and Jennings. I did manage to get those done. You won't believe what I owe the lovely young lady at the police department for her help.''

''Spare me those details.''

Trey grinned and continued. ''There's nothing at all on Winters or Jennings, but there is a record for a Joseph Jennings. Sarah is apparently his guardian.''

''That's her brother,'' Mac said. ''Raine said Sarah's been raising him for the last several years.''

''Well, he's been in some trouble over the course of those years,'' Trey noted. ''With the sheet he's got, the next time he strays over the line of the law, he's going to need a darn persuasive lawyer to keep him out of jail.''

Mac grunted. ''What about Klassen?''

''No record of criminal activity, but I've been asking around to people I know in the art world. I keep coming up with that same rumor about him being short of money.''

Mac leaned back and stared into space morosely. He couldn't help feeling as if they were spinning their wheels. What if it was, as Raine had said all along, a random crazy out there who had picked her out to be persecuted? He sighed and shook his head. Eliminate the obvious, that was their only choice. When they had proof that those with access to Raine weren't guilty, then they would shift their focus elsewhere.

In the meantime, he'd be with her every step of the way, keeping her safe. He'd make sure she was never alone. Until this was over. When he walked away, she would be very much alone, in a way she hadn't been before this mess had started. And there was no way he could make up to her for that.

Mac walked Trey to the door. He'd no sooner closed it behind his friend than Raine came down the stairs.

"Who was that?" She nodded toward the door.

"Trey." She had that look about her again, the one that said she wasn't quite ready to deal with the details of the world. Something had interrupted her in the middle of her painting. He was getting to where he could tell when she was distracted, her mind still on her work. She seemed a little far away, even when looking right at him. All her emotions were reflected in those large, expressive eyes. When she'd been arguing with him earlier they'd been full of sincerity and, he feared, pain. And when he'd dried her off from her shower yesterday morning, they'd been dazed with a desire so strong it took only the memory of it to draw an answering response from him.

"I just remembered," she said, stopping in her descent down the stairs. "I have to go out tonight for dinner with André and some art patrons. It's a long-standing engagement. I can't get out of it."

"What's it for?"

One delicate shoulder rose. "It's just a way for André to stir the pot before the show. He'll have invited several couples, all big spenders in the art circle. They'll also be issued special invitations to the exhibit. I'm to appear and be pleasant and try not to drive business away." Her tone was wry. This was not an outing she looked forward to. But André was the quintessential agent, always looking for a way to expand his artists' marketability. He was also a master of free publicity, and she wouldn't be a bit surprised to find a representative from a newspaper or a magazine there. She suppressed a sigh. No, this was definitely not the kind of evening she looked forward to. She wouldn't blame Macauley for wanting to sit this one out.

"I take it this is important?"

She shrugged again. "It's a command performance, really. André goes to a lot of effort to sell my paintings. The least I can do is cooperate on the rare occasions he dresses me up and trots me out to prospective buyers."

His mouth quirked in sympathy. Then he shocked her by saying, "What time do we have to leave?"

"We? You don't have to go, Macauley. I wouldn't put you through it, believe me. It's going to be dreadfully dull. Since I don't have a car anymore—" that thought made her frown "—I can call André and he'll pick me up."

"I told you that you'll go nowhere without me."

"I just thought," she said, her voice dwindling, "since André would be with me . . ."

Rather than tell her that André Klassen was one of the last people he'd leave Raine alone with right now, Mac merely said, "I can't protect you if I'm not by your side. So what time do we have to be there?"

"We're due at Clancy's Restaurant at seven," she murmured.

He inclined his head. "I'll have to stop by my place to change clothes, so we'll need to leave early." He consulted his wristwatch. "Can you be ready in an hour? Or, better yet, just gather up what you'll need and bring it along. That way we can change at the same time."

The thought of being in his apartment, both of them getting ready to go out, together, was filled with an alluring intimacy. Her throat dry, she managed to nod.

When she turned to go upstairs he headed to the office. Reaching the desk, he picked up the walkie-talkie he used to communicate with the men in charge of patrolling the grounds. He told them his plans for the evening and arranged a signal of three short honks of the horn to announce his return home. He wanted them to be aware, even in the dark, of the identity of his truck and the driver. He didn't want any mix-ups.

He'd barely finished when Raine entered the room. She was carrying a small suitcase and a garment bag. It occurred to Mac that tonight would be the first time he'd seen her in a dress. He was enough of a chauvinist to look forward to the sight with anticipation.

Raine finished dressing in record time, and left the spare bedroom. She freely admitted to herself the curiosity she was feeling about where Mac lived. Wandering through the scantily furnished rooms, she looked around for hints of the man who lived there. There were few to be found.

Nothing hung on the walls; there were no plants to soften the austerity of the bare essential furniture. Three photographs stood atop a television set, and she crossed the room to study them. One showed Mac with an older couple, who she guessed were his parents. She thought she recognized the same hints of stubbornness lurking around both men's jaws. Another picture showed the couple together, and yet another was of the woman alone. And that was all there was. She peeked into the kitchen, but it was as bare as the rest of the rooms. It was like being in a stranger's home, a stranger who put nothing of himself on display.

She didn't know why the Spartan-like apartment should surprise her. Mac gave little of himself away at any time. But she had expected there would be something of him in his home. The fact that it was as expressionless as he usually appeared made her want to cry. Did he spend so little time here that he didn't think it worthwhile to make it more comfortable, more of a home? Or was the emptiness of the apartment supposed to be a mirror of the man?

She didn't want to believe that, although she guessed that he did. There were enough times when she'd caught the bleakness in Mac's eyes to know he was capable of feeling far more emotion than he gave himself credit for. Maybe that was the whole problem. For some reason Macauley O'Neill had decided he didn't deserve any positive emotions. Whatever it was that rode him so hard at times wouldn't let him forget for long enough to experience anything besides guilt. She wondered if it ever would.

Mac stepped into the room and stopped as if he'd hit an invisible wall. He'd been tortured the whole time he dressed by teasing fantasies of what it would have been like to dress with Raine in the same room. There would have been something inherently sexy in watching her ready herself. He'd driven himself crazy with images of her struggling into her dress, asking him to clasp a necklace at the nape of her neck. He'd even fantasized watching her spray herself with a delicate scent of perfume.

Except that she wasn't wearing a dress. His eyes traveled over her small form slowly, taking in the turquoise jumpsuit with the wide silver belt. It was not figure-hugging, but the cut of the fabric draped softly over her fragile curves. It was very nearly backless, with the kind of defiance for gravity that drove a man crazy wondering just what kept it on. She turned then to face him, and he saw that the silver was repeated in a design across her breasts. Dainty silver sandals were on her feet, and she carried a matching purse.

He dragged the direction of his eyes to her face and said the first thing he could think of. "You did something to your hair."

He almost grimaced at the inane comment that had slipped out in an effort to cover what he'd *really* been thinking. But it was true. Her hair was a mass of curls on top, and added to the picture of utter femininity.

"So did you," she said teasingly. Very little, but he'd at least made an attempt to brush the waves back. They still glistened wetly from his attempt. He'd shaved, and she was peculiarly touched by this variation in his usual routine. His smooth jaw tantalized her, tempted her to drag the tip of her tongue across it. His suit was dark, his shirt cream and his tie muted. He looked even more dangerous than he had the first time she'd seen him, and no less uncivilized.

"Do you keep that suit as a disguise?" she joked in a shaky voice.

"It's my bank suit," he explained disgruntledly. "Trey insists we dress like this when we have an appointment with the banker. Never could figure out why. The banker should be looking at our assets, not our clothes."

"Believe it or not, Mr. O'Neill," she said, strolling toward him and hooking her arm through his, "those clothes show your assets off to great advantage."

His eyebrows climbed. "So do yours, honey. Especially," he added, his tone wicked as he led her out the door, "when you turn around."

He frowned as he helped her into the truck. He went to the other side and climbed in. She looked incongruous in the cab, like a delicate splash of color. "I should have taken the time to go by the company to get my car."

She turned startled eyes to his. "What for?"

"Well, it's nothing special, but it would have been a little more comfortable riding. And it would have been a much classier way to arrive at the restaurant."

She shrugged. "What difference does it make?"

He looked at her. She really seemed to mean it. Appearance didn't count much with Raine Michaels. He changed the subject. "Why don't you tell me what to expect tonight?"

The sigh she gave told him how little she was looking forward to the evening ahead. "Well, the food is always good at Clancy's. I'm afraid that will be the highlight. This will really be nothing more than an advertisement for the exhibit I have coming up. André will have invited several people he'd like to have attend the show.'' She grimaced. ''Don't be surprised if he's arranged for a photographer to be there. He's great at dropping hints at newspapers to get some free publicity.'' She turned her eyes to him. ''That's usually my least favorite part of these affairs.''

He wondered all of a sudden how his own presence at the restaurant was going to play out. How would Raine explain him to André? He could imagine the look on Klassen's face when he saw Mac tonight, and something inside him curled in satisfaction. It wouldn't break his heart to put Klassen's too perfect nose out of joint.

They arrived at the restaurant, and a valet took the truck to park it. Mac spotted Klassen standing in the courtyard near the door, apparently entertaining the dozen or so people surrounding him. All seemed to be hanging on his every word.

André looked up, a practiced, polished smile of welcome when he saw Raine. ''Well, at last! Here's our guest of honor!'' The smile abruptly froze when his gaze passed her and clashed with Mac's amused one. For one instant the careful mask slipped and the loathing he felt was apparent.

Then Mac's attention was snared by the flashbulbs going off. Four reporters left André's side and scurried toward Raine, tossing questions like grenades. And when he heard their words, it was Mac's turn to freeze, anger turning the blood in his veins to molten lava.

''Miss Michaels, what has your reaction been to these threats that have been made against you?''

''How has the danger surrounding you affected your current work?

''Do you trust the police to keep you safe?''

Chapter 11

Raine stopped short, blinded by the glare of flashbulbs. Mac put his arm around her and guided her through the journalists who were waiting with notebooks in their hands and pencils poised.

"Miss Michaels has no comment," he said tersely, attempting to get her to the door.

"Mr. Klassen reports that he's been quite worried about your safety recently. Is it true you've been receiving threats in the mail for several weeks?"

"Don't say a word," Mac muttered in her ear. They reached André's side and could go no further, as the man was half-blocking the entrance of the restaurant. "Step aside, now," Mac ordered the man through clenched teeth. Nothing would give him greater pleasure than to smash his fist into Klassen's gleaming capped teeth. He had little doubt that the man had engineered the whole thing, part of a media blitz that would bring more interest to his client and, in turn, line his own pockets.

"Raine, what in God's name possessed you to bring him?" Klassen whispered urgently.

Raine turned her head to address him sharply, but Mac cut in. "What's the matter, Klassen? Upset because I stopped you from turning this into a media circus?"

"That's enough, both of you!" she said under her breath. Turning to face the press, she gave a warm smile. "Thank you for your concern, but I'm all right. Yes, there have been some anonymous letters, and the police have been called in to deal with them. I trust that they will have something to report shortly. And none of this is affecting my work. I can be quite single-minded when I'm painting. I hope to see you all at the exhibit." Giving a friendly wave, she sidled by André and entered the restaurant.

Mac started to follow her, and André had to move aside or be run over. He stayed behind, and his urbane voice could be heard answering more questions. Mac caught up with Raine and muttered, "I thought I told you not to say anything."

"I was not interested in helping you make a scene out there," she informed him, her eyes flashing.

"You've got it all wrong," he answered grimly. "It was Klassen who was making the scene. And arranged it, too, if I don't miss my guess. Why he would pull such an asinine stunt is another matter."

She sighed and raised her hand to her right temple. It was already beginning to throb with a headache. "It's typical for André to have a reporter or two around, I told you that."

His mouth tightened. What was even more typical for Klassen, he imagined, was to milk every event in his path for the resulting publicity. He didn't seem to care overmuch about the possible effects it could have on Raine. For someone who'd convinced her earlier that the threats weren't to be taken seriously, he was sure taking advantage of them in a big way today.

André came in then, followed by two couples who'd been outside. "Raine, dear, shall we go in? Several people have arrived already and are waiting to meet you."

Raine smiled at him, but turned to Macauley. "Mac?"

He moved to her side, noting the way Klassen's mouth twisted with displeasure at the sight. Then they entered the private room where they were to dine.

It was already filled with twenty or so people, and all heads turned when André announced, "Ladies and gentlemen, may I introduce Miss Raine Michaels?" In an aside to Mac he said smoothly, "You'll excuse us, I hope?" He took Raine by the elbow and guided her toward the guests, making introductions.

Mac was content to hang back and observe the crowd. It was a moneyed bunch, that was apparent. The glitter from the jewelry on these people rivaled the glare from the flashbulbs outside. Decked out in outfits ranging from sequined short dresses to nonchalantly tattered jeans, all the women wore the confidence that beauty and wealth can bring. As for the men . . . His gaze narrowed as he observed one man on the wrong side of sixty slide his hand up Raine's bare arm as he was talking to her. The man seemed more interested in the artist than in the work she did.

Reaching out with two fingers, he snared a glass from a white-jacketed waiter's tray. He made a face as he tasted its contents. Champagne was a taste he'd never acquired.

As he set the glass down on a table behind him, a voice at his side said, "You don't strike me as the champagne type."

Turning his head, Mac looked down into the faded blue eyes of a man who appeared to be in his seventies. He was a full head shorter than Mac, and there was nothing left of his hair except for a fringe of white that ran from ear to ear. He would have looked as if he could make a living impersonating one of Santa's elves at Christmas time, if it hadn't been for his bearing. If the others in this room shone with wealth, this man radiated power.

"You're right," Mac answered finally. "Champagne's not my drink."

"Whiskey, Scotch?"

"Scotch, neat," he responded.

The stranger nodded in approval. "A man after my own heart," he said. He raised a finger, which brought a waiter immediately to his side. "Two Scotches," he ordered. The waiter hurried away.

"I'm Harold Bonzer, by the way," the man said.

Raine's benefactor. He hadn't known the man was going to be here tonight. Mac took the hand held out to him. "Mac O'Neill."

Shaking his hand, Harold eyed him intently. "I saw you come in with Raine. I've never seen her with an escort before. Have you known her long?"

"Not long, no," Mac answered shortly, reaching out to take one of the glasses the waiter had silently come back with.

When it became clear that he wasn't going to say more, Harold chuckled. "A man who keeps his own counsel, eh? That's a rarity in a crowd like this."

Mac looked at him speculatively. "Raine has mentioned you," he said. "She gives you a great deal of credit for her success."

Real pleasure lit the man's face at the compliment, although he shook his head. "Raine Michaels was going somewhere. I just happened to be the one who recognized it and promoted her talent a little."

"I understand you've also helped launch Sarah Jennings's career."

"Ah, Sarah, yes. That's how I met Raine, you know. It was at a showing I arranged for Sarah."

Mac took a drink from the glass he was holding, his eyes skimming the crowd. "She and Raine seem very close."

"An unlikelier pair I've never met," Harold murmured.

The remark captured Mac's attention. "I'm surprised you'd say that. After all, they both have similar interests, as well as talents."

Harold shrugged. "But they've very different personalities, haven't they? Raine's content to let her talent speak for itself, while Sarah is much more ambitious. It's to be expected, I suppose. She's had a rather tough time, losing her parents at a young age and taking on her brother to raise. An experience like that leaves a mark on a person."

"Every experience leaves a mark on a person," Mac said bluntly.

The man's eyebrows rose. "Quite so," he agreed. He surveyed Mac shrewdly for a moment. "What line of work did you say you were in?"

Mac took another drink from his glass. "I didn't."

Harold Bonzer's face was wreathed in a beatific smile. "You're a careful man, Mac O'Neill. You don't happen to need a job, do you?"

Mac shook his head, bemused. "I'm afraid I don't know much about the art world."

The man looked surprised. "The art world? I have an interest in it, of course. I enjoy surrounding myself with beautiful things. But I'm in finance. And I'm always on the lookout for a man who listens more than he talks."

"I'm afraid I know less about finance than I do about art," admitted Mac. "I'm in the security business."

"That explains it," murmured Bonzer, eyeing him keenly.

"Harold, it's so good to see you again." Raine came up and greeted him with a hug. "And you've obviously met Mac."

"Yes, I have, and I approve," he told her. "It's about time you started spending time with someone, away from your paintbrushes."

Raine cast an uncertain eye toward Mac. Harold was jumping to the same conclusion Sarah had, but Mac seemed unconcerned. He merely cocked an eyebrow at her look. Then Harold claimed her attention, for the better part of twenty minutes, until seating began for dinner.

André motioned for Raine to sit beside him.

"Harold, why don't you sit at Raine's other side? That way you can continue your conversation," André invited. But Bonzer waved the suggestion away. "Raine's already spent enough of her time entertaining old men. Put Mac next to Raine. I'll sit on his other side."

The suggestion obviously didn't sit well with André, but he did as Harold suggested. After the guests were seated, steaming platters of seafood and steak were placed before each of them.

"Meal choice number three," Raine murmured into Mac's ear. He turned his head at the teasing remark, and she didn't pull away. Her lips were scant inches from his own.

"Not quite the same ambience I'm used to," he answered, his eyes on her mouth.

Raine caught her breath at the sizzling look in his ice blue gaze. The heat that infused her veins owed nothing to the steam rising from her food. When he raised his eyes to meet hers the conversations around her faded away. Her focus narrowed to his mouth, the well-formed thin upper lip, the fuller bottom one. Memories of that mouth on her own surged through her.

"Raine." André's impatient voice startled her, and she turned toward him.

He indicated her plate. "Try some of the scallops. They're really quite good here."

Raine looked at him blankly for a moment, then at her plate. She couldn't help feeling that André's innocuous remark was intended to draw her attention from Macauley, and she wondered at the petty ploy. He had seemed very put out ever since he'd seen Mac with her tonight. However, he was used to arranging things to suit himself and to having her fall in with his plans. Perhaps that would explain his pique at Mac's appearance tonight. He simply didn't like surprises of any kind.

"Tell me," André invited as he reached for his glass of champagne, "how did you happen to come here tonight with O'Neill?"

The question seemed to validate the conclusion she'd just arrived at about his annoyance. But it also smacked a bit of possessiveness, and Raine was not going to allow that. "Mac was kind enough to offer me a ride," she answered carefully, keeping in mind Mac's warning not to reveal his real role. "My car is out of commission," she said, smiling grimly at the understatement, "so I really had no other way here."

"What's wrong with your car?" he inquired.

"I haven't talked to an insurance adjuster yet, but I believe the term I'll hear is totaled," she answered. "I had an accident a few days ago and my car will probably not recover."

"An accident?" André's expression was horrified. "Was anyone injured?"

She shook her head, although the memory of the incident was enough to make her tense. "It was a hit-and-run. But luckily, I wasn't really hurt."

"You should have told me," André scolded her like a mother hen. "I would have come and picked you up tonight. There's no reason for you to feel desperate."

Mac had been listening to the exchange. He leaned forward to address Klassen. "I was glad to help out."

André's face tightened, and Raine inwardly sighed. She always seemed to be caught in the middle of these kinds of skirmishes. First it was André and Greg, now Macauley and André. She wished she knew what caused these hard feelings. No doubt it had to do with testosterone overload, but she found it quite tedious. And totally unnecessary.

The rest of the evening passed with excruciating slowness. After the dinner André stood up and reminded all present of the date of Raine's show. The party was breaking up. Raine heaved a sigh of relief and smiled brightly as she rose and spoke to some of the departing guests.

Mac rose, too, but stayed in place, watching the rest of the room's occupants.

"Mr. O'Neill."

He turned to face Harold Bonzer.

"It was a pleasure to meet you tonight. I hope I'm going to see more of you. Will you be at Raine's show?"

Mac smiled. "That depends."

The older man chuckled. "Never give too much away, O'Neill. I like that. I just might give you a call myself. I always have the need for a good security expert."

"You do that, Mr. Bonzer." The two men shook hands. Harold walked over to Raine and said something, and she gave him a hug. Seeing Klassen alone for the moment, Mac sauntered over.

"This was quite an event you orchestrated," he told him.

The man didn't bother to conceal his dislike. "Yes, despite the fact that one uninvited guest showed up."

Mac raised an eyebrow. "Surely you're not referring to me? Raine was so certain that she was free to bring an escort to this shindig."

"Don't flatter yourself, O'Neill. You were a means to an end tonight. The next time Raine needs a ride somewhere she can call me, or another one of her *friends*."

"You know," Mac said, with deceptive mildness, "something's been bothering me tonight. All those reporters you had here. I can't figure out if you're really such a publicity hungry son-of-a-bitch that you couldn't pass up the chance to get some free coverage, or if you're even more devious than I thought."

André clenched his jaw. "What are you getting at?"

Mac stepped closer. "Maybe this was a ploy of yours from the beginning. Did you send those threats yourself in order to cash in on the resulting publicity? Never mind that Raine would be terrorized in the meantime. If it sold an extra painting it'd all be worth it to you, right?"

Looking as if he was weighing his chances if he threw a punch, André snarled, "You're a lunatic, O'Neill. I don't know how you insinuated yourself into Raine's life, but I will see that your tenure there is short-lived. It certainly wouldn't do her image any good to be linked to a man who's delusional."

"Just a warning, Klassen." Mac's voice was soft and deadly. "You better not have had anything to do with those threats. Because if you did, I'll be coming after you. Understood?"

"Well, André, it was an undisputed success tonight, didn't you think?" Raine's voice was overly bright. While she hadn't been close enough to hear the words the two men exchanged, the tone had been unmistakable. "You're a genius when it comes to this sort of thing."

"He's got the publicity down pat, that's a fact," Mac said.

"Raine." André brushed a kiss on the side of her face. "I hope you're ready for your big night."

"Just about," she agreed. "My last work is almost done."

"Good, I'd like to drop by and look at what you've accomplished. Then we'll have to make arrangements for the paintings to be picked up and delivered to the gallery...."

"Great. You call me, all right?"

Mac's hand came to the small of her back, and he guided her away. Raine ignored the shiver of electricity that skated down her spine at his touch. She waited until they got to the front door and Mac had given his keys to the valet. When she spoke her tone was weary. "Please don't tell me that you had words with André to-night."

Mac's eyes were searching the street in front of them. "We spoke, yeah."

She waited, but he left it at that. "Now why do I feel like that's the understatement of the century?"

"I let him know that I was less than pleased with his publicity trick tonight, if that's what you're getting at." The black truck pulled up in front, and the valet hopped out.

As they headed to the freeway Raine said, "I don't understand why you made so much of my answering a few questions. I warned you, after all."

"Because, Raine—" his voice was sardonic "—the less media exposure on this whole mess, the better. I can't think of any good that could possibly come out of having those letters splashed across the papers. If anything, it could encourage the person who's do-ing it to be getting that kind of attention. It could even trigger some sort of copycat threats."

"That sounds a little farfetched," she said skeptically.

"Publicity won't make the detective's work, or that of the postal investigators, any easier," he maintained. "And the fact that Klassen used it to gain media attention seems a little sick to me. I'd think it would to you, too."

Raine was silent. She'd been dismayed that André had chosen to go public like that, but she accepted it. It was, after all, in keeping with his character. She'd never been comfortable with that side of the business, the glitz and tinsel that sold newspapers—and pro-moted her paintings. But she'd entrusted those kinds of decisions to her agent. Macauley didn't seem to approve of André, and the feeling, she'd noted, was mutual.

"I don't know what on earth ever happened between the two of you to generate such dislike. I've never seen André angrier than he was at the end of the evening."

"He thinks he owns you, Raine." Mac's look was a warning. "You'd better open your eyes. The man feels his control goes far beyond selling your pictures. He tried to get rid of me once be-fore. He threatened to have me taken off the job, claimed that my crew was too distracting."

She made a disgusted sound. "That's just the way he is, Ma-cauley, it doesn't mean anything. He's very singular and focused. That's probably what makes him such a good agent. I managed my life very nicely before you came into it. I can manage my friends, thank you very much."

"I know you don't want to hear this, but you're going to have to ask yourself if Klassen would have had anything to gain by sending those letters himself," Mac said in a hard voice. "The publicity stunt he pulled tonight might give clues about his motive."

She stared at him as if he was crazy. "That has got to be the most half-baked, ridiculous…" She closed her eyes as a thought hit her. "Tell me you didn't voice that suspicion to André."

His set jaw was all the answer she needed. She groaned feelingly. "I don't believe you! You don't give up, do you? No wonder he looked like he was going to explode! Macauley, how could you! I've told you before, André is more than my agent, he's my friend! At least he was before you went after him tonight."

"It's a possibility," he maintained.

"Oh, and then he decided to run me off the road because a picture of my folded up car would make such a good headline? A dead artist is worth more to him than a live one, is that it?"

Mac leveled a look at her. "You said it, I didn't."

She stared at him, speechless for a moment. "You have never stopped suspecting my friends, have you? You didn't ban André, Greg and Sarah from the house, but it wasn't because I'd convinced you that they could be trusted, was it? It was so you could watch them closer."

He didn't deny her allegation, and that seemed to infuriate her even more. "Admit it, Macauley, for once in your life drop that damn smug silent act of yours and just admit it! Say out loud, 'Yes, Raine, I suspect one of your closest friends of terrorizing you for weeks and of then trying to kill you!' Maybe saying it out loud will help you hear how ludicrous it sounds!"

"You can't be unemotional about this. I understand that," he said evenly.

Tears smarted in her eyes, and she blinked them away furiously. "No, I can't. I happen to take friendship a little more seriously than that. But I don't doubt *your* ability to remain unemotional, Macauley. You've had plenty of practice at that, haven't you?"

Her words hung in the air, and he tightened his jaw against the truth of them. Yeah, right, he was a master at remaining unemotional. He'd perfected the technique and he'd never lost his objectivity. Unless you counted that time in Central America. He'd learned a lesson then he'd never forgotten. A man like him wasn't allowed the same reactions and feelings as others. He had to think with his head and his gut and disregard anything else. Disaster had struck the only time he'd ignored that stricture. He couldn't take that chance again, not with Raine. She didn't seem to realize that by concentrating on her, rather than her safety, he could jeopardize rather than protect her. He wouldn't take that chance.

"Not accepting people at face value is what makes me good at my job. That's exactly what's going to keep you safe."

It was no use arguing with him, she thought. He was a man to whom the job was everything, and he didn't spare a lot of time worrying about the niceties while he went about doing it. She should be happy to have that single-minded intensity directed toward her safety and her protection. But it was impossible to still the desire to have it focused on *her,* for her own sake. And she continued to be troubled by the fact that it was unfair for her friends to be under suspicion, simply because they were her friends.

"Don't ask me to help you," she said bitterly. "And don't ask me to believe, even for a minute, that one of my friends has anything to do with this."

He was silent. He wouldn't ask that of her. It was the least he could do, and if keeping his suspicions to himself saved her some grief, well, that was fine by him. God knew he'd caused her enough grief himself.

The ride back to her home was silent after that. Darkness had long since fallen, and the security lights were shining brightly as they approached her house. It looked, Raine thought sourly, as though they had lit the place up to land small aircraft in the yard. She hated this—she hated all of it. These lights called attention to the fact that she had more to fear these days than mere night. Much more.

The partially finished fence looked like a black skeleton across the front of her property. Macauley gave three short blasts of the horn as he entered her drive, causing her to jump. She snuck a look at him. She might hate the security measures they had been forced to take, but she could never hate him. She was still staunchly loyal to her friends, and he made her angry with his suspicions of them. But even arguing with him, faced with his implacable will, she couldn't help trusting him. Believing in him.

Loving him.

She sighed and got out of the truck without waiting for him to come around to help her. They walked to the house, still without words. She felt as tightly drawn as a wire, despite the lateness of the hour. This wasn't going to be a night where sleep came easily, despite the exhaustion that weighted her limbs. Turning on lights in her path, she headed to the kitchen and poured herself a glass of milk. She flicked a light switch near the back door, unlocked the door and let herself out onto the patio.

She sat down and looked into the distance broodingly, sipping occasionally from her glass. When she'd seen Macauley pace this area at night, he hadn't had the lights on, she remembered. He'd blended into the darkness in a way that said he was comfortable there, a familiar visitor to total blackness. Or maybe he thought he didn't deserve to live in the light, the way he felt he didn't deserve so many other things.

He stood in the doorway for a time and watched her. She was in a melancholy mood, he could sense it. Not really angry with him anymore, but almost . . . resigned. He found he preferred her anger. He could deal with her sparks, the way she could flare up at him and, more often than he was comfortable remembering, goad him into flaring back. No woman had ever had that kind of effect on him, because nobody else had gotten that close.

He'd been told that his temper was a fearsome thing. But Raine Michaels wasn't afraid to go toe to toe with him and give him hell right back. The trait shouldn't have been seductive. But it was.

"Plotting my demise?" he finally questioned, and stepped out on the small patio with her. She didn't move a muscle, and he knew she'd been aware of his presence.

"I'll never agree with the way your mind works," she responded. Then her head moved slowly to face him. "But I'm too darn lazy to dig a six-foot trench. You're safe with me."

"I'm not so sure," he murmured cryptically. A woman who could infiltrate his sterile world and kick more into life than his libido could hardly qualify as safe. Although all signs pointed to the fact that his libido was also alive and well. His hormones were on red alert all the time when he was around her, and often when he wasn't.

"Where were you last stationed before you left the Army?" she asked suddenly.

He knew then, in that instant, that she'd been out here brooding about him. She'd been holding back a lot of questions since the night he'd let her know, in no uncertain terms, that he didn't much like answering them. He'd spent a career being close lipped and watchful. It had saved his butt on many an occasion. But she'd put things together about him as easily as if she'd written his biography. He no longer questioned that ability of hers. And tonight he wasn't going to fight it. He'd refused to give anything of himself to her. A few answers seemed little enough.

"Central America."

She turned her eyes to him, silently waiting for him to go on.

"It doesn't particularly matter where. There are lots of little countries there with shaky governments, and at one time or another I was in all of them. They all shared the same poverty, and the same desperation. There were always people waiting for a chance to make money, and opportunities were plentiful, if they weren't too particular about the law. Most of them weren't." He'd known men who would slit their grandmother's throat for a dollar, and others working alongside them who did what they did because they needed the money for their families, for their children. Sometimes, in the dark of night, the motives of the latter seemed more admirable to him than his own.

"Our country has interests in who controls those governments. The people our politicians want to see in power there aren't necessarily good men or wise men. But for some reason they fit with our political agenda. It was my goal to make sure those people stayed in power." Constantly moving, he'd assessed the political climate of the country and, when he had to, arranged events that would help the local government stay in control. The goals hadn't been his own, but he'd carried them out faithfully.

And in the process lost his soul.

Raine's eyes were wide as they met his. "What happened to you there?" she whispered. Every instinct she had told her that whatever it was had shaped his view of the world ever since. Was continuing to shape it.

"I miscalculated the danger in one locale. A bomb went off in the hotel where I was staying. Trey dragged me out of the rubble, got me to a hospital." After a pause, he went on in a flat tone, "I may have blown my cover. The bomb may have been placed there for me, or it could have been one more senseless act of random violence that had been going on in that country. I'll never know. Forty-seven people died that night."

"You blame yourself?" She didn't need his answer, she read it in his silence. This, then, was the cause for the demons that still tormented his conscience.

"Yeah," he said finally, staring past her, past the lights, into the darkness. "I blame myself."

She wished suddenly that she'd never brought up the past, hated herself for putting that look on his face. What right did she have, after all? She, better than anyone, should know the pain that resulted from revisiting the past. It was like pulling the scab off a wound that wouldn't quite heal. The anguish didn't fade with time, nor did the memories. She almost hoped he'd tell her to go to hell, then clam up again. At least she wouldn't have to face the bitter regrets on his face or be a witness to his suffering.

But she stopped herself in the midst of her self-castigation. She knew from experience that the past had to be faced before the future could be dealt with. Macauley had to forgive himself before he'd ever feel he deserved anything good life could offer him. That was a truth he'd have to learn to accept. She was more than a little surprised when, after a long silence, he continued.

"There was a woman. I'd rescued her from some guerrilla troops roaming the town, and she was—" he hesitated for an instant "—grateful." Gratitude was what he thought she'd felt, but that was something else he'd never be sure about. It could have explained the accidental way they'd kept meeting. Surely she'd made her interest clear. Or she could have been sent to destroy him. He'd last seen her two hours before the bomb had gone off. He had no way of knowing whether she'd been in the hotel.

"Did she die in the explosion, too?" Compassion warred with jealousy, and the latter was an unfamiliar, distasteful emotion. She didn't want to hear Macauley say he'd loved this woman, that she'd been the only one to slip beneath his guard.

"I don't know. Trey seemed to think that she may have arranged it." His smile was self-mocking. "You could call it a going-away present for me. I never saw her again. I was Stateside shortly after leaving the hospital. But I found out later that she had a brother in the very guerrilla faction I supposedly rescued her from."

"You blame yourself for trusting her."

"Trust wasn't a word I'd use," he corrected her. "But I didn't necessarily mistrust her. And that might have been my biggest mistake."

He was a man who would learn well from mistakes, she thought. A man who would fight to avoid repeating them. "Did your superiors think you were at fault?"

"There was never enough evidence to prove who set the bomb, or why. It was accepted as just one of those things." His mouth twisted. "Successes or failures weren't measured in little things like the number of people who died. My job was to meet goals." His voice dropped. "I was very good at my job."

"So there is no one in the world who is blaming you for what happened at that hotel except yourself?" she inquired daringly. "Sometimes we're our own toughest judge and jury, Macauley." She didn't want to ask more, afraid of the answers she'd get. But the question that was burning inside her slipped out anyway, signaling her interest, and other emotions she didn't dare share. "Did you love her?"

He heard the note of yearning in her voice and hated himself for being responsible for it. He walked toward her until he stood before her. He parted her legs with one knee and stepped between them. Putting a hand on either side of her, he lowered his face to hers. "Love had nothing to do with it," he said huskily. "I didn't care enough about her to worry about whether or not I could protect her and still do my job. But she was a distraction, one I couldn't afford at that moment." She was gazing at him mutely, and he wished he could read what was going on behind those wide eyes of hers. "I thought at the time that she was responsible for my reflexes being sluggish, my suspicions being soothed. But now I've met a lady who shoots the whole thought of objectivity to hell. One who could tempt a starch-collared priest. You should be running, baby. As fast and as hard as you can. Because a bodyguard overly interested in your body isn't going to do you a whole hell of a lot of good."

That pouty mouth of hers was trembling, and her lips parted slightly. Her eyes were fixed on his, and he knew that the glow of barely suppressed desire in hers was reflected in his. His mouth was halfway to hers before his ears picked up a sound that shouldn't have been there.

One second he was above her, mouth close to hers, and the next he was propelled into action. "Get inside," he ordered. Without waiting for a response he gripped both elbows and lifted her from the chair. He ushered her into the kitchen, and she heard, through the walkie-talkie he'd left on the counter, a voice say, "Car's coming up the drive at a pretty good clip, Mac!"

"Stay here," he said firmly and ran down the hallway and out the front door. She obeyed for less than a minute. When she heard the shouts and squeal of car tires, she ran after him.

By the time she threw the door open, one side of her front porch was already engulfed in flames.

Chapter 12

Raine slammed the door and raced toward the stairs. Flipping light switches as she went, she stumbled into a spare bedroom and threw open the closet. She dragged down extra blankets, ran to the bathroom and threw them into the tub. The faucets were turned on full blast, soaking the blankets thoroughly. Then she gathered them up, dripping wet, and ran downstairs. When she stepped out on the porch, she saw Macauley there with the two men who patrolled the property at night. One held a garden hose in his hand, and the steady stream of water he was spraying turned the flames to searing, hissing furls of steam. She dropped her load and shouted, "Help me with this."

Mac turned to see her struggling with a large wet blanket. "I thought I told you to stay put," he said frustratedly. Even as he spoke he took the blanket from her and began beating at the flames with it. The other man stepped toward her, picked up the second blanket and attacked another area of the fire. "Call emergency and ask for a fire truck, and the police. And then stay inside," Mac ordered.

She obeyed part of the command. When she'd finished the phone call, Raine went out to the porch, drawn involuntarily. She watched, numbness setting in as the men fought for control of the blaze. Just as they would conquer it in one area, flames would shoot up from another. Slowly, the men gained ground. When nothing remained but glowing embers, the blankets were discarded. The man with the hose sprayed the porch and the surrounding area thoroughly, dousing even the most fervent sparks.

She stood staring emptily at the soggy mess that used to be part of her porch. The flames had licked their way across the railing and left the porch floor charcoal. Smoke had blackened the white siding of the house in spots. The soot and grime on the once shiny paint seemed a perfect commentary on the turn her life had taken lately.

"You okay?" a voice rasped in her ear. She didn't have to turn her head to know it was Macauley at her side. She didn't answer.

He drew her into the circle of his arm and led her toward the door. "Let's get you inside. Smith, Anderson," he called to the two men still standing outside. "I'll need to talk to you in the office."

Raine allowed herself to be led into the house, but once Mac got her to the front hallway, he didn't seem to know what to do with her. He cocked his head. "Is that water I hear running?"

She didn't move. "I wet the blankets upstairs."

He lowered his head to gaze intently into her eyes. Bringing both hands to her elbows, he rubbed up and down her bare arms in a gentle caress. "Why don't you go up and turn it off, honey," he suggested. "Better yet, take a long bath and relax. It's over." She appeared to weigh his words solemnly for a moment before turning silently and climbing the stairs.

Mac observed her retreat with worried eyes. She was too calm, too quiet and much too obedient. He knew the combination spelled possible shock. He'd have to watch her carefully.

Going to the office to confront his men, he demanded, "Well?"

"Looked like a late-model sedan, no plates," Anderson told him. "I chased it down the drive, but once it hit the road it was gone. Two passengers in the front seat."

"Both dressed in dark clothes and ski masks," Smith put in.

Hearing sirens approaching, Mac and the men went to the porch.

"There's glass all around here," Anderson said.

"Probably bottle bombs," Mac grunted.

"Pretty basic," agreed Smith. "Pour in some gasoline, stuff in some cloth and ignite. Instant torches." The man broke off abruptly.

Following the direction of Smith's gaze, Mac turned and saw Raine standing in the doorway. Walking swiftly to her side, he ran a finger along the soot on her jawline. "Doesn't look like you got that bath taken," he said softly. When she didn't respond, his arms went around her of their own volition. Cupping her head in one hand, he coaxed it to his chest. He bent his head, and rested his chin on her hair. He closed his eyes tightly, rocking a little. His hand swept up her bare back. It was chilled beneath his palm, despite the balmy temperatures outside.

"I wanted to be here when the police arrive."

Her voice sounded a bit more normal and he felt fierce relief. She was recovering from the shock of witnessing someone trying to torch her house. No matter how often he witnessed it, he never ceased to be amazed at her strength. But he couldn't help worrying at her surface calm. Some time when the shock wore off, she was going to crash. All he could do was be there for her when that happened.

The police car and the fire truck arrived simultaneously. When the two officers and the fire fighters joined them, Mac filled them in on the events of the evening.

"They were yelling at each other when they saw us coming," Anderson stated. "I heard one shout, 'She's not alone.' They were in a hurry to leave then."

"I'm sure they expected her to be by herself," Mac stated grimly. "No one had reason to believe otherwise."

The firemen looked around and pronounced the area saturated enough to prevent any embers from igniting. The officers took notes, asked a few more questions, then joined the fire fighters in surveying the damage. After promising to pass the information on to Detective Ramirez in the morning, the officers took their leave. The squad car was followed down the drive by the fire engine.

Raine returned to the house and huddled in a chair. All of a sudden she was cold, as if she'd been caught in a draft. She rubbed her eyes, which burned from a combination of smoke and stress, and stared straight ahead. It had been a while since she'd felt this fear, but she remembered its effects well. Intense enough to cripple a person, it could make her afraid to engage in a normal day's activities. She'd spent more than a decade working through that fear. She wondered bleakly how long it would take to undo all she'd accomplished.

That was how Mac found her. He didn't immediately see her when he entered the family room, and he scanned the area sharply. She was in the corner, in such a small ball that only the color of her jumpsuit made it possible to pick her out. He immediately crossed to her.

"I'm cold," she murmured plaintively.

Reaching down and picking her up, he turned and dropped into the chair, arranging her on his lap. His arms surrounded her, and her head went instinctively to the hollow of his shoulder. He didn't question the wisdom of his move. She needed to be held, and maybe he needed this as much as she did.

"Probably shock, as much as anything," he said against her hair. "You need a hot shower to warm you up, and a shot of whiskey to put you to sleep."

She wrinkled her nose against his shirt. "No, thanks. Whiskey wouldn't make me sleep, it would make me unconscious."

He wasn't so sure that wouldn't be a good thing. If ever a woman deserved a few blessed hours of unconsciousness, it was her. He didn't know how to make sure the scene tonight didn't trigger a flashback when she finally did manage to sleep. Passing out just might be the answer to avoiding that particular problem. But he wasn't surprised that she'd refused that solution. She wasn't the type to hide from her problems in the bottom of a bottle.

"I don't know what to do anymore, Macauley." Her voice was weary. "And I just keep wondering why. I can't figure out what I did to elicit this kind of hatred from somebody."

His arms tightened around her. "You didn't do anything," he said fiercely. "You've been targeted by someone with a sick mind whose motives are clear only to himself. Don't start blaming yourself for this."

"I'm scared," she whispered. "I mean, I'm really, really scared. It's crazy, because not even the accident shook me up like this. Part of me stands back and observes all this as if it's happening to a stranger. And then I realize with a jolt that this is *me*. This is all happening to me." She was silent for a while before she spoke again. "I was never afraid to stay here alone, you know? Once I had the house all set up so I didn't have to worry about being caught in the dark, it was always my haven. As soon as I'd approach the driveway a kind of peace always settled over me. I'm afraid I won't ever feel that again in my home, even when this is over."

"You won't be alone here while there remains any hint of danger," he said. Her admission of fear echoed a silent one of his own. Fear for her, for her safety. If she had been alone tonight, if she'd been sleeping, this act could have resulted in her death. The whole house could have gone up in flames, with her in it. He felt sweat pop out on his forehead at the thought. He could have lost her tonight, so easily. The threats were getting too real, and far too close. He hated having her afraid, and he knew what it took for her to admit it to him. He didn't much care for the feeling himself.

Somehow objectivity didn't seem to matter anymore. There was nothing objective about the rage he felt each time someone tried to hurt her. Emotion, an uncomfortable amount of it, had crept into this job at some point, and damned if he knew what to do about it. His instincts had always been his mainstay, and every instinct he had was screaming at him. This woman was more dangerous than any he'd ever encountered. Seductive because she saw through him, through the defenses he'd built for years. Alluring in her vulnerability, and in her curious strength. And too damn sexy to be out on her own.

Regardless of what people thought of him, Mac O'Neill did have a few scruples. That's what had had him holding Raine at arm's length, but those scruples were pretty tattered these days. The danger of her situation seemed to weave a cocoon of intimacy around them. His role as her protector drew him nearer, even as he tried to resist the pull. He didn't know how much more of this she could take, and he was wondering how much more *he* could take.

One thing was sure—sitting like this with her was playing hell with the one remaining ethic he had. Everything in him demanded that he reassure himself she was all right, in the most primitive way a man could. He wanted to lay her down and run his hands all over her, in a tactile exploration that would lead to more than his recognition of her well-being. Danger was a powerful aphrodisiac, but his fear for her was an even greater one.

She stirred then, and her hip pressed against his groin. He stifled the groan that was on his lips.

Raine raised her head. "I think I'll go up now and take that bath you were suggesting."

He had to agree, since it had been his idea. But the image of her in the tub, bubbles spreading alluringly to allow teasing glances at sweet secrets, danced through his mind. "Good idea," he murmured. "And then you'll come down for that drink I mentioned. It doesn't have to be whiskey."

"Thank heavens for that," she muttered.

"But it will complete the relaxation and help you get some sleep. Okay?"

She nodded, and he helped her to her feet. She walked from the room and only then did he move, almost painfully to the kitchen. She might not want a whiskey, but he'd never felt more in need of

a drink. Unfortunately, he didn't dare take one. He didn't need any
of his senses dulled. He shifted uncomfortably. Although he'd
welcome dulling his awareness of Raine.

She lolled her head back in the tub and turned on the tap with
her foot. When she'd replenished the hot water in her bath, she
turned it off again. Macauley had been right, she thought lazily.
For the first time all evening she could feel tense muscles lose a little of their stiffness. Not completely, of course. There was only so
much hot water could do, after all. But being held in his arms had
started the process.

Blocking all thoughts from her mind for a few precious moments, she engaged in the repetitive task of soaking the bath sponge
in the water and squeezing it gently out again. Over and over her
hands repeated the simple action, and she watched it hypnoti-
cally. It wouldn't do to fall asleep in the tub, but there really was
no danger of that. Her trancelike state was her mind's way of es-
caping the events of the last few hours. She didn't want to think
about the fire or the threats, or the persons responsible for them.
She didn't want to wonder about their motivations. And she didn't
want to feel afraid anymore.

She didn't feel afraid while Macauley held her. Those were the
only times since the rape she could remember feeling completely
and utterly safe. It didn't make sense to feel that way with a man
like him. She'd known from the start that he had a wall around his
emotions. But she'd sensed so much more since then.

He was holding his desire for her at bay. It wasn't ego that told
her that. There had been too many times when she'd read his true
feelings on his face. Or lower. Heat suffused her cheeks, and it
wasn't caused from the hot water she'd just added. Only a couple
of short days ago Macauley had joined her in this room, and the
mask of desire stamped on his features had been the most seductive sight she'd ever seen. She knew there was no chance he would
happen in tonight. Macauley O'Neill assuredly never made the
same mistake twice.

That was how he viewed their night together, she knew. A slip
of the natural guard that was so much a part of him. She doubted
he was aware that the control he exerted over his emotions served
to remind others to curb their own around him. Doubtless, he
wouldn't care. Emotion wasn't logical or reasonable or rational.
All the words that described almost every action he took.

Except on those rare occasions when he was tempted to forget them.

She rose then, the water sluicing off her, and stepped from the tub. She reached for a towel and dried herself, slipping into a short, silky robe she'd brought in. She stopped, catching her reflection in the mirror. He would assume the high color in her cheeks was the result of the warm bath. Only she knew it had been caused by memories of him touching her.

Macauley O'Neill. She'd told him once that the name sounded like a poet. Now she wondered if it described a saint. How much would it take to tempt a saint? she wondered. How much to tempt a man who held himself to higher ideals than any plaster of Paris martyr had ever harbored?

Perhaps tonight, if she could summon the courage, she'd find out.

Mac prowled around the kitchen restlessly. He'd scavenged through her cupboards and found some brandy. That would do, he thought judiciously. One drink would have just enough kick to get her completely relaxed. Two would complete the trick, and three—well, three would mean she'd need some help getting to bed.

He pursed his lips consideringly. Better not push it. Three might guarantee her a solid night's sleep, but would mean far less than that for him if he was forced to get anywhere close to a bed with Raine and then leave her.

The thought of putting Raine to bed gave rise to a more pleasurable solution to the problem tonight. Exhaustion could be arrived at by much more mutually satisfying means than brandy.

He pushed away from the counter, impatient at the way his mind kept coming back to one thing. One woman. It wasn't a possibility, and it wouldn't be fair to her to offer his protection, give her his body and walk away. A needling idea tormented him, one that slyly suggested walking away might not be necessary, but he knew better. She'd put her life back together over insurmountable odds. He was just beginning to be able to sleep through a solid night, and it had been four years since he'd come home. Once his parents had spoken of grandchildren, had teased about a daughter-in-law, but his mother never spoke of it now. She knew, somehow, in that indiscernible perception a mother has for her child, that something inside of Mac was gnawing away, and it couldn't all be obliterated by the love of a good woman.

Wanting something had never made it happen. That's what Shawna O'Neill had always told him, and he knew from experience that wanting to be whole again, wanting to be the kind of man someone like Raine deserved wasn't going to be enough. And only a bastard would ignore that.

He rubbed a hand over his face, and was half surprised to see the grime on his palm. He hadn't cleaned up after the fire, and he didn't think it would be such a good idea to share the bathroom with Raine. He opened a drawer and pulled out a kitchen towel. Shucking his shirt, he turned on the faucet, cupped some water in both hands and splashed his face and chest. Then he washed his hands, and with careless disregard he wet the towel and dragged it across his torso.

Feeling slightly fresher, if not totally clean, he turned off the water and reached for another towel. He heard a noise behind him and looked over his shoulder. All the blood in his body pooled behind his fly. She was standing in the doorway, and her skin was rosy from the bath. She was wearing a green silky shift that had narrow straps, and every hormone in his body attested to the fact that she was wearing little, if anything, beneath it.

"It occurred to me that you weren't going to be able to find any whiskey in here anyway." She nodded toward the cupboards. "So I really didn't have anything to worry about."

She had plenty to worry about, he wanted to tell her. If she had a notion of the kind of thoughts running through his head right now, he'd guarantee she'd be plenty worried. He picked up a glass from the counter and thrust it at her. "Here." His voice was raspy. "It's brandy. Drink it."

She moved toward him to take it, and his eyes narrowed assessingly. He'd never noticed her hips move with that seductive sway before, and he wondered for just a second if it was purposeful. Then she took the glass from his hand without managing to touch him, and he berated himself for his imagination. He wiped the excess moisture from his chest carelessly, then threw the towel with the other in the corner on the floor. He watched as she leaned against the edge of the table and looked from the contents of the glass to him.

"You didn't by any chance slip a mickey into this, did you?" she asked, only half joking.

"If the brandy does its job, you won't need one. But if you don't trust me, I'll take a drink from it first to prove it."

"Oh, I trust you." Her voice was soft, her gaze direct. "Completely." She moved the glass to her mouth and sipped.

His gut clenched at her words, and at her meaning. *She trusted him.* She could have been talking about his ability to keep her safe, but he knew she wasn't. She'd told him on more than one occasion that he was a better man than he gave himself credit for. He'd never wanted so much to believe that himself. He made himself look away. "You're going to have to drink more than that."

Bracing herself, she swallowed half the contents of the glass. The burning sensation brought tears to her eyes and a gasp to her lips. She shuddered. "It's awful," she said. "I never understood how a person acquired a taste for this stuff."

"Mostly they acquire a taste for what it does for them."

She nodded. There were many ways to forget. She'd been lucky she'd gotten help all those years ago before she'd chosen this one. She drank the rest of the brandy, better prepared for the taste this time. Then, crossing the room, she set the glass on the counter near his wrist.

Mac went still, his nostrils flaring. She was close, and he could smell the hint of lilac in the soap she'd used. Her pulse was beating rapidly in the spot below her jaw, and he couldn't help noticing that her nipples were taut beneath the shift. He thought of that for a moment, of how the material must have rubbed the delicate tips to cause that kind of reaction. He would never have accredited her response to himself.

Turning away abruptly, he picked up the bottle and poured her another healthy shot. What the hell, he thought a little frantically. The sooner she was out of commission, the sooner he could get to his own room alone. And spend the night howling silently at the moon like some damn animal in agony.

He gritted his teeth at the thought. Turning, he almost shoved the glass toward her. She took it, but didn't back away this time. Now she was close enough for him to observe through the glass the sight of her lips parting to accept the liquid. Her upper teeth were visible, and then he focused on the tip of her tongue. As she moved the glass away from her lips, it came out to sweep the errant drops of liquid away.

He watched that unhurried movement intently. The method he'd chosen to relax her was having the opposite effect on him, he realized grimly. His muscles were bunched up into knots, and his groin was drawn tight. He turned away from the sight and reached for his shirt. As he picked it up he noticed it was streaked with soot and he wadded it up and threw it with barely restrained force onto the pile of towels he'd already discarded.

Raine noticed the fury of his movements and watched him uncertainly. He seemed different tonight somehow. His eyes were hooded and intense. He looked as if he was the one in need of relaxation. All of a sudden she questioned the wisdom of her half-formed plan tonight, to see what it would take to make Macauley O'Neill lose his famed control. She was no longer certain she wanted to be responsible for letting all that tightly coiled energy loose.

She escaped his intent gaze by closing her eyes and taking a large swallow. She coughed as the brandy went down, choking a little, and her wrist tipped, spilling the remaining liquid down the front of her gown.

His eyes narrowed to ice blue chips. The brandy traced a path over one nipple and arrowed to her stomach. His gaze followed the trail it took, observing the widening of its path as the thin material soaked up the liquid. He didn't make a move to get her a towel to dry herself. He was out of helpfulness for the night.

Raine wiped away tears from the corner of her eyes. The brandy had taken a burning wrong turn down her windpipe, and it didn't look as if she'd have to worry about drinking the rest of it—she was wearing it instead. She crossed over to Mac and took a dish towel out of the drawer. She dabbed at the wetness with embarrassment. She was a total washout as a femme fatale. Instead of giving her courage, the brandy had loosened her muscles to the point of clumsiness. She raised her eyes to meet his gaze, and her movements gradually stilled.

Macauley's face was taut and wild, and he was watching every move she made with the intent look of a bird of prey. And then he looked in her eyes, and the towel fell, forgotten, from her hand.

Desire. She knew intuitively what she saw in those glittering blue eyes, and the recognition fanned her own. It wasn't an emotion she'd had much familiarity with in the past. But it was impossible to mistake. She'd learned all she knew about the feeling from him.

She reached out a shaky hand to touch him and, if possible, he went even stiller. She traced the strong breastbone that delineated his torso. One thumb brushed gently across the taut nub on his chest, and he hissed. The sound caused her eyelids to droop, and her hand slid lower. He caught it in his own.

"Time to get you to bed," he said, his voice a hoarse rasp.

She knew there was no sensual hidden meaning in his words, and she could have wept. She was inexperienced, but enough of a woman to know that he wanted her. And enough of a realist to know he wasn't going to allow himself to act on his desire.

She preceded him out of the kitchen. He went through the routine of the last few weeks. He locked the back door and flicked the light off behind her. Checking the door to the garage, he efficiently moved to the front, locked it and set the alarm. He caught up with her where she'd hesitated at the stairs, and unthinkingly reached by her to flip off the lights. He heard her gasp and knew immediately what he'd done. He'd witnessed her careful progress through the house enough times. Before turning off the light for the room in back of her, Raine always flipped on the one ahead. One hand reversed his careless act, but not before her body had slammed against his, her fingers grasping at the waistband of his jeans.

He knew, with his head, that he'd startled her with the abrupt descension of darkness. He never would have been so careless if his mind hadn't been shattered in a million different pieces from watching her a few minutes ago. But even knowing that her need for him stemmed from her fear couldn't dim the tidal wave of arousal that finally burst forth.

His hand dropped of its own accord and traveled quickly to fasten on her waist. He pulled her even closer, lowered his mouth and found hers. The simmering desire he'd been fighting boiled out of control, and reason receded. Her lips were sweet with the remnants of the brandy, and without thought he pressed them open and swept the taste of the liquor from her mouth with his tongue. He couldn't blame the brandy for the speed with which her taste went to his head. Her hands, which had had such a death grip on the waistband of his pants, moved upward to clasp around his waist.

Without releasing her lips, he slipped his arm below her buttocks and lifted her up a step, so she was closer to his own height. He angled his mouth for a closer fit, and the demand it made was implicit. His tongue skated over hers and then returned to claim it.

Her knees grew weak, and Raine's arms climbed to twine around his neck, one hand entangling in the longer hair at his nape. The speed with which his dam of desire had burst dizzied her. But its strength erased the single moment of panic she'd had in the darkness, and it was forgotten in the surging pleasure of his touch.

The moisture on the front of Raine's nightgown dampened his skin, and Mac broke the kiss as he remembered how the wetness had occurred. Panting, he drew the material of the shift tightly across her breast and lowered his mouth, finding the spot where she'd spilled. He sucked strongly, a little roughly, the brandy on the material coating his tongue as he lashed the pebbled hardness of her nipple beneath.

A broken cry came from her, and she twisted against his mouth. This was what she'd wanted, his control broken, his reason gone. For a moment, earlier, she'd been almost frightened by the thought of unleashing his passion. But now she couldn't get enough of it. She'd never expected that she could inspire such emotion in a man, nor that she'd want to. But Macauley's loss of control sent shivers of exhilaration shooting through her veins.

The narrow straps of her shift were lowered down her slim arms, and Mac raised his head. The fabric was wet from his mouth over her breast, and he observed the pouting nipple thrusting against it. Then he pulled the material down to her wrists and turned her so her back was against the railing. He went down on one knee in front of her and drew his chest across her breasts.

Sparks flew inside her at the rasp of his hair-roughened torso dragging against her sensitized nipples. Her breath caught at the exquisite sensation, so pleasurable it bordered on pain. And then she felt herself being held closer, her shoulders arching over the railing as wet heat enclosed her nipple. The suction of his mouth caused a corresponding weakness in her limbs.

Mac raised his head slightly and looked down at her with slitted eyes. Her pretty breasts were shapely, almost conical, her pink nipples drawn to firm points. His hand replaced his mouth on the breast he'd abandoned, massaging it as his other hand plumped its twin for his lips.

His lips tugged at her, and the searing heat was suddenly too much Raine. She twisted in his arms. The shift had slid down to her wrists, and suddenly she couldn't bear to have her hands confined. She wanted them free, like his. She wanted the pleasure of skating them over his skin, finding the places that made him moan. When he raised his head again she wiggled from the narrow straps, her hands gliding up his chest.

He watched as the silky fabric caught on her narrow hips, draping enticingly. He curled his fingers into the material and gave it a little tug, sending it to pool at her feet. He squeezed his eyes shut tightly, fighting for control. She wore only a scrap of midnight blue panties, more lace than fabric, which hinted enticingly at the mysterious shadow beneath them.

The blood in his groin pounded demandingly. He cupped her mound in one large palm and pressed once, then again. She gasped and twisted against his hand. The other slipped behind her and palmed one lace-clad buttock, squeezing gently. Raine opened her mouth against his chest, dragging the tip of her tongue across one taut male nub, wanting to bring him a measure of the torment he was subjecting her to. Her hands stroked his chest, kneading his muscles, before dropping to his waist.

When one delicate finger drew a pattern in the whorl of hair above his navel, Mac drew in his breath sharply. He found the taut bundle of nerves between her legs, and his thumb tapped against it, eyes glinting with satisfaction when she bucked against him. He repeated the motion over and over.

Raine's hands clenched for an instant at his waistband, then with shaky fingers she released the button of his jeans. She lingered on the hard long length pressed tightly against the fly, fingers rubbing gently up and down. His mouth came down on hers fiercely, and she lowered the zipper.

His breath hissed against her lips when he felt her small hands reach inside the jeans to hold him. His control shredded when, an instant later, the jeans were pushed impatiently off his hips and she was cradling all of him between her hands.

With a primitive, unconscious movement he pushed heavily into her touch. He reached a hand down to close over hers, teaching her the motion, groaning when she mimicked the action perfectly.

She couldn't get enough of him. Her wandering fingers traced his length, then returned to squeeze gently. Then her breath was lost as her panties were drawn down her legs.

"Step out of them," he rasped, and she obeyed mindlessly. He insinuated a knee between her legs, parting her for the return of his hand. This time he let his fingers slide through the delicate folds until he found the slick, damp heat of her. He eased a finger inside her and watched her go wild in his arms.

She moaned and her inner muscles clenched. He used his knee to widen her stance, and his other arm snaked around her back, pulling her closer. He took her mouth in a deep, wild kiss, at the same time probing more deeply with his finger. His thumb rubbed rhythmically in accompaniment to his finger, and she whimpered into his mouth at the dual assault.

He wanted her hot, writhing, ready for him. He wanted to wipe out anything that had come before this moment and leave only a lasting, searing memory of the two of them. But she was wet silk against his hand, and the feel of her straining against him, the sound of the little whimpers she was making torched his own control. He wanted her now—here and right now. He didn't want to wait, couldn't take a few precious moments to move her to a bed. He pushed his jeans and briefs off and kicked them away. Reaching for her again, he lifted her up with one arm beneath her buttocks.

He turned her away from the railing and pressed her back against the wall. He was between her legs, the tip of his shaft just nudging her tight entrance, when a modicum of reason skated across his mind. Not only had he surrendered his last remaining vow to do what was best, what was right for Raine. He wasn't taking enough care with her, not being gentle enough. He didn't want to bring back traumatic memories. Squeezing his eyes tightly together, he threw back his head and clenched his teeth. His body was heaving, his muscles trembling as he fought the passion-induced haze.

She sensed the precise moment he had second thoughts. Her eyes flew open, and the sight of his big body trembling with effort against hers almost snapped her last link to sanity. "No, Macauley," she whispered fiercely, achingly. She didn't want his thought, or his gentleness. She wanted him the way he'd taken her the first time, sensual longing without thinking. She'd accept nothing less from him now. She moved slightly, and the blunt tip of his sex probed her. His forehead fell to lay against hers. His chest heaved as he drew in great breaths of air. "Now," she panted. "Right now. Like this."

There had been an instant, just an instant, when he actually believed he'd be able to pull away, to do the decent thing and leave her. But her words managed to convince him as nothing else could. She moved experimentally against him, and he groaned. He pulled her legs around his hips, bracing her bottom with one arm. Then he let reason fade as he obeyed his screaming impulses and surged strongly into her.

Her teeth closed on his shoulder, but he didn't feel the sting of pain. Sweating and shaking, he held still in her and slipped one hand between their bodies. Finding her sensitized nub again, he pleasured her with his fingers until she was moaning and writhing, moving wildly on him. Only when he could feel how close she was to completion did he let his body take over.

His next thrust was deeper, and Raine cried out brokenly. He caught the sound in his mouth and surged into her again. Reflexively she tightened her legs around his waist and clung to his wide shoulders. Her muscles were coiled so tightly, she felt as though she'd explode. She moved against him frantically, accepting his thrusts and searching unconsciously for something just out of reach. His hips slammed against hers again, and suddenly her senses exploded. Waves of ecstasy transported her to a place she'd only experienced with him.

Feeling her delicate convulsions around him was all it took to shatter Mac's control. With one more wild, deep thrust, he crested, and reality faded away.

Chapter 13

Their breathing slowed after long minutes. When Mac finally raised his head from Raine's shoulder, she was almost afraid to open her eyes. Only now did she remember the regret that had stamped his face after the first time he'd made love to her. She wasn't sure she could tolerate it again. She forced herself to open her eyes, steeling herself against what she'd find in his.

He stared at her and reached up a hand to brush the hair from her forehead. The tenderness of the motion almost made her weep. Brushing a kiss across the skin he'd just bared, he began to withdraw from her body. She gasped a little at the feeling of desolation that swept her at the separation. As if reading her mind, he didn't back away as he lowered her body down his. Instead he scooped her up, and regardless of the clothes strewn behind them, walked deliberately up the stairs.

He didn't stop until he'd reached her room. Then he knelt on the bed and laid her carefully down. She didn't let go of his shoulders. She wasn't going to let him leave her without saying a thing. He was going to have to speak the words, although if he apologized to her this time, she knew she would break down.

He studied her face in the dim light that spilled into the room from the hallway. After several long moments he spoke. "I'm not sure this is what you needed tonight, Raine." His voice was low.

She scooted up to a sitting position. One hand went to his jaw. It was so rare to see him completely clean-shaven that she gave into an urge she'd had all evening and ran the back of her hand along his cheek lingeringly. Looking straight into his eyes, she murmured, "I needed *you*, tonight, Macauley. Only you."

He closed his eyes tightly for a moment. An emotion washed over him that he couldn't identify, didn't dare identify. She'd needed him. He knew she wasn't talking about protection from the person threatening her. She meant him, Mac O'Neill. He'd never been needed like that before, wanted for himself only, and the feeling was gut-wrenchingly alluring.

It was also quite possibly the most frightening thing he'd ever had to face.

"I'll be right back," he muttered and pushed off the bed.

Raine let out a shaky breath. She'd just taken a huge risk, and he'd almost run from her room. But not before she'd witnessed the effect her words had on him. They had meant something to him, she was certain of that. She just wasn't certain what.

She'd faced many of her own fears over the last few years. But learning to let another person walk up behind her and facing her fear of the dark hadn't left her nearly as vulnerable as laying her heart out to this man. He wasn't comfortable with emotion, not from others, and most certainly not from himself. She didn't know why she'd expected any different reaction from him. Or why she let it hurt so much.

He entered the room again, a wet cloth in his hand. Seating himself on the side of the bed, he bent over her and slowly, carefully drew the cloth between her thighs. They clenched reflexively at the intimate gesture. It was ridiculous to feel embarrassed after what they'd shared, but she couldn't control the feeling. She looked into his face. His expression was a little grim, but determined. Slowly she relaxed and he completed the task, his face a mask of intense concentration.

When he'd finished and pulled away, she forced herself to remain silent. She wasn't going to beg him to stay with her; she wouldn't allow herself to. Raine wasn't sure she would be able to stop once she started pleading. His back was turned toward her as he sat on the edge of the bed, and she could see the muscles play across the broad expanse. He looked like a man fighting a war with himself, and her heart ached painfully for him.

Then his muscles untensed. He turned deliberately and lay beside her, drawing her close to him. With one hand he pulled the sheet over the two of them. Then he arranged her against him, pressing her face to the hollow of his shoulder and anchoring her to him with one strong leg across both of hers. His arm wrapped across her waist.

Recognizing the inner struggle that had taken place, she realized what this decision had cost him. Her heart squeezed with joy as she snuggled into his embrace. One lone tear trickled from the corner of her eye. "Macauley," she whispered achingly.

A feather-light kiss brushed against her hair. "Sleep, baby," he ordered huskily. "I'll stay. Just sleep."

Her breathing gradually slowing, her body relaxed against his. Mac fought slumber as he held her. The feel of her in his arms, soft and trusting, was too sweet not to savor. He stared into the blanket of darkness, waiting for the guilt to begin, for the regret to take over. Reason had a way of seeping insidiously back into a mind that had only moments ago been lost to passion. But the guilt, though hovering at a distance, for once stayed at bay. This had felt too damn right, too inevitable to regret. His mind was racing in furious circles, trying to reconcile what he knew was right with taking what he wanted.

Because all he wanted was the woman cradled in his arms right now.

Raine came awake to the delicious aroma of coffee. Her vision was the last of her senses to become alert. Slowly she managed to open her eyes.

Macauley was sitting next to her on the side of the bed, waving a mug of coffee under her nose. Her eyes dropped again, a smile creeping across her lips. The happiness that filled her was idiotic, and impossible to suppress. "I've said it before," she murmured lazily. "You're a handy guy to have around."

"Always glad to be of service, ma'am," he drawled.

One of her eyes popped open and then the other. She studied him suspiciously. His face was impassive. There was no way of guessing if the double entendre had been intentional or not. She sighed and rubbed her eyes. Sitting up in bed, she rested against the headboard and reached out for the mug he was offering her.

"Mmm," she said appreciatively, after she'd taken a sip. "Thank you. But where's yours?"

"I've already had half a pot," he answered dryly.

He was wearing a pair of jeans and nothing else, but she could tell that he'd been up for a while. His hair was still damp, and curling slightly in back. And he had obviously had a recent shave.

She reached out and ran a finger along his chin. "Twice in twenty-four hours," she said teasingly. "What's the occasion, O'Neill?"

"If it calls for that kind of reaction," he muttered, "I need to shave more often."

"Not on my account," she assured him. "I've developed a real appreciation for that slightly sinister look you affect."

His look wasn't amused, but she smiled anyway. "What have you been doing since you've been up?" she asked. "I mean, besides drinking gallons of coffee and pruning that beard of yours?"

He cocked an eyebrow. "Sassy this morning, aren't you?"

She stretched, not quite innocently, and her leg beneath the sheet glided over to touch his hip. "Yep. What are you going to do about it?"

He felt a jolt of electricity from her touch, even through the bedcovers. He wasn't going to consider answering that question. What he would like to do about it didn't bear thinking of, much less discussing. Having a conversation of any kind in her bedroom this morning probably hadn't been a real wise move.

His mouth twisted. Wise moves hadn't exactly been his forte lately.

He moved off the bed. "I thought," he said, his voice slightly hoarse, "you might want to get away for a little while today. Unless you need to work, of course."

She studied him in surprise. That suggestion was almost the last she would have expected from him. Waking up to find him there with coffee had allayed her fear that he was going to withdraw completely, as he had the last time they'd made love. The fact that he wasn't had fragile hope blooming inside her.

"I think I can spare a few hours," she finally responded. "Just don't tell André I'm loafing, though."

"He won't hear it from me," Mac promised dryly.

"Actually, I'm almost done with my last piece. Just a few more hours will do it. So I'm okay on time."

"Good." His voice was filled with satisfaction. "Then get cleaned up and dress for swimming."

"We're going to the beach?" Her amazement grew.

"That," he said, as he moved toward the door, "is exactly where we're going. We'll have to stop on the way and pick up some lunch. How fast can you get ready?"

"A half hour."

He stopped in the doorway and issued her a disbelieving look. "There isn't a woman on earth who can move that fast, honey. The truck leaves in an hour. Better get your tush out of bed if you want to be in it." Mac ducked out of the room while she was still sputtering.

"Chauvinist!" she called after him. She could picture the cocky grin on his face as his answer floated back.

"Fifty-nine minutes and counting."

Muttering to herself, Raine flung back the covers and put on her robe. She'd make him eat those words by getting ready in half the time he'd given her. But to do so, she was really going to have to fly.

Twenty-five minutes later she pulled a coverup over her swimsuit and slipped into a pair of sandals. As she picked up the beach bag she'd packed, she heard a male voice call her name from downstairs. "I'm coming," she shouted. Running down the stairs, she scolded, "That wasn't even a half hour, you're not as patient as you—" She stopped in her tracks as Greg ambled out of the den.

"Raine." His earnest brown eyes were worried. "What in heaven's name happened here? Your porch is a charred mess."

"I know," she replied, biting her lip. The night she'd spent in Mac's arms had successfully driven the trauma of the fire from her mind, at least for a while. "Someone drove out here last night and left several bottle bombs as calling cards. But I'm all right," she hastened to add, stemming his next question. "Mac—I mean," she stammered, "the police and the fire department came. There wasn't too much damage done."

"This is horrible!" he exclaimed, pushing his glasses up the bridge of his nose. "My God, Raine, you could have been killed!"

"Things could have gotten serious," she admitted. "I was fortunate that help arrived in time to keep the fire from spreading to the house. I really believe that some of the, um, security measures we've taken around here scared them off." She supposed at the beginning Macauley's presence in her life could be loosely defined as a security measure, she mentally excused herself. "Did you bring something out that needed my signature?" she asked quickly, nodding toward the file folder in his hand.

Her change of subject didn't entirely wipe the worry from Greg's face, but he answered, "Well, yes, I thought it might be a good time to go over those papers I've been talking about, but I see you're ready to go out."

It suddenly occurred to Raine that she was standing in the very spot where she and Macauley had made love last night. Color suffused her face, and she looked around surreptitiously. She released a relieved breath when she noted that the clothing they'd left strewn around had been picked up. Then her eyes lit on her panties, on the floor next to the staircase. Although Greg hadn't seemed to notice, to Raine they seemed a banner proclaiming last night's lovemaking.

Turning her gaze to Greg, she said with an overbright voice, "Actually, I was planning to go to the beach today. But if we can run through this quickly, I can spare you half an hour or so. I'll join you in the den."

He looked at her a little oddly, but turned to precede her into the room. As soon as his back was to her, she bounded down the rest of the steps and scooped the telltale scrap of material up, shoving it into her beach bag with shaky hands. Then, casting one more quick glance around for Macauley, she followed Greg into the den.

"I'm glad we're doing this now," he was saying. "You really can't afford to let this go much longer. Especially with your new exhibit coming up. You're realizing some nice profits from your paintings, Raine, and since you won't let me talk you into some new deductions..."

"We've been over this, Greg," she said dryly as she sat down on the couch. "I don't need a second home. Or a boat large enough to house a family."

"That's what I mean," he continued doggedly. "So I've outlined some other ways that will help defer your tax load. When your new pieces start selling, we need to have a clear plan for investing that money in a way that will reap the greatest return for you." He sat next to her and laid his folder on the coffee table in front of them. Spreading some sheets out in front of him, he explained his suggestions enthusiastically.

Raine looked up in relief when Mac entered a half hour later. Turning to Greg, she said firmly, "It sounds great, as usual, Greg. You're a genius. Now, show me where to sign and you'll be able to get back to work."

"And we'll be able to be on our way to the beach," Mac drawled, drawing Greg's attention to him for the first time.

The man's gaze swung to the door, then to Raine, then to Mac again. "O'Neill." Greg's voice was confused. "What are you doing here?"

"He's taking me out for some sun and sand," Raine told him. At Greg's shocked expression, she added wryly, "I really do have a life outside of painting, you know, although it doesn't seem like it sometimes."

Her words seemed to finally filter through Greg's shock. He looked at her, his puzzlement still obvious. "What? Oh, I know. I just . . . I didn't realize . . ." He finally stopped stammering and looked at Mac, consternation written all over his face. "I thought you were finished with your work here."

"You did?" Mac murmured, his eyes intent on the other man.

"I mean . . . the last time I was here it looked like you were getting done. Is there still a lot left to do?"

"Just odds and ends," Mac replied, smoothly forestalling a reply from Raine. "My only job today is to get Raine away from here for a while. She needs a break."

It was obvious that his answer didn't satisfy Greg. He shot a troubled look at Raine.

"Greg?" she asked quizzically. He always became flustered easily, but right now he was acting especially strange. "May I sign now?"

"Oh, of course." He hurriedly bent over the papers he'd been explaining to her.

He indicated a few places, and she signed her name. Then she smiled at him. "Thanks so much for bringing these over today. You were right. I needed to make some financial plans, but I kept putting it off. Lucky for me you're so dedicated."

Greg seemed reluctant to leave, and Raine walked him to his car. Mac grabbed the bag she'd packed and the cooler he'd set in the doorway and hauled them out to his truck. Raine joined him, and a few minutes later they were on their way.

"Greg was acting odd this morning," she mentioned, a frown on her face.

Mac looked at her. "How can you tell the difference?"

"Be nice," she scolded him. "He's a very pleasant young man, and an excellent accountant. He just gets easily agitated. I'm sure seeing the porch and hearing about what happened last night rattled him."

Returning his gaze to the road, Mac shook his head. "Greg Winters is not a young man. I'd bet he's older than you. And if you want to know the cause of his agitation, look in the mirror."

It took Raine a second to grasp his meaning. Then she swung her head to look at him. "Me? Why would I fluster him? I'm about as threatening as a housefly."

"I didn't say you threaten him, Raine. But you do bother him. Surely you're not so naive that you can't figure out why?"

When she didn't answer, he sighed. "C'mon. He hangs around you as much as he can, looking like a lovesick puppy dog. He comes up with excuses to leave his office when he should be working and runs out to see you. What do you make of that?" He could tell by her frown that she was uncomfortable with his pursuit of the subject.

"We're . . . just friends. Greg knows it will never be more than that, and he's accepted it. He and I have talked about it before."

"You may have talked about it, but I wouldn't be too sure about his acceptance of that fact," he replied. "He was gibbering because he couldn't figure out where I came into the picture, and he didn't like the thought of you going anywhere at all with me."

Her brows lifted. "You mean you've had words with him, too?"

"He hasn't been as anxious to slit my throat as Klassen is," Mac said thoughtfully. "Although knowing that I'm going to spend the day with you probably has him harboring some homicidal thoughts toward me at the moment."

"You know, O'Neill, that suspicious nature of yours can be a real pain."

He resisted the urge to remind her that his suspicious nature was also quite possibly going to keep her alive. He pulled into the parking lot of a drugstore. "You'd better come in with me," he said. He didn't want to let her out of his sight. He'd been outside talking to the men when he'd identified Winters's car coming up the drive, and had entered the house only moments after Raine had shown the man to the den. He'd felt like a spy as he hung around outside the room, but he'd been loath to leave the two of them completely alone. Especially after what Trey had discovered in the man's apartment.

With the idea of picking up some sunscreen, Raine obediently accompanied Mac into the drugstore. She wandered away from him and selected some sun block. Then she picked up a daily paper, took her items to the counter and paid for them. She opened up the paper as she waited for Mac to finish his shopping. When she got to the arts and entertainment section, her own face stared back at her. Local Artist Threatened was the headline above the picture. She groaned mentally. Darn André for giving that information to the press! She should have known it was too sensational for the media to ignore. No doubt she'd have to field yet another phone call from her father when he got hold of this. She knew she wouldn't have to warn him to keep this news from reaching her mother. Lorena never saw a newspaper that Simon hadn't screened first.

Raine shot a look at Macauley, who was heading for the checkout counter. Surreptitiously, she replaced the paper before joining him. There was no need to call the article to his attention. It would only serve to elicit another nasty remark about André. She joined him in line, and Macauley put his selections on the counter, pulling his wallet out to pay. For the first time Raine looked at what he was buying, and slow heat suffused her cheeks. The clerk rang up the box of condoms in front of her without a second glance. But Raine couldn't stop her gaze from flying to meet his.

Tiny twin reflections of herself shone in his dark glasses. She remembered how carefully he'd protected her that first time and, more enticing, she remembered just how hot it had been last night, how out of control. There hadn't been time, or thought, for protection. There'd been nothing between them, and a flashback of his velvety hardness inside her made her mouth tremble.

Something wild leaped inside Mac as he read the look on her face. Her expression was tantalizingly, innocently transparent. His blood began to pound as he read her thoughts. Never before had he failed to protect his partner. Not when he was a randy teenager, little more than a walking hormone, and never as an adult. Last night had been a first for him in that respect, and the lapse was disturbing. It was bad enough to realize he'd lost control so easily that he'd never given protection a second thought. But that wasn't what had his jeans growing so tight now. No, that particular discomfort was due to the exquisite memory of how tightly she'd sheathed him, and how mind-blowingly fantastic it had felt to take her without anything between them. It was that memory, and not the concern over lack of protection, that had kept him awake for hours after she slept. He was no longer able to fool himself that he could withstand the lure Raine held for him. But he wasn't going to take a risk with her again, and that vow had made this stop necessary.

"Sir?"

His head snapped to the clerk. She repeated the price for his purchase, and he quickly extracted a bill from his wallet and handed it to her. Shoving his change into his pocket, he slipped his wallet in place. Grabbing the sack in one hand and Raine's elbow in the other, he growled softly in her ear, "Let's go."

They made one more stop, for a bucket of fried chicken and fixings, and then headed toward the coast. For the duration of the trip, Raine remained shaky from the silent, heated exchange. She usually lamented over how hard Macauley was to read. But in the drugstore his thoughts had been erotically clear.

When they finally stopped, she hopped out of the truck, eager to enjoy the spectacular view. Belatedly remembering that she had left him with everything to carry, she hurried back. He handed her her beach bag, stacked the food on the cooler and climbed out of the truck.

"Mac, there's a sign that says this is private property," she told him worriedly.

His long legs kept moving. "It is. I just finished a job for the owner last month."

She had to trot to keep up with him. "He said you could use it?"

One corner of his mouth went up when he thought of the owner, and of Mark Rayburn's gratitude when the job had been completed successfully on time. "He was . . . grateful," Mac acknowledged laconically. Access to the prime beachfront property was the least of what he'd offered Mac. He'd also been willing to introduce him to his daughter. Mac had accepted the first offer and declined the second. "He's rarely here to use it himself. He has six other houses, I think."

Raine scrambled down the dunes of sand, which had formed from the constant breeze off the ocean. "It's beautiful," she said, her voice hushed. Huge craggy rocks jutted up from the water. The waves crashed over them, sending splintered sprays of foam racing to the shore. More rocks dotted the beach, combining with the dunes to create an isolated, private paradise. "I can't believe your client needs so many homes when he has one with a view like this."

Mac set down his load and extracted two soft drinks from the cooler. When he turned back, his mouth went as dry as the sand beneath his feet. Raine had taken off her coverup to reveal a fairly modest bright blue one-piece suit. It was cut high on the thighs, showing off her slim legs to advantage. Other than that, there was nothing the least bit daring about it. Mac was used to his female companions showing quite a bit more skin at the beach, either in a thong bikini or in nothing at all. He couldn't remember any of them eliciting this kind of reaction from him. He watched her slim hips move as she took two large beach towels from her bag and spread them out on the sand.

He went over and dropped down on one. "You like it here?" he asked.

"It's gorgeous," she said sincerely. "I adore the water. There's something so calming in watching the rhythm of the tide. If my finances had allowed it, beachfront would have been my choice when I bought my property. But the first time I saw my house, I felt that same kind of peace. It was a good choice for me."

He'd been thinking about this all last night, and again this morning. But now, broaching the subject with her, he felt as though he was picking his way through a mine field. "What I mean is, if you like it here, you could stay for a while. We both could. It would just take one phone call to the owner. Just until this whole thing is over."

She grew still as his meaning became clear. "You mean hide here." Her voice was flat.

"No. I mean make sure you aren't a target anymore. Keep a low profile. After the fire last night that should appeal to you."

"Should it?" She turned to look at him. "Is that why you brought me here?" It was important all of a sudden for her to know. "Did you just want to get me out of the house so you could talk sense into me? Talk me into running away?"

His chest grew tight at the hurt that flickered across her face. It didn't seem as if he could do anything right around her, and he cursed himself for his clumsiness. "It's an option," he said evenly. "You wanted to be apprised of all aspects of the case. You wanted to make the decisions. Well, this is a choice."

She stared hard at him and then slowly relaxed. He was telling her the truth. And he was making it incredibly easy for her. All she had to say was yes. It was that simple. And he would see to it that whoever was harassing her wouldn't even know where she was. No one could get to her, and she wouldn't have to be afraid anymore. It would be so easy to agree.

"I can't," she said softly, looking away. "I appreciate what you're trying to do, but I just can't. Try to understand, Macauley. I stopped running a long time ago, and it wasn't an easy habit to break. I can't let myself begin again." She knew she couldn't adequately explain her determination to stand up to the threats in her own way. Certainly it wasn't bravery on her part. It was more a need to fight against being overtaken by a fear that could be as crippling as any disease.

He was quiet for several minutes. His voice, when it came, was low. "All right. But if the time comes when I don't believe I can protect you adequately in your own home, I won't ask."

She looked at him wordlessly.

"I'll pack you up and take you somewhere else, argument or no."

And she knew he wouldn't hesitate to do so. She appreciated the fact that he'd allowed her to make this decision. Not long ago, he would have faced her with a fait accompli. She wondered if he realized the significance of giving her this choice.

After a time she murmured, "I love the sound of the ocean." She turned to look at Mac. "Sarah and I have been to Cancun three times. It's great. Beautiful white beaches and rowdy bars downtown." She smiled in remembrance. "Every time we go to the marketplace she tries to talk me into a tattoo."

At his swift look down her body, she laughed. "She hasn't convinced me yet. I'm not quite that adventurous. But I do like to return there. My idea of a perfect vacation would be to be out in the ocean on a seaworthy boat. I'd like to just drift, putting in to shore when I felt like it."

Her tone was almost wistful, and her description appealing. It was damn close to what he'd had in mind for himself, before he'd agreed to take on another job. Before Raine.

They drowsed in the sun for the next couple of hours. Raine put on sunglasses against the glare of the sun, and to hide the fact that her gaze wandered, again and again, to Mac's bare chest. He lay sprawled out on his back, looking like a sun god fallen to earth. His chest was already brown, and she remembered suddenly the remark he had made once about an all-over tan. Her eyes traveled down his torso to where his waist narrowed in the black trunks. His body would be firm, smooth and warm. Her hand was tempted to touch him, but she couldn't quite work up the courage.

Sensing her gaze on him, he turned on his side to face her. He took his glasses off and surveyed her soberly. Reaching out with one finger, he traced the line where her suit met the top of her breasts. She caught her breath at the action.

"Did you know all of those people at Klassen's party last night?"

His question came out of the blue. And the movement of his finger made it difficult to formulate an answer.

"I . . . no. That is, André introduced me to most of them. A few—" Her voice broke off when his finger dipped into the valley of her cleavage. "A few I'd met . . . before."

"There was an older man last night you were talking to." His voice was expressionless, completely at odds with the liberty his errant finger was taking. "He had his hand planted on your arm the whole time." He paused a heartbeat before adding almost soundlessly, "I didn't like it."

She remembered. She hadn't enjoyed the feel of his hand on her bare skin, and had moved away as quickly as possible. "I've had to learn to handle myself in a crowd like that."

Mac's gaze was on the journey his finger was taking as it trailed inside her suit and skated over one nipple. Then his eyes returned to hers. "I didn't like it," he repeated flatly. Nor did he like the accompanying sensation of jealousy. It had been an emotion so unfamiliar that it had taken him a while to identify it. Jealousy was an unproductive emotion, a dangerous one. Jealous men acted rashly; they made mistakes. He couldn't afford to make a mistake with Raine.

He hoped he wasn't making one now, by allowing her to stay in her home. He'd weighed all the risks as he'd lain awake last night, and again this morning. He thought it would be fairly safe. After all, Raine wasn't alone out there—she had him. She wouldn't be hurt as long as she followed his orders. It still would be a couple of weeks before the fence would be completed and the gates operational. But if this mess escalated, he'd remove her despite her protests.

His thoughts scattered when he felt her small hand on his chest. He reached over and removed her sunglasses. She could never hide her emotions from him if he could see her eyes. His stomach clenched when he read the desire simmering there. Her nipples stood up under the thin material of the swimsuit. He touched them, and she shuddered. He smiled slowly. She was innocently responsive to him, and she couldn't disguise her reaction. The thought filled him with a purely male satisfaction.

He bent over her and pulled the swimsuit off both shoulders. Then he stopped, caught indecisively between pleasurable choices. He wanted to kiss her pretty breasts, but he tortured himself first by just looking at her. When they'd made love last night it had been too frantic, almost out of control. Today he wanted to take his time, to find all the secret places on her body that responded to him. Leisurely, he cupped one breast, enjoying the way it filled his

palm. It was delicate, just as she was, and warmed by the sun.
When he put his lips to her nipple and rolled it with his tongue, she
made that little whimper in the back of her throat that had an immediate, electric effect on his groin. Maybe this wasn't going to be
as leisurely as he'd planned.

He moved closer to her, and she wriggled her arms free of the
swimsuit straps so they could roam freely over his broad torso. The
hair on his chest rasped her fingertips as she combed through it.
She traced the muscles that defined his chest, then circled the nipples. She lost her breath as he raised his head and removed her
swimsuit. Her eyes flew open, and she watched him stare at her
with frank appreciation. There was something a little pagan about
being stripped bare in the sunlight for a man's enjoyment. No, not
just a man, she corrected herself fuzzily. Macauley. His hand began sliding up one thigh, across her stomach and down the other.
Long, soothing strokes. But there was nothing soothing in the wake
of fire left in his path.

Her hand went to the waistband of his trunks, and one finger
dipped inside. Stroking his belly with that one finger, she asked
huskily, "Aren't you forgetting something?"

His eyes were slitted with pleasure. "You do the honors." Her
gaze flew to his, and he knew in that moment that she had never
undressed a man before. But before he could berate himself for
pushing her, he saw interest light her eyes. She was intrigued by the
prospect. He lay back on the towel and watched her.

As fascinating as his invitation had been, Raine didn't quite
know how to go about carrying it out. Her fingers went to the
waistband of his trunks and then faltered. She glanced at his face
uncertainly. What she saw there was encouraging. His eyes were
hooded, his nostrils flared. He was finding pleasure in just watching her undress him. The knowledge gave her courage. Her hands
again pulled at his trunks, and this time he lifted his hips to aid her.
The action put the long, hard length straining inside the suit just
inches from her mouth.

Her lips parted, and she hesitated. Then slowly, she released his
throbbing manhood from the material encasing him and pulled the
trunks down his muscled legs. He kicked free of them.

Raine stayed where she was, half bent over him, unable to move.
There was something particularly sexy about a man who would lay
back and let a woman enjoy his body. He had neatly reversed their
positions, and despite her unfamiliarity with the role, she wasn't
going to waste the opportunity.

She caressed his muscled thighs, skirted his straining manhood and stroked his belly. Then her fingers trailed downward again, closer this time, but still avoiding his hard length shyly. He withstood the teasing trail of her fingers for long minutes, feeling himself grow thicker and harder with each pass. Finally he groaned, "Raine."

Her eyes met his.

"Touch me," he begged huskily. "C'mon, baby, you're driving me crazy. Or don't you want to?"

"Oh, yes," she breathed, allowing her fingers to close around his hardness at last. "I do want to."

A strangled moan was her only answer as she gave in to the temptation of his body and explored him as intimately as he had her the night before. Then she bent her head and whispered her lips against the velvety tip of his manhood in a kiss as light as butterfly wings. Again and again she returned there, until Mac's flagging control demanded an end to her play.

He snaked an arm around her waist, tumbling her on top of him. Then he captured her mouth in a deep, wet kiss that spoke of his eroding patience. One hand went to her bottom, pressing her more firmly against him, and she squirmed beneath his touch, wanting to be even closer. He stroked a finger between her legs, finding the proof of her readiness in the moist dew at her entrance. She bucked against him at the touch, and his last thought of leisurely lovemaking went up in smoke.

He pulled his mouth away from hers and reached for her beach bag. Dumping the contents, he found one of the foil-wrapped packages he'd tossed in there. She took it from his hand. Their eyes meeting, she opened the packet and moved so that she could put it on him. The action spoke of bone-shattering intimacy, and she knew she was trembling.

He pulled her astride him when she finished, and she blinked at the unfamiliar position. "This time you control it," he rasped. "I don't want to hurt you."

"You haven't," she whispered, even as she experimented with the position. She fitted him to her carefully.

"I could. It doesn't take much with you to make me lose my head, and I don't want to be rough with you." His breath hissed out when he felt her ease down on him slowly. He could feel sweat pop out on his forehead.

She absorbed another inch of him and then another. He could feel her delicate inner muscles pulse in adjustment. When she'd accepted all of him, he heard her gasp at the sensation, and his hands went to her hips. He held her steady as he surged upward, and her gasp became a cry. The rhythm of his thrusts was wildly intoxicating, driving him deeper and deeper within her. Raine gave herself up to the abandoned energy. Her knees clasped his hips tighter and tighter, until the ultimate explosion wrung a cry from her lips. She fell forward, and he lifted within her one more time. Then the tiny convulsions inside her triggered his own climax, and his hands gripped her hips as he drove upward one last time.

They lay depleted of energy in the aftermath, Raine still sprawled above him. The rush of the surf on the sand and the balmy breeze from the ocean combined with the privacy afforded by the rocks and dunes to create an intimate, private cocoon. Mac finally stirred, turning on his side and slipping out of Raine's softness. Nothing would have given him more pleasure than to remain buried inside her, sinking into sleep even as they were still joined. But the protection was fast losing its effectiveness, and there was no way he was going to allow himself to put her at risk again.

She made a murmur of protest, but he pulled her close to him and she contented herself by laying her head against his chest.

"Are you all right?" he asked in a low voice.

She raised her head slightly to look into those ice blue eyes. They hadn't changed color, but they weren't cold now, and they weren't expressionless. They were filled with concern for her, and a faint glimmer of regret. "You could never hurt me," she whispered, brushing her lips across his. "Never."

He remained unconvinced. His eyes held hers and he said deliberately, "I'm afraid I'm going to be too rough, and that you'll..." He swallowed hard and said thickly, "I don't want anything to remind you of that night. I'd never forgive myself if anything we did triggered those memories for you."

"The rape was a long time ago," she said, softly but firmly. "And I've come a long way since then. But nothing you could do would ever remind me, Macauley. Nothing." His concern for her brought an aching tenderness, and she somehow knew that he had given her what he had no other. She wanted to give him something in return. So she gave him the truth. "In my nightmares, I always saw the outline of his shape looming over me. Shadows blending into shadows. But now if I wake from one, I remember the way you looked that first night, bending over me. Your shoulders were broad enough to block out the moonlight, but I wasn't afraid. Not of you, Macauley. Never of you."

He squeezed his eyes shut tightly at the words. She gave him such gifts so sweetly, without reservations. She left herself vulnerable with such offerings. Most people kept a little something of themselves in reserve, so as not to risk too much. She apparently had never learned that lesson. Her words seeped into him, seeming to fill the huge void that had become his life in recent years. The knowledge was scary, but too damn tantalizing to resist. And even then she wasn't done.

Her hand stroked his jaw tenderly. "I love you, Macauley O'Neill. Nothing will ever change that." She pressed her mouth to his when he would have spoken. Kissing him slowly, she drew his bottom lip into her mouth and ran her tongue across it. "I don't expect anything in return. My love is a gift, freely given."

He spoke anyway, around the huge knot her words had caused to form in his throat. "You don't have one ounce of self-preservation, do you? You picked a hell of a guy to give your love to, Raine. A broken-down ex-soldier who's lost his soul."

"I did pick a hell of a man to give my love to." Her inflection changed the meaning of his words. "Don't you worry about me. I think I can survive one Macauley O'Neill."

Her words made a mockery of his concern, even as they highlighted it. Maybe she was right. Maybe he should stop worrying about keeping her safe from him.

Maybe it was time to start worrying about how *he* was going to survive without *her*.

Chapter 14

"Wow, that's some remodeling project going on out there." Sarah prowled to the front window. "The fence is sure going up fast. And what in heaven's name happened to your porch? It looks like you let a barbecue get out of hand."

Raine joined her friend at the window. "The fence is ugly, isn't it?" Her voice was flat. There would be an intercom system, Mac had informed her, linking visitors at the gate to the house. No car could gain access to the drive unless someone in the house pressed the appropriate button. "I feel ridiculous. It's going to look like something from Lifestyles of the Rich and Infamous. But after the fire last week, Mac didn't leave me much choice."

Sarah frowned. "You had a fire on the porch?"

Raine nodded. "Luckily for me, Mac was here. He helped put it out before too much damage was done."

Sarah's concern was momentarily waylaid by her insatiable curiosity. "Mac was here? What was he doing here at night? Or need I ask?"

Turning away from her friend's inquisitive gaze, Raine crossed to the sectional and dropped down on it. "I had no car, remember? And never will have that particular car," she added in an aside. "The insurance adjuster called yesterday, and it's been totaled out. So on top of everything else, I have to go car shopping.''

''And?'' Sarah prompted.

Raine sighed. ''Mac offered me a ride to André's dinner that evening. We hadn't been home long when a car roared up the driveway. The occupants threw some sort of bottle torches up on the porch and took off again.''

''Someone did this on purpose?'' Sarah seemed to sway a little before sinking weakly into a chair. ''Did you at least get a good look, so you can identify them?''

Shaking her head, Raine explained, ''They wore ski masks.''

''Raine, this is getting scary.'' Sarah's pretty face was full of worry. ''I don't know how you can stand this. First the letters, then the accident and now a fire. I would be a gibbering idiot by now if I was in your place. How do you bear staying here alone? Especially at night?''

Hoping her cheeks reflected none of the heat she felt in them, Raine simply murmured, ''I'll be all right.'' Darn it, she wasn't good at lying, especially to her best friend. Aside from Mac's instructions to keep his role here secret from her friends, she now had her own reasons for keeping the information to herself. Her relationship with Mac was too new and much too tenuous to share with anyone else, even someone as close to her as Sarah was. Especially since Raine was so uncertain just what the relationship entailed.

Dubiously, her friend peered at her. ''You don't look all right. You're flushed. And how come you're not painting today? Has all this affected your work? I would be a nervous wreck with all that's been going on.''

''Actually,'' Raine said brightly, glad for the subject change, ''I happen to be finished. André was thrilled when I called and told him. As a matter of fact, I'm expecting him to come by today so we can discuss how we're going to transport my paintings to the gallery next week.''

Sarah looked stunned. ''I don't believe you.'' She shook her head wryly. ''You manage to complete all the paintings in spite of being terrorized for months, and I can't work if I so much as get a hangnail. Sometime you'll have to let me in on your secret.''

''It's a relief to know everything is ready,'' Raine confided. ''At least at my end. André can be pretty demanding, and if I was behind schedule at all he'd have me pulling my hair out. At least now it's all in his hands.''

"I'll say it is," Sarah replied. "I think I noted his fine hand in the articles that made the newspapers a few days ago. I was a little surprised he would play up the fact that you'd been threatened the way he did. At least, I assume he's the one who told the journalists about that."

"You assume right," Raine said dryly. "And I wasn't pleased about the publicity, either. Mac was furious with him."

Sarah looked at her knowingly. "Mac, again, hmm? Funny how his name keeps cropping up. Are you sure there isn't more here that you'd like to talk about?"

Raine cursed her careless tongue. "I mean, after all the security measures he's implemented around here, he thought it was pretty careless of André to make the threats public. He's afraid it will attract the wrong kind of attention."

Sarah shrugged. "Well, it was typical André, I must say. I don't envy your working with him. His fussiness would drive me crazy—although, I have to admit, he gets results. Actually, I may be looking for a new agent myself."

"You're dropping Vanessa?" Raine was surprised. Vanessa Bancroft had represented Sarah for years. Raine had never heard Sarah express dissatisfaction with the woman's work before.

Sarah shrugged. "I don't know. I'm thinking about it. I really didn't do as well as I should have at my last exhibit. And she doesn't market me as aggressively as André does you. I'd like for her to work more closely with Harold than she does. If she would keep after him I'm sure he'd sponsor another show for me soon."

"I didn't realize you were ready for another exhibit."

Sarah got up and strolled to the window, peering outside. "Well, I could be if I had something to work toward. Anyway, I haven't decided for sure whether to replace Vanessa. I'm just thinking out loud."

Raine mulled over Sarah's words, troubled. She wondered if the real reason behind Sarah's dissatisfaction was money. She seemed to have chronic financial problems, despite the fact that her sculptures were starting to command respectable prices. Raine suspected that Sarah handed over a great deal of money to her brother, who wasn't too motivated to make any of his own.

"Speaking of money—" Sarah spoke over her shoulder "—when was the last time you spoke to Greg?"

"Sometime last week, I guess. He came over and I signed some papers. Why?"

"Because I was in his office yesterday." Greg was also Sarah's accountant. "And he seemed very weird to me."

Raine smiled slightly. "He always seems weird to you." Sarah lacked the patience to deal with the man's shy eccentricities. But she'd always been pleased with his work.

Turning to face her, Sarah continued, "No, I mean even weirder than usual. He was real distracted. I kept having to repeat myself, which was annoying. But then I happened to ask if he'd seen you, because I hadn't talked to you last week, and he got..." She shrugged. "Very strange. He practically snapped my head off, which isn't like him, and he didn't want to talk about you at all, which is *very* unlike him." She cocked her head curiously. "Did you two have a fight or something?"

Frowning, Raine shook her head. Darn it, until the craziness in the past few weeks, Greg *had* seemed okay about the two of them remaining only friends. She definitely was going to have to talk to him soon. However uncomfortable the scene might be, he was a dear friend of hers and she didn't want a void to develop between them.

She belatedly answered her friend. "We didn't have a fight. But I think there might have been a misunderstanding. I'll have to call him."

"You'd better," Sarah agreed. "The poor man probably won't be able to function until you do. Well." She sighed, looking out the window one last time. "I'm beginning to lose hope that the men putting in that fence are ever going to take their shirts off. And if I don't miss my guess, that's André's car coming up the drive. I guess I might as well go home and do something productive."

"Talking to me isn't productive?" Raine teased as she walked her friend to the door.

"Oh, very," Sarah assured her. "But, unfortunately, it isn't getting my latest sculpture done, so I'm going to take a lesson from you and get down to some serious work."

"I'll call you," Raine promised.

"Hi, André." Sarah greeted the man poised on the porch as she swept by him. "Bye, André."

André barely batted an eyelash at Sarah's whirlwind departure. "I'm afraid I received some rather distressing news today, Raine," he began without preamble.

Immediately a knot formed in the pit of her stomach. It was obvious that something had unsettled him. His usual urbane manner seemed almost flustered, and Raine couldn't remember ever seeing him in such a state.

"What . . . what it is it?" Dread laced her words. "Is it another threat?"

Belatedly André seemed aware of the effect his greeting had had on Raine. "No, nothing like that. I'm sorry, I didn't mean to alarm you that way. Let's go in and sit down. Together we can get this latest development ironed out."

Mac appeared in the doorway just as they'd both been seated. "Your mother's on the line, Raine. Do you want to call her back or take it now?"

She bit her lip, torn, then shook her head. "I'll have to call her back."

But André disagreed. "No, go ahead and take the call, Raine. I seem to have upset you, and that was the last thing I meant to do." He flicked his fingers dismissively. "As I said, we have something to discuss, but you and I will get it taken care of. Get your call out of the way first."

Raine hesitated, and then said, "All right, I'll just be a minute. And then you can tell me the whole story." She brushed by Mac, giving him a warning look. "Be nice," she said in an undertone. He cocked an eyebrow at her.

"So, O'Neill," André said, as soon as Raine was out of earshot. "What a surprise it was to come here today and find your men back, working on yet another job for Raine." He gave a thin smile. "It almost makes one think you keep busy finding new ways to spend her money."

Mac leaned against the doorjamb and crossed his arms. "You don't think her security is worth spending money on?"

"Oh, of course. It's also a situation you can milk for all it's worth. A vulnerable woman living alone, one with a rich, overprotective father." His tone was meaningful. "That must seem like a dream come true for a man like you."

"A man like me." Mac's voice was thoughtful. "And what kind of man would that be, Klassen?"

"A very desperate man, perhaps," he suggested. "It seems rather odd the way you keep popping up in Raine's life. Each time something happens to frighten her, coincidentally, you're able to use the new incident to sell yet more security measures."

Mac clapped his hands slowly, sardonically. "Very good, Klassen," he said in mock admiration. "The best defense is a good offense, right?"

The man flushed. "It makes as much sense, I would say, as the accusation you leveled at me the last time we met."

"In your mind, maybe." Mac gave a feral grin. "I'm a bit harder to convince."

Raine came in, interrupting the verbal duel. "I apologize again for the interruption, André."

The man switched his attention from Mac to her and inquired politely, "How is your mother, Raine? Her health is stable, I hope?"

She nodded. "She's doing fine. But I think you better tell me what happened to disturb you so."

He sighed. "Well, this morning I called the gallery I'd reserved for your showing to go over some details and was shocked to learn that they had a break-in last night. Nothing was taken, but there was quite a bit of broken glass and paint thrown all over. Naturally, with our exhibit coming up so rapidly, I'm concerned about how quickly the owner will be able to repair the damage. I've already begun checking with some other galleries in the area. Of course, at this late date, it would be difficult to reserve another. Not to mention the problem with the publicity and invitations."

"You're saying the show may have to be postponed?" Mac asked.

André looked horrified. "Certainly not! There is entirely too much riding on this particular exhibit for us to postpone it. I'm afraid our only hope lies in the owner making the gallery presentable by the time we need it. You can be sure that I'll be in constant contact with him in the time remaining."

Raine was certain that he would. If nothing else, the owner of the gallery would make sure it was ready just to get André off his back.

"I'm still worried about security measures at that gallery, however," André fretted. "After all, what would have stopped those vandals from breaking in and doing all sorts of damage to any works inside? Or stealing them completely? I just wish there was time to find another reputable gallery."

"Did you talk to the owner about security measures?" Mac asked.

"He assured me, of course, that they had adequate protection. He seemed to think his alarm system and the quick response of the police saved the place from a looting. But I'm not completely convinced. At any rate," he said, switching his attention to Raine, "we'll follow the same procedure as always when it comes to transporting your works. You'll supervise the actual loading, of course. We'll probably be pressed for time due to the amount of work the gallery will be having done. So if you can have everything ready to go at a moment's notice, that will be a big help."

Raine agreed. After going over several more points with him, she saw him to the door. Mac hadn't moved from his position in the doorway, stepping aside only to let them pass. When she had bid goodbye to her agent, she came to stand before him.

"Okay, let's have it."

He looked at her silently.

"C'mon, Macauley, I know you well enough by now to know that something is bothering you. So out with it."

He surveyed her lazily. "Think you know me pretty well?"

She took a step closer, and her hair brushed his mouth as she turned her head up to his. "I'm beginning to."

He dropped a quick, hard kiss on her lips, then led her to the couch. "I don't particularly like coincidences. The very gallery that you had reserved for your showing got hit last night, only days before your exhibit."

"I know," she admitted. "I didn't want to seem paranoid, but I couldn't help wondering. Your suspicious nature is starting to rub off, I'm afraid. But if the vandals had really wanted to target me, why didn't they wait until my paintings were there? Why hit the gallery now?"

"To keep your exhibit from taking place?" he suggested.

"But that doesn't make sense," she argued. "Up to this point everything has been designed to frighten me."

"Or to hurt you," he reminded her quietly. "Hurting your career is another way to get at you."

"Maybe." She bounced up restlessly and roamed around the room. "It's hard to predict what's going to happen next. It certainly never occurred to me that the gallery could be a target."

"I'm going to call Detective Ramirez and inform him of the break-in. We're going to assume, for now, that it's connected with you somehow. I wanted to talk to him and see if he's come up with anything lately, anyway." He thought for a moment, then added, "To be on the safe side, I don't want you delivering the pictures the way you usually do with André. It seems to me, if someone wants to stop your showing, the next logical step would be to make sure your paintings never reached the gallery."

"But someone would have to be very familiar with my arrangements to know when and how we would be loading," Raine argued.

"Whoever is behind this knew what gallery was hosting your exhibit," he reminded her.

"That information has been in the papers, Macauley. The way I transport my pictures hasn't."

"You'd be surprised how easy some information is to get, if you ask the right questions. Let's just be cautious, shall we?"

She rubbed her forehead tiredly. He was right, as usual. "What did you have in mind?"

"We've got a van at the office. I'm sure it can be used to carry your pictures to the gallery. You can supervise the loading and tell me how it can be done without damaging anything."

She nodded slowly. "All right." A permanent chill seemed to be settling inside her. She wondered how much longer they could be expected to fight an unknown harasser, trying to predict his next move and counteracting it. It was as exhausting as it was scary. The incredible irony of it was she couldn't even look forward to the end of the threats. Because that would be when Macauley would walk out of her life forever.

Once Raine was occupied in another part of the house, Mac took the opportunity to phone Ramirez. When questioned, the detective admitted that they hadn't found any leads on the person responsible for firebombing Raine's porch.

"I was going to give her a call, though," Ramirez told him. "The postal investigator has pinpointed the general locale in which the last letter originated."

Mac could feel himself grow tense. "What did he find out?"

After hesitating, the detective said, "I can't discuss that with you, Mr. O'Neill. I have to talk to Miss Michaels. Is she there?"

Silently cursing the man's procedures, Mac told him to wait and went looking for Raine. He found her in the kitchen. She looked up at his entrance.

"We are really going to have to break down and get some groceries," she informed him. "It's to the point where we're going to be eating leftover leftovers. I don't know about you, but my stomach is starting to rebel."

"Later," he said. "Right now Ramirez is on the line for you."

His voice was terse, and she gave him a wary look as she hurried by him. "What's he want?"

"I don't know. He wouldn't say."

She picked up the receiver of the phone in the kitchen. "Detective Ramirez, this is Raine Michaels. How are you?"

Mac walked by deliberately and went to the office. There he picked up the phone and unabashedly listened to the conversation.

"The postal investigators have pinpointed the Los Angeles locale where the last letter was mailed," the man was saying as Mac picked up the phone. "At this point, it will be almost impossible for them to catch the person in the act of mailing another letter. But we are trying to match prints we found on the letter with—"

"Raine," Mac cut in smoothly. "Maybe you ought to tell the detective about what happened at the gallery."

"Gallery?" the man repeated. "What gallery is that?"

Raine filled him in on what André had told her. "We're not sure," she said hesitantly after she'd finished. "But Mac thought the coincidence might mean it was linked to me."

"When is your showing scheduled?"

"Next week."

"Sure sounds like it could be related," the detective said. "At any rate, it won't hurt to be extracautious."

"I will," she promised wryly.

"We did find some human hairs in the car that was abandoned after the driver ran you off the road. Unfortunately, we're going to need a suspect before we can make any matches there. I wish we had more good news for you, Miss Michaels."

Mac hung up the phone as they said their goodbyes. A few minutes later Raine was in the doorway.

"What's the matter?" he asked sharply, noting her expression.

Approaching him slowly, she waited until she was next to his desk before answering. "What was that all about?"

He leaned back in his chair in a show of nonchalance, but his stomach clenched reflexively. "What?"

"You interrupted the detective as he was talking about fingerprints."

Mac shrugged. "Sorry. Anyway, all he said was that they were checking for prints."

"But whose prints?" she asked shrewdly. At his silence, she went on, "You might as well tell me. Detective Ramirez will eventually."

He nodded slowly. "Yeah." Coming to a decision, he indicated a chair near his desk and said, "Sit down, Raine."

Not releasing his gaze, she obeyed. He looked down, studying his knuckles. His obvious reluctance alarmed her.

"What is it, Macauley? Tell me."

Taking a deep breath, he met her gaze squarely. "I asked them to explore a possible link between the person who's making the threats and . . . Brian Burnett."

She went absolutely still. Not so much as a muscle twitched, but her eyes . . . God, the look in her eyes made Mac want to yank out his tongue with pliers. And then he wanted to fold her in his arms and hold her tightly enough to keep the world at bay. But he didn't move. He knew how fruitless such a move would be.

But that didn't stop his gut from knotting up at the haunted look on her face.

"I never told you his name," she whispered.

"I know." His voice was low.

"He . . ." She drew in a deep breath. "You think he lives in L.A. now?"

Mac watched her carefully. "He does."

She was visibly fighting not to show it, but he could read her shock as reaction set in. Her hands began to tremble, and she clasped them tightly in her lap. "I never even considered him," she whispered, as if to herself. "I mean . . . it just never occurred to me." She stopped and collected herself. When she looked at him again, her gaze was steady. "I think you'd better tell me the rest of it."

Watching her carefully, Mac told her how her father had hired the investigator as soon as he'd heard about the letters. Her mouth firmed, but she remained silent.

After he'd finished she said, "And you just decided to keep all of this from me?"

"I didn't know about it until we went to see your father that day. That was the first he told me of it."

"That was a while ago, Macauley. Are you saying it slipped your mind since then?" Her voice was caustic.

"No."

Her semblance of calm suddenly shattered. "Then maybe you could explain why you kept this from me," she lashed out. "And please don't forget the part about how you rationalized your reasons for keeping me in the dark. I'm particularly interested in hearing you explain why it was important for me not to know the identity of who might be stalking me."

With a frown, Mac suggested, "Let's talk about this later." He felt sick at causing her upset, but he'd make the same decision again, given the opportunity. There was no way of knowing, not even yet, if Burnett was involved. And he hadn't wanted to put her through this if he didn't have to.

"No!" At his sharp look, she lowered her voice, but her words were no less firm. "We aren't going to put this off any longer. I had a right to know everything about this case. This is my life we're talking about. When were you planning to tell me?"

"I wasn't going to tell you at all," he answered bluntly. "Burnett has been watched for weeks now. If nothing had linked him to the threats, I never would have mentioned him to you. Neither would your father. God, Raine, why would we put you through that hell again unless we were sure? If I had my way, you still wouldn't know. Not unless and until Burnett was in cuffs."

Tears of frustration pooled in her eyes, and her fists clenched. "Don't do that to me," she said painfully. "Don't try to shield me from life and tell me you're protecting me, that it's for my own good. No one can do that for a person, Macauley. No one. Believe me, I know, and I won't let anyone treat me like that again. I've worked too hard facing what's wrong with my life to let someone else make the decisions for it. I'd expect this behavior from my father. He's never going to change." The look in her eyes was accusing. "But I expected more from you." She got up and walked away.

"Raine." She disappeared out the doorway. He got up and went after her. "Dammit, Raine, wait." She continued to climb the stairs without turning, and when she got to her room, the door closed behind her with a bang of finality.

He slammed his fist against the doorjamb, scowling in the direction she'd disappeared. He'd known she would be shaken by hearing Burnett's name, especially in connection with her case. But her reaction went deeper than that. He went to the office and dropped into his chair tiredly. He propped his elbows on the desktop and rested his chin on his clasped hands.

It wasn't her reaction he was having difficulty figuring out. It was his own. He was too involved here, he'd known that for some time. It was hard to dispute it when witnessing her pain was like taking a punch to the gut.

His phone rang, interrupting his morose thoughts. Eyeing it balefully, he gave a second's consideration to throwing it out the window. Instead he picked up the receiver.

"Hey, Mac, how's it going in the easy life?" Trey joked.

"Just dandy," Mac replied sourly. "Have you run the company into the ground yet?"

"Still working on it," Trey answered. "Things have settled down in the last several days. As a matter of fact, I've just finished checking up on the list of Burnett's cronies you got from the guy investigating him. Nice bunch of characters." When there was no response on the other end, Trey said, "Mac? You there?"

Mac let out a deep breath. "Yeah. You were saying?"

"Like seeks out like, I guess. Burnett hangs out with a few other ex-cons, none of whom are gainfully employed or above doing something illegal for a few bucks. One's been convicted of armed robbery. All of them are bad news."

"So if their good buddy Burnett asked them to help him terrorize a woman he hated, they wouldn't ask questions?"

"Only how much," Trey answered. "What does the investigator have to say?"

"Nothing new," Mac said. "Burnett hasn't been out of L.A. since the tail started on him. There's no record in the private investigator's log of Burnett using a post office or even a corner mail drop. Of course, there's no way of knowing if he mails things at work or what mail goes out from his home."

A low whistle came from the other end of the line. "Now what?"

"The police are trying to match a set of prints as we speak."

"What are you going to tell Raine?"

Mac was silent.

"Mac? You are going to tell her, aren't you? She's going to have to know."

"She knows."

Trey digested his tone. He didn't need to ask any more questions to be aware that something was very wrong. "I'm sure she's upset, but she'll be okay. It sounds like this will be over soon, and then she'll have her life back."

Later, contemplating the ceiling, Mac went over his friend's words. He wasn't sure he could believe them. He didn't even like to think about what was going through Raine's mind right now. Surely old wounds were renewed just at the mention of that bastard Burnett. But she was a fighter. And a survivor. He knew she'd come out of this stronger than before.

He just wished he was as sure that she'd forgive him.

Chapter 15

An uneasy truce settled between Raine and Mac for the next few days. It seemed as if she was going out of her way to avoid him, but he didn't press the issue. He'd gone to her room looking for her one afternoon. She hadn't been there, but he noticed a night-light plugged into the wall. He'd never seen it before and could only assume that its appearance was linked to Burnett's possible implication in her case.

He stared at the light for a long time, his stomach churning. It seemed to represent a direct hit at her equilibrium, and he wanted to smash it, just as he wanted to smash whoever was responsible for terrorizing her. After a while, he turned jerkily away. He couldn't help her with this, she'd made that clear. She was adamant about being responsible for her own life, but it was damn hard not to go to her and promise her that nothing was ever going to hurt her again.

Hell, he couldn't make a promise like that to her, even if he wanted to. Life had a way of throwing nasty little surprises at a person, and ducking them just didn't work. He felt helpless, and the feeling was unfamiliar. It was also damn frustrating.

He'd taken her to the grocery store just this morning. Not that she'd been expressing much of an interest in food lately, but she needed to eat. She was too slight to be able to afford any weight loss. He thought he'd detected a glimmer of a smile when she watched him push that damn cart around the aisles, especially after he'd rammed into a display of soup cans. But she'd helped him pick up the cans without a word.

Her silence was wearing on him. He wasn't a man to whom apologies came easily, but there was a side of him that was uncomfortably aware she deserved one of some kind. And there was another side that wanted to possessively announce that he would continue to do whatever it took to protect her, both physically and emotionally.

He wandered into the kitchen and found it empty. Checking the clock, he judged that it wasn't too early to start dinner. Maybe if he felt real adventurous, he'd deviate from meal choices one through four. And if supper turned out well, he might even take a bigger risk, and bring up the subject that had caused this distance between them.

Raine entered the kitchen later to find it encased in waves of steam. Macauley was at the stove, in front of a huge pot of boiling water. He was concentrating on another pan, stirring absently as he read from a cookbook he'd taken from her shelf.

She raised her eyebrows dubiously. The sight of him reading from Betty Crocker was intriguing, but she couldn't help but be a little alarmed at what he might have thrown together. He'd bought enough groceries at the store this morning to feed a family of five for a month. They'd had a short discussion about it, which had concluded when he'd announced she needed to eat. Obviously he'd been serious.

He turned his head to look at her. "About time you showed up." Continuing as if she'd spoken, he said, "Yes, as a matter of fact, you can help. There's a loaf of French bread that needs to be buttered and put in the oven."

Raine went to the counter and looked at the loaf he'd indicated. It looked as though it had been victim to a samurai warrior, and her mouth curved. The slices were smashed, and crumbs littered the counter around it.

"I've already mixed the garlic butter. The book says that all you have to do is butter the bread, put it in foil and throw it in the oven for a few minutes. Better hurry up. This stuff might be done soon."

She did as he requested, and he stood aside for her to open the oven door. She rose and peered through the steam pouring off the pot.

"We're having spaghetti," he announced unnecessarily.

"Yes. Well, it certainly seems . . . abundant."

He frowned at the cookbook. "They don't tell how to figure the portions, so I just threw in the whole box."

She firmed her mouth, which was threatening to tilt upward. "You must be hungry."

He glanced at her sharply. "Aren't you?"

"Oh, yes." He didn't look convinced, so she added, "I'm starved, actually."

Macauley looked relieved and went back to stirring whatever was in the pan. "Good. I think there's going to be plenty."

Silently agreeing with him, Raine set the table.

"How do you know when this stuff is done, anyway?" he muttered, waving a hand through the steam.

Raine went over and turned the heat down under the pot. "It depends on how you like to eat it."

"Well done."

She turned a startled look to him. He was still concentrating on the sauce he was stirring.

"Okay," she drawled, shaking her head in bemusement. "I'd say it's about ready then."

He insisted she sit down while he served her. She gave a little gasp at the amount of spaghetti he heaped on her plate, but after glancing at him she subsided. It was an interesting meal. The bread had enough garlic in the butter to ward off vampires for the next decade. And the sauce... Well, the spaghetti sauce was unlike any she'd eaten before.

"Did you follow a recipe when you made the sauce?" she questioned.

He shook his head and twirled another forkful of spaghetti. "I didn't have time. You had a jar of sauce in the cupboard. It tasted a little funny at first, but I added some Italian seasoning to it. Why?"

"It's...delicious," she said weakly. She ate as much as she could, but when she finished it didn't look as if she'd made a dent in the helping he'd given her.

"You aren't finished?" he questioned when she pushed her plate away.

"You gave me enough to feed three," she pointed out. "I'm not used to eating like this."

He nodded in satisfaction. "That's okay. We can refrigerate the leftovers and reheat them tomorrow."

Smiling weakly, she got up and began to clear the table as he finished his meal. Glancing behind her to be certain he wasn't looking, she crossed to the wastebasket and pulled out the empty sauce jar. The label read, Taco Sauce—Extra Spicy.

"What are you doing?"

She whirled around guiltily, holding the jar behind her back. "Nothing."

He got up from the table with his plate. "Did you drop something in the wastebasket?"

"Yes. I mean, I thought I did. But I didn't."

He looked at her oddly and set his plate on the counter. Then, before she could guess his intention, he reached out and drew her hand forward. Taking the jar from her, he read the label, a frown on his face. "I'll be damned. I kept trying to think of what that taste was." He looked up and cocked an eyebrow. "Was that, by any chance, your first experience at Mexican-Italian dining?"

"As a matter of fact—" She fought against giggling and lost. "It was. But it was definitely memorable."

He grunted and let the jar drop into the trash before clearing the rest of the table. "You weren't even going to say anything," he accused her. "You were just going to go on letting me believe that everything was fine."

"Everything *was* fine," she assured him. "After all the trouble you went to to cook a different meal, I wasn't going to ruin your effort by complaining. Besides, it wasn't that bad."

He stared at her. "Didn't want to hurt my feelings, huh?"

Still smiling, she shook her head.

"So, what you were actually doing could be interpreted as protecting me, couldn't it? In a way."

Her smile faded away as she interpreted his meaning. "It's not the same thing, Macauley." At his expression she insisted, "It's not. I was sparing your feelings. You were trying to control mine."

He got a dishrag and went to the table, scrubbing vigorously. "You're right. It's not the same. But you can't blame me for not wanting to tell you something that would tie you up in knots. Maybe I should be sorry for keeping Burnett's possible involvement from you, but I'm not. And if that makes me controlling, then I'm guilty as hell."

She looked away. The days had dimmed her anger at him. It hadn't been the first time, after all, that she'd been cosseted from life. But she'd always known that her father's unfortunate attempts at protecting her from her past had stemmed from his love for her. Even in her most optimistic moments she couldn't assign that motivation to Macauley. Love was the last thing he'd accept from her, and the last thing he'd offer.

Finishing his task, Mac tossed the cloth into the sink and leaned his hips against the edge of the table. Folding his arms across his chest, he said reflectively, "You know, an objective man might have told you about Burnett right from the start." He paused for a meaning-laden instant before reminding her silkily, "I think you'll recall exactly when I lost my objectivity. Like it or not, you can't have it both ways. I'm involved, Raine. And I can't apologize for trying to protect you."

Her eyes went wide and soft at his words. He wanted to take those few steps to her side and put an end to all the torment she must have been going through for the past few days. He remained rooted where he was.

And then she spoke. "When I heard Burnett might be involved in this thing, it did bring back some memories I'd prefer to forget." Her voice was as soft as the look in her eyes. "How do you protect someone from memories, Macauley? You can't stop my thoughts or the flashbacks. Just as I can't do it for you."

She'd turned the tables on him neatly. She went to him then and laid a hand on his arm. "Don't you think I'd like to free you from those demons that haunt you, too? But you're the only one who can step away from them. I can only be here. And I want to be," she said achingly. "You once told me that you'd stay as long as I needed you. Well, how long are you willing to stay for? Because I'm not going to stop needing you, not even when this is all over."

His voice was ragged. "You don't know what you're asking."

"I think I do." She knew exactly what she was asking, and she knew how impossible a dream it was. Oh, she didn't doubt that he felt something for her, but she wouldn't want to put a name to it and examine it in the light of day. Guilt and regret rode the man hard, and tinged every other good thing in his life. Macauley O'Neill wasn't a forever kind of man.

She knew all of this with her head, but the realization slashed at her heart. She'd told him once before that her love came with no strings, and she'd meant it. She hated putting this look on his face. Right now he resembled a man caught between two equally tortuous choices, and she hurt for him. Perhaps he had been partially right. Though she knew there was no way to shield him from old demons, she couldn't deny wanting to. Yes, if it was at all possible, she'd want to protect him in any way she could.

It was this emotion that drove her to walk into his arms and reach up on her tiptoes to place a soft kiss on his mouth. His eyes slid shut, and his arms closed around her immediately, crushing her to him. She pulled his shirt loose from his jeans and slid her palms up his chest, needing suddenly to touch him.

"Raine." His voice sounded choked.

"No," she whispered. "No more words. Just us, Macauley."

He caught her mouth with a deep, wild kiss that was tinged with desperation. Inside him a clock was ticking away each minute he had left to spend with her. She was too damn generous for her own good, offering herself and allowing him to give back only as much as he dared. When she pulled slightly away, her eyes were slumberous with desire. Knowing that he'd put that look there had the blood pooling behind his belt. She took his hand in hers and led him to the stairway. He paused at its foot for a moment, trying to remember just why this was so incredibly unfair to her. Then she walked ahead of him, her slim hips swaying, enticing him to forget all but her.

She represented everything he never thought he'd have and had assumed he didn't want. Raine was pure and sweet, with a hidden, unexpected depth to her that caught a man unaware. Her curious blend of strength and vulnerability brought out his most primitively protective instincts, as well as his admiration. She was as far removed from the women he'd known as it was possible to be. And something about her had a hold on him he couldn't shake. Didn't want to shake.

Booted feet deliberate on the treads, he followed her up the stairs.

The next day André called, and Raine told him of her plans for delivering the pictures. He made his displeasure about the change obvious, but faced with her insistence, he grudgingly agreed. They arranged to meet at the gallery later in the day.

Hours later, Mac and a gallery employee were busy unloading the van. Raine carefully removed the paintings from their protective cases and leaned them against the wall to await hanging.

"What in heaven's name were you thinking of?" Raine's head jerked up, startled by André's outraged voice. She hadn't seen him enter the gallery. He took her by the arm and fairly dragged her to the other side of the room, stopping in front of the painting of Macauley. Pointing at it with a shaking finger, he demanded, "Whatever possessed you to deviate from your usual style? Not to mention the subject matter, which is completely unsuitable."

She tried to calm him down with humor. "Unsuitable? Somehow I don't think that will be the adjective you'll hear used to describe this picture."

"Well, it won't do, Raine," he said querulously. "I simply won't have it. I'll send you back home in my van and you can select another painting to take its place. Surely you have an earlier work that would be appropriate. And we'll send *that* back with you."

Her good humor vanished abruptly. "No, André, we won't. I paint what I feel, when I feel it. That's the quality that brings a painting alive. Haven't you told me, on many occasions, that one can't dictate inspiration?"

He became placating. "Of course, I've said that. But I thought you understood that this show was of particular importance. People expect a certain style from you. If you want to remain marketable, you have to be true to the element in your pictures that makes them popular."

She shrugged. "If that's all that's bothering you, don't worry. This painting isn't for sale, anyway."

At these words he turned apoplectic. "Not for sale? You must be joking."

"No," she drawled wryly. "Actually, my sense of humor walked out the door about the same time this conversation started."

"You're beginning to build a respectable reputation, Raine. But you aren't in a place in your career where you can afford to be temperamental."

She looked at him warily, wondering if it was more than just her painting of Macauley that was upsetting him. He was always highstrung before a show, but right now there was a wild look in his eyes she'd never seen before. Perspiration dotted his upper lip, although the temperature in the gallery was quite comfortable. "I can afford anything I want, André," she said, deliberately misunderstanding his words. "My tastes are quite simple. And I wanted to paint a picture for *me*. It's not going to lead to the collapse of the art world as we know it. Relax. You've outdone yourself with the publicity. The gallery has been cleaned up on time. Everything is sailing along perfectly."

"I haven't approved of the effect that man has had on you from the first," he muttered, glaring across the room toward Mac, who'd fallen into conversation with the gallery owner.

"Mac O'Neill and his effect on me, have nothing to do with you," Raine said firmly, reclaiming his attention. "I appreciate all you've done for me, but I won't let you start dictating what I do and do not paint. I can't work that way. I don't think you really want me to."

"Of course not," he said stiffly. "You're free to paint as you wish. But it was my duty as your agent to warn you that such a flagrant departure from your normal style might not be welcomed by your public."

Her public. Raine's mouth turned up. André made her sound as if she was royalty. "It's one picture," she reminded him gently. "And it's important to me to have it included in the show." Seeing Macauley heading for them, she quickly draped the soft tarp over it.

Mac's eyes went between the two of them shrewdly. But he didn't comment on the obvious tension in the air. "What else do you need to do here?" he inquired of Raine. "All the pictures have been unloaded."

"Well, I usually supervise the hanging of them, but I'm sure André can handle that. He has a much better eye than I do." She touched the agent lightly on the arm. "Would you do that for me, please, André?" It was an obvious peace offering, and after a moment, the man nodded shortly.

"As you wish." Turning on his heel, he walked rapidly away.

Mac watched him go. "Seems a little more wired than usual," he observed. "Which is saying something, for him. What's got him so worked up?"

"I'm not really sure," Raine said slowly, her eyes still on her agent. "He's always jumpy before a show, but his behavior to-day..." Shrugging, she looked at Macauley. "I guess I'm finished here. We can go home."

His gut clenched at her words. Home. He hadn't had one to speak of since he was a boy living with his parents. Years of military barracks, and then less than luxurious accommodations in whatever hellhole he'd been assigned to, could hardly be called home. Neither could the apartment he lived in now. It was as empty as he was, as his life had been before he met Raine. Usually it was a relief to get back to his own place after one of these jobs, but it was going to seem like a vacuum when he went back this time.

His job protecting her was almost at an end. It was more than Ramirez's assurances that told him that. The case was rapidly winding down, he could feel it. The certainty filled him with desolation. Because he knew he'd walk away from her then. She'd been through too much in her life already to be saddled with a man who had his own ghosts. A man who had been empty inside for too long to have anything left to offer her.

"Ready?" She smiled at him, and the clouds of despair receded for the moment. She had a special way of looking at him, as if he was something he knew he wasn't, could never be. But when she smiled at him just that way, he thought dangerous thoughts. As if maybe he could be what she wanted, if he tried hard enough. That was risky thinking, self-delusional and masochistic. He was what he was, and her belief in him didn't make him any different.

But knowing all that didn't make him immune to that electrical pull between them. "Yeah," he said, laying a heavy arm across her shoulders and leading her to the door. "I'm ready."

There was a car in the drive when they reached home, and Mac eyed it sharply. Anderson jogged over to their van as they pulled up at the gate.

"I let Detective Ramirez in about twenty minutes ago. He said he needed to talk to both of you."

Mac glanced at Raine and observed the way she swiftly swallowed and imperceptibly straightened. He nodded, pressed the button on the control he'd placed in the van that would release the gate's mechanism and drove up to the house. He kept a tight hold on Raine's hand as they walked into the house.

"Detective," Raine greeted the man as they entered the room.

"Miss Michaels." Ramirez rose as they entered. He was dressed today in a tan double-breasted suit that made him look more like a game show host than a cop. "I'm glad I didn't miss you. I've got some good news for you today."

"Well, good. We could use some of that, couldn't we?" She looked at Mac. His face was set in the expressionless mask that had been so common when they'd first met. She turned to Ramirez.

"We were able to match a set of prints on the last letter you received." He waited a heartbeat before adding, "They belong to Brian Burnett."

She wasn't aware that Mac had moved until she felt his hands on her shoulders. He drew her against his chest, as if offering her his strength. She blinked, a little stunned.

"He was arrested last night. We've got him in jail here now. You won't have to worry about being threatened anymore, Miss Michaels."

Numbly, Raine shook her head. "I knew it was a possibility after what you said the last time, but I just don't understand why. Why now, after all these years?"

"Apparently he saw some articles about you in the paper or some magazine." The man added almost apologetically, "He's carrying quite a grudge against you. Blames you for his time in jail." The man shrugged. "Go figure. Anyway, he saw his chance and did a little digging, I suppose. Came up with your address and decided to start terrorizing you. You can't figure how these guys' minds work, ma'am. Just be glad we got him when we did."

"What about when she was run off the road?" Mac demanded. His body was tense behind hers, but his fingers on her shoulders remained gentle. "Who set fire to the porch and tried to trash the gallery? It wasn't Burnett. The private investigator Simon Michaels had watching him can vouch that Burnett never left L.A."

The detective shrugged. "You told me yourself that Burnett had lots of unsavory friends who could have perpetrated those incidents at his command. After doing time he must have smartened up enough to want to establish an alibi for himself."

"Has he—" Raine cleared her throat. Her words had come out hoarse. "Has he admitted to all this?"

The man shook his head. "He's still proclaiming his innocence. To hear him tell it, he's a model citizen these days. It's going to be tough to maintain that, though, with his prints all over that letter." He rose to his feet. "Anyway, I wanted to let you know as soon as possible. You've been through enough these last few weeks. I didn't want to leave you in suspense any longer."

She managed a smile. "Thank you, Detective. I appreciate everything you've done."

"I'll let myself out," he told her. "You have a good show at that gallery, okay?"

Raine thanked him again, and he left. She sagged against Mac's chest, and he moved his hands from her shoulders to clasp them around her waist. "I can't believe it's over," she murmured. "And to have him involved in this . . . How in God's name could he have twisted it all around so that the rape was my fault?"

He hugged her fiercely, his head lowering to lay against hers. "Who knows what goes on in a sicko's mind? It's over now. He'll never hurt you again." The words were meant to calm himself, as well. The rage that had buoyed in him at the detective's words was murderous. He'd dearly love to have ten minutes with Burnett and save the county the expense of a trial and a lengthy incarceration.

Sensing the churning emotions that raged through him, Raine said questioningly, "Macauley?" She turned in his arms and looked into his face. "Are you all right?"

He shook his head at wonderment at her question. "I think that's supposed to be my line."

She put her arms around him and hugged him tightly. "I'm okay. I really am. I just can't believe this is over."

"It is over," he whispered into her hair, and the words taunted him with another meaning. The reign of terror was at end, and so was her need for protection. It was over. Relief warred with the now familiar despair. This would likely be the last time he felt her delicate curves pressed up against him, and the thought filled him with another kind of rage. He'd been haunted by flashbacks since he'd left the military, but he suspected they were nothing compared to the torturous nights he had ahead of him. Tantalizing memories of her would wisp across his mind like delicate ghosts, memories of the way she moved or laughed. He'd remember the first time he'd taken her, and seen her eyes widen at the sight of his body over hers. He felt his pulse turn thick and heavy.

His mouth sought hers and was almost rough in its need, desperate in its seeking. She returned his kiss without hesitation, with that sensual generosity that was so much a part of her. She painted his bottom lip with her tongue, then took it between her teeth to worry it gently. But gentleness wasn't what he wanted from her, and it wasn't in him to return.

He sank to his knees and took her with him. Never releasing her mouth, he removed her clothes and discarded them. He backed her against the sofa and bent her over the cushion so her breasts jutted upward to his mouth. He ravished them both in turn, using his tongue to paint erotic pictures on her nipples. She moved beneath his lips, writhing and crying out at the sensations. He tightened his hold on her, emotion sluicing through him, and wished this moment could last forever.

Her hands made a mockery of that wish, roaming frantically over his chest and back, urging him to abandon the control he needed so desperately to reach for. Dragging his mouth away from her breasts, he strung a trail of kisses up her neck and fastened on her mouth again. The kiss was hot, deep and wild. He held nothing back, couldn't, even if he'd thought of it. He was shaking, but so was she. He used his one remaining grasp on sanity to reach for his jeans. He managed to extract the foil packet from his pocket and sheathe himself. Then he reached for her and pulled her beneath him.

Raine made a soft, desperate sound and drew up her knees, urging him forward with hands that were frantic. He closed his eyes and gritted his teeth as he buried himself within her. Deep. And tight. So very tight.

His hands went to her hips and he lifted her to receive his thrust. The sensory bombardment was almost too much to bear, and he clenched his jaw. It was more than sex, it was a connection between them that was as heady as it was inexplicable. Their fusion filled the emptiness in his soul and erased the specters from his mind. He wanted to savor the completeness, and he braced himself on his forearms, attempting to fight the mind-shattering sensation. He bracketed her face in his hands and covered her mouth with his in a slow, searching kiss.

But she wasn't going to let him wait for the first, fierce, electrifying rush to ease. Hands clutching his shoulders, she lifted her hips, rocking her pelvis hard against his. Mac roughly locked one hand beneath her bottom, sliding the other under her head to keep her mouth sealed to his. His breathing trapped in his heaving chest, he lifted her hips higher, then rolled his hips against hers. Raine uttered a wild cry, and he drank it, wishing he could draw all of her in and keep her there inside him. When she countered his thrust, a haze blurred all his thoughts, and only one need remained. He wanted to erase the horror from her mind, drive away the memory of the man who'd made her life a hell once again. Trying to hang on, he dragged his mouth away and gritted his teeth as she moved convulsively beneath him. He surged into her again, trying to maximize her pleasure, drawing it out until he felt her movements turn more erratic and frantic.

She cried out softly, and her inner convulsions pulled at him. Giving in to the passion, his face contorted, and he gave one last thrust before emptying into her.

Their breathing remained choppy for long minutes. Eddies of pleasure were still chasing down his spine when reason returned to taunt him. His time with Raine had come to an end. He was unable to deny it. The knowledge pounded inside his skull.

The last time. The last time. The last time.

It was over.

Chapter 16

Raine mingled with the guests at the gallery with a smile that felt strained and plastic. There was enough of a crowd to satisfy even André, and indeed, he seemed in his element. Far from the almost frantic wreck he'd been just yesterday, today he appeared the smooth, genial host. She wished for just a fraction of his poise. She wished, above all, that this night was already behind her.

Her parents wouldn't be here tonight. They'd left almost immediately after she'd told them of Burnett's arrest for the cruise her father had been planning. She didn't mind. The knowledge that her mother was experiencing some rare good health was far more comforting than their presence here tonight would have been. Her brothers would come later in the week, on a night that was a little less hectic for her.

She hadn't seen Macauley all day, although she'd been aware of the constant stream of people in the house. Trey had been holed up in the office with him, and so had some of the other men. She'd looked out the window once that afternoon, and seen men loading the van. She'd known they were carrying his things out of her house, and she'd dropped the curtain as a wave of pain had swept over her. The visual reminder of his withdrawal from her life was too much to bear.

When Harold had called and offered to send a limo for her, she'd gone in search of Macauley. She didn't know what she had been hoping for, but she didn't get the chance to talk to him. She ended up telling Trey of the plan, and he'd agreed to pass the information on to Mac. She'd dressed and left the house that evening without ever running into him once.

She wondered, for what seemed the hundredth time, if he was in that big a hurry to get away from her. She dreaded reaching home again tonight, to find it empty of him and of his belongings.

"The showing looks like a success."

At the diffident voice behind her, Raine whirled around. "Greg!" she exclaimed delightedly. She took his hand impulsively and squeezed it. "I'm so glad you came."

The man blushed to his receding hairline. Pushing his glasses up his nose with his free hand, he said, "Well, I appreciated your calling and inviting me specially." He took a deep breath and looked at the floor. "Look, Raine, the last time I saw you I acted kind of like a jerk, and . . . Well, I guess I need to apologize."

"No," she informed him, "you don't. You've put up with me when I've acted worse, remember? You've never lost patience with me no matter how long it took me to understand tax options."

He laughed nervously. "But seriously, I wanted to tell you that our friendship is important to me. I'd hate to have anything happen to ruin it."

"Nothing will," she assured him.

"What are you two doing chatting while Raine is supposed to be the queen of this ball?" Sarah strolled up and scolded them. "She's supposed to be schmoozing all these deep-pocketed guests into buying up every one of her paintings. That's what I would do."

"I'm afraid André is going to have to be in charge of that department," Raine told her ruefully. "I flunked schmoozing in school." Her gaze went past her two friends and caught a familiar sullen face. "Sarah, is that Joe?" It had been a couple of years since she'd seen Sarah's brother, but she thought she recognized the young man who disappeared into the crowd as she spoke.

Sarah nodded without turning. "He insisted on coming with me. He's learning to appreciate culture. Maybe there's hope for him, after all."

"Well, if you ladies will excuse me, I'm going to take a look at the paintings. I'll talk to you later, Raine. Nice seeing you again, Sarah." With those words Greg ambled away.

Sarah looked after him with raised eyebrows, then at Raine. "He seems back to normal, or at least what passes for normal for him."

"Whatever he was angry about, he seems to have gotten over," Raine allowed. "I'm glad. I would hate to be on the outs with him. He really has been a good friend to me."

"Well, he's not the only one who wants to see your latest masterpieces. I think there are several here I've never seen before. I'm going to wander. I'll talk to you later." Sarah strolled away.

Raine was stopped by a couple she recognized from the dinner André had hosted and politely listened to their praise of her work. Walking with them to a piece they'd expressed an interest in, she answered what questions she could before suggesting that they direct the rest to André. Her attention garnered by yet another couple, she smiled regretfully and took her leave.

"I'm afraid I'm going to have to steal this talented woman away from you for a moment," a voice said from behind her. She smiled in gratitude as Harold Bonzer offered her his arm in a courtly manner and strolled away with her.

"Thank you," she whispered.

"Not at all." He patted her hand. "I can always tell when you need rescuing. You get this desperate look on your face, as if you're planning your escape." He eyed her with kindliness. "You're not cut out for this kind of thing, are you?"

Raine laughed ruefully. "This is my least favorite part of the process, but a necessary one, I know. I'm just lucky that André can take up the slack on my behalf."

"Don't you worry." He steered her toward a corner of the room. "Your talent speaks for itself. As a matter of fact, I'm no different from that couple I stole you away from. I wanted to ask you about this picture." He stopped in front of the painting she'd done of Macauley.

She should have known that, having left the hanging of the paintings to André, he'd put this one in the most inconspicuous spot possible. But it seemed to fit here, somehow. She studied it, trying and not quite succeeding to see it without a prejudiced eye.

It was nighttime in the picture, and Macauley was standing in front of a window identical to the one in her bedroom. He wore only jeans, the button unfastened. His face was unsmiling. The darkness that filled the room shrouded him in shadows. He cast shadows of his own. He looked like an avenging angel come to earth. Her own dark warrior. The caption on the card she'd prepared for the painting read, Out of the Darkness. She'd painted him with all the emotion he evoked in her, and looking at the picture was always going to be a bittersweet reminder that he had refused her invitation to take that final step away from the shadows that existed in his soul. For the first time she questioned her wisdom in planning to keep this piece. The constant reminder of what she'd gambled, and lost, would do nothing to fill the void in her heart.

"This is a different piece for you, Raine." Harold's voice was mild as he surveyed the picture.

"André pointed that out to me," she retorted. "But I did this one for myself."

Harold eyed her shrewdly. "You've made a wise choice. Despite his toughness, he's a good man. I'm an excellent judge of character, so take it from me. Don't let this one get away."

Raine smiled sadly and led him from the picture as others began to drift in their direction. "I'm afraid I no longer have a way to make him stay."

Harold looked at her sharply, opened his mouth and closed it again. Then he looked across the room and smiled broadly. Bending closer he murmured, "Maybe you have more pull than you give yourself credit for."

Mystified, Raine followed the direction of his gaze and was shocked to see Macauley standing across the room. Hungrily, her eyes drank him in. He was wearing his bank suit and looked a little rough, a little uncivilized despite the fashionable clothing. Then his eyes caught hers, and she felt a very physical jolt. Her mouth went dry.

"He just came in," Harold informed her. "Something told me the boy wasn't as foolish as you'd have me believe."

"You're misinterpreting his presence here," she said shakily. She tore her gaze from Macauley with effort. "He hates loose ends, that's all." She should have known that he wouldn't be so callous as to leave without a word. He wasn't a coward. He'd see this through to its inevitable, heart-aching conclusion.

"We shall see," the man said cryptically. "We shall see. Would you mind excusing me for a moment, Raine?"

She nodded, but her eyes had already moved back to Macauley. He was standing in front of one of her paintings, his hands in his pockets, his eyes narrowed in concentration. She wondered what he saw there, and what he was feeling.

She wondered why he was here.

Not attempting to resist the invisible magnetism of his presence, she began to make her way through the crowd toward him. She was stopped frequently by guests who recognized her and wanted to congratulate her on the showing. Before she was halfway across the room, Greg came to her side and said in an undertone, "André wants to see you in the office."

She glanced at him, then toward the office. "All right," she said reluctantly. Casting one last glance toward Macauley, she was shocked to see his ice blue gaze trained on her. His face was brooding, and he was studying her with the same intensity he'd given her paintings. For an instant, she was helpless to move. She was dimly aware that all her yearning was present on her face, for his hardened in response.

"Raine, he asked that you come now," Greg insisted. He succeeded in capturing her attention, and the contact was broken. When she glanced over her shoulder as Greg led her away, her view of Macauley was obscured by the crowd of people.

As he watched Winters lead her away, Mac was aware of a surge of primal emotion. He didn't like to see Greg put his hands on her. It wouldn't have made any difference who it was. He was primitively aware that he didn't want to see any other man touching Raine.

She'd looked almost unrecognizable dressed as she was tonight. He knew she was more comfortable in blue jeans and T-shirts than in the short, glittery red dress she was wearing tonight. But he couldn't deny the effect she had on him when he saw her wearing it. Hell, if he was honest, she had a similar effect on him no matter what she wore. Or didn't wear.

Bonzer had called the house earlier today and talked to Mac before he'd spoken to Raine. Mac had agreed to the idea of the limo. Surely Raine would be as safe in that as it was possible to be, especially since the older man had promised to send his own driver. There was really no reason for Mac to be here tonight. Burnett was in custody; Raine was no longer in danger. There had been a million details to tie up at her place today.

But he couldn't stay away.

He'd tried to rationalize to himself that things just didn't feel right to him yet. Despite Burnett being safely behind bars, there was still the fact that the man had an alibi for each and every time someone had physically threatened Raine. If Ramirez and Trey were right, and some of Burnett's friends were responsible for carrying out the more physical threats, Raine could possibly still be in danger. Who knew where those culprits were right now? At least, that was the reason he'd given himself for not moving out of her house tonight, instead coming here.

But once he'd seen her again, he'd known he'd lied.

Whatever had pulled him here had nothing to do with her safety and everything to do with the power she had over him. He couldn't let go, that was the truth. And the hell of it was, despite her earlier declaration of love, she was giving every indication of a woman who was willing to allow him to go. She hadn't sought him out today, though she must have seen the men loading his things into the van. She hadn't begged and she hadn't pushed. She'd stood back and let him make his own decision.

Damned if he'd ever thought there'd come a day when he'd want a woman clinging to him, but, he thought, aggrieved, it would have been nice in this instance. Maybe it would have alleviated this gnawing sense of indecision, the edginess along his spine that nagged about details overlooked.

He elbowed his way through the crowd to go in search of her. But the mill of people had obscured his view, and he wasn't certain which direction she'd gone with Winters. He found a corner to wait in and leaned against a wall. When he looked up, he was faced with his own likeness.

Shock rooted him in place. Seconds ticked by as he stared, stupefied, at the painting she'd done of him, without his ever having the slightest inkling. He pushed away from the wall, coming to stand before the picture for a better view. The instant he recognized the scene in the painting, his stomach clenched in remembered response. Though he'd been in her room many nights since, the night depicted here was the first time he'd made love to her.

His breathing grew choppy as he studied the painting. All the emotion that Raine had so freely offered to him was reflected here. She'd told him in a hundred different ways that she loved him, and it was on display, for the entire world to see. His gaze dropped to the caption, and reading it was like taking a punch to the gut.

Out of the Darkness. It could mean the treatment of night and shadows in the picture, but he knew there was a deeper meaning. He felt raw, exposed, yet strangely humbled that she had turned her awesome talent on him. The picture seemed to represent his last chance to leave the guilt and regrets aside and take what she was offering.

His throat tight, he abruptly turned and practically ran over a woman who'd come up behind him. Her sleek, dark hair was perfectly coiffed, and her dress tightly sheathed a curvy body. When he would have muttered his apology and gone by, she laid a hand on his arm to stop him.

"That's quite a tribute," she purred, indicating the painting with an elegant hand. "Do you know Miss Michaels . . . well?"

"Why?"

Rather than being put off by his terse tone, she seemed to find it intriguing. Her hand on his arm tightened. "The picture evokes all kinds of emotions, darling. One has to wonder if that's because of the subject, or because the artist painted what she was feeling herself. Either way," she said, her long, taloned fingers kneading his arm sensuously, "as soon as I saw it, I knew I had to have it. I believe André is discussing the deal with Raine as we speak."

Without regard for niceties, he pulled his arm from her grasp. "You'll have to excuse me," he muttered brusquely, striding away. The thought of this woman, or someone like her, buying that painting made him want to throw something through the nearest window.

His need to see Raine, to talk to her was greater than ever. Resuming his search, he left the room and turned down a hallway. Light spilled from one door at the end of it that stood partially open. The shade flapped softly at the window inside. He stopped in the act of entering when he realized the room was occupied.

"That is my last word," Raine was saying firmly. "I told you yesterday that painting wasn't for sale, and I won't change my mind. I don't care what she offered to pay for it."

"I just wish you'd see reason," André answered, his voice sharp. "You could always paint another, Raine, if you wanted one for yourself. This offer is very generous."

"It's also out of the question," she answered unequivocally. "And that's final, André. I won't change my mind."

After a long pause, he heard André say, "Perhaps it's time I shared something with you, Raine. I really didn't want to burden you with my worries, but . . . I've been having some financial problems recently. I'm counting on this show to help bail me out. I don't mean to push . . ."

The hell you don't, Mac thought caustically. He fought the urge to barge into the room and take Klassen by the throat. But Raine wouldn't welcome his taking the decision out of her hands. He had been a slow learner when it came to that lesson, but he'd learned it well.

"But every little bit is going to help. If you can possibly see your way to selling this painting, it would be a tremendous boost for me. I never dreamed that there would be a buyer for it, but since there is . . . I hate to sound as though I'm trespassing on our friendship, but it's very important to me. Would you at least think about it?"

Not trusting his response if he listened to another word, Mac slipped away. He didn't want to think of that painting in anyone else's hands. It was too damn personal, revealing too much of both him and Raine. But he didn't have the right to make any demands on her, now less than ever.

Feeling as though his skin had grown two sizes too small, he went into the large room. The guests were dwindling, leaving in couples and small groups. Sarah waved gaily at him as she left with a dark-haired young man Mac didn't recognize. He nodded laconically in return.

"Well, it's been quite a night," Harold Bonzer said expansively, stopping next to him. "I was glad you made it tonight. Couldn't quite believe Raine when she said she didn't think you'd be here."

"To tell you the truth," Mac replied remotely, "I'm not quite sure what I'm doing here, myself."

"Give it time, son," the older man advised, his eyes twinkling. "I'm sure you'll figure it out."

"Something doesn't feel right," Mac murmured, his edginess increasing as he surveyed the dozen or so people left. The tightness in his gut hadn't lessened since he got here. If anything, it had grown worse. Greg Winters walked by, nodded at him and went out the door.

"You've got some thinking to do," Bonzer answered. "Nothing is going to feel right until you reach a decision on whatever it is churning in your craw."

Mac turned a jaundiced eye on him, but the man laughed and clapped him on the shoulder. "My driver is already here. I'm going to collect Raine and take her out for a celebratory drink at Sheena's. Do you know the place?"

Mac nodded. A small, intimate eatery, it was just around the corner.

"Good. Why don't you meet us there? Maybe between now and then you'll figure out just what it is that's bugging you." Chuckling, the man walked away.

Going out for an intimate drink with Raine, especially with Bonzer in tow, was the last thing Mac thought was going to cure this itchy feeling. But he knew he'd go. He'd seize the opportunity to be with Raine, even if they weren't alone.

The last of the guests left, and still André and Raine hadn't come out of the office. Fighting the urge to go and drag her away with him, he strode to the rest room. When he emerged and returned to the front door, the white limo was pulling away from the curb. André was locking the front door.

"I never thought you were such an art lover that you'd be the last one out of here," the man snapped, barely civil.

"I have varied tastes," Mac replied tauntingly. Striding toward his van, he hoped like hell that Klassen wasn't going to join them tonight. He felt like crawling out of his own skin, and a good fight sounded like a satisfying way to cure the feeling.

Entering Sheena's, Mac squinted in the dimness. Seeing Bonzer in the corner, he approached the table.

"Where's Raine?" asked Bonzar.

"Raine?" Mac repeated, uncomprehendingly. "You said she was coming with you."

Harold shook his head. "I thought so, but at the last minute she decided to go look for you and see if you'd agree to come tonight."

"Damn," Mac swore, turning to stride rapidly away. He met André at the door. "Give me the gallery keys," he demanded.

"Have you finally taken complete leave of your senses, O'Neill?" Klassen demanded.

Remembering what the gallery owner had told him when he'd questioned him about security, Mac grabbed André's shirt. "Give me the damn keys. Raine must be locked in there, and the damn lights are on a timer. They'll be going off any minute."

Klassen jerked out of Mac's grasp. "There wasn't anybody left in the gallery when I closed up. And if she was there, she's fully capable of calling us here."

Mac didn't waste any more time arguing. Thoughts of Raine alone, even for the slightest amount of time, in near darkness in unfamiliar surroundings made his muscles contract. He already knew too well how the news of Burnett had affected her. He'd seen the night-light and recognized the ghosts that refused to be banished. He didn't want her to be traumatized any more. Lowering his face to Klassen's, he gritted out, "Last chance, Klassen. Give me the keys, now, or I'll take them off your unconscious body."

Recognizing the threat in Mac's face, André reached into his pocket and pulled out a set of keys. Mac snatched them away and ran out the door. Deciding it was quicker on foot, Mac avoided the parking lot and loped around the corner. The gallery was in sight. Even as he caught sight of it, the lights in the building dimmed automatically. Cursing fluently, he put on more speed.

Raine held the heel of one red pump in her hand and childishly kicked the rest of the shoe across the rest room. Closing her eyes and sighing, she leaned heavily against the wall. This could only happen to her, she thought fatalistically. Every other woman in the world managed to dress up occasionally without courting minor disasters. But when it was her turn, fate always took a satirical turn. She'd spent the last ten minutes in here trying without result to force the heel onto the shoe. It was time to admit defeat.

She might have avoided this if she'd just gotten in Harold's limo, as planned. But she hadn't been able to resist the urge to search out Macauley. Her intent had been to see that he joined them, but she hadn't found him in the large room of the gallery. Stopping in the rest room to freshen her makeup, she'd turned her ankle and neatly snapped her shoe into two useless pieces.

She slipped out of the other shoe, rescued the first from where she'd kicked it and left the room. She padded almost silently down the corridor, and when she got to the gallery's large room, she stopped, nonplussed.

It was completely empty. She hurriedly checked the other rooms, the office, rest rooms and storeroom. All empty. Feeling more and more like a second-class Cinderella forgotten at the ball, she heaved a heavy sigh and went to the door to let herself out. She could manage to get to Sheena's herself. It wasn't far, and the streets were extremely well lit. However, she was going to look darn funny limping along without shoes on.

The door didn't move under her hand. Surprised, she used more strength, pulling with all her might. The set of front double doors remained immobile.

And then, just when she was cursing the fates, the lights went out.

The sudden blanket of darkness sent an all-too-familiar wave of panic through her. Her reaction was as inevitable as it was unavoidable. Her breathing grew erratic, her palms clammy. Taking deep breaths, she tried to calm herself. The doorway outside the gallery remained lit. She wasn't in total darkness. She looked over her shoulder slowly. The rest of the gallery was as black as a tomb.

She peered into the dim light that came through the doors, trying to find the light switch. She didn't see it. Moving to the wall nearest the door, she stepped a little deeper into the room, feeling her way on the wall. No luck.

Stopping, she wrapped her arms around herself and looked in the direction of the corridor leading to the office. She knew she could find her way easily, even in the dark. But she couldn't seem to force her feet to move.

All I have to do is get to the phone, she told herself reassuringly. *I know where the phone is. I know! Just move. There's nothing here, just move, darn it!*

The first step she took felt as though she was moving underwater. Her limbs felt heavy and lethargic. She stopped. Her heart was pounding, her breath coming in quick, short spurts. She hadn't felt this panicked in a long time. Despairingly, she wondered if just finding out who had been responsible for the threats was going to undo all the gains she'd made through the years.

Her spine stiffened. That wasn't going to happen; *she wouldn't let it.* With physical effort, she forced herself to take another step, and then another. Her progress was slow and laborious. Halfway to the office it finally occurred to her that she hadn't had to do this at all. Surely once everyone arrived at the restaurant, it would take only minutes to figure out what had happened. Someone would be coming for her.

She looked over her shoulder toward the doors. The light seeping through them beckoned like an oasis on a desert. She turned resolutely away. The need to continue went beyond the need to find a way out of here. She had something to prove, at least to herself. She wouldn't allow herself be a coward.

When she reached the hallway, she took a great breath. She was almost there, and yet it seemed as though the farther she came on her journey, the harder it became for her to continue. Inching toward the door, she moved with very little noise, save for her ragged breathing. When she reached the office door, she clasped the doorknob as though it was a lifeline and pushed the door open quickly, reaching for the light switch at the same time.

Her body went limp, and her eyes closed in relief as light flooded the room. She leaned heavily against the wall, her heart pounding as rapidly as if she'd finished a marathon. It was several moments before she opened her eyes again, and moments later before her adrenaline-loaded brain observed the other figure in the room, by the desk.

"Sarah!" she gasped.

Sarah was staring at her, dismay written on her face.

"Raine! What . . . what are you doing here?"

Her pulse was just beginning to resume its regular beat as she explained ruefully, "I was in the rest room and got locked in. I was just going to call Sheena's to tell someone to come get me." She frowned quizzically at her friend. "I thought everyone had left."

Sarah gave a shaky laugh. "Were we born under the same star, or what? Would you believe that I came back tonight because I thought I'd left my purse? I was in the office looking for it and never realized that everyone else had gone."

Confusion warred in Raine's mind. "But you weren't here before the lights went off. I looked around." Noticing the vapor rising from a jar on the desk, she frowned and took a step closer. "What's that?"

Sarah didn't answer.

Raine took a step closer and stopped. "It looks like acid, Sarah. I know it wasn't here when I came in earlier."

In the face of her friend's continuing silence, a feeling of dread began to seep through Raine's system. "Sarah?" she whispered, her gaze rising to meet her friend's.

But Sarah's gaze was fixed on the wall beyond the desk. The shade on the window was pressed inward, and someone was crawling over the sill. He jumped lightly to the floor and turned around, saying, "Sarah, you idiot. Turn off that damn light before someone sees it."

Joe Jennings's voice stopped abruptly when he saw Raine. Then a grim smile crossed his face, and he addressed his sister again. "Looks like things are going to turn out my way, after all."

"No, Joe," Sarah said sharply.

"Shut up!" he ordered. Sarah's mouth trembled, but she remained silent. "Get over there and turn off the light. Come here, Raine."

Raine didn't move.

"I said get over here!"

Sarah moved to obey her brother and turned off the switch.

Even forewarned, Raine couldn't stem her panic at the abrupt darkness. As she stood immobile, even her mind seemed frozen. Then a hand yanked her by the shoulder and pulled her off balance. A hard arm crooked around her throat.

Raine's throat clutched and she went still. This was a scene from her nightmares, a stranger in back of her, touching her, the very

real element of evil surrounding her. Her frozen state lasted only
for a moment, until reaction set in, and she fought wildly to free
herself.

"Damn you," Joe cursed, as one of her backward kicks made
contact with his leg. She raked her fingernails over his arms, her
actions fueled by panic and renewed adrenaline. "Stop!" He removed his arm from her neck and grasped both her wrists, yank-
ing them behind her.

A flashlight clicked on, and Joe and Raine were caught in its
beam. "Joe, let her go!" Sarah insisted. "This isn't going to
work."

"Of course it will work," he retorted, panting from his struggle
with Raine. "This solution will be a more permanent one, is all. We
don't need to worry about ruining the pictures. We can get rid of
her once and for all. I failed in the car, and the fire didn't do the
trick. But this is almost too perfect. It can be arranged to look like
an accident. Poor Miss Michaels got locked in here at night and got
disoriented in the dark. She panicked. Surely there's something in
here she could trip over and hit her head. Head wounds are so
dangerous, you know."

"Sarah, for God's sake," Raine choked out, the horror of the
situation too much to comprehend. "You can't possibly want to go
along with this!"

Sarah sounded dazed. "The fire? And the accident? God, Joe,
you swore to me you weren't involved with them! I told you I
wouldn't be a party to anything that would really hurt Raine." Her
voice was beginning to rise. "I told you that from the beginning!"

"You don't *tell* me anything, sister Sarah!" he lashed out. "If
it hadn't been for me, you'd still be crying in your vodka martinis
about your career going to hell. Remember how well you were doing when Harold Bonzer was sponsoring your shows, before he'd
ever heard of your dearest friend? You can't even get a commitment from him to plan another, now that she's on the scene. Isn't
that what you told me when the money your sculptures brought in
started to slow to a trickle? Didn't you cry and curse Raine Michaels for being the cause of your career drying up?"

The words swirled through Raine's mind, chasing through the
panic-induced fog. "No," she said disbelievingly. She wished
frantically to see Sarah's face. But the ray of light was the only clue
she had to her friend's location. "That's not true, Sarah. Tell him.
You've done great these last few years, you've told me yourself."

"I told you." Sarah's laugh sounded a little wild. "That's just it, don't you see? But what I told you and what really has been happening are two completely different things. You don't know how many times I've cursed the day you met Harold at one of my shows. He was interested in *me*. It was my career that was taking off. And then, once he met you, it was all over. He started concentrating on you. Everything was for you."

"But you just had a show last year," Raine insisted desperately. Her fear left a cold, metallic taste in her mouth. "Harold sponsored that. He's still interested in your development as an artist. That proves it."

"He told her that he wouldn't be doing another," Joe said then, his voice tinged with malice. "He was going to concentrate on Raine Michaels. The great Raine Michaels. She thought she was well enough established to make it on her own, but she overestimated herself. My life-style can't afford another year like the one she just had."

"But..." Sarah's voice seemed disjointed, coming from the darkness. "This isn't the way, Joe."

"It's exactly the way," he disputed her words. "Without her to concentrate on, Bonzer will switch his attention back to you again. Especially when you tearfully show him the sculpture you'll do of your dear friend. The old fool won't be able to resist it. And when it becomes known that he's again sponsoring you, the money will start flowing once more."

Raine shook her head, dazed. "Sarah, I can't believe you arranged all of this." She was filled with incredible pain at this evidence of her friend's deceit.

"No!" Sarah cried, "It's not my fault! I didn't mean for all of this to happen!" Joe laughed, an ugly sound. "I told Joe about the letters you were getting. It was my idea to copy them and step up the pace, but I never wanted to hurt you! I just thought you'd be too shaken up to work. And then when your show couldn't come off on schedule, you'd lose credibility with Harold. He'd turn to me once more." Her voice turned petulant, colored with hysteria. "You have so much already! I just wanted my turn again!"

Mac was still several yards away from the building when he noted a light in the office. *Good girl,* he thought with relief. Raine had managed to walk through the dark hallway to the office to get to the phone. He knew the kind of courage that had taken. He'd barely finished the thought when the light went out. He paused, frowning. Though he had the utmost respect for her strength, he couldn't believe that she'd made a phone call from the office and then blithely walked into the darkness. Something was wrong.

Suddenly the feeling he'd had all night made terrifying sense. In his mind's eye, he saw the office again when Raine had spoken to André. And remembered the window shade flapping. The window had been open.

He crouched down and sidled along the building to the window. It was still open, and he could hear voices inside. What he heard was enough to curdle his blood.

Damn it, Sarah Jennings was involved in this? He'd never really considered her a serious threat to Raine, but from the conversation drifting through the window, she'd been storing up resentment toward her friend for some time.

He'd heard enough. Turning from his post, he ran softly toward the front of the building. There was no time to waste.

"Forget the acid, we'll come back for it later," Joe told his sister impatiently. "Lead the way with that flashlight and let's find a good place for Raine's accident."

The light's beam turned away from them, and Joe used his grip on Raine's wrists to propel her forward. The adrenaline that had been pounding through her for the last several minutes had her heart beating wildly in her chest. How long could it be, she wondered wildly, before André or Harold missed her? Had Macauley joined them? She knew without doubt that he would come for her, if he had.

She had to try to buy time, to allow an opportunity for help to arrive. Her body needed no commands from her brain to progress slowly through the hallway. She was encased in her two worst nightmares, and in her panic couldn't determine whether her greatest fear was the darkness around her or the man behind her.

"Move, bitch," Joe said in her ear. He forced her forward more quickly until they were standing with Sarah in a corner of the gallery's large room. "All right, Sarah, find one of those little tables they have scattered around here. We can arrange the scene to look like she tripped over it."

The flashlight beam shone in Joe's face, illuminating Raine's at the same time. She welcomed the glare in the otherwise dark room.

"I'm not going to let you do this, Joe." Sarah's voice sounded thin but determined. "It's over. It never should have started."

"Don't start babbling now," her brother growled. "It's over, all right—for Raine Michaels. I've already told you how it's going down. Don't make me repeat myself, Sarah!"

The beam of light moved away, and Raine could hear something scrape across the marble floor.

"You got it?" Joe asked. "Dammit, give me that light. I can't see a thing."

"Sarah, think," Raine blurted out, still unable to believe the extent of her friend's duplicity. "Whatever you blame me for, you can't want me dead! We've been too close. For God's sake, think!"

"She's right, Joe." Sarah's voice wavered. "You know she's right."

"There's no choice now. Do you think she wouldn't tell what went on tonight? She has to die. And when she does, it won't be long until the money from your sculptures starts rolling—"

The beam of the flashlight bounced crazily as Sarah brought it down on her brother's head. Grunting in pain, he stumbled, letting go of his grip on Raine's hands. With a snarl of rage he turned and backhanded his sister with a vicious slap that sent her reeling. The flashlight flew in an arc across the room, before shattering at its contact with the marble floor.

The gallery was once again completely dark, and Raine started to run for the faint light that beckoned from outside the front doors. She hadn't gotten more than a few feet before her arm was grabbed and she was pulled backward.

Joe's voice panted in her ear. "You're not leaving yet. Or ever."

She screamed with all the pent-up terror and adrenaline inside her, and then a force knocked both of them to the ground. She lay stunned for a moment, and then rolled as far away as she could before climbing to her hands and knees, peering frantically into the darkness. She could hear Sarah sobbing somewhere in the room, and the sounds of a struggle taking place.

Disoriented in the tomblike room, Raine tried to head away from the action. Then there was the unmistakable sound of a fist making contact with human flesh, and the struggle came to a conclusion.

Raine's head jerked up, and she forced herself to go completely still. Scarcely daring to breathe, her ears strained for the next movement. She'd have to be quick. Once she had a clue where Joe was, she'd have only one chance to get to the office window to make her escape.

"Raine? Where are you?"

She swayed a little at the sound of the voice coming from the shadows. "Macauley," she whispered tremulously, disbelievingly.

He found her in the darkness and captured her in a tight embrace. Then, with unerring accuracy, he tipped her head back and sealed her mouth with his own.

She clung to him tightly, welcoming the almost bruising strength of his arms. Her mind was still confused by his presence here, dazed still further by the sensation of being held by him again.

"It's going to be all right, Raine," he murmured huskily, rocking her slightly in his arms. "It's going to be all right, I promise. Do you trust me?"

Her answer was immediate, and aching with tenderness.

"Always."

Epilogue

The waves were gentle, rocking the boat like a large cradle. The aqua waters off the shore of Cancun sparkled in the sunlight. The boat's distance from the white beaches turned the people into brightly clothed specks.

Mac handed Raine an icy-cold glass of lemonade. He dropped down on the deck mattress next to her with a can of Dos Equis in his hand, supremely, confidently naked.

She blushed and looked away, but not before her eyes had painted him with a quick, thorough glance. "You could have at least dressed when you went to get the drinks," she scolded feebly. Unable to prevent it, her eyes snuck back to him, and she gave silent thanks that he hadn't. What he lacked in modesty he made up for in sheer masculine beauty.

"No, thanks. I don't want any tan lines." He cocked an eyebrow. "You were working on a cute little all-over tan yourself until a few days ago."

"Yes," she retorted in a scandalized voice, "until Alberto left the steering wheel and came back here to ask you something." She put her glass down and punched him with a gentle fist. "You assured me that would never happen."

He laughed appreciatively in remembrance. "I covered you up

in time, didn't I? And I explained to him once more that he must never do that. It won't happen again."

"I'm not taking any chances," she said loftily. Leaning back on her mattress, she gave a contented sigh. "You know, in some ways this has been the most perfect month of my life."

His voice was quiet. "I'm glad." He hadn't left her side since that nightmarish night in the gallery. He'd arranged this trip quickly, with ruthless efficiency. They'd dealt with the police swiftly, and after a few days he'd had Raine on a plane heading south. He hadn't known how long it would take for the ghosts to fade from her expressive golden eyes. They hadn't disappeared completely, but they'd definitely faded.

Yes, they'd faded, he thought with satisfaction. And sometime since he'd met her, his own ghosts had started to fade, too. He'd been much too busy taking care of her in the last few weeks to spend any time on regrets. In his concern for her, he was finding it surprisingly easy to let go of some of the guilt he'd borne for so long.

"It still hurts," she whispered softly, gazing pensively at the water. "Sometimes I catch myself thinking of things to remember to tell Sarah about, and then I remember . . ."

"I know," he responded quietly.

"I'm glad she won't go to jail," she said, her eyes meeting his.

He nodded. "You were right about the kind of help she needed. The judge must have agreed, too. Trey says she's been remanded to a psychiatric institution." He hadn't liked listening to Raine defend Sarah to the police. But the results attained by the court-appointed psychiatrist had supported Raine's long-time suspicion of abuse. Raine was convinced that the years of physical abuse Sarah had suffered from her brother had taken a serious emotional toll on the woman. "After Burnett had begun the threats, Sarah must have decided to copy the idea. When you were completely terrorized, she figured you wouldn't be able to work. But I think it was definitely Joe's decision to take the idea to the extreme."

"Getting rid of me completely."

His face went harsh at her words. "Yes." God, the final episode in the gallery still had the power to wake him at night, sweating at the realization of how easily he could have lost her. It had been the most difficult thing he'd ever had to do, to wait in the darkness, knowing Joe had his hands on Raine and being aware of the man's intentions. It had been impossible to tell in the darkness whether Joe had a weapon, so he'd had to wait for his chance to take him off guard. Sarah's action had given him the opportunity he needed. He hadn't expected her to come to Raine's rescue and strike her brother with the heavy flashlight. It had provided the opening he'd been waiting for. Joe had turned Raine loose, and Mac had sprung.

He smiled grimly. Getting his hands on Joe had been primitively satisfying. If it hadn't been for his need to hold Raine again, he couldn't be sure Joe would have left the gallery alive.

"What will happen . . ." her voice faltered a little, and she made a visible effort to steady it. "I mean, to the others?"

He frowned, fiercely wishing she'd leave the subject alone. But he knew better than to shield her from unpleasantness, had learned his lesson well from her. Still, it was with visible reluctance that he answered. "Burnett will go back to prison," he said with certainty. "With his record, there won't be any plea bargains. And there's an awful lot of circumstantial evidence linking Joe to the physical attacks on you. The hairs found in the abandoned car matched his. His girlfriend drives a late-model sedan that matches the description of the one Anderson saw the night your porch was set on fire. I think they have enough to send him away for a long time."

He fell into a brooding silence, and she could read his thoughts from the ferocity of his expression. It wasn't in his nature to forgive easily, and he'd taken his role as her protector very seriously. But she'd learned a long time ago the fruitlessness of dwelling on the past. She turned to her side, facing him, and reached out to smooth her hand over his hard shoulder. "It's over now," she reminded him gently.

He turned his head slowly to gaze at her, and the intensity in his eyes made her breath catch. He raised himself up on one elbow, bringing his face very close to hers. "No, it's not over," he said, his low voice giving her words a very different meaning. "If there's one thing I've decided in the last month here with you, it's that I don't want it to be over. Not for us.

"All I've thought about in the last twenty-nine days has been you. And if I was honest with myself, I'd admit that I thought of damn little else for quite a while before that." He leaned closer and pressed a long, deep kiss to her mouth. Raising his head slightly, he rasped, "My life had been empty for a long time before I met you. I deliberately kept it that way. But I have a feeling that if I let you walk away, I'd find out what true emptiness is."

Her lips parted, wonder skating over her features as hope unfurled its fragile bloom within her. "I'm not going anywhere," she whispered, her lips near enough to brush his as she formed the words.

"You told me once that your love was there for the taking. Are you still offering it?"

She wrapped her arms around his sun-kissed back. "It's always been yours, Macauley," she told him achingly. "All you had to do was reach out for it."

His mouth grazed hers as he said shakily, "I don't know much about love, Raine, but I figure you have about the next seventy years to teach me."

She stroked his cheek lovingly and saw the pure emotion blazing in eyes that had once been so expressionless. "You know more about love than you think."

He gazed steadily at her, wanting to freeze the moment into his memory. If he had her talent he would paint her like this, sunlight spilling all around her. "I like to see you like this," he murmured, "surrounded by light."

She smiled serenely against his lips as they claimed her own. He was thinking of her fears, she knew, and the shadows that had tormented them both. But somehow she didn't think she would mind the darkness anymore, now that Macauley would be there beside her.

* * * * *

COMING NEXT MONTH

Silhouette

SPECIAL EDITION

TM

THE MacKADE BROTHERS

the exciting series by

NEW YORK TIMES BESTSELLING AUTHOR

Nora Roberts

The MacKade Brothers are back—looking for trouble,
and always finding it. Coming this March,
Silhouette Intimate Moments presents

THE HEART OF DEVIN MACKADE

(Intimate Moments #697)

If you liked THE RETURN OF RAFE MACKADE (Silhouette
Intimate Moments #631) and THE PRIDE OF JARED MACK-
ADE (Silhouette Special Edition #1000), you'll love Devin's
story! Then be on the lookout for the final book in the series,
THE FALL OF SHANE MACKADE (Silhouette Special Edition
#1022), coming in April from Silhouette Special Edition.

These sexy, trouble-loving
men heading out to you in
alternating books from
Silhouette Intimate Moments and
Silhouette Special Edition. Watch out for them!

NR-MACK3

Bestselling author

RACHEL LEE

takes her Conard County series to new heights with

A CONARD COUNTY *Reckoning*

This March, Rachel Lee brings readers a brand-new, longer-length, out-of-series title featuring the characters from her successful Conard County miniseries.

Janet Tate and Abel Pierce have both been betrayed and carry deep, bitter memories. Brought together by great passion, they must learn to trust again.

"Conard County is a wonderful place to visit! Rachel Lee has crafted warm, enchanting stories. These are wonderful books to curl up with and read. I highly recommend them."
—*New York Times* bestselling author
Heather Graham Pozzessere

Available in March, wherever Silhouette books are sold.

CCST